HIGHLAND LOVER

Gregor watched the tip of Alana's tongue move over her full lips and felt his insides clench with desire. He suspected she was too innocent to realize the invitation she had just offered him, but he intended to accept it. There was little chance he would gain all he hungered for, but need and curiosity made him eager to take whatever he could right now and hope there were no heavy consequences for doing so.

Gregor brushed his lips over Alana's again and felt her shiver faintly. Slipping his fingers into her thick, soft hair, he began to kiss her. Very quickly he needed more than the sweet, restrained closed-mouth kiss he was giving her, and he lightly nipped at her bottom lip. Alana gasped softly and he took quick advantage of her slightly parted lips.

Alana nearly shoved Gregor away, but the urge proved a very fleeting one. The way he stroked the inside of her mouth soon had her clinging to him, silently demanding more of the same. Desire swept through her body. She was not so innocent that she did not know where such intoxicating kisses could lead her . . .

Books by Hannah Howell

Only For You

My Valiant Knight

Unconquered

Wild Roses

A Taste of Fire

Highland Destiny

Highland Honor

Highland Promise

A Stockingful of Joy

Highland Vow

Highland Knight

Highland Hearts

Highland Bride

Highland Angel

Highland Groom

Highland Warrior

Reckless

Highland Conqueror

Highland Champion

Highland Lover

Published by Zebra Books

Hannah Howell

HIGHLAND LOVER

ZEBRA BOOKS
Kensington Publishing Corp.
www.kensingtonbooks.com

ZEBRA BOOKS are published by

Kensington Publishing Corp.
850 Third Avenue
New York, NY 10022

All Kensington titles, imprints, and distributed lines are available at special quantity discounts for bulk purchases for sales promotion, premiums, fund-raising, educational, or institutional use.

Special book excerpts or customized printings can also be created to fit specific needs. For details, write or phone the office of the Kensington Special Sales Manager: Attn. Special Sales Department. Kensington Publishing Corp., 850 Third Avenue, New York, NY 10022. Phone: 1-800-221-2647.

ISBN 0-8217-7759-9

First Printing: June 2006
10 9 8 7 6 5 4 3 2

Printed in the United States of America

Chapter 1

Scotland, Spring 1475

"Oof!"

Oof? Dazed and struggling to catch her breath, Alana decided she must have made that noise herself. Hard dirt floors did not say *oof.* It was odd, however, how the rough stone walls of the oubliette made her voice sound so deep, almost manly. Just as she began to be able to breathe again, the hard dirt floor shifted beneath her.

It took Alana a moment to fully grasp the fact that she had not landed on the floor. She had landed on a person. That person had a deep, manly voice. It was not dirt or stone beneath her cheek, but cloth. There was also the steady throb of a heartbeat in the ear she had pressed against that cloth. Her fingers were hanging down a little and touching cool, slightly damp earth. She was sprawled on top of a man like a wanton.

Alana scrambled off the man, apologizing for some awkward placement of her knees and elbows as she did so. The man certainly knew how to curse.

She stood up and stared up at the three men looking down at her, the light from the lantern they held doing little more than illuminating their grinning, hairy faces.

"Ye cannae put me in here with a mon," she said.

"Got noplace else to put ye," said the tallest man of the three, a man called Clyde, who she was fairly sure was the laird.

"I am a lady," she began.

"Ye are a wee, impudent child. Now, are ye going to tell us who ye are?"

"So ye can rob my people? Nay, I dinnae think so."

"Then ye stay where ye are."

She did not even have time to stutter out a protest. The grate was shut and that faint source of light quickly disappeared as the Gowans walked away. Alana stared up into the dark and wondered how everything had gone so wrong. All she had wanted to do was help to find her sister Keira, but none of her family had heeded her pleas or her insistence that she could truly help find her twin. It had seemed such a clever idea to disguise herself as a young girl and follow her brothers, waiting for just the right moment to reveal herself. How she had enjoyed those little dreams of walking up to her poor confused brothers and leading them straight to their sister. That had kept a smile upon her face and a jaunty spring in her step right up until the moment she had realized she had not only lost her brothers' trail, but also had absolutely no idea of where she was.

Feeling very sorry for herself and wondering why her gifts had so abruptly failed her just when she needed them most, she had been cooking a rabbit and sulking when the Gowans had found her. Alana grimaced as she remembered how she had acted. Perhaps if she had been sweet and had acted helpless, she would not be stuck in a hole in the ground with a man who was apparently relieving himself in a bucket. Maybe it would be wise to tell the Gowans who she was so that they could get some ransom for her and she could get out of here. Appalled by that moment of weakness, Alana proceeded to lecture herself in the hope of stiffening her resolve.

Gregor inwardly cursed as he finished relieving himself. It was not the best way to introduce himself to his fellow prisoner, but he really had had little choice. Having a body dropped on top of him and then being jabbed by elbows and knees had made ignoring his body's needs impossible. At least the dark provided a semblance of privacy.

He was just trying to figure out where she was when he realized she was muttering to herself. Clyde Gowan had called her an impudent child, but there was something in that low, husky voice that made him think of a woman. After she had landed on him and he had caught his breath, there had been something about that soft, warm body that had also made him think of a woman, despite the lack of fulsome curves. He shook his head as he cautiously stepped toward that voice.

Despite his caution, he took one step too many and came up hard against her back. She screeched softly and jumped, banging the top of her head against his chin. Gregor cursed softly as his teeth slammed together, sending a sharp, stinging pain through his head. He was a little surprised to hear her softly curse as well.

"Jesu, lass," he muttered, "ye have inflicted more

bruises on me than those fools did when they grabbed me."

"Who are you?" Alana asked, wincing and rubbing at the painful spot on the top of her head, certain she could feel a lump rising.

"Gregor. And ye are?"

"Alana."

"Just Alana?"

"Just Gregor?"

"I will tell ye my full name if ye tell me yours."

"Nay, I dinnae think so. Someone could be listening, hoping we will do just that."

"And ye dinnae trust me as far as ye can spit, do ye?"

"Why should I? I dinnae ken who ye are. I cannae e'en see you." She looked around and then wondered why she bothered since it was so dark she could not even see her own hand if she held it right in front of her face. "What did they put ye in here for?"

Alana suddenly feared she had been confined with a true criminal, perhaps even a rapist or murderer. She smothered that brief surge of panic by sharply telling herself not to be such an idiot. The Gowans wanted to ransom her. Even they were not stupid enough to risk losing that purse by setting her too close to a truly dangerous man.

"Ransom," he replied.

"Ah, me, too. Are they roaming about the country plucking up people like daisies?"

Gregor chuckled and shook his head. "Only those who look as if they or their kinsmen might have a few coins weighting their purse. A mon was being ransomed e'en as they dragged me in. He was dressed fine, although his bonnie clothes were somewhat filthy from spending time in this hole. I was wearing my finest. I suspect your gown told them your kinsmen might have some coin. Did they kill your guards?"

Alana felt a blush heat her cheeks. "Nay, I was alone. I got a little lost."

She was lying, Gregor thought. Either she was a very poor liar or the dark had made his senses keener, allowing him to hear the lie in her voice. "I hope your kinsmen punish the men weel for such carelessness."

Oh, someone would most certainly be punished, Alana thought. There was no doubt in her mind about that. This was one of those times when she wished her parents believed in beating a child. A few painful strikes of a rod would be far easier to endure than the lecture she would be given and, even worse, the confused disappointment her parents would reveal concerning her idiocy and disobedience.

"How long have ye been down here?" she asked, hoping to divert his attention from how and why she had been caught.

"Two days, I think. 'Tis difficult to know for certain. They gave me quite a few blankets, a privy bucket that they pull up and empty each day, and food and water twice a day. What troubles me is who will win this game of ye-stay-there-until-ye-tell-me-what-I-want-to-know. My clan isnae really poor, but they dinnae have coin to spare for a big ransom. Nay when they dinnae e'en ken what the money will be used for."

"Oh, didnae they tell ye?"

"I was unconscious for most of the time it took to get to this keep and be tossed in here. All I have heard since then is the thrice-daily question about who am I. And I am assuming all these things happen daily, not just whene'er they feel inclined. There does seem to be a, weel, rhythm to it all. 'Tis how I decided I have been here for two days." He thought back over the past few days, too much of it spent in the dark with his own thoughts. "If I judge it aright, this may actually be the end of the third day, for I fell unconscious again when they threw me in here. I woke up to someone bellowing that it was time to sup, got my food and water, and was told about the privy bucket and that blankets had been thrown down here."

"And 'tis night now. The moon was rising as we rode through the gates. So, three days in the dark. In a hole in the ground," she murmured, shivering at the thought of having to endure the same. "What did ye do?"

"Thought."

"Oh, dear. I think *that* would soon drive me quite mad."

"It isnae a pleasant interlude."

"It certainly isnae. I am nay too fond of the dark," she added softly and jumped slightly when a long arm was somewhat awkwardly wrapped around her shoulders.

"No one is, especially not the unrelenting dark of a place like this. So, ye were all alone when they caught ye. They didnae harm ye, did they?"

The soft, gentle tone of his question made Alana realize what he meant by *harm*. It struck her as odd that not once had she feared rape, yet her disguise as a child was certainly not enough to save her from that. "Nay, they just grabbed me, cursed me a lot for being impudent, and tossed me over a saddle."

Gregor smiled. "Impudent, were ye?"

"That is as good a word for it as any other. There I was, sitting quietly by a fire, cooking a rabbit I had been lucky enough to catch, and up ride five men who inform me that I am now their prisoner and that I had best tell them who I am so that they can send the ransom demand to my kinsmen. I told them that I had had a very upsetting day and the last thing I wished to deal with was smelly, hairy men telling me what to do, so they could just ride back to the rock they had crawled out from under. Or words to that effect," she added quietly.

In truth, she thought as she listened to Gregor chuckle, she had completely lost her temper. It was not something she often did and she suspected some of her family would have been astonished. The Gowans had been. All five men had stared at her as if a dormouse had suddenly leapt at their throats. It had been rather invigorating until the Gowans had realized they were being held in place by insults from someone they could snap in half.

It was a little puzzling that she had not eluded capture. She was very fast, something often marveled at by her family, could run for a very long way without tiring, and could hide in the faintest of shadows. Yet mishap after mishap had plagued her as she had fled from the men, and they had barely raised a sweat in pursuing and capturing her. If she were a superstitious person, she would think some unseen hand of fate had been doing its best to make sure she was caught.

"Did they tell ye why they are grabbing so many for ransom?" Gregor asked.

"Oh, aye, they did." Of course, one reason they had told her was because of all the things she had accused them of wanting the money for, such as useless debauchery, and not something they badly needed, like soap. "Defenses."

"What?"

"They have decided that this hovel requires stronger defenses. That requires coin or some fine goods to barter with, neither of which they possess. I gather they have heard of some troubles not so far away and it has made them decide that they are too vulnerable. From what little I could see whilst hanging over Clyde's saddle, this is a very old tower house, one that was either neglected or damaged once, or both. It appears to have been repaired enough to be livable, but I did glimpse many things either missing or in need of repair. From what Clyde's wife said, this smallholding was her dowry."

"Ye spoke to his wife?"

"Weel, nay. She was lecturing him from the moment he stepped inside all the way to the door leading down here. She doesnae approve of this. Told him that, since he has begun this folly, he had best do a verra good job of it and gather a veritable fortune, for they will need some formidable defenses to protect them from all the enemies he is making."

Alana knew she ought to move away from him. When he had first draped his arm around her, she had welcomed what she saw as a gesture intended to comfort her, perhaps even an attempt to ease the fear of the dark she had confessed to. He still had his arm around her and she had slowly edged closer to his warmth until she was now pressed hard up against his side.

He was a very tall man. Probably a bit taller than her overgrown brothers, she mused. Judging from where her cheek rested so nicely, she barely reached his breastbone. Since she was five feet tall, that made him several inches over six feet. Huddled up against him as she was, she could feel the strength in his body despite what felt to be a lean build. Considering the fact that he had been held in this pit for almost three days, he smelled remarkably clean as well.

And the fact that she was noticing how good he smelled told her she really should move away from him, Alana thought. The problem was, he felt good, very good. He felt warm, strong, and calming, all things she was sorely in need of at the moment. She started to console herself with the thought that she was not actually embracing him only to realize that she had curled her arm around what felt to be a very trim waist.

She inwardly sighed, ruefully admitting that she liked where she was and had no inclination to leave his side. He thought she was a young girl, so she did not have to fear he might think she was inviting him to take advantage of her. Alone with him in the dark, there was a comforting anonymity about it as well. Alana decided there was no harm in it all. In truth, she would not be surprised to discover that he found comfort in it, too, after days of being all alone in the dark.

"Where were ye headed, lass? Is there someone aside from the men ye were with who will start searching for ye?" Gregor asked, a little concerned about how good it felt to hold her even though every instinct he had told him that Alana was not the child she pretended to be.

"Quite possibly." She doubted that the note she had left behind would do much to comfort her parents. "I was going to my sister."

"Ah, weel, then, I fear the Gowans may soon ken who ye are e'en if ye dinnae tell them."

"Oh, of course. What about you? Will anyone wonder where ye have gone?"

"Nay for a while yet."

They all thought he was still wooing his well-dowered bride. Gregor had had far too much time to think about that, about all of his reasons for searching for a well-dowered bride, and about the one he had chosen. Mavis was a good woman, passably pretty, and had both land and some coin to offer a husband. He had left her feeling almost victorious, the betrothal as good as settled, yet each hour he had sat here in the dark, alone with his thoughts, he had felt less and less pleased with himself. It did not feel *right*. He hated to think that his cousin Sigimor made sense about anything, yet it was that man's opinion that kept creeping through his mind. Mavis did not really feel *right*. She did not really *fit*.

He silently cursed. What did it matter? He was almost thirty years of age and had never found a woman who felt *right* or *fit*. Mavis gave him the chance to be his own man, to be laird of his own keep and have control over his own lands. Mavis was a sensible choice. He did not love her, but after so many years and so many women without feeling even a tickle of that feeling, he doubted he was capable of loving any woman. Passion could be stirred with the right touch and compatibility could be achieved with a little work. It would serve.

He was just about to ask Alana how extensive a search her kinsmen would mount for her when he heard the sound of someone approaching above them. "Stand o'er there, lass," he said as he nudged her to the left. "'Tis time for the bucket to be emptied and food and water lowered down to us. I dinnae want to be bumping into ye."

Alana felt immediately chilled as she left his side. She kept inching backward until she stumbled and fell onto a pile of blankets. She moved around until she was seated on them, her back against the cold stone wall. The grate was opened and a rope with a hook at the end of it was lowered through the opening. The lantern this man carried produced enough light to at least allow them to see that rope. Gregor moved around as if he could see and Alana suspected he had carefully mapped out his prison in his mind. She watched as the bucket was raised up and another lowered down. As Gregor reached for that bucket, she caught a faint glimpse of his form. He was indeed very tall and very lean. She cursed the darkness for hiding all else from her.

"We will need two buckets of water for washing in the morn," Gregor called up to the man, watching him as he carefully lowered the now-empty privy bucket.

"Two?" the man snapped. "Why two?"

"One for me and one for the lass."

"Ye can both wash from the same one."

"A night down here leaves one verra dirty. A wee bucket of water is barely enough to get one person clean, ne'er mind two."

"I will see what the laird says."

Alana winced as the grate was slammed shut and that faint shaft of light disappeared. She tried to judge where Gregor was, listening carefully to his movements, but was still startled a little when he sat down by her side. Then she caught the scent of cheese and still-warm bread and her stomach growled a welcome.

Gregor laughed as he set the food out between them. "Careful how ye move, lass. The food rests between us. The Gowans do provide enough to eat, though 'tis plain fare."

"Better than none. Perhaps ye had better hand me things. I think I shall need a wee bit of time to become accustomed to moving about in this thick dark."

She tensed when she felt a hand pat her leg, but then something fell into her lap. Reaching down, she found a chunk of bread and immediately began to eat it. Gregor was obviously just trying to be certain where she sat as he shared out the food. She did wonder why a small part of her was disappointed by that.

"Best ye eat it all, lass. I havenae been troubled by vermin, but I have heard a few sounds that make me think they are near. Leaving food about will only bring them right to us."

Alana shivered. "I hate rats."

"As do I, which is why I fight the temptation to hoard food."

She nodded even though she knew he could not see her, and, for a while, they silently ate. Once her stomach was full, Alana began to feel very tired, the rigors of the day catching up to her. Her eyes widened as she realized there was no place to make up her own bed and doubted there were enough blankets to do so anyway.

"Where do I sleep?" she asked, briefly glad of the dark, for it hid her blushes.

"Here with me," replied Gregor. "I will sleep next to the wall." He smiled, almost able to feel her tension. "Dinnae fret, lass. I willnae harm ye. I have ne'er harmed a child."

Of course, Alana thought and relaxed. He thought

she was a child. She had briefly forgotten her disguise. The thought of having to keep her binding on for days was not comforting but it was for the best. Thinking her a child, Gregor treated her as he would a sister or his own child. If he knew she was a woman, he might well treat her as a convenient bedmate or try to make her one. She brutally silenced the part of her that whispered its disappointment, reminding it that she had no idea of what this man even looked like.

Once the food was gone, Gregor set the bucket aside. Alana heard him removing some clothing and then felt him crawl beneath the blankets. She quickly moved out of the way when she felt his feet nudge her hip. After a moment's thought, she loosened the laces on her gown and removed her boots before crawling under the blankets by his side. The chill of the place disappeared again and she swallowed a sigh. Something about Gregor soothed her, made her able to face this imprisonment with some calm and courage, and she was simply too tired to try to figure out what that something was.

"On the morrow we will begin to plan our escape," Gregor said.

"Ye have thought of a way out of here?"

"Only a small possibility. Sleep. Ye will need it."

That did not sound promising, Alana mused as she closed her eyes.

Chapter 2

Alana grimaced as she finished washing, patted herself dry with a cloth, and began to don her clean but damp clothing. The Gowans catered to her and Gregor's need to keep clean, but there was nothing they could do about the all-pervasive damp. Or the chill, she mused, wrapping her damp plaid around her shoulders. After three days in the dark hole the Gowans had tossed her into, Alana felt as if that chill had settled deep into her bones. The only time she felt even partly warm was when she was curled up in Gregor's arms, pressed close to his warm body.

And that was beginning to be a pure torment, she thought as she brushed and braided her hair. All too often she had to sharply bite back the confession that she was a woman, not a child. Alana did not understand how she could be so hungry for a man she had only known for a few days, one she had never seen and who told her very little about himself. In most ways, he was a complete stranger to her, and yet, she felt as if she had known him for years. Each time she felt that hard length pressed against her backside, she wanted to move against it and ached for it to be born of a desire for her, not for some chimera in his dreams or a need to relieve himself. It was utter madness. Worse, she could think of no way to cure herself of this insanity.

It was past time for the man to devise a plan of escape, she decided, especially since she had not come up with one. Since he had spoken of it the first night she had joined him in the pit, he had never really spoken of it again. The few times she had ventured to mention it, he had said only one thing—patience, lass. Just how patient was she supposed to be? If he had a plan, he could share it with her, and if he did not, why did he not just admit it? She would be disappointed but would not fault him for not being able to find a way out of a very deep hole in the ground.

"Best ye move to the bed, lass," Gregor said. "Our meal is arriving."

Alana cautiously groped her way toward their rough bed. She doubted she would ever learn to move about in the dark as easily as Gregor did no matter how long she stayed here. Stumbling into the bedding, she quickly sat down and watched as the faint shaft of light appeared overhead.

"Ready to tell us who ye are?" asked the Gowan man who was lowering down the clean privy bucket.

"Nay," replied Alana, proud of how she resisted the growing urge to scream out her full name, give precise directions to her people, and demand to be pulled out of the darkness.

She frowned a little when Gregor's response was little more than a grunt of agreement to her words as he exchanged the clean bucket for the soiled one. He stood as he had for the last three days, staring intensely at the rope as the Gowan man raised the privy bucket and then lowered down their food. And again as he exchanged the dirty water for clean water. It puzzled Alana, for he was far too intense in how he watched the whole tedious process. Although she could not see his face, she almost felt his concentration and could see it in the taut stillness of his lean form.

Their guard left, taking that faint light with him, and Alana shivered with fear as she always did. She fought for calm, but still sighed with relief when Gregor sat down next to her. Each time that light disappeared, her fear of the dark reasserted itself. It embarrassed her that she required Gregor's presence to harness it again. It seemed so cowardly, yet it was not a fear that could be reasoned with. She could only hope that Gregor was not aware of how deep and strong that fear was, although why that should be important to her Alana did not know.

"I have a plan now, lass," Gregor said as he divided the food between them, carefully placing her share in her lap.

"And just when did ye devise this plan?" she asked calmly, even though her pulse quickened with hope. "Before or after ye assisted in changing the privy bucket?"

"So sharp for one so wee," he murmured, grinning. "I was watching the raising and lowering of the buckets."

"I noticed that. I cannae see much in that wee flicker of light, but it did seem that ye were most interested in that."

"I was studying it all verra closely. It took me a while to decide on the best way to judge it."

"Judge what?"

"The distance up to that hole."

"Too far for either of us to reach it."

"Aye, but, mayhap, nay too far for the two of us."

Alana took a moment to think about that as she finished the bread she had just filled her mouth with. "What do ye mean by the *two* of us?"

"How tall are ye, lass?"

"Five feet."

"And I am six feet and a few inches."

"How proud ye must be," she muttered and then sighed out her irritation, "but how does that matter?"

"Your height added to mine might be enough to get ye up to that opening."

"To do what? Gnaw through the thick iron bars?"

"The grate isnae locked or barred." He could feel her grow tense even though she was not sitting up against him.

"Are ye certain of that?"

"Aye. Why should they bother? 'Tis too high to reach, or so they believe. And these walls cannae be climbed. I tried several times ere ye arrived and got naught for my effort save more bruises. I am a verra good climber, but e'en I need the odd niche or outcrop or so to grab hold of as I climb. The few there are are too far apart and not easily grabbed hold of."

"So how do ye plan to get us out of here?"

"I think that if ye stand upon my shoulders, ye will be able to reach that grate."

Alana looked up, envisioning the grate in her mind since it was too dark to see it now. It was made of a very thick iron. Barred shut or not, it would be difficult for her to move it, especially since she would be standing on a man's shoulders and not on firm, steady ground. She was also not that fond of heights but felt she could overcome that unease if offered the chance to escape. Alana was just not sure this plan gave them much chance.

"'Tis a heavy thing to try to push up and out of the way," she murmured.

"I ken it, and 'twill be a struggle for such a wee lass, but there is no other choice. I cannae stand upon your shoulders."

"Quite true. 'Tis worth a try."

"'Twill probably take several tries because of the lack of light. 'Tisnae easy to do anything in this dark. We should give it a try after we sup."

"Why wait?"

"If we succeed, 'tis best if we try to leave the keep come nightfall. After the last meal is delivered, we can also be certain no one will be coming down here for hours. If we fail, it will also give us time to hide all possible sign of what we were trying to do. After having come up with a plan, I dinnae want it to fail simply because the Gowans caught us at it and secured the hatchway better."

"Should we attempt to hoard a little food?"

Gregor sighed. "We should, but I still worry o'er attracting the rats."

"I certainly dinnae want them for company, but I havenae heard much scratching about within the walls. Mayhap they have given up since ye have been here nearly a week and we havenae left anything out for them."

"True. It may also be that, since the Gowans have only recently begun to play this game, the vermin havenae discovered a way in here. We shall give it a try. Mayhap if we wrap it securely in cloth and keep it close they willnae sniff it out and come ahunting for it."

The mere thought of rats crawling about their prison made Alana shiver. She loathed the creatures. Unfortunately, she and Gregor did need to at least try to hoard a little food for their escape. If they got free of this place, they would have to move swiftly and stealthily, which would make hunting for any food very difficult. She had little doubt that the Gowans would set out after them. Although she did not believe the Gowans would follow her and Gregor too far, there would probably be several days during which she and Gregor would spend a lot of their time running and hiding. For that they would need food, if only to keep up the strength needed to run fast and hide well.

"'Tis a shame we willnae be able to get the horses," she murmured.

"Aye," agreed Gregor. "Howbeit, I think e'en these fools would notice if I tried to slip a horse or two past the gates."

Alana laughed softly and then frowned as a sudden complication in his plans occurred to her. "If I can get up there and open the hatch, how do we both get through it? Once open, I can pull myself up and out, but I cannae pull ye up after me."

"Ah, weel, that is a weak point in my plan."

"'Tis nay a weak point, Gregor. 'Tis a gaping hole."

"Sarcasm is unbecoming in a female," Gregor said and grinned when she muttered a curse in response to that pious and condescending remark.

"So is punching someone offside the head," she muttered.

He ignored that. "I think we could use one or two of the blankets as a rope of sorts if ye can find naught to use up there. Once we ken if ye can move that lump of iron, we can tie the blankets about your waist ere ye climb out of here. If I recall it aright, above us are several things ye could tie the end of a rope to."

"Ah, that may serve."

"The first problem we need to solve is how to hold ye steady enough upon my shoulders so that ye can open that cursed grate. How much do ye think ye weigh?"

"Seven stone, mayhap a little more."

"I can lift that easy enough, but I have ne'er tried to balance such a weight upon my shoulders. But dinnae worry. I will catch ye if ye fall."

Alana did not feel particularly comforted by that reassurance. Six feet was not a great distance to fall, but the ground was hard. She still had bruises from landing on Gregor when the Gowans tossed her into the dungeon. Obviously unwilling to damage their prize too much, they had lowered her down by her wrists first, but it had still hurt when the man holding her had let her go.

For a brief moment, she battled the urge to tell Gregor that she could not do it, but then she lectured herself sternly to banish that surge of cowardice. They needed to escape this place, and not just to save their families the expense of ransoming them. She needed to get out of the unrelenting dark before she began to cling to Gregor like some terrified infant. Each time the Gowans brought that blessed shaft of light and took it away again, she drew closer to that point. Her fear of the dark grew sharper and took longer to shake free of.

It was also necessary to escape the chill and damp of their prison. Alana was surprised that Gregor was still so hale and strong after spending a week in such a dismal place. The man appeared to be annoyingly untouched by conditions she knew were slowly robbing her of the good health she had enjoyed before entering the prison. If fear of the dark did not drive her to attach herself to Gregor like a leech, then the chill creeping into her bones would.

The thought that she was a pathetic weakling settled itself in Alana's mind. Cold and damp were ever pervasive, annoyances she had thought herself inured to. She hastily shook that troubling thought aside. There had always been fires to warm one and dry clothes at hand. They were blessed with neither in this dark pit. If one could not get warm and dry from time to time, it was only to be expected that the cold and damp would settle in deep and hard. It was also not surprising that Gregor held up better than she did, for he was much bigger and had more meat on his bones.

"What are ye scowling about now?" asked Gregor as he carefully packed away some of their food, a simple chore that was proving very difficult to do well in the dark.

"How do ye ken what expression is upon my face?"

"Ye make a little noise when ye are irritated."

"A little noise?"

"A soft, weel, grunt, or the like."

"Ladies dinnae grunt."

"Of course not. My mistake."

She ignored that remark, for the words were heavily weighted with amusement. "What are ye doing?"

"Attempting to secure some food. A simple chore. Or it would be, if we had a wee bit of light," he grumbled and then asked, "So, what has annoyed ye?"

Alana sighed. "I was just thinking on what a puling weakling I am." Gregor made an odd choking noise and she decided it was probably flattering that he would find such a statement amusing. "I always told myself the dark *unsettled* me. Weel, I cannae lie to myself anymore. It frightens me. As for your plan to escape? Standing on your shoulders to try to open a way out of here is a good idea and I shall do my best, but thinking of how high up I will be also frightens me. I am weary of the cold and the damp, can feel it in my verra bones. Each time one of those fools asks if I will now say who I am, I have to fight verra hard to say nay. A part of me wants to cry out my name, where I am from, give them a clearly drawn map to get to my people, and demand that they be quick in the doing of it. And that part gets bigger every day. 'Tis a coward I am."

Gregor had to bite back a laugh as he sat down next to her and put his arm around her slim shoulders. She sounded extremely irritated with herself. He could understand that well enough, for he had battled with a few of his own fears in those days he had been alone. Being alone in the dark with no way out and nothing to do made one think about oneself and see oneself far too clearly. Gregor suspected few people would find that comfortable.

"I suspicion many people are made uneasy by the dark and by being up high," he said. "Each is a fear I think we are all born with and we ne'er fully shake free of. There is naught wrong with being afeared of something, only in letting it control you. As for the cold and the damp? There is naught wrong with ye for feeling that. So do I, and I grow most weary of it."

"Ye have been here longer than I have."

"And I have a lot more flesh for it to sink its teeth into. Takes a lot longer for it to burrow down into my bones, but 'tis there. Nay, lass, ye are no puling weakling for that either. Ye havenae wept, or needed a wee sharp slap to restore your wits, or complained incessantly."

Alana said nothing, just subtly pressed a little closer to him. For warmth, she told herself. She was not sure she believed all his kind reassurances, but they were comforting all the same. The urge to have a screaming, hair-pulling fit lurked inside of her, but his presence helped cage it. Alana did not think it would be wise to tell him so, however. If nothing else, it would not be fair or kind to put the weight of such a responsibility upon his broad shoulders. There was a good chance he was using her presence in a similar way, so there was no need to belabor the matter.

For a fleeting moment, she wished she had never left home, and then she accepted the fact that she simply could not have continued to wait for some word from her sister. Hearing that Keira was a widow, that her home had been taken by a man whose evil reputation was widespread, and then hearing nothing from her for months had been hard to bear. Her fear for her sister had grown stronger with each day that passed without word or sight of Keira, only more rumors and all of them bad. The only thing that had kept Alana from blindly rushing off to find her twin immediately was the feeling that Keira was still alive. That and her dreams.

She frowned as she realized she had had no dreams of her twin since setting out after her brothers. That should trouble her more than it did, yet she simply could not believe that Keira was dead. Alana still felt drawn toward her sister and suspected she would begin to sense in exactly what direction to go once she was free again. Yet it was odd that, in all other ways, she had lost that bond she and Keira had shared all of their lives. It made her feel intensely alone, and she pressed even closer to Gregor.

"Troubled, lass?" he asked.

"Nay, not truly," she lied, still uncertain if she should tell him exactly why she had been alone and such easy prey for the Gowans. "I think the chance to escape is so tantalizing, I fear to let myself believe in it too much."

Gregor idly rubbed his hand up and down her slender arm. "I think I ken what ye mean. Now that we have a plan, we must face the daunting possibility of failure."

She nodded, feeling the soft wool of his plaid rub her cheek. Alana knew just how bitter failure tasted. Her arrogant plan to lead her brothers to their sister had been a failure of monumental proportions. It was something that still stung her pride and puzzled her as well. She really should not have failed so badly. All her skills and gifts had deserted her, and that made no sense. It was as if whatever power had granted them had abruptly taken them away, but she did not understand why.

Alana inwardly shrugged. She could still sense that her twin was alive, could not believe that the other half of her was gone forever. There had to be some purpose to it all, some reason God and fate were conspiring to keep her from joining her sister at this time. Perhaps Keira needed to pass some test, to learn some great truth about herself, and having her twin at her side could make that difficult. Or, she mused, perhaps *she* needed to pass a test. Alana did not like that idea at all and hastily asked for Keira's forgiveness for hoping it was her sister who was being tested. Keira was pretty, kind, and clever, much more able to pass such a test of her spirit and courage.

Although she loved her sister dearly, felt that Keira was truly her best friend and ally, Alana ruefully admitted to herself that she often suffered the pinch of envy concerning Keira. Keira was the one who looked so much like the matriarch of their family, being vividly beautiful with her black hair, fair skin, and green eyes. Alana was little and brown. Keira had the true gift of healing whereas Alana was just a good healer, using knowledge and skill well but lacking the touch and strong instincts Keira had been blessed with. Keira had the sight. Alana only had a bond with her twin that occasionally stirred dreams and strong intuitions. Although neither of them had a bad temper, Keira was the gentler one, the sweeter one. Alana knew her tongue could be as sharp as a knife's edge. Although she knew it was nonsense, knew she was as beloved by her family as Keira was, Alana occasionally felt that, as the second born, she had entered the world in Keira's shadow and had never left it. She sighed, dismayed by her own foolishness.

"That was a mournful sound, lass," Gregor said. "Are ye sure ye arenae troubled?"

"Nay, I am just thinking on how long we must wait until we may try to escape," she lied, embarrassed by her thoughts.

Gregor did not need to see clearly to know he was being lied to, but he did not press her. "Weel, what say ye to a game of chess to pass the time?" he asked, leaning back against the wall and tugging her along with him.

"Aye, I am prepared to beat ye soundly yet again," she said. "Ye may make the first move."

"How gracious ye are," he drawled, suspecting her confidence was warranted, as he had not won a game yet.

He closed his eyes, pictured his much-prized chess set in his mind, and struggled to decide upon his first move. If he was very lucky, he might take longer to lose this time. His victory could then be found in keeping them both well occupied during the too-long wait ahead of them.

Alana lay sprawled on top of a cursing Gregor and struggled to catch her breath. It was obviously going to take them a while to learn the trick to it all, to gain the strength and balance to act as one while she stood upon Gregor's shoulders. Her only consolation was that he was not any better at it than she was. He could hold her up well when she stood still, but the moment she attempted to move the heavy iron grate, he lost that control. The first three times she fell he had caught her easily enough. This time, however, even that had gone wrong.

"I think four times is enough for tonight," Gregor said, trying to will away the pain in his head, which had hit the hard ground with enough force to bring him perilously close to unconsciousness.

"I concur," Alana replied in a voice still hoarse and unsteady after having all the breath knocked out of her. "Mayhap on the morrow, betwixt meals, we should practice moving about whilst I am on your shoulders."

"Might be wise."

Forcing herself to move off him, Alana sprawled at

his side. "We need to learn to move as one—one verra tall person."

Gregor briefly laughed. "Aye. Holding ye up there isnae so hard. Standing as steady as the floor whilst ye struggle to move that cursed grate will require some practice. Do ye think ye *can* move it aside?"

"Aye. 'Tis heavy, true enough, but I can do it. I must needs figure out how to push it aside without toppling us is all. There is a trick to it, I am certain of it."

"Fine, then. On the morrow we will practice moving with ye on my shoulders and ye can try to puzzle out what that trick is."

"And then, after we sup, we try again?"

"Aye. And the next night, and the next, until we get it right."

"Oh joy."

Chapter 3

"I can almost hear it laughing at me."

"'Tis a lump of iron, Alana," said Gregor. "It cannae laugh."

"'Tis a lump of iron that has defeated me for three nights. 'Tis laughing."

Gregor almost laughed and then winced as Alana touched one of the many bruises he had acquired as she got onto his shoulders. He knew she also suffered from their many stumbles in their efforts to escape, but she was stubborn. In truth, Gregor had the distinct feeling that each failure only made her more determined. He was the one who put a stop to their efforts after several tries each night, if only out of fear that one of them could be seriously hurt if they did not take a rest from it. Last night Alana had been knocked unconscious for several tense, frightening minutes when, after he caught her as she had stumbled from her precarious perch upon his shoulders, they had both come up hard against the stone wall of their prison. When she had gone limp in his arms, he had suffered a moment of blind terror he had no wish to taste again.

It had seemed such a simple plan but was proving to have far too many unforeseen complications and dangers. When one was landing upon rock and hard ground, the distance one fell did not matter quite as much as how one landed. As they had struggled again and again to move that lump of iron keeping them from escaping, Gregor had realized Alana was right. The weight of the thing was not as big a problem as the angle they were approaching it from. Alana not only had to find the strength to lift it, but also to then push it aside. That required some stretching and twisting of her small body, and that was where their trouble would begin.

The moment Alana began to straighten up, one small bare foot on each of his shoulders, Gregor grasped her ankles. Thinking it might steady her more as she worked, he slid his hands up the front of her legs. With his arms slightly curved around her legs, he firmly clasped the front of her slim thighs. He felt Alana jerk ever so slightly and the muscles in her slender legs tautened beneath his hands.

"Good lass," he said. "Keep yourself as taut as a bowstring. 'Twill help lessen our chances of stumbling."

Stumbling was the very last thing Alana had been thinking about as she had felt those big hands move up her legs. She almost looked down to see if she was on fire, such was the strength of the heat his touch stirred within her. There was nothing seductive about his touch, but that did not stop her pulse from leaping. *He is just trying to hold ye steady as ye struggle with this cursed lump of iron*, she told herself, but herself did not seem inclined to listen. The heedless part of her that desired the man was not interested in the struggle to escape; it wanted him to stroke her legs again.

Alana forced herself to concentrate on moving aside the contrary iron grate that barred their escape. Her hands were sore, covered with scratches and bruises, but she had done her best to hide those injuries from Gregor. Once she realized she could stand on his shoulders without shaking in fear and that she could reach the hatch, she became determined to succeed. Instinct told her that Gregor would try to halt her attempts if he knew what abuse her hands were suffering. He had almost done so when she had taken that little sleep after slamming into the wall, but she had managed to talk him out of quitting. If he knew about all the other injuries she was aching from, Alana felt absolutely certain he would give up.

Slowly, Alana lifted the grate. Stretching herself up as far as she could, she began to push it aside. Distracting though it was, she had to admit that Gregor's new hold upon her legs did keep her steadier. She took several slow, deep breaths, willed every ounce of strength she had into her arms, said a little prayer, and shoved the grate. The sound of heavy iron landing on stone rang in her ears, but it took her a moment before she fully realized she had, at long last, succeeded. Disbelief rose up and she used her hands to confirm her success, feeling around the opening—the now completely unobstructed opening.

"I did it," she whispered.

Just as Alana opened her mouth to more loudly announce her success, she found herself yanked off Gregor's broad shoulders. Left a little breathless by that abrupt dismount, she could barely utter a squeak of surprise as he enfolded her in his strong arms for a vigorous hug. She was still reeling from the heady effects of that embrace when he set her on her feet and moved away. A moment later she felt blankets being draped around her shoulders. Alana told herself that the fact that Gregor seemed completely unaffected by that embrace should not feel like such an insult.

"Now, lass," said Gregor, "I ken it willnae be easy to do what ye must in the dark. Ye must be verra careful whilst ye move about up there."

"I ken it. 'Twould be far too easy to get turned about and fall back down here."

"Aye, and since I cannae see, I cannae be sure I could catch ye."

"Catch me, is it? Aye, I think that does sound a wee bit better than *let ye fall on me*."

Gregor laughed softly and reached out, groping around a little until he touched her on the arm. "Up ye go, then."

As carefully as she could, Alana climbed up him until she stood upon his shoulders again. The faint knot of fear she felt over being in such a high and precarious position was a lot easier to ignore this time. The promise of freedom proved a very good cure for that uneasiness.

Cautiously raising her arms, she moved them around until she felt the edge of the opening. Alana started to pull herself up. Just as she decided she would need to ask Gregor to lift her up higher, he slowly did so. It took but a moment to pull herself up and out of the pit. She sprawled facedown on the cool stone floor, struggling to calm herself, excitement and jubilation making her almost light-headed. Alana was tempted to do a little dance, but suspected she would probably dance right over the opening to the oubliette and fall down on a waiting Gregor.

Her delight faded as she became all too aware of the darkness surrounding her. Somehow she was going to have to grope her way around until she found something to tie the blankets to. Then she would have to cautiously find her way back to the hole and lower the rope of blankets down to Gregor without falling in. This was not going to be easy, she thought as she began to slowly inch her way along the floor.

Gregor paced, stopped and stared up toward the opening of their prison, and then paced some more. He could hear just a few soft sounds indicating Alana's careful movements. There was no outcry, no hint that some Gowan had stumbled upon her, and that was good. What was not good was the waiting. He was all too aware of how difficult Alana found it to move about in the dark.

Recalling her ineptitude, he quickly placed himself beneath the opening and forced himself to stay there. It was indeed very possible that Alana could get confused in the dark and end up stumbling back into the hole. There could be a few more bruises to collect before they got free.

He cursed. Freedom was still a long way away. Once out of their prison, they would have to get out of the keep. Gregor had not been able to study the keep and its grounds as he was brought in, and Alana had seen only a little. That meant they were going to have to depend far too much on luck in getting out. At the moment, standing in an oubliette he had been held captive in for over a week and nearly betrothed to a woman he no longer wished to marry, Gregor was not sure he ought to put much trust in his luck.

And just why he was suddenly so reluctant to wed Mavis he did not know. He would like to believe his reluctance was due to too much time to think and a bachelor's natural hesitation to marry, but he knew it was more than that. What he truly wanted was what his brother and cousin had—a true mating of heart, mind, and soul. Gregor had thought he had accepted the fact that he was not destined to find that, but it was clear he had not. Mavis was a good woman who would bring him land and coin, but she was not his true mate.

Scowling up at the opening to his prison, Gregor had the feeling that his true mate was up there crawling around in the dark and softly cursing. Every instinct he had told him she was not the very young girl she pretended to be. She was too mature in her thoughts and speech. Although careful to shield all clues to exactly who they were, they had exchanged stories about their lives, and hers indicated that she had been around a lot more than twelve or thirteen years. Of course, if he was wrong, that could prove heartily embarrassing. A man did not like to think that his true mate was a child not much older than one of his own. He certainly did not want to discover he had been having some very licentious dreams about a child.

"Gregor! Best ye stand back a bit."

That was *not* a child's voice, he decided. "Why? I cannae be hurt by blankets."

"'Tisnae blankets I will be lowering down to ye. I found the bucket rope and 'tis a thick one. Oh, and I wasnae able to untie the knot holding the bucket onto the end."

Gregor quickly stepped back. A heartbeat later he heard the bucket lowered, swiftly. He put his hands up just in time to stop the swinging bucket from banging into his head. Alana was clever, good company, and had been the source of some very welcome heat in the night, but she was dangerous to a man's health, he mused as he untied the bucket. She certainly gave him one thing he had never gotten from another woman— a lot of bruises.

He tied their packs to the end of the rope. "Pull our supplies up, lass. After ye remove them, lower the rope back down and I will climb up it."

Wincing at the pain in her hands, Alana pulled up the rope. She struggled to untie the simple knot Gregor had made, her fingers no longer so nimble and a little slick with blood. After tossing the rope back down, Alana dragged their packs away from the hole and then searched for something to wrap her hands in, as well as for her stockings and boots. Properly cleaning and tending to her damaged hands would have to wait. Alana just prayed that they were not as badly tattered as they felt.

She was just wrapping strips torn from her nightshift around her hands when she heard Gregor pull himself up out of the hole. When she heard him put the grate back over the hole, she almost told him that she doubted even the Gowans would be fooled by that for long, but hastily bit back the words. It was probably wise to cover the hole while they were stumbling around in the dark looking for a way out. It had been a danger that had loomed large in her mind as she had crawled around looking for something to tie the blanket rope to and as she had tried to find the hole again in order to lower down to Gregor the rope she had found.

When Gregor did not immediately join her, Alana sat still and listened carefully. He was moving away from her and she was just about to speak out to him to let him know where she was when she heard him softly exclaim in delight. A familiar scratching noise echoed in the dark and, a moment later, she winced as a light flared. Blinking slowly as she struggled to adjust to the sudden presence of light, she watched Gregor set the torch in its holder and begin to search the room encircling the opening to the oubliette. Another soft exclamation escaped him as he found what were possibly his own sword and dagger, and then he turned to face her.

Alana felt her breath catch in her throat. Despite the rough beard growth on his face, Gregor was a very handsome man, too handsome for any woman's peace of mind. Although she had guessed that he was tall, lean, and strong, she had never imagined such perfection. A broad chest, trim waist, lean hips, and long legs made for the sort of manly figure that caused a lass's heart to pound. Hers certainly was. As he moved slowly closer, she could see the smooth grace of his movements, the agile strength revealed in every step.

There appeared to be no imperfections in his face, either. Long, shining black hair framed a face designed to make women foolish. From his broad forehead to his strong jaw, his was a face created with clean, expertly carved lines. His dark brows held the hint of a curve and were neither too thick nor too thin. His lashes were just long and thick enough to soften the stark manliness of his face. His mouth was well shaped, with lips just full enough to aid those lashes in adding a softness to what could have been a cold, harsh face, and to sorely tempt any woman with blood in her veins. As he stepped close enough for her to clearly see the color of his eyes, she had to declare them the crowning jewel in this vast array of dizzying perfection. His eyes were sized just right to be neither too small nor too large, and flanked his long, straight nose in exactly the right place. They were also a beautiful color—a silvery blue that made her want to sigh like some besotted idiot.

And that was the problem, she mused sadly. She *was* besotted, deeply and probably irrevocably. He was everything she thought perfect in a man. The man she had come to know in the dark was only more impressive in the light. Even as she felt her heart pound with burgeoning emotions, wants, and needs, she felt her stomach clench with grief. He was too perfect for a small, brown woman whose family fondly called her "wren."

Gregor studied Alana carefully, his opinion that she was no child hardening into near certainty. Hers was not an elegant beauty, but he had already suspected that. Adorable though it was, it was definitely a woman's face he looked at, one he suspected would hold fast to a youthful look far longer than many another. Her hair was a deep, rich brown, reminding one of fertile fields and elegant wood. Just as he had guessed from occasionally touching it, it was long, hanging past her waist, thick and unruly. It looked too great a weight for her long, slim neck to carry. She looked as small and dainty as she had felt. Gregor suspected there was some binding beneath her gown, having stolen a quick feel of her back one night while she slept and feeling the ridges of something beneath her gown. He was curious as to how fulsome she might be, guessing that she might be as small there as she was elsewhere with her tiny waist and slender hips. Gregor knew his curiosity would not be satisfied, however, until she fully trusted him.

It was her small, oval face that held most of his attention. Big, golden brown eyes were the first thing to catch and hold his interest. Thickly lashed and set beneath daintily arched brows, they were almost too big for her face, which added to that air of sweet innocence she carried. A small, straight nose led to a mouth that put the lie to that look of childlike purity. It was a lush mouth, a hint too wide and with a fullness of lip that begged for kisses. He was just wondering why there was a look of sadness in her pretty eyes when he noticed the binding on her small, long-fingered hands.

"What has happened to your hands, lass?" he asked.

"Ah, I fear I scraped them a wee bit as I crawled about on the floor," she replied. "They are fine as they are for now. When we stop for a rest later, much later, I will tend to them more precisely. So, what now?"

Deciding not to press her about whatever injury she had suffered, Gregor looked around. "First we should see if there is a bolt-hole. Most of these old tower houses have one. It would speed our way out of this trap. If we cannae find one, we will have to try to creep out of the keep and then out the gates."

"A verra uncertain journey," Alana murmured, "but lingering here too long could also be too dangerous, aye?"

"Aye, so we willnae spend too long searching for a secret way out of here."

Gregor found another torch, lit it, and handed it to Alana. She stood up and immediately began searching. Yet again she proved an excellent ally, he mused as he began to search for some way out aside from the most direct and most dangerous route. They not only needed to escape the Gowans unseen, but to put as much distance as possible between them and the Gowans before their escape was discovered. With no horses, that was not going to be easy. Counting slowly in his head, he hoped to grasp some idea of time passing as he carefully worked his way around the dark bowels of Laird Gowan's keep. He could hear Alana moving things as she hunted, but she asked for no aid, so he concentrated on his own hunt.

When Gregor decided they had wasted enough of their too-precious time, he turned to look for Alana. It made him uneasy when he could not immediately see her. That unease was beginning to flare into a panic when Alana suddenly appeared from behind a stack of barrels. He started toward her, telling himself that he would take time to examine that moment of fear—later.

"What have ye found?" he asked.

Grabbing Gregor by the arm, Alana tugged him closer so that he could see behind the barrels. "Our bolt-hole." She sighed. "I fear it is no fine tunnel one can walk through, though. And I couldnae see too far inside of it, but I fear we may be crawling along amongst many vile creatures that take quick advantage of such long-unused spaces. I think whoe'er leads the way could carry this lamp I found, however, and that may help."

"Aye. Most, er, vile creatures flee before the light."

Studying the tunnel revealed by the recently moved

barrels, Gregor bit back a curse. There was a good chance it could lead them out of the keep unseen, and they had no choice but to take that chance. It would be nothing less than torture, however. Even with the lantern, it would be dark enough to disturb Alana. As for himself, he had always shunned small, enclosed spaces. The idea of crawling along that tunnel, surrounded by rock and dirt, chilled him. He could almost hope a few Gowans caught up with him and Alana for, after going through that tunnel, he would be more than pleased to kill a few of them.

"We should go now," Alana said.

He could hear the reluctance in her voice and wholeheartedly shared it. "I was hoping for something bigger," he said as he lit the lantern.

Something that reminded one a little less of a grave, she mused.

"We must hope the Gowans have kept it in better repair than the rest of the keep," he muttered as he handed her the lantern.

She held the lantern as he doused the torches. Coward that she was, she had taken one look into that tunnel and had hesitated to tell Gregor what she had found. She did not want to go in there. She did not want to stay, either. Alana told herself that all she needed to do was be brave for a little while longer and then she would be free.

The moment they entered the tunnel, Gregor in the lead, Alana pulled the small wood door shut behind her. For a brief moment she felt choked with panic, with an overwhelming urge to get out of the tunnel as fast as possible, but she fought that fear. This could be their only chance to escape and she could not allow her weakness to steal it away.

As Gregor started to crawl along, she moved to keep pace with him, if only to stay within the small circle of light. That light and Gregor's presence were the only things helping her to keep her fears tethered. She fixed her gaze upon Gregor's backside. Taut, well shaped, and firm with muscles, it was a pleasure to watch it as he moved. Many scorned the wearing of hose and doublet as an English affectation, but at this precise moment, she had to appreciate the fit of his clothes. Embarrassing though it was to discover that she definitely had a wanton streak in her, she could not stop the unmaidenly thoughts that were filling her head. Such thoughts as how she would like to see him naked also kept her cowardice under control. Alana did wonder, however, why he was so finely dressed, for he had mentioned no important meeting or even a visit to the king's court.

She shook aside the unease that thought caused, smothering the intuition her kinswomen had always told her to heed closely. There were many good reasons for him to be dressed so fine. Even vanity could explain it. Alana did not know why her mind kept whispering that his finery had something to do with a woman, unless it was simply because such a man undoubtedly had women falling at his feet. If not for the fear that he would simply step over her to reach a prettier, more fulsome woman, she would fall there, too.

Alana was sternly lecturing herself concerning wanton thoughts and ill-judged infatuations when she realized Gregor had halted and was now kneeling. She sat back on her heels and watched as he struggled to open a thick oak hatch above his head. When it began to open and sprinkled him with dirt, she quickly snatched the lantern out of the way of what she suspected would be an increasing deluge. Gregor hastily moved out of the way as her suspicion proved correct, but Alana was too preoccupied by the lack of any new light that had entered the tunnel along with the debris to enjoy being right. Freedom was apparently going to be as dark as captivity. She had hoped for a glowing full moon at the very least.

She waited tensely as Gregor took a cautious look, inching his head up into the opening. "Where has it opened to?" she whispered.

"Outside, but a few feet from the walls," he replied as he crouched beside her and put out the lantern. "Ten yards away lies the shelter of the wood. We can crawl or run to it. Your choice."

"I choose whate'er ye think will be safer."

"How about a wee bit of both?"

"Lead on."

By the time they reached the shelter of the wood, Alana felt battered and bruised. She did not think covering such a short distance had ever taken her so long or hurt so badly. When she felt the first drop of rain upon her face, she nearly cursed aloud.

"Now what?" she asked, glaring up at the sky.

"We run," Gregor replied.

"For how long?"

"Until we cannae run another step. Then we have a wee rest and begin to run some more."

"Oh joy."

Chapter 4

Why had she thought that getting out of the pit the Gowans had tossed her into would mean she would be warm and dry? Alana asked herself as she fought to keep pace with Gregor. She was wet, cold, and tired. Very, very tired. Dawn had come and gone hours ago, yet on they ran. Gregor allowed a few rests and a regular change from a fast pace to a slow one and then fast again. Alana knew she was an excellent runner, could go fast and endure a hard pace for a long time, but she feared she had passed her endurance miles ago.

The chill of the rain had begun to sink deep into her bones, joining forces with the well-settled chill of the prison. She ached from the cold, ached from weariness, and ached from pushing herself far beyond her strength. She wanted to lie down someplace warm and dry and stay there for a day or two, perhaps even a full sennight.

It occurred to her that she was not even sure where they were running to, but she was too tired to ask Gregor. Alana decided that as long as it was away from the Gowans, it would be good enough for now.

Later she would take up the hunt for her sister again. Exhaustion had so dulled her wits and senses, she doubted she could find her sister even if she stood only feet away.

When Gregor paused to take a drink of water from his wineskin, Alana stumbled to a halt. A moment later, she felt her unsteady legs collapse beneath her. She was too exhausted to even curse as she sat down on the cold, muddy ground. Although she knew it was unwise to sit, she could not find the strength to get back up. Then she began to shiver and a soft roaring filled her ears. She looked up to see Gregor staring at her while holding out the wineskin and felt herself slowly topple onto her back.

Gregor cursed and knelt by Alana's side. He slid his hand beneath her shoulders and lifted her partly up out of the mud. The way her head lolled against his arm, the complete limpness of her body, told him she was unconscious. When he started to brush the mud from her face, he cursed again. The skin beneath his hand was hot despite the cool rain falling on them.

"Och, poor wee lass," he murmured. "I pushed ye too hard, didnae I."

He picked her up and set her down beneath a tree where the ground was not quite so muddy. Using his plaid, he formed a blanket sling so that he could carry her and yet keep his hands free. It took several tries, but he finally got her settled against his chest so that her legs dangled off to his sides and would not impede his stride. Picking up their belongings, he set out to find them someplace where they could hide from the Gowans until she recovered.

Fate smiled upon him and, within an hour, he found a small stone cottage. When no one responded to his pounding upon the door, he opened it and cautiously looked around, but saw no sign of life. Although the cottage was small, it looked sturdy and its thatched roof was still intact. Gregor quickly laid claim to the abandoned shelter. He set Alana down on the floor and, pulling out the few blocks of peat he always carried with him, he started a fire. Wood or more peat would be required soon, but first he had to get Alana dry and settled near the meager fire.

Thanking God that he had had the foresight to secure two blankets in the oiled sacks he and Alana carried, Gregor turned his attention to getting Alana out of her wet clothes. He prayed she remained unconscious until he was done, for he felt certain she would object most strenuously to being undressed by a man.

He tugged off her boots and stockings and then rubbed the damp from her legs just vigorously enough to restore some warmth to her limbs. Although she was slender and her legs appeared rather long despite her lack of height, Gregor felt his conviction that she was not what she appeared to be grow a lot stronger. The legs he now rubbed dry were far too shapely to be a child's.

When he removed her cloak and gown, he softly cursed. Her shift was as wet as her outer clothing. Gregor tugged it off her and then sat back on his heels and stared at her. She wore a delicate, more feminine style of a man's braies, but that oddity was not what really grasped and held his attention. There were several layers of linen bandages wrapped around her chest. He had little doubt that it would not be some wound he found when he unwrapped her.

Forcibly recalling himself to the need to finish getting her warm and dry, he drew his knife and cut away the sodden bindings. Plump little breasts were revealed to his appreciative gaze, the dark rose tips hard from the chill air. His mouth actually watered with a hunger to taste those long, tempting nipples. The marks the binding had caused were an ugly scar upon her soft skin.

Gregor forced down the lust heating his blood as he prepared to remove the last of her clothing. Knowing he was about to uncover a woman's secrets and not just infringe upon a young girl's modesty, he was still surprised at how fiercely the sight of a fully naked Alana affected him. Her thighs were firm and slender. Her hips were gently curved and her stomach was flat and smooth. Between those beautiful thighs was a tidy little vee of brown curls that held a strong hint of red. She was perfection, he decided.

He then realized he was panting. Disgusted at how he was acting no better than a stag in rut that had just scented a doe, he quickly finished drying Alana off. Setting her down on a blanket, he dug through her belongings until he found a clean, dry shift and hastily put it on her. He then covered her from her chin to her tiny feet in the second dry blanket.

To further tamp down his lust, he looked at her hands, carefully unwinding the dirty bindings. A soft curse escaped him as he saw how badly scraped they were. Using some of the water from his wineskin, he gently bathed the scratches, careful to remove all grit and dirt. Deciding it might be best to leave her hands free of bandages, he patted them dry. He just wished her fever were as easy to tend to. There was a lot more he would need to do to keep the fever from settling in too deeply, but his knowledge of such things was scarce.

Standing up, Gregor began to more closely inspect the cottage. It took him only a few moments to decide that it had only recently been deserted. There was still some peat and wood in a box near the fireplace. The fact that the little cottage even had a fireplace was surprising, and he had to wonder what it had been used for. After building up the fire, he pulled a rough bench closer to it and draped her wet clothes over it so that they would dry. He then returned to his explorations.

The fact that the cottage had a sturdy wooden door should have alerted him to the possibility that this was no mere cottar's hut, he realized. Opening one of the thick shutters on one of the three windows, he found glass panes, a true luxury. Although the mattress upon the bed was stuffed with straw, it was thick and clean. A poor man would have taken such a fine mattress with him. Gregor then recalled how the cottage was tucked deep within the woods with no area cleared for farming or the raising of animals. He began to think he had stumbled upon some laird's retreat, perhaps even a place where he housed his lemans out of sight and reach of his wife. It was pure luck that the man was between lovers at the moment, Gregor mused.

He shook his head as he removed his wet clothes, rubbed himself dry, and donned some fresh dry clothes. After arranging the second bench in front of the fire, he laid his own clothes over it to dry. When he had wished for shelter for himself and Alana, he had never expected to find something this fine. The Fates were definitely smiling on them.

Stepping into the room at the back of the cottage, Gregor found himself in a small kitchen. Whoever had lived here last had left only a few things behind, but they could prove useful. He was impressed by the fact that the fireplace was actually two sided, the kitchen side being constructed more for use in cooking. Here, too, was a supply of peat and wood. As long as the Gowans did not find them, he and Alana could stay here in comfort until she regained her health and strength.

Opening the door at the back of the room, Gregor saw what had obviously been a kitchen garden, and there was a well. Not wanting to get wet again, he set a bucket just outside the door to catch the rain. What collected in it would serve well enough until the rain eased and he could go to the well without getting soaked to the skin.

Just as he began to shut the door, an animal bolted into the house and disappeared into the front room, moving too fast for him to see exactly what it was. His hand on his knife, he entered the room and stopped to stare at the creature huddled near the fire. Whoever had lived here had left behind their cat. The fact that the animal had known exactly where to go to find warmth was reason enough to believe it lived here. It was wet, dirty, and terrified, but it did not move as Gregor cautiously approached it.

It took a while, but the cat finally allowed Gregor to rub it dry, which cleaned most of the dirt off its gray fur. For a moment, he had thought that it was growling at him and that he was about to suffer a mauling for his care, but he soon realized that the rough, deep noise was not a threat; it was a purr of appreciation. He fetched the cat some water in a battered wooden bowl and cut up a little of the venison he had hoarded from his last meal in the oubliette.

"'Tis fortunate ye are that I have a liking for cats,"

Gregor said as he sat down near Alana. "Ye havenae cleaned up so verra bad, either. Leaving ye to fend for yourself is a poor way to thank ye for keeping the rats out of the meal, aye?" Gregor took a drink from his wineskin. "And 'tis a sad day indeed when I am reduced to talking to a cat," he grumbled.

The cat blinked its big yellow eyes at him.

Gregor shook his head and turned his attention back to Alana. He placed his palm against her forehead and cheeks and then frowned. She definitely had a fever, and a dangerously high one, if he judged it right. He told himself that the fear knotting his insides was born of a natural concern for a lass too young to die and one who had been a good companion as well.

He rose and walked to the bed. Deciding that until he could gather more wood, he would be unable to build the fire up high enough to heat the whole room adequately, he moved the mattress close to the fire. When he took the blanket off Alana to spread it over the mattress, he studied her for a brief moment.

"She is a bonnie, wee lass, cat," he murmured as he settled Alana's limp form on the mattress and tucked the other blanket around her. "Wee enough to play the child, although I dinnae ken why she couldnae trust me with the truth."

The cat gave him such a disgusted look, Gregor suspected it was a female. "I shouldnae be surprised if *I* have a fever. Thinking ye ken what I am saying has to be a sign of delirium."

Recalling one thing he had seen done for someone with a fever, Gregor fetched the bucket he had set out to catch rain. He searched out the other shift he had seen in Alana's pack, took it out, and tore it into strips.

Heartily wishing he knew more about healing, Gregor began to bathe Alana with the cool water in the hope of bringing down her fever.

"Artan?"

Startled by that unexpected voice and the sharp annoyance he felt over her calling out another man's name, Gregor stared into Alana's fever-glazed eyes. "Nay, 'tis Gregor."

"When did the Gowans allow us to have a light in our pit?"

"We arenae in the pit now, lass. We escaped, remember?"

For a moment, she frowned and glanced around her. "Oh, aye. We escaped. Did we get verra far?"

"Far enough for now, and I think this will prove to be a good hiding place."

"Ah, that is good to hear, for I am feeling verra tired."

"Who is Artan?" Gregor heard himself ask and inwardly cursed.

"My brother. Thought ye were him for a moment. Foolishness, for he didnae e'en ken I was following him."

"Why were ye following him?"

Even though her eyes were closed again, Gregor waited for her to speak. He sighed when, after several minutes had passed and she made no effort to say anything else, he realized there would be no answer to his question. She had apparently gone right back to sleep. Although he knew sleep was best for her, he regretted the lost chance to get some answers to the many questions he had.

When he finished washing her down, Gregor fetched himself something to eat. He ended up sharing nearly half of his meager ration of meat with the cat and decided he was much too soft of heart. After stepping outside just long enough to relieve himself, he wiped off the small amount of rain that had fallen on him and returned to Alana's side.

He had never felt so helpless, and he hated the feeling. Fever could be a deadly thing, and he did not even know how to tell if her fever was of that ilk or just a natural reaction to being exhausted, cold, and wet. Even if he was able to find some herbs to use, he did not have any idea which ones would heal her. In his ignorance, he could easily poison her. Gregor was not even sure wiping her down with cool water and forcing her to drink whenever possible did much more than give him something to do. As he began to bathe her fever-flushed face yet again, Gregor promised himself that he would take the time to learn a little more than how to ease the bleeding of a wound until a skilled healer could be fetched.

"I think we must fetch Grandmere," Alana said. "I dinnae feel weel."

"I cannae fetch your grandmere, lass. I dinnae ken where she is." When Alana became a little fretful, Gregor decided it might have been wiser to lie to her.

"Then ye must find my sister Keira. Mayhap Cousin Gillyanne or Cousin Elspeth. I truly dinnae feel weel and they will ken what to do."

"I shall search them out. Ye rest. 'Tis what ye need most now."

"Aye. Sleep is a good healer, but one of their potions would be good, too."

Gregor hoped she had gone back to sleep when she grew still again. He also hoped she did not recall what he had said. If she had the wit to catch him in a lie, it would become difficult to keep her calm.

One of the names she had mentioned was familiar to him, and he frowned. His brother Ewan was married to a woman who had a sister-by-marriage named Gillyanne. It could be just a coincidence, yet he did not think the name was that common. If one considered that Alana seemed to be calling for a healer and that the Gillyanne he knew was a healer, such a coincidence became more of a possibility. And if it was the same Gillyanne, that made Alana a Murray, he mused, and scowled. What was a Murray lass doing traveling alone and disguised as a young girl?

That was a question he would not get an answer to soon, he thought as he collected his now-dry plaid. Settling himself on the mattress next to Alana, he spread the plaid over them and decided to get some rest. One thing he did know about a fever was that it often got a lot worse before it got better. There was a good chance he would find little time to sleep in the next few days.

Gregor winced and then cursed as one of Alana's small fists connected sharply with his jaw. She was a lot stronger than she looked, he thought, as he struggled to pin her down. He had managed to get several hours of sleep before the fever madness had struck Alana. Since then he had only been able to catch an hour or so of rest now and again. After two long days and nights of that, he was both exhausted and frightened. He did not like to see anyone die, save for a few enemies he had known, but the thought of Alana dying left him feeling cold and empty in a way he did not understand. He breathed a hearty sigh of relief when she grew still, only to start cursing when she then began to weep.

"I must find Keira," she said, her voice thick and hoarse as she cried.

"Your sister?" he asked as he slid his arm beneath her shoulders, lifted her up a little, and tried to get her to drink a little water.

"Aye, my twin. She needs me, but they wouldnae let me look for her."

"Ah, and so ye went to hunt her down by yourself." Gregor sat next to her, kept his arm around her shoulders, and held her close to his side.

"I can find her. I am certain of it."

"So, there is another wee lass roaming the country, aye? One just like you?"

"Nay. Keira is beautiful and clever and sweet and has a true healer's touch. I am just a wee brown lass."

Gregor looked down at her in surprise, but her eyes were closed again. "Ye are a bonnie wee lass."

"Nay, just a wee lass. Keira is the bonnie one. Everyone loved Keira, and I cannae find her."

"Ye will, lass. Cast off this fever, get weel and strong again, and we shall go ahunting."

She did not really answer him, only muttered something about lack-witted brothers and smelly Gowans and fell asleep again. Gregor gently settled her back under the blanket and his plaid. As he stood up and stretched, he studied her. She was pale except for the scarlet tint of the fever in her blood, her hair was a dull brown as if her illness had stolen away all hue and shine, and her full lips looked as if they had been burned by the sun. Alana was definitely not looking her best, and yet, he had no difficulty seeing the beauty of her. He had to wonder who had given her the idea she was just a "wee brown lass." He also wondered why he wished to find the one who had convinced her she was so plain and beat them until they could see more clearly.

Shaking away that thought, Gregor gently tied her down. He needed to leave her alone for a while as he searched out some food and wood. Although finding such things as a bucket, rope, and a few wooden plates and tankards had been helpful, he had found no livestock and only a few edibles in the tiny kitchen garden. Not only did he need something to eat, but some sort of broth was needed to feed Alana. She could not continue to fight off the fever unless she got some sustenance.

If not for the dangerous illness that had befallen Alana, Gregor would have thought them blessed. The snare he had set out earlier had caught a fat rabbit, and a more thorough search of the garden had uncovered a hearty assortment of vegetables and a few herbs he recognized. Though some were not fully mature, they were more than adequate for his needs. Even better, Alana was still sleeping when he returned, which allowed him the time to prepare the food and set it in the battered pot that had been left hanging in the fireplace.

It was as he was finishing his meal that Gregor noticed something odd about Alana. Her skin appeared to glisten where the light from the fire touched it. Setting down his bowl, he quickly moved to her side and felt her forehead. She was cool and covered in sweat. Gregor was so relieved at this sign that Alana's fever had finally broken, he nearly cheered. He stepped around the cat that was greedily licking his bowl clean and fetched water and cloths to clean the sweat from her skin.

By the time Gregor got Alana clean and settled between dry blankets, he was knotted up with lust. It both annoyed and puzzled him. Despite the opinion of his eldest brother Ewan, Gregor had never had any trouble controlling his lusts. The fact that Alana was in need of his care, that she was ill and dependent upon him, should have been enough of a tether upon his baser feelings, but that tether had consistently failed him. He had never been so easily or fiercely stirred by the sight of a woman's body or the feel of her skin. It would be easy to blame it on the fact that he had not had a woman in weeks, but Gregor could not convince himself of that. Something about Alana set his blood afire.

And that was something he had to think hard about, he decided as he draped the shift he had just rinsed clean over the bench to dry. Since the moment he had met Alana, his doubts about the wisdom of marrying Mavis had grown. Gregor knew that the possibility that Alana really was the child she pretended to be had helped keep his feelings for her in check, but that restraint had been shattered the moment he had removed her binding.

Gregor settled himself next to Alana, grimacing when she curled up next to him. When they had shared a bed before, she had been clothed and he had thought she might be the child she claimed to be. Now, she was naked and he was well aware of every soft, womanly curve of her body. Feverishly, achingly aware. It was a hunger that seemed to possess every part of him, and not just his heedless groin.

In the past, he would simply have seduced her, fed his lusts, and walked away. That was not a game he could play with Alana, and not simply because she might well be a Murray, a wellborn lass with a vast army of kinsmen behind her, ready and willing to avenge any insult to her. Alana meant something to him, although he was not exactly sure what or how deep that feeling went. The unsettling feeling that if he made love to Alana, he would not be able to walk away also prompted him to be cautious.

He had some hard decisions to make, but he was too exhausted to make them now. Later, when his wits were sharp again and he was not feeling so needy. A few facts were needed as well, he mused as he closed his eyes. Facts such as exactly who she was, why she was wandering about alone, what had happened to her sister, and if she already belonged to someone. The thought that Alana might already belong to some other man chilled Gregor, and he hurriedly pushed that thought from his mind. Aye, he thought, there were decisions to make, and as soon as Alana was awake and clear-eyed, he would get the answers he needed to make them.

Chapter 5

There was a hunchbacked man sleeping next to her. Alana closed her eyes and slowly opened them again. He was still there. When the hump upon his back moved, she nearly leapt out of the bed. The fact that she was too weak to move so quickly was all that kept her in place long enough for good sense to prevail.

The man sleeping next to her had long, shining black hair. His scent was familiar to her. Even the weight of the arm draped around her waist and the sound of his breathing were familiar. It was Gregor sleeping next to her, she realized, and smiled faintly. She had fallen asleep to that not-quite-a-snore sound he made too many times not to recognize it now that she had a moment to think clearly.

Then Alana frowned. Since she did not believe someone could grow a lump upon his back in but a day or two, what was that lump? Cautiously, she lifted the covers, and her newly recovered calm immediately dissipated. The gray cat staring at her from its warm, comfortable place upon Gregor's broad back did not disturb her at all. The fact that she was completely naked did, however. It disturbed her a lot.

She quickly lowered the covers, resisting the strong urge to see if Gregor was also naked, and clutched the blankets to her chest. A slight movement at her side drew her attention and she slowly turned her head. Alana found herself staring into Gregor's beautiful eyes and felt herself blush.

"I am naked," she whispered.

"Aye, lass, that ye are," replied Gregor, idly wondering just how far down that deep blush went.

"Why am I naked?"

"Because ye were all asweat when your fever broke and I didnae think ye should be left lying in a damp shift. The other shift wasnae dry enough, either, and I had to rip up your third shift so that I would have rags to wash ye down with." As he watched the import of those words sink into her mind, Gregor was amazed at how her blush deepened, for he would not have thought she could get any redder.

"I had a fever?" Alana asked and immediately began to recall several things that she had thought were only strange dreams. "Ah, I think I do recall feeling ill. How long was I feverish?"

"Nearly three days."

Alana stared down at her hands, still clutching the blanket tightly against her chest, and idly noticed that those hands were no longer bandaged and were nearly healed. She knew she ought to be deeply embarrassed by the knowledge that Gregor had cared for her for nearly three days. Now she could recall the feel of a cool cloth bathing her skin, easing the heat that ravaged her body. There would have been other intimacies as well. Yet all she could think of was that he now knew she was no child. Her breasts might not be large, but he could hardly have missed them when he removed her binding.

He knew she had lied to him. Perhaps *lie* was too strong a word, she thought. She had simply not corrected his assumption. Alana inwardly cursed. It *was* a lie and it revealed a lack of trust she truly had not felt. It was going to be difficult to explain why she had not told him the truth, especially since she was not completely sure of the why of it herself.

She looked at him again. He was watching her closely, the hint of a smile curving his mouth. At any other time, she would have found the sight of the cat's head poking out from beneath the blanket amusing. It was watching her as closely as Gregor was. Alana wondered if there was any chance they could simply ignore the lie.

"Ye have a cat upon your back," she said and could tell by the look in his eyes that Gregor knew what game she tried to play. That look also told her it was not going to work.

"I am aware of that," he drawled.

"Where did it come from?"

"Whoever lived here obviously decided to abandon it when they left. How old are ye, Alana?"

The abrupt question startled her so that she answered without hesitation. "Two-and-twenty."

Gently turning so that the cat removed itself from his back, Gregor lay on his side facing her. "Why are ye searching for your sister?"

"How do ye ken that?"

"Ye told me."

She obviously became far too talkative when gripped by a fever, Alana decided and grimaced. It was also clear that she had revealed enough that it was foolish to try to hold fast to her secrets now. Since she and Gregor were united in trying to escape the Gowans, it was better if he knew the whole truth anyway.

"Aye, I am looking for my sister, my twin sister Keira," she said. "We have heard nothing from her since her husband died several months ago. Weel, nothing but some very alarming rumors. Her husband had been cruelly murdered, her lands had been taken by a vile mon, she had been wounded badly and fled, or died, or was being held prisoner. Dark tale after dark tale."

"Did none of your people go to her keep to find out the truth?"

"Two. When the first did not return, another went. He returned but only lived long enough to tell us that Keira was not being held captive, that rumor said she had been wounded but had escaped, and that the devil himself held fast to her lands."

"And so ye set out to find her?" Gregor rose from the bed before he gave in to the strong urge to take her into his arms.

Alana stared at him as he got out of the bed. He wore only his braies. As he stretched, she watched the muscles in his broad back and long, well-shaped legs flex and felt as if her fever had returned. She had to bite back a soft protest when he began to dress. The man was such a pleasure to look at, it seemed a sin to cover all that beauty. She forced her wanton thoughts aside and put her mind back on the matter of the search for Keira.

"My brothers Artan and Lucas decided to go ahunting for Keira. I wished to go with them. Keira is my twin, after all. She would wish me to be at her side, especially if she was hurt. No one would heed my wishes, however. So I slipped away and followed my brothers, intending to join with them once we were far enough away from home so that they could-nae send me back."

It was not the full truth, and she felt a little guilty about that. Caution was necessary, however. People clung to a lot of superstitions concerning twins. Sometimes people still set the second born out to die or killed the child themselves. Learning just how close a bond there could be between those who had shared a womb only added to those unreasonable fears. Although Alana could not sense such foolish-ness in Gregor, she reluctantly admitted that she was too great a coward to test it.

Gregor built up the fire and set the pot of stew over it to warm. "And ye lost your brothers' trail?"

"Aye, although I believe I could have found them if the Gowans hadnae arrived."

"Considering the danger they may be riding into, are ye truly surprised that they didnae wish ye to ride with them?"

He had turned to face her again and was giving her one of those manly looks, the one that said she had be-haved like a witless female driven by emotion and not wisdom. It made her teeth clench. Alana took a few deep breaths to calm her rising temper. Considering the trouble she had stumbled into, he probably thought his opinion justified. It was tempting to point out the fact that he, a big strong man, had stumbled into the same trouble, but she bit back the words. She recognized what the hard set of his jaw meant. Arguing with him would gain her nothing more than a throbbing headache.

"Keira is in trouble. 'Tis my duty to be with her."

Although he could understand her need to help find her sister, Gregor still thought she had acted recklessly. He had the feeling she did, too, but he would probably be ten years dead before she admitted as much. There was nothing to gain in arguing the matter, anyway. He was more interested in who she was and what she planned to do once they had shaken free of the Gowans.

"Do ye have the strength to dress yourself?" he asked, deciding to wait until after they broke their fast to question her some more.

"Aye," she replied, certain she could at least get herself more modestly covered before she might be forced to ask him for some help.

Gregor handed her her clothes and then left the cottage to tend to his personal needs. Now that she was no longer insensible, he knew he would have to be more considerate of her modesty. He would also have to find the strength to keep his lust tightly leashed if he did have to help her. He could only hope that she regained her strength quickly so that she could tend to herself without any help from him.

By the time Alana had donned her shift, braies, and hose, she was so weak she was shaking. She sprawled on her back and struggled to steady herself. The fever had obviously badly sapped her strength. It would probably be several days before she and Gregor could leave this cottage, and that worried her. Alana was sure the Gowans were hunting for them. This sanctuary could all too easily become a trap. Thick-witted though the Gowans were, she doubted the men would

allow her and Gregor another chance to escape if they
captured them. The dark, damp pit would be made
even more secure.

Alana shivered at the thought of returning to that
lightless prison. It shamed her a little, but her first
concern when considering the possibility of being
imprisoned again was not for her sister. It was for her
own sanity. Alana hoped she proved as robust as she
usually did and regained her strength quickly. She
was eager to put herself far out of the reach of the
Gowans.

Gregor returned just as she was reaching for the
rest of her clothes. Alana blushed, but did not refuse
his aid when he moved to help her. Despite a few moments of rest, she was still feeling unsteady, and
pride would not get her dressed.

Embarrassment kept her silent as Gregor wrapped
her in a blanket and carried her to a small stone privy
behind the house. Considering what intimate quarters they had been sharing until just a few days ago,
and all he must have done for her as he tended her
fever, Alana did not know why she was embarrassed.
She supposed it could be because now she was not
sick and it was not dark.

When Gregor carried her back into the house, he
set her on her feet but kept a firm grip upon her
shoulders. "Can ye stand here for a wee while, lass?
I am going to put the bed back together."

"Aye." She leaned against the wall. "At worst, if
my legs prove too weak, I will just slide down the
wall and sit upon the floor."

He laughed softly but hurried to get the mattress
back on the bed, making it up with the blankets as he
had when it had been on the floor. There was now

much more wood at hand and the weather had improved, so he felt he no longer needed to have her sleep right in front of the fire. By the time he walked back to Alana, she actually was in danger of sliding down the wall to sit upon the floor. He picked her up and carried her to the bed.

"The fever has badly weakened me," Alana murmured as she sat on the bed, her back against the wall and the blanket spread over her legs.

"It had set in hard, true enough," Gregor said and moved to get her some of the broth from the rabbit stew. "Try a wee bit of this. If it sets weel in your belly, then later ye can try some of the heartier fare that was cooked in it."

Alana sipped at the broth and welcomed how it warmed her insides. It was not the best tasting she had ever sampled, but it was good enough for now. Most men knew how to make camp food, and Alana had to admit that Gregor had obviously tried to make something to tempt her appetite. She counted herself fortunate that he had not simply roasted the rabbit on a spit and handed her a slab of meat to gnaw on. Alana hoped that it would not be long, however, before she could savor the heartier fare that Gregor was enjoying.

Gregor took her empty bowl, set it aside with his, and sat down beside her on the bed. "Now, lass, mayhap ye will answer a few questions for me."

"Mayhap," she said, "if ye will do the same."

"Aye, fair enough, but I think ye can go first. Exactly who are ye?"

Since there was really no sense in continuing to keep her name a secret, she replied, "Alana Murray of Donncoill. And ye are?"

"Gregor MacFingal Cameron."

"Three names?"

"MacFingal is of my father's creation because he had a falling-out with his Cameron kinsmen. I think ye may have heard of a few of my kinsmen. My brother Ewan is married to Fiona MacEnroy, sister to Connor MacEnroy, the laird of Deilcladach, who is wed to—"

"My cousin Gillyanne!" Alana stared at him, nearly gaping in surprise, and then she frowned. "Ye dinnae look verra surprised by such a strange twist of fate."

"Ah, weel, ye spoke of some of your kinswomen whilst ye were feverish. Gillyanne was one of the names ye mentioned, and that is why my surprise isnae as great as yours."

Alana wondered a little nervously about what else she might have said, but resisted the urge to ask Gregor. If she had said something too embarrassing and revealing, she would just as soon not know about it. She had dealt with enough feverish people to know the one tending to them could become an unwilling confidant, privy to a great many secrets. One of the few secrets she still held fast to at the moment was the growing attraction she felt for Gregor, and she prayed she had not babbled about that.

"Fate is definitely playing a game with us," she murmured.

"Fate, luck—good and bad—and a few ill-thought-out decisions. Ye shouldnae have followed your brothers, and I shouldnae have been traveling alone."

"Why were ye traveling alone?"

That was not a question Gregor felt inclined to answer, at least not with the complete truth. "The only escort I could get were men I didnae ken weel. Since there wasnae any talk of troubles in the land I intended to ride through, I felt I could make my way home alone."

The way Gregor did not meet her gaze as he answered her question made Alana think he was not telling her the full truth. At first, she felt angry over his lack of trust and then scolded herself for being a hypocrite. She was not telling him the whole truth, either. He could simply be reluctant to tell her that he had been returning home from some tryst. Since she did not want to hear about any woman in his life, not even some fleeting entanglement based upon an equally fleeting lust, she decided not to press him on the matter.

"Why were ye pretending to be a child?" he asked.

Pleased with the diversion from thoughts of Gregor with another woman, Alana replied, "I thought I would be safer. I cannae say the Gowans would have treated me differently if they kenned I was a woman, but it was probably best that I ne'er tested them."

"I am surprised your kinsmen didnae set out in search of you."

"Ah, weel, they did, but I eluded them. They didnae persist too long, so they must have found the message I left behind telling them exactly what I was doing."

"But ye also lost your brothers, aye?"

"Aye, but I am certain I would have found them again if the Gowans hadnae captured me." She could tell by the look upon his handsome face that he had some serious doubts about her claim.

"Where do you think your sister is?"

"I am nay sure. All I am sure of is that she isnae dead and she needs help."

"Then we shall look for her. And for your brothers. It seems as if any who set out for Ardgleann find trouble. Now that ye have begun your search, 'tis best if ye finish it, but nay alone. Now, there willnae be any husband or betrothed rushing about looking for ye, will there? I dinnae wish to be caught up in that sort of trouble." Gregor found that he loathed the idea of any other man having a claim to her.

"Och, nay. No husband and no betrothed."

At least not yet, she added silently. Her father had been ready to find a husband for her and she had been ready for him to do so. Alana suspected her father was not acting on that plan at the moment, but she was not sure how much he had accomplished before she left Donncoill. She felt certain any choice he did make would still require her approval before any firm betrothal agreement was made, however. Since she had not given her consent to anyone, she decided that little complication did not need to be mentioned. If nothing else, she did not want Gregor to know that her father had to find a husband for her because no other man had asked for her hand. It might be the way of things for others, but Murray women were allowed to choose their mates and she found it lowering that she had never even had a choice offered to her.

"It was hard for me when Keira married and went to Ardgleann," she said, and found she still felt the pinch of that loss. "It was hard for her, too, but as most women do, she wanted her own home and children. Donald MacKail seemed to be a good mon. Yet, what few letters she wrote didnae carry any real hint of happiness. Something wasnae right. I was certain of it. I finally requested that I be allowed to come to her, for just a wee visit, to see how matters stood with mine own eyes. I am nay sure if she e'en received that letter, for soon after we were hearing of some mon named Rauf Mowbray taking Ardgleann, that Donald was dead, probably murdered, and that Keira had gone missing. We assumed she had fled from Ardgleann and was returning to us. As I told ye, soon even more rumors drifted our way, darker ones about what a beast Mowbray was and that Keira had been badly hurt."

"And then it was decided that your brothers would hunt for her? Did no one suggest taking an army to Ardgleann?"

"Aye, of course they did, but it was decided that it would be best to wait until we kenned what poor Keira's fate was. From what little we could learn of Mowbray, challenging him could get Keira killed if she was still within his grasp. Plans were being made for battle when I left, but naught would be done until we kenned what had befallen Keira."

Gregor shook his head. "Difficult, especially if she is hiding from Mowbray. And aye, I have heard some verra dark things said of the mon. Your people are probably right to think he would just kill her if he was confronted and threatened. If e'en half of what is said about the mon is true, he is the verra worst of outlaws. His men are as weel." He put an arm around her shoulders when she shivered. "A mon declared an outlaw by the crown walks with death at his shoulder. He kens any mon can kill him with impunity and so cares little what crimes he commits. The fact that

Mowbray still lives implies that he isnae an easy mon to corner or defeat."

"And now he has a keep to shelter in."

"Aye. Your kinsmen are wise to wait until they ken more about your sister, about Ardgleann, and about Mowbray."

"I ken it, but it doesnae make it any easier to bear."

When she struggled to hide a wide yawn behind her hand, he smiled faintly and got off the bed. It was wise to put some distance between them anyway. When he had not been certain of her age, his lustful feelings had been easy enough to curtail, if only because it had horrified him that he might be feeling that way toward a child. Now that he had seen the beauty beneath her clothes, a need to make love to her seemed to have become a permanent part of him. Even when she had been feverish, it had been nearly impossible to ignore the allure of that lithe, soft body he bathed with cool water. He had to sternly remind himself now that she was only newly recovered, that she was still weak, and that the very last thing she needed was some lusty fool mauling her.

"Rest, lass," he said as he gently urged her to lie down. " 'Tis best and will help ye regain the strength the fever robbed ye of."

Even as he tucked the blanket around her, she was asleep. Gregor shook his head when the cat leapt up onto the bed and curled up against Alana's back. Lucky cat, he thought. He would like to be there, his arms wrapped around her slender body and his own body sated and warm after a hearty bout of lovemaking.

Time to go ahunting, he decided as his body tightened with a need that was nearly painful. He collected the hunting bow and arrows he had taken from the

Gowans and left the cottage. Gregor did not particularly care if he actually caught anything, but he needed to get away from Alana and clear the fog of lust from his mind. It was time to make some hard decisions.

Guilt wracked him as he fully accepted the fact that he could not marry Mavis despite the strong lure of her dowry. That had caused him to waver in his decision more than once, but no longer. Mavis was a good woman, and she deserved better than a husband who could never give her his whole heart. He was still not sure if Alana was his true mate, but he knew for certain that Mavis was not. The ferocity of the need he felt for Alana was proof of that. He had never felt anything like that for Mavis and doubted he ever would, no matter how many years he was married to her and how good a wife she was. As soon as he returned to Scarglas, he would send word to Mavis and her father that the betrothal would not go ahead. He would send Mavis a more personal missive explaining his reasons more gently and as honestly as he dared.

That left him with the question of what to do about Alana. She was a free woman of two-and-twenty, a woman who had been ready to be courted for years now. Gregor did not feel confident of his courting skills, however. Even with Mavis, he had done little wooing except of her father, for he was the one who controlled the purse. Somehow Gregor did not think the few flirtatious games he had played with Mavis—and had played with other women—would impress Alana. He was going to have to come up with a whole new plan, and one that would help him decide if Alana was truly the mate he had been looking for but would not offer any false hopes of a future in case she proved

to be the wrong one. And one very large part of that
plan would be seduction, for he had no intention of
getting all the way to Scarglas without at least once
tasting Alana Murray. Preferably more than once.

Chapter 6

A small fist struck Gregor sharply in the nose, the pain making his eyes water. He cursed and quickly moved to restrain a thrashing, muttering Alana. For a moment he feared she had become feverish again, despite her steady improvement of the last three days. He felt none of that heat in the slim body pinned beneath his, however. The way their bodies were pressed together was certainly making him feel feverish, but she felt blessedly cool. Although he silently cursed himself for a lecherous swine, he enjoyed the way her lithe body was moving against his for a few minutes before he attempted to wake her from what he now realized was a nightmare.

"Keira!" she cried as she tried to break free of his grasp.

"Hush, lass. Hush," he murmured. "'Tis but a dream."

"She is in trouble! She needs me!"

"Nay, nay, 'tis but your worry for her now plaguing your dreams."

Whatever the dream was, it held Alana tightly in its

grip. Gregor brushed light kisses over her face as he murmured soft, calming words against her skin. She tasted like more, her skin as sweet and smooth as cream. It was not until he brushed a kiss over her lips that he realized she had finally grown still. Gregor opened his eyes to find her staring at him, her expression one of shock. Beneath that shock, however, he felt sure he could see the glint of desire.

Alana woke from a frightening dream about Keira to the warm touch of Gregor's lips against hers. His hard body was sprawled on top of hers in a way that turned her thoughts decidedly warm, even a little lewd. This time there was no doubt in her mind that a certain very hard part of his long body was not caused by a dream or a need to relieve himself. The kisses she had felt upon her face were proof of that. It also explained why her dark, troubled dreams had slowly turned sensual. Keira and the man threatening her had faded, replaced by images of herself and Gregor, naked and wrapped in each other's arms.

Those images remained seared into her mind, fading not at all as she woke up. And now his mouth was but an inch or two away from hers. Alana knew she ought to push him away, but she did not move. Inexperienced though she was, she felt certain Gregor wanted to kiss her and she intended to let him. It was not just that brief, sensual dream that urged her to hold still and, hopefully, prompt him to act upon that intention she could read in his fine eyes. She had been wanting Gregor to kiss her for days, even before she knew what he looked like. In anticipation of a toe-curling kiss such as her cousins had so often sighed over, Alana licked her lips.

Gregor watched the tip of Alana's tongue move

over her full lips and felt his insides clench with desire. He suspected she was too innocent to realize the invitation she had just offered him, but he intended to accept it. There was little chance he would gain all he hungered for, but need and curiosity made him eager to take whatever he could right now and hope there were no heavy consequences for doing so.

He brushed his lips over hers again and felt her shiver faintly. Slipping his fingers into her thick, soft hair, he began to kiss her. Very quickly he needed more than the sweet, restrained closed-mouth kiss he was giving her, and he lightly nipped at her bottom lip. Alana gasped softly and he took quick advantage of her slightly parted lips. The way she tensed for a moment told Gregor she had probably never had a man's tongue in her mouth, and the thought that he was the first to give her such a kiss was a heady one, intensifying his desire for her. He prayed he could keep his desire tethered enough not to frighten her.

Alana nearly shoved Gregor away when he stuck his tongue in her mouth, but the urge proved a very fleeting one. The way he stroked the inside of her mouth soon had her clinging to him, silently demanding more of the same. Desire swept through her body. She was not so innocent that she did not know where such intoxicating kisses could lead her, but she decided she could wait a little longer before putting a stop to things.

Then Gregor moved his hand away from lightly stroking her side, up her ribcage, and onto her breast. The intimate touch sent fire streaking straight to her loins. What shocked her, however, was that she could feel *his* desire almost as strongly as if it were her own. She could almost smell it as well. Although she had heard about such a thing from her grandmother and Aunt Elspeth, she had never fully believed it. She certainly had never expected to feel such a thing herself. Alarmed by the strangeness of it all, she placed her hands on his broad chest, ignored the tantalizing feel of all that smooth, taut skin beneath her hands, and pushed.

He tensed and then slowly eased himself up on his forearms. Alana did not really need to see the light flush upon his cheeks and the way his eyes had darkened to a deep storm cloud blue, or even hear how heavily he was breathing to know how hard he was trying to rein in his desire. She could feel it. She suspected she looked much the same, especially since she carried the weight of his desire as well as her own.

If her grandmother and aunt were right, this man staring down at her, his long hair falling forward to brush against her cheeks, was the man she was made for. Gregor MacFingal Cameron was her mate. Just what she should do about that, she did not know. Her next steps could determine her entire future, and she needed to think hard on the matter. Tempting though it was, she could not let passion rule her. Her grandmother and aunt had been willing to gamble that the passion in their chosen man went deeper than his loins, but Alana was not sure she was that brave or daring. Recalling the tales of all the trials, tribulations, and heartbreak both women had suffered before finding happiness, Alana was even less certain of her own daring.

Gregor stared down at Alana. Every part of him was demanding that he ignore the silent rebuff implied by those soft hands gently pushing against his chest. He fought hard to subdue that heedless, greedy part of him. She had every right to halt their love-play. He took comfort in the fact that her desire obviously flared as quickly and fiercely as his own, even if it was a little embarrassing that she had more control than he did.

It was too soon, he told himself as his breathing grew steadier and the hard knot of need in him eased ever so slightly. Alana was a wellborn maiden, her innocence proclaimed by the inexperience of her kiss. This was not a woman one pushed too hard. Her desire was still a stranger to her and to use it against her would do more harm than good. She needed to be coaxed, gently seduced, and taught to revel in her passion, not shy away from it. Since the women he had known in the past had needed none of that, being neither innocent nor shy, Gregor was not sure he possessed such skills. With the heady taste of her kiss still lingering in his mouth, however, he was more than willing to learn them.

"Och, sorry, lass," he murmured as he rolled off her.

"Sorry?" Alana felt his expression of regret like a hard blow to the chest.

"Aye, I lost all control." He dared a quick kiss upon her cheek. "Ye are a bonnie lass and I wished a taste of ye. 'Twas ill done of me to steal one whilst ye were barely awake and still all atremble from a bad dream."

She breathed an inner sigh of relief, pushing away that unwelcome stab of pain his words had caused. For a moment, she had feared he was apologizing because he had kissed *her,* had simply turned and reached out for the warm female body at his side without really knowing who it was. That would have meant those feelings that had so alarmed her, that sense that she had felt his passion as well as her own, were born of no more than her own imagination. Although the idea that she could share his feelings in such a way made her uneasy, she had been sharply disappointed to think she had been so very wrong about that. His apologizing for taking advantage of her when she was more asleep than awake was acceptable, although she did not think he looked all that guilty.

"Aye, it was a verra bad dream," she said quietly, unable to think of anything to say concerning the kiss and his apology. She did not regret the kiss at all and did not wish to push him too far away by saying the wrong thing.

"It concerned your sister?" Gregor asked.

Alana sighed and wondered if she ought to tell him to stop stroking her hair. She decided to act as if there was nothing unusual about such a caress, for it felt good and she selfishly wished it to continue. "Aye. Keira was in danger. A man was threatening her. There was such an evil air about him that it chilled me." She frowned. "There was someone else there who attempted to help Keira, a young girl, but the man easily tossed her aside. He put his hand upon Keira's throat and began to squeeze. I could taste her fear, e'en feel her growing need for air," Alana whispered.

Gregor was startled by the vividness of Alana's nightmare. It was not filled with impossibilities, omens, or demons born of some hidden fear, as most were. This sounded more like a *seeing* than a dream, more of a foretelling than an imagining.

Then, suddenly, he recalled a few of the things he had heard of the Murrays. It was said that many of them had *gifts*, from a healing touch to the sight. Alana was also a twin, and there were enough of those within his own clan for him to know that, sometimes, they could seem to know each other's thoughts or feelings without a word being spoken.

It appeared Alana was not going to lay claim to any *gift*, however. Gregor was not sure he liked her having one. Such things made him uneasy, even if he did not believe that they were the devil's work as so many others did. That fear was probably the reason she was cautious, but he realized he did not like her hiding things from him. He could not allow her to hide this from him, no matter how unsettling it was for him. Gregor just hoped this *gift* was one that was restricted to what was happening with her twin sister. A true seer would be a very uncomfortable person to be around.

"A verra clear dream, lass," he said. "'Struth, I would call it a vision." The way she paled slightly and cast him a wary look told him he was right.

"Nay, 'twas but a bad dream."

"Ah, lass, ye are a verra poor liar. I do ken a wee bit about the Murrays and the *gifts* so many of them are blessed with. Ye dinnae need to fear my kenning it."

"Nay, 'tis Keira who has a gift. She has the healing touch, ye ken. I am just verra close to Keira."

"Aye, verra close indeed. 'Twas such a bad dream that made ye risk trailing after your brothers, wasnae it?"

Alana sighed, briefly closed her eyes, and then looked at Gregor again. He was not going to accept her evasive replies. She had spoken too freely concerning her dream and there was no retreating from her own words. There was a chance that Gillyanne had spoken of the Murrays' many gifts, ones sprinkled about the clan a little more often than they liked, considering the dangerous superstitions people were afflicted with. Alana could see no sign that Gregor was troubled by such things, but she did sense that he was uneasy. That she could accept, for such things made her a little uneasy as well.

She nodded, capitulated, and began speaking the full truth. "Aye, it was." Alana was not quite sure why he smiled at her so beautifully, but she felt compelled to return the expression with a faint smile of her own. "I wasnae surprised when word came that she might have been hurt and had gone into hiding. I had seen it in a dream. It was the evil mon who wanted to hurt her this time, although in my first dream he was all arrogance and strutting brutality."

"And this time?"

"That was still there, but I sensed a desperation in him as weel. The anger of the defeated, if that makes any sense."

"It does. Defeat can enrage some men."

Gregor realized his unease had faded. He was mostly intrigued now. Alana still spoke of it as a dream, but it truly was a *seeing* and they both knew it. He was a little surprised over how pleased he was that she had ceased to deny it, but decided it all had to do with trust. By acknowledging such a dangerous secret to him, she revealed that she trusted him not to shun or betray her. To be gifted with such trust would please anyone.

"The other mon wasnae in this dream, either," she said.

"What other mon?" he asked.

"The beautiful mon who was also hurt. My first dream was of Keira being hurt, but I had another. In that dream the beautiful mon was hurt and Keira was tending his injuries. They walked away together," she murmured and then frowned, still puzzled over what that meant.

It annoyed Gregor to hear her keep referring to that other man as the beautiful man. "What did this mon look like?"

"Och, weel, beautiful." Since Gregor did not look at all happy with that vague description, Alana struggled to recall exactly what the man had looked like. "Dark copper hair, blue-green eyes, and verra clear, perfect features. Tall, lean, graceful, and strong." She shrugged. "Beautiful. Odd, but it seemed to irritate Keira."

It certainly irritated Gregor. He did not like the thought of such a man wandering through Alana's dreams, even if it was in the company of her sister. Suddenly, he had to swallow a laugh. He was jealous of a man in a dream. A heartbeat later, he frowned, deciding that that was not really all that amusing. He had never suffered from jealousy before, and he did not like it. Matters between him and Alana were growing complicated very quickly and, worse, she seemed completely unaware of it. It was humbling for a man who had almost always had any woman he desired, and with very little effort on his part.

"Ye see most clearly in your dreams, lass," he said. "'Tis that and the fact that there was naught odd or confusing in your dream that told me it really wasnae a dream, but a *seeing*. Do ye have them often?"

"Nay. The ones I do get concern Keira. 'Tis why I dinnae consider it a true gift, but more as part of being Keira's twin, just part of the bond we share as we shared a womb. She has had one or two about me. We have always been able to ken when one of us faced some danger."

That was far more acceptable to him than a full gift of the sight. Gregor could even understand it more easily as simply a close bond between siblings. "Aye, I understand that, for my cousin Sigimor has a twin and there were times when he claims he just knew his twin was in trouble. I have two brothers who claim a similar ability to ken such things about each other."

"I need to find her," Alana said softly, the cold horror of the images in her dream making her voice tremble with the fear she felt for her sister.

Gregor put his arm around her waist and tugged her closer to him. "*We* will find her. Ye cannae return to wander about the country alone, lass, and weel ye ken it. Ye were most fortunate the Gowans respected your guise as a child. Sad to say, others wouldnae have cared that ye werenae a woman grown yet and taken ye as one. Stupid the Gowans may be, but they obviously have some honor in them. Ye cannae expect that from everyone ye may meet, and ye willnae be finding your brothers soon, either. Nay, ye will have to search for them, too. I will help ye in your search."

"But ye were headed home," she protested, although she would welcome his help.

"There was no compelling need for me to reach Scarglas. I can go home later."

It would be good to have a strong man at her side as she searched for Keira. Alana hated to admit it, but when she had lost her brothers' trail, she had been afraid. Finding herself all alone in a land she did not know was not an experience she wished to repeat. When the Gowans had appeared she had become almost painfully aware of her own utter helplessness. Clever and fast she might be, but she had faced the harsh truth that sometimes, that was not enough to survive.

There would undoubtedly be a few problems born of having Gregor at her side for longer than it took to escape the Gowans. She would have no chance of curing herself of her strong attraction to the man. It would be almost impossible to make any cool, well-reasoned decisions about him if he was with her night and day as he was now. It had not been easy to control her infatuation when they were imprisoned together, even though it was dark and he had thought her a young girl. Worse, she had awakened from her fever to find those feelings were still strong. The brief embrace they had just shared had only made matters worse, for she could still feel his touch, still taste the heady warmth of his kiss.

She inwardly shrugged after another moment's thought. If this was the mate fate had chosen for her, there was little she could do to stop her heart from reaching out to him. Whether she was at his side for mere hours or long weeks of travel, her heart would go its own way. Although she had always held fast to a doubt or two concerning her kinswomen's tales of finding the perfect mate, of knowing just when it happened and having little control over one's emotions, she had also always dreamed of such an experience. She had just expected her perfect mate to be a more ordinary man, one much more suited to a little wren of a woman.

Alana hastily pushed those thoughts aside. The most important thing facing her right now was finding her sister. If she lost her heart to some man along the way and then had it thoroughly broken, it was inconsequential when weighed against Keira's life. The dream she had just suffered through would linger in her mind and chill her blood until she saw Keira again, alive and well. Once that was accomplished, she could begin to deal with whatever else fate had handed her.

"'Twill be a comfort to have some help," she finally said. "That dream showed a mon trying to choke the life out of Keira, yet I still cannae feel that she is dead. Still, I truly need to see her with mine own eyes ere I can rest easy. There is a darkness in her life right now, and I must see that she has escaped him or help her do so."

"We *will* find her, Alana," Gregor said. "We will get your answers for you and put that dark seeing to rest." He again dared to steal a brief kiss, a hasty brushing of his lips over hers. "Now, rest. Tomorrow or the next day we begin our journey."

"Why the uncertainty about when?"

"I wish to be sure that ye are strong enough and that your first day of travel isnae in the rain."

"Ah, a good plan," she murmured as she turned onto her side, her back toward him.

"Thank ye," he drawled.

"One should always have a plan."

"Did ye have one when ye set out after your brothers?"

"Aye." She scratched the cat's ears when he curled up against her chest. "I told ye. I was following them until we had gone too far for them to send me back. Then, I would join with them in the search for Keira."

Gregor bit back his opinion that repeating what her plan had been did not make it sound any more sensible. "Why did ye think they would need your help?"

"Because of the bond I have with Keira. I was sure I could find her."

"Ah, of course. The dreams."

"Aye, and, weel, just a feeling, a pulling on my heart, if ye will. Keira and I have always kenned where each other was as we grew up. It didnae completely fade away when she got married and moved away to Ardgleann. In truth, I wasnae surprised when I heard the rumor that she had been hurt. I had felt her pain, felt that something was wrong with her. I had thought it was but grief o'er what had happened but, nay, it was more, and I sorely regret that I did naught. I should have acted the moment I got that feeling." She sighed and closed her eyes, feeling sleep tighten its hold on her. "Still, it wouldnae have made any difference, I am thinking. No one would have listened, just as they refused to heed me when I assured them that I could find her."

"A strange stand for your people to take, considering how many of them have an odd gift of their own."

"So I thought. 'Tis fate playing games with me. Those who should have heeded me did not. I lost my brothers' trail e'en though I am a good tracker. And despite my having excellent hearing and a keen sense of danger approaching, the Gowans rode right up to where I was camped. Then, although I am fast, have good endurance, and can hide in the veriest shadow, they had no trouble catching me. Each step of the way there was trouble. I have ne'er been so plagued with stumbles and barriers."

Since Alana was not given to false conceits, Gregor accepted that she had the skills she claimed. He had also seen her run and knew she had endurance as well as speed. If he were a superstitious man, he would think some unseen hand was moving her along like a piece upon some chessboard, doing all it could to steer her along a set path. It did seem that she had suffered an extraordinary turn of bad luck, the sort that cried out for an explanation. He inwardly shook his head, refusing to give in to any superstitious whims. It was all exactly as it seemed to be—bad luck.

"Keira could be anywhere," he said, turning the conversation back to the matter of finding her sister. "She was hurt and afraid when she left Ardgleann. How can ye ken *where* she is hiding?"

"Our bond, remember." Alana hid a yawn behind her hand and felt the fog of approaching sleep start to cloud her mind. "And aye, she was hurt. Of that I have no doubt. So, how far could she go? I ken she would have gotten herself off Ardgleann lands, but after that, I dinnae think she would have gone much further. If we head for Scarglas, I am certain I will be able to, er, sniff her out, although I dinnae ken how I can be so certain of that. I just am."

Gregor was not sure how she could know such a thing, either, but felt no urge to question her certainty. She was planning to head in the very direction he wanted her to go—toward Scarglas. Although he was not yet absolutely sure this was the woman who *fit*, as Sigimor was wont to say, he grew more so every day. He wanted to get her to Scarglas, and he strongly suspected that by the time they reached his home, he would be wanting to keep her there.

He raised his head and peered over her shoulder, smiling faintly when he saw that she had fallen asleep while he had been tangled up in his own thoughts. The cat was curled up against her chest, its head upon

her breasts. Her slim arm was curled protectively
around the beast. Gregor shook his head as he gently
settled himself against Alana's back, grimacing as she
nestled her backside against his still-aching groin. It
was going to be a long night. If at all possible they
would leave in the morning, he decided. Too many
more hours spent alone with Alana in the cottage,
curled against her all night and close to her all day
with little to distract him, would surely cause him to
lose his mind. It was time to head home.

Chapter 7

"We cannae take the cat, Alana."

"We cannae leave the poor lad behind, Gregor. 'Twould be too cruel."

Gregor stared down at the cat that sat by Alana's feet, leaning slightly against her leg and purring. The animal had the wit to choose the best ally, he thought. He, too, had not liked the idea of leaving the animal behind. Since the cat obviously had been treated like a pet by the previous owner of the cottage, he suspected it would not fare well on its own. However, he had accepted the cold fact that it had to be done since he and Alana had a long, hard journey ahead of them, on foot and with the Gowans undoubtedly hunting them. They could not take a cat along on such a journey. Alana and the cat obviously thought otherwise.

"A cat cannae make such a journey," he said, feeling compelled to offer one last protest.

"Weel, 'tis verra possible he may wander off or the like, and I ken we cannae waste any time hunting for him, but at least we can try to bring him along. I can carry him in a sling I can make from a blanket so we dinnae have to fret o'er his ability to keep up with us."

"I believe I will fret o'er being caught by the Gowans again instead."

He had to bite back a laugh at the disgusted look she gave him. She even glanced worriedly at the cat as if afraid the beast might have been offended by so callous a remark. The cat looked smug.

"People dinnae take cats on journeys," he said.

"Aye, they do. My cousin Gillyanne always takes her cats with her whenever she travels. And my Aunt Elspeth also traveled with a cat. 'Tisnae so unusual."

Gregor decided it would not be wise to say what he was thinking, that just because her kinswomen did something did not mean it was normal. "Ye must agree, here and now, that we willnae waste any time looking for or waiting for the beastie, at least nay until we are off the Gowans' lands. I willnae be sent back into that pit for the sake of that cat."

"Agreed. He will be a good wee traveler. I am certain of it."

Shaking his head, Gregor helped her tie on a blanket so that it formed a sling that hung down her front. It surprised him a little when the cat calmly allowed itself to be put inside. Alana then willingly accepted the pack of her belongings and supplies, but Gregor was determined to keep a close eye on her. She was only four days healed of her fever and he did not want her growing too weary.

After shutting up the cottage, he started on his way, Alana walking calmly at his side. They had walked for several miles before Gregor gave in to the urge to look at her. She walked at a good, steady pace and showed no sign of weakening. What made him swiftly look away, however, was the sight of the cat. It sat comfortably in the sling, facing forward, with little more than its head sticking out of the folds of the blanket. Neither the cat nor Alana seemed to think it was odd of them to travel so. Gregor was afraid that, if he looked too often, he would soon start laughing too hard to keep walking.

He began to wonder if he was a little odd as well. Every instinct he had told him this little woman was *right*, that she *fit*. Even when he listed her weaknesses, such as a fear of the dark and of heights, he quickly recalled how she had never given in to either fear. Tiny though she was, she was obviously strong and hardy. The fever had laid her low, but only for a short while, and he could see no real weakness there. She simply did not have the bulk needed to fight the effects of penetrating cold and damp for days at a time. Gregor was still somewhat surprised that he had not taken ill as well.

There was, in fact, nothing he could say or think about her that could dim the attraction he felt for her. She was utterly different from any woman he had ever known, yet he found those differences only fascinated him. Despite the unfed desire he suffered from, he was at ease with her and he trusted her. He could not say the same of any of the women in his past. Even Mavis did not make him feel completely at ease, and he did not know her well enough to say that he trusted her, either. All the more reason to back away before the betrothal between them was finalized.

"I wish I had hidden the bulk of my coin more cleverly," Alana said as she idly scratched the cat's head.

Yanked abruptly from his thoughts, Gregor had to

think about what Alana had just said for a moment before asking, "Why?"

"Weel, so that the Gowans didnae find so much. More coin would surely aid us now. It might even buy us a horse."

"Ye brought a heavy purse with ye, did ye?"

"Heavy enough. A horse would make this journey a great deal easier."

"True, but it could also help the Gowans find us."

"Ah, of course." Alana nodded slowly. "A horse would leave a much clearer trail to follow."

"It would," said Gregor. "It would also be something they could all too easily hear about."

"True, especially whilst we still linger upon their lands. Do ye ken where their boundaries lie?"

"Nay, I can but guess."

"Mayhap we could stop in a village and ask someone."

Gregor shook his head. "If 'tis a village upon Gowan land, we could easily find ourselves caught and held for the laird. It has been a sennight since we escaped, and word of that could have spread far and wide in that time. We shall have to try our best to stay out of sight of anyone, e'en the poorest shepherd, until I can be more certain of where we are."

"And if we cannae stop at a village or speak to anyone, that will be a lot harder to do, aye?"

"Aye, I fear so. I ken which direction to head in, but I am nay sure how far from my original path I was taken. Do ye ken where ye were when they caught ye or how far and in which direction ye were taken?"

"Nay, I fear I dinnae. Do recall that I was following my brothers, nay making my own way, and I lost them, didnae I." She shook her head, hating to admit that, but knowing it was foolish to keep denying it. "When the Gowans first rode up, I was that surprised that it wasnae my brothers coming to say, *Ha! We have caught ye out, Wren!* 'Twould be just like them to do such a wretched thing once they caught me following them. But 'tis just as weel they werenae close at hand."

"Why do ye say that? They might have succeeded in keeping ye out of the hands of the Gowans."

"Aye, but then there probably would have been a lot of dead Gowans and, annoying though they were, I am nay sure they deserved that harsh a punishment."

Gregor stared at her, not sure if she was boasting or not. "Ye seem most sure of that."

Alana nodded. "Verra sure. My brothers are verra good fighters and a little too quick to anger. They would have seen what the Gowans did as a grave insult. They trained with some of my mother's kinsmen who live deep in the Highlands in some verra remote and rough places. Since Donncoill is fair to bursting with Murray lads, my father offered anyone who wished it a chance to train elsewhere. My brothers thought it would suit them weel to do so. They saw it as a chance to have an adventure. They returned as weel-trained warriors, but were verra rough and wild in their ways. Papa has worked verra hard to civilize them a wee bit."

"Civilize them? I would have thought that fierce warriors who dinnae quail at the thought of a hard fight would be most welcome at any keep."

"Oh, my father doesnae wish to change that. 'Tis just that, weel, it did appear as if that was all they were trained to do. As Papa says, he sent off two beardless boys who had a few manners, and got back two savages who think a discussion consists of knocking a mon down until he agrees with what ye say."

Gregor laughed. "Sounds like many of my kinsmen."

"There is a gentleness in my brothers, but I think they wouldst rather cut out their own tongues than admit to it." She glanced over the clothes Gregor wore, from the fine white linen shirt visible beneath his partly unlaced doublet to his elegant hose and fine boots. "They wouldnae wear such fine clothes, thinking them too English. They mostly wear their plaids and rough deer-hide boots. Mama made them don some braies beneath that plaid." Alana smiled a little when Gregor laughed again. "She wouldnae tell me what she said or did to convince them, but she must have been verra persuasive, for they didnae argue much at all."

"Do ye have any other siblings?"

"Aye. Four. All younger. Three other brothers and another sister. And ye?"

"Dozens. Near all of them brothers. One thing my father does weel is breed sons." He grinned briefly at her expression as he helped her over a fallen tree branch. She looked an even mixture of shocked and intrigued. "My father wasnae faithful to any woman until he married Mab. Many think he was trying to breed his own army. A lot of us, myself and my siblings, e'en feared he was a bit mad. But, nay, 'twas an old betrayal that started him down that path. He was and is a good father, although we didnae see that clear until recently."

"His bastards live with ye?"

"Aye, at least everyone he kens about."

"Weel, that is verra good of him."

"'Tis indeed, although it doesnae excuse him from

recklessly breeding so many, making enemies at
every turn, and being unfaithful to every woman he
bedded or wedded. He still refuses to completely
mend matters with our kinsmen and take back the
name Cameron."

As they walked, Gregor told Alana several tales
concerning his father. Now that they no longer felt
the need to hide exactly who they were, he could
speak more honestly about his life and family. He
could even speak about how things had changed
since Fiona had come to Scarglas, and all for the
better. The fact that Alana could be amused by such
tales, despite her occasional shock, made him feel
good in a way he could not truly describe. Gregor decided it was because there would be no difficulty in
having her live at Scarglas with him if he found that
he wanted her to.

They had just finished sharing a laugh over how,
when there was a full moon, his father and some of
the other men would daub themselves with blue paint
and dance naked within a circle of stones, when they
reached the edge of an open field. It was almost
completely surrounded by an equally open moorland
upon which sheep grazed. Gregor gently urged Alana
to kneel down behind some bramble bushes while he
carefully surveyed this new obstacle.

"I dinnae see anyone," Alana said. "Not e'en
around that wee cottage at the far end of the field."

"Nay, neither do I, although one would think that
someone would be about, working or tending to that
flock of sheep," he said.

"True. We could go around," she murmured,
unable to keep all of her reluctance to do so out of
her voice.

"We could, but we would add several hours to our journey, which is long enough as it is."

That was the hard truth, Alana thought with a sigh. Neither she nor Gregor might know exactly where they were, but they knew it was a very, very long walk from where they wanted to be. She briefly considered asking him to steal a horse and then hastily shook that thought aside. Necessity did not make stealing any less of a crime or a sin, unless it was done because one was starving. They were not starving. There was also the chance that stealing a horse would simply put even more people on their trail.

She wished she knew how long a journey they had to make. At least she could then mark off each day. Until they knew exactly where they were, however, that would be impossible. What they needed was some landmark, but Alana doubted they would see one soon since they had to stay away from all well-traveled routes in order to escape the Gowans.

When Gregor slowly stood up, she quickly got to her feet as well. "Do ye think it is safe to move on?"

"Nay, but we only have a few choices," he replied. "We could stay here until dark, go round, or take our chances that we can cross that field without being seen. Or, if we are seen, that it doesnae raise any hue and cry."

"I think we should just march boldly onward." Alana shrugged when he looked at her and cocked one eyebrow. "A brisk march. If someone sees us, they will probably wonder o'er who is crossing their field, at least for a wee while. Then, they might hail us, but since they arenae e'en in sight now, that would probably be from a distance. We would have a head start when we have to run away."

Gregor grinned briefly. "'Tis as good a plan as any I could come up with. Do ye think ye can run verra fast whilst carrying that cat?"

"Aye, he doesnae weigh much."

"Then let us march boldly onward," Gregor said as he took her by the hand and started forward across the field.

By the time they reached the other side of the field, Alana felt as if every muscle in her body was taut enough to snap with her very next step. They had not even gotten half the way across before she decided her plan had been a bad one, and she had grown more convinced of that each step of the way. A man had stepped out of the cottage, but he had only watched them. She suspected he was simply making sure that she and Gregor did not steal anything, but it had only added to her unease.

"Weel, if the Gowans come round here, they will be able to easily mark our trail," said Gregor. "Or that mon has already set off to find them and tell them that he has seen us."

"If he kenned the Gowans are seeking us, why didnae he come after us?" Alana asked as she cautiously edged her way around a muddy area between the edge of the fields and the small strip of moorland between them and the woods they sought.

"Why should he risk getting hurt? 'Tisnae his purse that will be enriched by our capture."

"Ye dinnae think the Gowans are offering any boon for our capture?"

"Nay. The whole game of capture for ransom was begun because their purse was empty. I cannae think they would be willing to part with anything they have or hope to gain."

"Nay, probably not." She looked back at the field and the sheep. "Yet if these are part of the Gowans' lands, they shouldnae be so desperately poor. 'Tis good land, I think, and those sheep look fat and hale."

"The Gowan laird may nay have the wit to make the most of what he has, or these arenae his lands. I cannae believe we have already left Gowan land, however. I darenae. If nay their land, 'tis their neighbors' or their kinsmen's, as open to them as their own. Best we move along quickly for a while, and we should try hard to leave as little a trail as possible."

Alana inwardly cursed the Gowans in ways that would have shocked her family as she increased her pace. An adventure lost a great deal of its allure when one had to spend much of the time running and hiding, she decided. Since the alternative was to stop and confront the Gowans, she did not voice her complaints aloud or slow her pace. She just hoped it was not too many more miles before Gregor decided they were safely out of the reach of the Gowans.

A soft groan escaped Alana as she sat down on the mossy ground beneath a huge pine tree. She managed a faint smile as the cat climbed out of the sling and looked around. The worry that the cat would wander too far away and get lost came and went quickly. The cat had plainly hated being deserted, and Alana suspected it would stay very close at hand so that it did not get left behind again. As soon as she had rested for a little while, she would make her final decision on a name for the beast, she decided and yawned.

"Weary, lass?" Gregor asked as he sat down next to her.

"My feet certainly are," she admitted.

"Aye, I ken that feeling weel." He wrapped his arm around her shoulders and tugged her closer. "I concede. That cat has taken to journeying verra weel indeed," he said, diverting her attention from how he held her close before she could venture any protest. "Of course, he hasnae had to do any walking."

"True. I have been trying to think of a name for him." Alana knew she ought to move out of his grasp, but she realized she had become increasingly greedy for his touch and was far too selfish to refuse it when it was given. "We cannae keep calling him *the cat.*"

"He doesnae seem to mind."

"He is our fellow traveler. He deserves a proper name. Charlemagne will suit him fine, I think." She gave Gregor a narrow-eyed look when he made a soft choking noise, for she knew he was struggling hard not to laugh out loud.

She was about to scold him for laughing at her when she realized he had stopped. He was staring at her mouth with an expression that caused her heart to race. Alana knew he was going to kiss her. She also knew she was not going to stop him despite the sharp voice of warning in her mind. She knew she was playing with fire, but she was too hungry for the heat his kiss stirred to care.

When he teasingly brushed his lips over hers, she heard herself whisper a sound of protest over how meager the kiss was. As he wrapped his strong arms around her, Alana realized that she was already far beyond just playing with fire and very close to embracing it wholeheartedly. After this kiss she would take a few steps back, she promised herself. One more taste of the desire he stirred within her and she would put some much-needed distance between them so that she could think clearly about how much she was willing to risk for this man.

It was not until Alana felt Gregor's hand upon her naked breast, his long fingers skillfully tormenting the aching tip, that she realized she had completely stopped thinking. She struggled to regain the wit to speak only to hear Gregor curse softly. When he removed his hand, she had to bite back a protest. The loss of his touch left her feeling chilled and disappointed. Even as she puzzled over that, he tidied her clothes and sat up, pulling her up with him. The fact that *he* had put a halt to their lovemaking began to settle in her mind and she flushed with embarrassment. She also felt highly irritated by the fact that he had so much control over his passion when she obviously had none at all.

"That wasnae weel done of me," Gregor murmured as he finished lacing up her bodice.

Alana thought he had done very nicely indeed, and then silently cursed. Her ability to defend her virtue around Gregor was nearly nonexistent and she should be highly concerned about that, not thinking about the quality of his lovemaking. And, she suddenly thought, if he was doing something he felt he had to apologize for, why did he keep doing it? There was no doubt in her mind that he had a great deal of experience in lovemaking, and she did not believe she was the sort of woman who caused a man's senses to be swept away on a wave of passion. Gregor did not look particularly guilt ridden, either. Just as last time, he mouthed the words but showed little conviction in them.

He was trying to seduce her, she realized, absolutely certain of her sudden decision. Alana was not sure what she felt about that. It was certainly flattering that such a man would wish to bed her, yet his reasons for doing so might be low and insulting. She was, after all, the only woman at hand. Just the passing thought that he might be making use of her only because she was convenient and female made her angry, and she glared at him. She might prove fool enough to toss her heart and virtue at the feet of a man who would break her heart and walk away, but she would not do so for a man who saw her as nothing more than a female convenient for rutting with.

Gregor watched the vast array of expressions chase over Alana's delicate features with fascination. He could only guess at what thoughts raced through her mind. When her eyes narrowed and the golden brown color turned nearly black, he did not have to have a keen understanding of a woman's mind to know Alana was absolutely furious. He just wished he knew which of his many sins had just angered her so that he could respond correctly to whatever she was about to say and act properly contrite while doing so.

"Ye are trying to seduce me," she snapped. "Have ye decided that, since I am within reach, ye may just as weel try for a wee bit of lustful companionship on your journey?"

Since he could not honestly deny her first statement, he turned his mind upon her second accusation. He did not need to act offended as he stood up and brushed himself off, for he really did feel somewhat insulted. "I willnae ask what kind of mon ye think I am that ye could accuse me so, for I suspicion your answer will only make me angrier. Now, I will give ye a wee bit of privacy whilst I find us some wood for a fire and, if luck walks with me, something to eat."

Alana felt guilty as she watched him walk away, and then told herself not to be such a complete fool. He might not be the callous lecher she had implied with her accusation about using her, but he *was* trying to seduce her. As she stood up and sought a place to tend to her personal needs, then washed up, she decided she would not apologize. She had a perfect right to be angry over his attempts to seduce her. If he did not like the conclusions she reached as to why he would do so, then he could tell her why. In truth, she dearly wished he would, for it would certainly make it easier for her to decide what to do concerning the desire she felt for him.

By the time they had finished dining on the rabbit Gregor had caught, Alana had discovered that Gregor could hold tightly to a pout. She had been within a heartbeat of apologizing for her words to ease the chill between them when he began to act more as he had before that confrontation. Relieved, she made no complaint when he arranged only one bed near the small fire. It was also becoming a habit for her to sleep with Gregor curled up against her back and the cat curled up against her chest. Exhausted from a full day of walking, she cuddled up against Gregor, wrapped her arm around the cat, and went to sleep.

Gregor sighed as he felt Alana relax in sleep. Her delightfully curved backside was pressed hard against his groin, tempting him and keeping his desire stirred. He was a little disappointed that she had offered no apology for thinking he would use her as if she were some alehouse wench one could have for a coin or two, but decided he was partly to blame for that suspicion. He gave her no words that would allow her to judge his feelings more correctly.

Alana did not see herself as desirable to a man so, naturally, she would question his desire for her. The way she spoke of herself had told him that days ago. He would have to try harder to make her believe that he found her very desirable indeed. Simply making love to her would not be enough to convince her of that, no matter how sweet it was. If he was to gain the prize he hungered for, he was going to have to do more than pleasure her body. He was going to have to win her mind and heart. He was going to have to work hard to win what he ached for. As he rested his cheek against her soft hair and lightly cupped his hand over her breast, Gregor decided it would be well worth the effort.

Chapter 8

It was a pretty little village, Alana mused as she stood on a small hill beside Gregor and stared down at the tidy collection of houses. She inwardly sighed when Gregor put his arm around her and held her closer to his side. She knew what game he continued to play with his constant touching and his kisses. He was still trying to seduce her. Alana was not sure how she felt about the fact that he was succeeding. It was disheartening to know that she was so close to succumbing to his seduction after only four days. She would have thought that a man, even one as handsome as Gregor, would have to offer more than pretty words and heated kisses to get her to relinquish her virtue. Obviously, she had been sadly mistaken.

Charlemagne meowed softly and Alana absently scratched his ears. She looked at Gregor, who scowled down at the village. It was clear that he was not eager to enter it. They both had a few coins, each having hidden some within their clothing and safe from the Gowans. She could not believe his hesitation was because they could not afford a night at an inn and a few supplies. Since they had been traveling for four long days, she could not believe they were still upon the Gowans' lands, either. The Gowans had not appeared rich enough to own so much land.

She had several reasons for wanting to enter the village Gregor watched so warily. It was hard not to beg the man at her side to let her go to the inn she could see so that she could have a hot bath. Alana also wanted something to eat beside roasted rabbit. She knew she was spoiled, that there were many people who would think themselves blessed if they had any meat at all to set upon their table, but she really was growing heartily sick of rabbit.

"Do we go into the village or creep around it?" she finally asked.

"We cannae still be on Gowan land," Gregor muttered.

"I wouldnae have thought so. If they owned so much land, they would be as rich as kings."

"And if we go down there, we may finally be able to gain some idea of exactly where we are."

"Aye, and that would be most helpful." She knew he was just speaking his thoughts aloud as he tried to come to some decision, but Alana hoped he would be quick about it.

"And I am heartily sick of rabbit."

"Och, aye," she agreed with far more force than she had intended to.

Gregor laughed, kissed her on the cheek, and started down the hill. "We shall take a chance," he said, "although what these good folk will think of a lass carrying a cat around like a bairn, I dinnae ken."

Alana ignored that. "Do ye think I could have a bath?"

"Aye, I believe that between us we have enough coin for a bath, a meal, and, if 'tis as safe as it looks, a room for the night. 'Twill be a pure pleasure nay to sleep upon the ground for a night."

A room? Alana thought, but did not say anything. She suspected there were a lot of good reasons to get only one room, and since they had been sharing a bed since she had joined him in the oubliette, it was foolish to fret over it now. There was probably not enough money for the luxury of two rooms anyway.

By the time they reached the tiny inn in the heart of the village, Alana was tired of all the startled, even wary, looks cast her way. She knew it was because of the cat she carried. Sadly, her chest was not the sort to get so much attention, she mused with a little smile and then scowled at a gawking lady. She did not understand why people thought it so odd that she carried Charlemagne with her. A lot of people traveled with animals, and a cat was not made to walk for mile after mile. She stood beside Gregor as he bartered for a room, food, and a bath with the round-bellied innkeeper, who kept staring at Charlemagne.

"The cat, too?" the man asked.

"Aye, Master Dunn, the cat, too," replied Gregor. "'Tis my lady's pet and verra weel behaved."

"Is it hurt? Is that why ye be carrying it about like that, m'lady?" Master Dunn asked Alana.

"Nay, it isnae hurt," replied Alana. "Cats cannae trot along beside ye for miles like a dog can, aye? So I carry him. He doesnae weigh much." She inwardly cursed as the man gave Gregor what was obviously a manly look of commiseration for having to deal with womanly nonsense.

"I have clean beds, ye ken," Master Dunn said. "I dinnae be wanting them infested with fleas."

Alana was about to protest that slander against her cat when she saw a dog walking toward them, a very large, very ugly dog. Afraid she was about to find herself in the midst of a squabble between the dog and Charlemagne, she tensed, readying herself to try and protect the cat. A slight movement in the sling drew her gaze downward. Charlemagne was hiding deep in the sling and lying very still. The dog sat down by the innkeeper's side and showed no sign that it knew there was a cat so close at hand.

"The cat is verra clean," Gregor assured Master Dunn as he looked at the dog and then glanced at the sling. "He is also a complete coward," he murmured.

"Thank God," whispered Alana and ignored Gregor's grin.

After another few moments of bargaining, the man led them up the stairs to a room. Alana set her pack down and, after making certain the dog had not followed them up the stairs, set Charlemagne down on the bed. She looked around the room and subtly checked the cleanliness of the bed as the bath was brought in. It was a plain room, but the innkeeper had not made an idle boast when he had claimed it was clean. She peered out the window and saw that they had a good view of the inn yard, something that could prove very useful. When Gregor stepped up behind her, she looked over her shoulder at him and was startled when he gave her a quick kiss upon the mouth.

"I will leave ye to your bath now, lass," he said even as he started toward the door. "Nay too long, though. The gracious Master Dunn charges dearly for what he considers needless luxuries, so I agreed to the one bath and a few extra buckets of heated water."

"I promise to be quick," she said.

"Good. I will spend the time trying to find out exactly where we are."

The door had barely finished shutting behind him when Alana started to remove her clothes. She was disappointed that she could not sink herself into the hot water and stay there until it cooled and her skin had puckered up like a wizened apple, but she was determined to savor the luxury despite that. A murmur of delight escaped her as she eased her body into the water. For a few minutes, she gave in to temptation and just enjoyed the warmth of the water penetrating her body, but then she recalled that Gregor would soon return to take his turn at the bath.

She was just lacing up the body of her only clean gown when Gregor rapped upon the door and she bade him enter. "Did ye discover anything useful?" she asked him as he stepped in, followed by two boys carrying in more hot water.

"Aye." Stepping closer to her, Gregor idly sniffed her damp hair. "I am to stink of roses, am I?"

Alana blushed, realizing that her scented soap had indeed left the bath smelling of roses, a scent no man would want to carry. "Sorry," she murmured.

"Ah, weel, 'twill fade. Leastwise, I pray it will, for I fear I must beg use of that soap ye used."

She had to bite back a laugh at the grimace he made as she pointed to her soap set carefully on its piece of linen to dry. "I shall now allow ye your privacy," she said.

Gregor frowned. "I am nay sure ye ought to

wander about alone." He grinned and winked at her. "Ye could stay and wash my back."

A blush heated her cheeks and Alana knew it was not due to that bold invitation, but how tempted she was to accept it. "I think not. Are we to stay the night here?"

"'Twas my plan, aye."

"Then I shall spend my time in the kitchens seeing if I can get us some food to take with us for what few pence I still have. It might cost less if I went to the merchants, but I dinnae think it would be wise to be seen by so many. I am counting on the woman in the kitchen being eager to pocket a few coins Master Dunn kens naught about."

Gregor nodded but still frowned with unease as he watched her leave. He shrugged it aside and hastily shed his clothes. She had left him some fairly warm water, so he added only a bucketful before he climbed into the bath. Sniffing her soap, he chuckled as he recalled Sigimor making the observation that a wise man always carried his own soap. He had to wonder what scent Sigimor had had to carry once that had prompted such wisdom. As he began to wash, he decided her soap did not smell so bad and its scent was light enough that it should fade quickly. He had certainly smelled far stronger and more flowery scents on some of the men who clung to the king's court and fancied themselves men of fashion, true gentlemen of the world. Too many of them, however, seemed to ply the heavy scent in a vain attempt to hide the smell of a long-unwashed body.

One thing he heartily approved of in Alana was her cleanliness. She did not complain about becoming dirty, but she did not hesitate to get clean again at the very first opportunity. He had never been that particular before, but he knew that, if he went to another woman now, he would sorely miss that scent of clean skin touched with roses. Gregor sighed as he started to wash his hair. He had the strongest feeling it would be far more than the scent of her skin that would turn him away from another woman now.

His seduction of Alana was proving more difficult than he had imagined it would be. He had no doubt in his mind that her passion ran as hot and fierce as his own, but her innocence and her inability to believe in the depth of his desire for her were proving very stalwart shields. Gregor was not sure what key was needed to unlock his prize. It did not help his cause that she knew he was trying to seduce her and that he was unable to offer her any more than passion as a reward for her innocence. He could make her no promises. Not only was he still somewhat uncertain about what he felt or wanted, but Mavis still stood between them. It would not be right to offer Alana any promises of a future until he had let Mavis know that there would be no marriage between them.

He stepped out of the rapidly cooling water and began to rub himself dry with a coarse linen cloth. The fine line he walked between wooing Alana and not offering promises he had no right to offer yet was beginning to make him dizzy. When he held Alana in his arms, kissed her, and touched her soft skin, he felt the urge to promise her all manner of things he had never promised a woman before. Gregor knew that should tell him something, but he was not quite sure what it was. He had the feeling his heart and body had already decided that Alana was a perfect fit for him, but his mind was reluctant to concede. It might be wise to take a moment to try and understand why that was, he mused.

His wandering thoughts were abruptly shattered when Alana burst into the room. She carried a large sack and Gregor wondered how she had gathered so much of what he assumed was food for their journey. Then he noticed that she had come to an abrupt halt and was gaping at him. Suddenly recalling that he was naked and, a quick glance confirmed, aroused, he supposed he ought to hurriedly cover himself. Instead, he grinned at her.

"Ye are too late to scrub my back, lass," he said, drawing her wide-eyed gaze up from where it had been fixed upon his groin.

Alana blinked at Gregor as she struggled to clear her mind of the sight of his naked body. She knew she had rushed up to their room to tell him something very important, but it had fled her mind. She feared that if she opened her mouth to speak, some very embarrassing words would tumble out. The way he was grinning so cockily told her he did not need to hear her tell him how beautiful he was. It struck her as odd that the sight of that tall, leanly muscular body in all its glory would make her want to leap upon him and demand he make love to her, even as the sight of his manhood standing so proud between his long legs made her quail. That part looked a lot bigger than it felt when pressed against her backside as he slept. Since God intended man and woman to go forth and multiply, she had to believe it would fit inside of her, but she found it difficult to believe she would enjoy it.

When Gregor started to dress, Alana slowly came

to her senses. She pushed aside the regret she felt over seeing all that manly beauty covered up as she began to recall just why she had burst in upon him. Her trip to the kitchen had gained her far more than the food she carried.

"We must leave here," she said even as she moved to shove the clothes she had shed before her bath into her pack. "Now."

"Why?" Gregor dressed more quickly as he caught her mood of anxiety and her need for action.

"Master Dunn is selling us to the Gowans."

"The Gowans are here?"

"Nay, not yet, but Dunn is having them fetched. He heard they were looking for a mon and a wee lass." She scowled as she recalled some of the man's words. "I heard him talking to one of his workers, sending him off to find the Gowans. Dunn is certain ye are the mon the Gowans are hunting for, but he said the lass with ye is no child. Then he said he could understand the Gowans' mistake, for I am as small as a child and nay more shapely than a knotted thread."

"He is clearly as blind as he accuses the Gowans of being."

Alana blushed with pleasure although she knew his words were probably no more than a well-practiced bit of flattery spit out to soothe her badly bruised vanity. "Mistress Dunn was outraged when she heard what her mon was doing, although nay really for our sakes. She grumbled about how it would ruin their business if word spread that Dunn was willing to sell anyone out to their enemies. That truly distressed her so that she gave me this sack of food, free, saying we wouldnae have time to get back the fee we paid for this room and the meal we willnae be eating. Then she told me to flee this place."

"And that we will. I am sorely tempted to steal a horse from Dunn's stables for this."

"I think he fears that someone might, for he has set those two braw laddies of his to watching the stable."

Gregor cursed. "Get the cat. I pray we can slip away from here without being seen." He quickly shoved his belongings back inside his pack as Alana settled Charlemagne in his sling. "'Twill be a bed under the stars again, lass."

As swiftly as possible, Gregor divided the food between their packs. Thinking of the meal and the bed he had paid for but would not receive, Gregor took the blanket from the bed as well. He prayed the Gowans were not too close at hand, for he and Alana were losing a lot of time just preparing to leave. Grabbing Alana by the hand, he led her out of their room and down the back stairs he had discovered while waiting for her to finish her bath. As he led her on a crooked route, weaving in and around the buildings of the village, Gregor kept a close watch for the Gowans. It did not really surprise him when the Gowans arrived before he could get Alana out of the village. His luck had been very poor of late.

Keeping an eye on the Gowans, who were wandering about the village near the inn, Gregor finally reached the far end of the village. The open space they now had to cross to reach the wooded hills where they could hide was not so very wide, but he knew it was wide enough to be a danger to them. It would only take one fleeting glance by a Gowan to espy him and Alana, for they would be fully exposed until they reached the trees. Since there was no other choice, Gregor exchanged a hard look of determination with Alana and then headed for the trees as fast as he could run. He was not really surprised to hear her keeping pace at his side, for he had already observed her skill in running, even while wrapping one arm around the cat's sling to hold it steady. Later he would smile over how the cat had its head jutted forward, its ears flattened against its head, and looked as determined as he and Alana did.

The moment they were within the shelter of the trees and the shadows they cast, Gregor paused to look back toward the village. He felt a brief surge of satisfaction when he saw no Gowans in pursuit, only to feel it washed away by a soft gasp of alarm from Alana. Gregor drew his sword as he turned around. The Gowans had obviously grasped enough wit to place a man in the woods to watch for them. That man held a sword on Alana. Gregor briefly tasted a fury so hot he ached to immediately cut the man down.

"Let us pass," Gregor said. "We are no threat to ye."

"My laird wants ye caught," the man said. "He needs the coin your ransoms can bring us and he cannae let ye escape without trying to catch ye again, can he? It wouldnae look good."

"Shall I step back and allow ye more room to cut this lack-wit into wee pieces?" Alana asked Gregor.

"If ye would be so kind, m'dear," Gregor murmured.

"My pleasure. Have at it, then."

It amazed Gregor that he had to swallow the urge to laugh. *Have at it?* Now that his fury over seeing someone threatening Alana had cooled a little, Gregor knew he did not want to kill this man. The fool was simply obeying his laird and would be wanting to capture him and Alana alive. Unfortunately, once the clang of swords filled the air, a man could easily forget such fine distinctions.

"'Twould be best if ye let us pass," Gregor told the man even as he and the man began to warily circle each other, each waiting for the other to start the battle that now seemed inevitable.

"Best for who? Ye and the wee lass? It certainly wouldnae be best for me." The man cast a fleeting glance toward Alana. "And when did the wee bairn grow breasts, eh? True, they are as wee as she is, but I am thinking she was alying to us, aye? She be no child. Och, weel, 'tis said that sometimes the smallest fruit be the sweetest. Tiny wee bumps that they are, I bet ye find them so. Mayhap I will as weel. No need for the poor wee lass to be cast back into the pit. Nay, she can stay aboveground and warm my bed. She may have nay more shape than a knotted thread, as the fine Master Dunn says, but she will do me for a wee while."

Gregor sighed and shook his head. "And here I was deciding that I wouldnae kill ye after all. Weel, now I willnae disappoint ye after ye have worked so hard to kill all the mercy in my heart."

After chancing a brief glance at Alana, Gregor dared not look her way again, and not just because it could cost him dearly in the fight he was soon to be in the midst of. Her gasp had caused him to fear that some other Gowan had arrived, but her expression as she glared at the man facing him told Gregor it had been outrage that had caused the sound. She looked prepared to argue with the Gowan man over his disparaging remarks concerning her size.

The man's sudden attack pushed all thought but survival from Gregor's mind. Although he quickly tested the man's skill and felt confident he could beat him, Gregor did not hold back or ease his vigilance. Even the most inept of swordsmen could get lucky, and this man was not completely inept. Just as that thought passed through his mind, fate decided he had become too vain and that he needed to be taught some humility. Gregor stumbled over a rock and heartily cursed when his opponent's sword scored his right side. He quickly recovered and knew the wound was not a serious one, but he also knew that a loss of blood could weaken him in time.

Alana cursed, fear a sour taste in her mouth as the Gowan man's sword slashed across Gregor's right side. She suspected it was not a deep or serious wound, for Gregor barely faltered, but the widening dark stain upon Gregor's doublet told her that it was bleeding freely, and that could prove dangerous. Both men were fighting hard and seriously and she doubted the Gowan man was about to suddenly recall that Gregor was to be taken for ransom, not killed.

It was a strange time for her to realize that her feelings for Gregor far surpassed a mere infatuation with his pretty face or a lusting for his fine, strong body, she mused as she searched for a weapon. Espying a thick branch upon the ground, she picked it up and began to creep toward the Gowan man. Both men were so intent upon each other they never even glanced her way. She would not be surprised to discover that they had both completely forgotten about her. This ought to remind them, she thought, and the moment she saw her chance, she clubbed the Gowan man on the back of the head as hard as she could. He stood very still for a moment and then slowly collapsed facedown on the ground.

Breathing heavily, Gregor stared down at his unconscious opponent and then looked at Alana. "I am nay sure that was a particularly honorable way to end the fight, lass," he said calmly.

"I dinnae care," she said as she tossed her rough club aside. "Gregor," she murmured in a concerned voice as she started toward him, "ye are bleeding."

"Aye, but 'tis only a scratch." He sheathed his sword.

"At least allow me to bind it." She hastily pulled one of the bindings she had once used upon her breasts out of her pack and wrapped it around him. "It really needs to be cleaned and looked at most closely—"

"I ken it, but, later, lass." Gregor knelt to relieve the Gowan man of his small purse, stuffed it into his pack, and looked toward the village. "For now 'tis far more important to get as far away from here as we can."

Alana knew he was right and tried not to worry about him as they hurried away. In her experience men could be very foolish about their wounds, ignoring them far beyond what was wise or safe. She knew they could not linger so close to the Gowans, but she was determined not to let Gregor push onward for so long that a minor wound became a dangerous one. A loud cry from behind them told her it might prove difficult to keep that promise to herself. It appeared that the Gowans had finally turned their attention to the woods.

Chapter 9

Gregor slumped against a tree and closed his eyes. Every muscle in his body was screaming in protest of how hard he had pushed them and he knew it would take a while before that faded. He heard a soft thump by his feet and looked down only long enough to make sure that Alana was still conscious. She had gracefully sprawled on her back on the grass by his feet, Charlemagne still cradled gently in her arms. Slowly, Gregor sank down until he sat beside her, his back still against the tree. He hoped he was right in thinking they had lost the Gowans, for he doubted he had the strength to even crawl away from them now.

"Have we lost them?" Alana asked when she had finally caught her breath.

"Aye, I think so. 'Struth, I think we lost them just before the sun set."

"That was o'er an hour ago."

"I wanted to be sure."

"And ye are sure now, are ye?"

"Aye, I am," he replied after a moment's thought.

"I doubt they will continue to search now that it is dark, either. So, we can rest for a while."

"Oh, good. Dinnae think I could move right now anyway, not e'en if the fools threatened to ride right o'er me." She slowly sat up. "Howbeit, I should tend to that wound."

"Truly, 'tis but a scratch, lass. My doublet took the worst of the blow."

"E'en the smallest of scratches can prove a danger if it isnae tended to."

There was no arguing that. Gregor remained where he was, watching as Alana collected a few strips of linen, water, and a small pot of something from her pack. He was pleased to see no needle and thread. As she returned to his side, he removed the rough bandage she had wrapped around him and then took off his doublet. Each movement caused him to wince with pain and he meekly accepted her aid in removing his shirt.

Alana quickly retrieved a candle stub and flint from her pack. She lit the candle and carefully studied the wound. "I dinnae think it needs stitching," she said.

"Thank God," Gregor muttered.

She ignored that. "E'en with all the running ye did, the bleeding has nearly stopped. I will clean it, put some of this salve on it, and bandage it. That should be enough. It would be best if ye can rest for a day or so, so that the wound can begin to close. Do ye think that is possible?"

"It may be." Gregor hissed a curse between tightly clenched teeth as she bathed his wound. Her touch was gentle, but he doubted that eased his pain by very much. "I will ken better in the morning."

"I pray we have thoroughly lost the Gowans, left them wandering in circles e'en now." She put salve on his wound as gently as she could, but still heard him grunt softly in pain. "E'en if ye werenae wounded, I would like a wee respite before beginning our journey again. I ken I will be aching in the morning."

"As will I, I suspect, and nay just from this wound."

"Hold this here for a moment," she ordered, placing his hand against the linen pad she had put over his wound. "I will make up our poor bed and ye had best lie down," she said as she wrapped the long strips of her linen bindings around him to hold the pad of linen in place over his wound. "This injury will be pulled and pained each time ye move, I fear. 'Tis in such a place that it willnae be ignored. It will close faster if ye can bring yourself to lie flat and still for a day or two."

"It didnae seem that deep," he murmured.

"It isnae, but it still bleeds, aye? If ye pamper it for a wee bit now and we continue our journey at an easy pace for a few days, after that it should heal weel. I doubt I need to tell ye that e'en a slow loss of blood, if continuous, can fell a mon and tempt a fever."

"Aye, I ken it, but ye will need help to set up our camp."

"Nay, I can do it." She smiled faintly at his look of doubt. "Trust me."

He nodded slowly. He might trust her to do it, but that did not mean he had to like it. Unfortunately, his side burned and he felt somewhat light-headed. Gregor knew he would be more hindrance than help right now. Slumped against the tree, he watched as she skillfully built a small fire and then brought him some bread, cheese, and cold venison to eat. As he ate, she made up a bed for them near the fire. Someone had obviously taken the time to teach her a few skills so that she could survive on her own. Gregor supposed that was a good thing, but it made him uncomfortable, for he had to wonder why she needed him at all.

She needed him to protect her, he told himself, and then grimaced as his cruel memory reminded him of why she was the one setting up their camp now. In his first battle for her sake, he had stumbled like some untried oaf and gotten himself wounded. She had ended the fight and downed their foe. It was a sad blow to a man's pride. While it was true that she had needed him to escape the oubliette and while she was feverish, it was also true that anyone could have done the same. Gregor did not know exactly why he so wished her to see him as necessary to her, but he did. There was one way left to him in which he could bind her to his side, but she was proving resilient to his seduction. He really did not wish to discover that he was not as good at wooing a lass as he had thought.

When she helped him to his feet, she put her arm around him and pressed close to his side. That cheered Gregor up, and he began to think of ways to take advantage of her closeness. It only took a few steps for him to realize he would not be taking advantage of her gentle solicitude this night. What had started as a nice embrace became a necessary support to keep him on his feet. He had clearly lost a lot more blood than he had realized.

Alana frowned at him as, once he was settled on their bed, she covered him with a blanket. "Ye are looking verra pale, Gregor."

"'Twill pass," he said. "I was just thinking that my wound must have bled more freely than I thought."

"The small wounds can fool ye that way. Many people think that because the blood isnae flowing freely, the wound isnae so verra dangerous, but ye can still lose too much blood if 'tis a slow, steady loss. My cousin Syme near died of a wound upon his ankle. He was out hunting and got stabbed in the ankle by something, but he just cursed the brief pain and kept on hunting. When he finally collapsed his boot was fair soaked with blood and he had left a trail of it behind him. 'Tis fortunate that my other cousins, Uilleam and Kelvin, were hunting with him. They got him to Grandmere verra quickly, but 'twas a near thing."

"A wound in his ankle?"

"Aye. Something poked a hole in just the right place. Grandmere says there must be one of those bleeder veins down there. I kenned about the ones in the throat and in the wrist and thigh, but I was verra surprised to discover there was one in the ankle."

Gregor watched her as she removed her boots and used a little water from their supplies to wash her face and hands. Fiona had said that most Murray lasses trained with Lady Maldie to become healers. It was clear that, although she claimed her sister was the true healer, Alana was not without skill and knowledge. He almost grinned. If he kept her, Alana would join with his father's wife Mab and Fiona, giving Scarglas three skilled healers. They would be the healthiest clan outside of the Murrays themselves.

"Nay," he said when she started to get beneath the blankets on his right side. "The other side would be better."

"Wheesht, of course." She quickly got into the

rough bed on his left side and tried to settle herself comfortably on the hard ground with her back toward him. "I could hurt your wound."

"Aye, I suppose ye could, but I was thinking on how I wouldnae be able to do this."

She smiled faintly when he curled his arm around her waist and tugged her up close to him. Her smile widened slightly when she felt him harden against her backside. No matter how vigorously she scolded herself or tried to tell herself that it was just a man's blind lust for anything female, she found that sign of Gregor's desire flattering and very exciting.

It was far past time to decide what she was going to do about him. She had had a sharp reminder today that no matter how handsome he was, how big and strong and skilled with a sword, he was just a man. He could bleed and he could die. All her lessons in healing had told her that it was just a surface wound, but knowledge and good sense had done little to ease the cold fear she had felt when that sword had cut him. Alana knew she was in love with Gregor. She needed to decide just how far she was willing to go to try to gain a return of her love.

First, she would stop fighting against his seduction. Alana suspected some of that decision was aided by the sight of Gregor naked that was now emblazoned upon her mind. Despite his rather imposing size, just thinking about Gregor naked made her feel uncomfortably warm. Her palms itched to touch all that dark, smooth skin stretched over taut, fit muscle. One look at his body in all its natural glory was enough to make her feel the greatest of wantons. Alana could not even imagine how wonderful it would feel to hold him close, skin to skin, and be free to run her hands all over him.

She suffered a brief flicker of fear as she recalled how large one particular part of him was, but easily pushed it aside. Although she was bereft of experience, she had knowledge enough to know that they would fit together. The first time would probably hurt, but passion always carried a price for a woman. It was the time after the breaching that she looked forward to, and all the times after that.

Alana knew she did not have to become Gregor's lover to win his love, but she suspected it would help a little. She also knew it might not gain her any more than a lot of pleasure followed by a kindly farewell, but she had to try. If she ended up alone, so be it, but at least she could comfort herself with the knowledge that she had done all she could to win his heart. There would also be some very pleasant memories to cling to when she was alone.

With her plans made, Alana felt sleep gently drag her into its folds. She smiled when Gregor slowly moved his hand up her midriff to cup her breast. He always did that when he thought she was asleep. Her last clear thought was that Gregor plainly found her *wee bumps* to his liking.

Her body was on fire. Alana thought it odd that her mind would tell her that was pleasurable when it ought to be telling her to run for her life. Then she woke up enough to understand what was happening. Gregor's hands were stroking her breasts and she could feel the heat of his mouth against the back of her neck. This time the movement against her backside was not so subtle. Gregor had woken up very hungry indeed.

For a moment Alana reveled in the feelings coursing through her. The touch of his hands and his lips felt so good. The way he rubbed against her caused a pleasurable aching in her groin. She remembered that she had decided to succumb to the passion between them and was just about to give herself over to it when she recalled his wound. One night of rest was not enough for it to heal. If she let him do what he wanted to now, he would probably bleed all over her. That thought was enough to give Alana the strength to move away from him.

She nudged Charlemagne out of the way, but instead of immediately fleeing the bed as she did every morning, she turned to face Gregor. It was easy to see the desire in his face. She had felt it as well. His passion, his need, seeped right inside of her and strengthened her own. Alana decided it was time to give him a hint that he would soon get what he needed, what they both needed. She wrapped her arms around his neck and gave him the most wanton kiss she could. The moment she felt her wits start to flee her head, she pulled away and scrambled out of bed.

"Alana!" Gregor called as she started to walk away.

"I must find some more wood for the fire," she said, and kept on walking. "Call if ye need any help."

What he needed was for her to come back and fulfill the promise of that kiss. Gregor was feeling both frustrated and confused. Alana had never been so bold, had never taken that first step. He had always coaxed her into his arms, wooed or stolen every kiss out of her. Her first bold step had been a big one as well. His blood was still burning from the heat of that kiss. It had declared a passion and a fire he was eager to taste more fully. It had declared acceptance; he was certain of it.

Gregor cautiously sat up, the wound in his side making each move painful, but he was relieved to find that he was no longer light-headed. Unfortunately, he was also in no shape to act upon what he was sure was an *aye* from Alana. Despite his weakened condition, the mere thought of finally being allowed to make love to Alana had him hard and aching. He felt as if he had waited for her for years instead of just a fortnight.

A few yards away from camp, he slumped against a tree and relieved himself. As he waited a moment to regain enough strength to return to his bed, he looked all around and listened very carefully, but caught no sign of anyone else in the area. He wondered if they had finally reached lands the Gowans did not want to venture onto. It would please him beyond measure if that were true, and not just because he was tired of constantly watching for them. He would need a little longer to regain his strength, and when he did, he intended to spend a few more days on those blankets answering the invitation of Alana's kiss.

Deciding he had rested enough to make his way back to the blankets, Gregor started walking back to their camp. He was so weak in the knees by the time he reached the bedding, only the thought that he could add to his injury kept him from just falling on top of them. As he sprawled on his back trying to catch his breath and will away the burning pain in his side, he ruefully admitted that it might take more than a day or two to regain enough strength for all he planned to do with Alana.

"I cannae believe that worked," Alana whispered, staring down at the three fish she had caught.

As she had collected wood for the fire, she had found the river. It was not a big one and could be easily forded in several places, but it was big and deep enough for fish. At first she had simply enjoyed the sound of the water tumbling along over the rocky slope and then savored its crisp, cold taste. Then she had caught sight of the fish. Years ago her cousin Logan had shown her how to catch a fish with her hands, as well as which fish were the ones she should catch. These certainly looked like the fish he said were good and, although she could never recall the names of the creatures, she had learned how to cook them.

Her success had surprised her and she was feeling quite proud of herself. Even the fact that her hands and legs were only just starting to warm up again could not dim her pride in her accomplishment. Only the way the poor things had lain on the ground gasping for so long cast a shadow over her joy, but her stomach was obviously merciless. It was growling in anticipation of the meal these fish would make. Hunger was making her a good hunter. She was, however, going to be very glad to return to a place where someone else had to hunt for the food.

"Oh, Charlemagne, dinnae ye dare," she said when the cat drew close to the fish. "Ye will have your share once these beasties are cleaned and cooked. And I believe I shall have Gregor tend to the cleaning of them. That shouldnae trouble his wound or weaken him."

Charlemagne sat down near the fish, his tail swiping the leaves as it flicked back and forth.

"No need to look so ill-tempered, m'lad. I said ye would get some, but later."

Alana put the fish into the small sack she had brought with her in the hope of finding something to add to their food supply as she had gathered wood for the fire. At several points along the path she had taken there were now little piles of wood she could simply pick up at her leisure and take back to camp. Looping the handle of the sack over her shoulder, she picked up the pile of wood nearest her and started back to camp, Charlemagne walking by her side. The animal rarely let her out of its sight, she realized, and she was not sure if she should be touched by that or a little wary. Shaking aside a brief moment of superstitious unease, something she had always considered herself far too clever to suffer from, she fixed her thoughts upon Gregor.

"Ah, Charlemagne, I think I am soon to make a great fool of myself," she told the cat.

Charlemagne swatted at a leaf that floated down from the trees.

"Aye, a fool who talks to cats as weel as a fool who plans to give away her weel-guarded innocence to a mon who may ne'er love her as she loves him."

Charlemagne paused to sharpen his claws on a tree trunk.

Alana sighed, heartily wishing she had one of her kinswomen to talk to. Considering the romantic history of many of her kinswomen, however, they would probably just advise her to do exactly what she was planning to do. She was going to take Gregor as her lover and pray, very hard, that his desire for her held the seed of love.

A heated anticipation raced through her at the thought of having Gregor make love to her. She was clearly beyond redemption now. It was a huge risk she was about to take, one that could leave her alone yet unweddable, and she simply did not care. She loved Gregor, she wanted him, and she needed him. For once in her life she was going to do exactly what she wanted and pray that the consequences would not be too great. She just hoped she did not cause her parents too much disappointment.

As she entered the camp and watched Gregor slowly sit up, his winces telling her that the movement pained him, she knew she would have the time to prepare herself well for the very large step she was going to take. Alana placed the wood near the fire, opened the sack, and set the fish down next to Gregor. She grinned at his look of astonishment.

"How did ye catch these?" Gregor asked.

He listened to her tale with growing surprise as she handed him a knife, clearly intending that he should clean the fish. Stunned, he did so silently while she readied the fire and a spit to cook them on. Being cared for by Alana Murray could well prove to be a very humiliating experience, he decided. He had never been able to catch a fish with his hands, let alone three.

"Where did ye get them?" he asked as she collected the cleaned fish and carefully set them on the spit to cook.

"There is a lovely wee river nay far from here," she replied. "'Tis a welcome source of water, though it is a bit colder than I like. I saw no sign of the Gowans or anyone else whilst I collected the wood, either."

Gregor slowly nodded, not really surprised. "I think we have finally lost them for good. At some time during our flight from them we must have finally crossed a boundary they willnae cross."

"But ye intend to keep a wary eye for a while yet, I suspect."

"Och, aye. They hunted us for longer than I had thought they would. I was so certain that they would have to give up at some time, but 'twill be a while ere I believe this chase is finally o'er."

"I shall keep a close watch as weel, but I truly believe we have gone beyond their reach. Will ye watch o'er these fish for me? I think I will go and collect some of the wood I stacked in wee piles all along my path."

"Aye, I can do that much, at least." He heard the sour note in his voice and was not surprised to see her lips twitch as she fought to suppress a smile. He sounded like a sulky child even to his own ears. "Hand me my pack ere ye leave, if ye would. I mean to shed these clothes and wear my plaid. 'Twill be easier on my wound."

Alana handed him his pack and hurried back into the woods. She strongly resisted the urge to spy upon him as he changed his clothing. It had taken all of her willpower to hold back the shameful advice that the best way to spare his wound any irritation from his clothes would be to lie about naked. Alana shook her head as she walked to the pile of wood that sat the farthest distance from the camp, determined to give Gregor enough time to change his clothes without her gawking at him. She never would have thought that she could be so enamored of the sight of a man's naked body, but she suspected she could happily stare at Gregor's for days. Years, a voice in her head whispered, but she ruthlessly silenced it. When she returned to the camp, Gregor sat by the fire. He was dressed in a simple white linen shirt, his plaid, and deer-hide boots. She decided she liked the look of him in this simpler attire. His other clothes had been very fine, but they had marked him too strongly as a man of the world, a courtier. Although he was still so handsome he made her heart ache, somehow he now looked more attainable.

There was a look in his eye as he watched her that told Alana the kiss she had given him might not be being spoken of, but it was not forgotten. Alana was certain he had read the invitation she had tried to give him by acting so boldly. If not for his wound, she suspected Gregor would be showing her just how clearly he had understood her silent message. She forced herself not to blush as she served him his share of the fish.

Every instinct she had told her that the Gowans were no longer a threat. That meant that she and Gregor could take their ease for a while and allow his wound to heal properly. Weather permitting, they could linger here for several days in comfort. Glancing around at the trees, the many violets winding colorfully around the bases of the tree trunks, and the clear view of the hills in the not-so-great distance, Alana decided it was the perfect place for a woman to be introduced to all the secrets of passion. Glancing at Gregor again, she decided she could not have chosen a finer teacher. All she had to do was wait for his wound to heal enough for him to commence with her lessons.

Chapter 10

"Alana."

Startled by that deep voice, Alana nearly dropped the fish she had just caught. She quickly tossed the fish up onto the bank and then looked at Gregor. He was leaning against the trunk of a tree, his arms crossed over his broad chest. She wondered how long he had been watching her and hoped he had not been close enough to hear her conversation with Charlemagne concerning the success, or lack thereof, of all her attempts to make Gregor know she was ready to be his lover. The fact that Charlemagne was draped over his boots did not detract from Gregor's manliness at all, Alana thought in bemusement.

"Ye had best step out of that water, lass. Your legs are turning blue."

She scowled at him, thinking that a very poor way to seduce her, but she got out of the water and hastily lowered her skirts. "A gentlemon wouldnae be peeking at a lady's legs," she said piously.

"Weel, I have ne'er claimed to be a gentlemon, and

I have plans to be looking at a bit more than your bonnie legs."

Even though she blushed over those bold words, Alana felt her desire stir. It was clear that Gregor really did not have to try very hard at all to seduce her. For three days they had lingered in this place, enjoying the peace and the unusually fine weather. Gregor had gotten stronger each day. He had also gotten bolder with his kisses and caresses, as had she, but he had always pulled back before they had gone too far. She knew he had done so because of his wound. The look upon his face now told her that he was as tired of pulling back from their desire as she was.

"Ye are a verra bold mon, Gregor MacFingal Cameron."

"And I plan to be a lot bolder," he drawled as he gently nudged Charlemagne off his boots.

"'Tis always good for a mon to have a plan," she whispered and could not fully repress a squeak of surprise when he lunged at her and pulled her into his arms. "We must take the fish back to camp."

"Who says we are gong back to the camp? This is a fine place."

"'Tis still daylight."

"I dinnae have the patience to go back to the camp or to wait for the sun to set."

Alana was about to say something about his eagerness, which she found highly flattering, but he kissed her and she quickly forgot what she was going to say. His hunger was evident in his kiss. His need was revealed in the way he pressed her body so close to his. As her desire for him flared into full life, she felt his desire for her flow into her veins, enhancing her own and making it fiercer, deeper.

She clung to him, returning his kiss to the best of her ability, as he slowly lowered her to the soft, mossy ground on the bank of the river. It felt as if every part of her, heart, soul, mind, and body, sighed in hearty welcome as he settled his long body on top of hers.

This moment had been approaching for three long days, their need for each other growing fiercer with each kiss, each touch, each heated glance. Alana had lost all hesitation long ago. She suspected she had been as impatient for his wound to heal as Gregor had been.

"Say aye, lass," Gregor murmured against the soft curve of her neck as he unlaced her gown. "Ye have been saying it with every sweet kiss, every soft caress, and every sigh for three days, but ye have never said the word. Say it now, Alana. Say aye."

"Aye."

If he had not been so desperate to hold Alana close, skin to skin, Gregor suspected he would have collapsed from relief. Despite every sign that she was ready to be his lover, he had still suffered a doubt or two. She was a virgin, a wellborn maid whose innocence was a fiercely protected prize intended only for a husband. He had offered her no promises of love or marriage. He still feared that, at the last moment, she would hesitate and ask him for those promises he was not yet free to give her.

He stripped her of her clothes with a little more speed than skill. Desperation and greed drove him. When he tossed aside the last of her clothes, he sat back on his heels and looked her over, ignoring the fierce blush that stained her cheeks. She was sleek and soft, her curves gentle ones. Compared to the women he had known in the past, Alana was almost childlike, but he had not thought of her as a child since the day he had cut off her bindings. Alana would probably never have lush, plump curves, but he found her slender shape beautiful.

Still staring at her, watching how her nipples hardened invitingly beneath his gaze, he threw off his clothes. Gregor knew he would have to keep a tight control on his need to be inside her. She was an innocent, and he needed to be gentle with her. He did not need to have had any experience with virgins to know that the first time was very important and could leave lasting impressions, good and bad. Despite all the sensual hunger gnawing at him, he was actually a little nervous. Somehow he would have to hold back his own aching need until he had stirred her passion to a height where the pain he would have to inflict would not leave her cold.

When he settled himself back in her welcoming arms, their flesh touching for the first time, he shuddered. A faint tremor went through her and he breathed an inner sigh of relief. It might not be so difficult after all. Alana appeared to be as eager and as hungry for this as he was.

"Ah, lass, ye feel so right," he murmured as he ran his hand down her side and stroked her hip. "I have been waiting for this from the moment I discovered ye were no child."

Now that he was not staring at her so boldly, Alana felt her embarrassment finally fade away. "I have given it some thought as weel." She lightly stroked his broad chest, savoring the feel of his warm skin beneath her hand. "Ye are a verra fine-looking mon, Gregor."

"And I have ne'er seen anything as fine as ye

lying here upon the moss with the sun gilding your soft skin."

He kissed her when she started to protest his flattering words. It stung a little that she doubted his words, but he understood. Her feeling that she was no beauty was an old one, bred somewhere in her past. It could be because of things said or done, or even born of her own fears and concerns, but it was set hard. It would take more than a few kisses or his lovemaking to banish such doubts. He would give her passion and, he decided, he would give her confidence in herself. Even if she did not stay with him—and the mere thought of that gave him an odd, sharp pain—he would be certain that she left him sure of her own beauty and sensuality. It was the least he could do for the gift she was about to give him.

Alana ran her hands over his body as he trailed kisses down her throat. She could not believe how good he felt. As a healer she had seen many a male body, but she had never felt such a craving to touch one before. The feel of his warm skin beneath her hands, the movement of his muscles as he shifted in her arms, and even the faint roughness of a scar beneath her fingers all delighted her and fed her desire.

When he covered her breasts with his big, lightly calloused hands and kissed the spot between them, Alana closed her eyes and lost herself in the pleasure of his touch. The hot, damp brush of his tongue over her aching nipples made her shudder and tighten her grip on his arms. A cry that was more delight than shock escaped her when he drew the hard tip of her breast deep into his mouth and sucked. The pleasure speeding through her body was so intense Alana was surprised she did not swoon. Instead, she slid her fingers into his thick, long hair and held him in place, silently urging him on as he began to feast upon her breasts.

He murmured soft, coaxing words against her skin as he stroked her belly, but Alana was not sure what he was saying. Then he slipped his hand between her thighs, and she tensed. By the time she could grasp the words needed to protest such an intimacy, she no longer wished to do so. It was a shocking intimacy but with each caress, her passion grew. All the desire she felt for him seemed to flow downward, pooling in that place he pleasured and tormented with his long fingers. Alana heard herself gasp and then moan softly when he slid one long finger inside her. Even as he began to kiss her, his tongue moving in her mouth in perfect rhythm with the finger he moved in and out of her, her body loudly clamored for more. The way he placed a second finger inside her only eased that growing need for a moment.

"Gregor," she cried as he returned his kisses to her breasts, "I need."

"Aye, I ken it, lass. I can feel your need." He removed his fingers, praying he had readied her enough to ease the pain he would soon have to inflict upon her. "So hot and wet," he whispered against her ear as he settled himself between her thighs and slowly began to enter her. "Wrap these bonnie legs around me, dearest." He groaned softly when she obeyed his hoarse command and he felt the soft skin of her inner thighs rub lightly against his hips.

Although she still felt the heat of desire in her veins, Alana also felt an uncomfortable stretching as Gregor pushed into her slowly, almost cautiously. "Ye are a verra large mon, Gregor," she whispered, trying not to tense for she strongly suspected that would only make it more difficult for both of them.

"Thank ye."

She laughed and then yelped as he abruptly thrust himself deep inside of her. In an instinctive gesture, she placed her hands upon his chest and tried to push him away, to put an end to the sting and discomfort he was causing her. He kissed her ever so gently and then lightly rested his forehead against hers. Alana realized he was waiting for her discomfort to ease, for her body to adjust to this intrusion. There was a fine tremor in his body as he fought to hold himself still inside her. She wrapped her arms around him and realized that her pain was already fading. For a moment, she closed her eyes and concentrated on the fact that she was now one with Gregor, that they were now as close as two people could be. The last of her pain slipped away and she felt her desire return. She looked at Gregor, at his tightly closed eyes and gritted teeth, and smiled. It was probably time for her to end his suffering.

Gregor wondered if this could drive a man insane. He was exactly where he had ached to be for over a fortnight, buried deep inside Alana. Feeling her tight heat around him was pure bliss. Not being able to move now that he was there was pure agony. He was sure it was the sort of torment that could bring on madness. Since she was not moving, he feared he had caused her a lot of pain, perhaps even enough to make her heartily regret saying aye. He slowly opened his eyes and caught her staring at him, a faint smile curving her kiss-reddened lips.

"Ah, ye are done with your wee nap, are ye?" she asked.

"Wretched lass." He propped himself up on his forearms. "I hurt ye."

"Aye, a wee bit. 'Tis gone now."

"Thank God."

He kissed her even as he began to slowly move inside her, thrusting gently as if he feared she would break. Alana wrapped her legs more firmly around him and quickly began to meet his every thrust, letting her body's greed guide her. Soon she wished him to be less gentle, less carefully controlled in his movements. Her whole body seemed to be tensed on the brink of some unseen edge. Alana moved her hands down Gregor's back and grasped his taut buttocks, trying to push him deeper inside her. That brought a deep groan out of him and suddenly his movements grew fiercer and less measured.

Gregor muttered something against her neck that sounded vaguely like an apology, but Alana paid it little heed. Her body felt as though it was reaching for something, although she did not know what. And then she felt all the taut need inside of her shatter, a sweet fire spreading throughout her body. She called out to Gregor, wanting him to share it with her. She could feel him with her a heartbeat later, his hoarse voice shouting out her name as the warmth of his seed flooded her womb. Alana clung to him, holding him deep within her, as she gave herself over completely to the pleasure he had brought her.

Gregor slumped against Alana, resting most of his weight upon his forearms. He was feeling both stunned and quite proud of himself. He had fulfilled his promise to bring her pleasure but was astounded by how much she had brought him. In all the times he had been with a woman he had never felt such passion, such fire, and such complete satisfaction. Gregor could still feel the thrill of his release running through his body. He felt wrung out, but knew he could be eager for more very soon.

This was what he had been searching for in the arms of all those other women. He had finally given up the search and decided to seek a little land and coin through marriage instead of some great passion or bonding. With Alana, he thought, he had found the richness of feeling that made Ewan and Sigimor such happy men. This was what he wanted, what he needed, and what he intended to have.

Words crowded into his mouth and he bit them back. He had no right to speak of a future yet. And, he realized, after having nearly betrothed himself to the wrong woman once, he was feeling hesitant to offer any promises to another. Gregor felt a strong need to be sure, absolutely sure. Alana certainly felt right, but that could be passion clouding his reason. He would be cautious this time. There was also the fact that, if he did offer any promises to Alana, he did not want her finding out about Mavis afterward. That would surely make Alana think he was far too free with such words and that his promises meant nothing.

Slowly easing himself out of her embrace, he turned onto his side and tugged her hard against him. She still had a hint of pleasure's blush upon her face and her brown eyes were rich with warmth as she looked at him. When she turned onto her side and kissed his chest, he felt a renewed twitch of desire.

"Is there any pain, love?" he asked, lightly stroking her hip.

"Nay, just a wee bit of a sting and, weel," she blushed, "I am a wee bit sticky."

Gregor laughed and stood up. He pulled her to her feet and ignored her blushes as he looked her over. There were a few red marks upon her breasts caused by the rough scrape of his emerging beard and only a little blood upon her thighs. He picked her up in his arms and walked into the river. It was sharply cold, but the day was warm and made the water feel almost pleasurable. Setting Alana down on her feet in the water, he used his hand to sluice water over her body and, ignoring her squeaks of protest, between her thighs.

"Ye have no respect for a person's modesty," she complained as he dragged her out of the water and dried her off with his shirt.

"None at all," Gregor agreed cheerfully and tugged her shift on over her head.

Alana watched him don his plaid and sighed. The lovemaking had been all she could have hoped for, but the afterward was very disappointing. Gregor had held her and gently stroked her skin as they had regained their senses, but there had been no love words. She sternly told herself that it was much too soon, that men were very slow to recognize any feelings beyond lust and an easy affection, but she was not sure she believed that excuse.

"Ye are looking verra serious, lass," he said quietly as he moved to stand in front of her. "Regrets?"

"Nay," she said and meant it.

"Good." He draped his arm around her shoulders and kissed her cheek. "Best we get back to camp ere Charlemagne steals your fish."

Seeing the cat creeping up on her fish, Alana hurried over to put her catch safely into her sack. She tugged on the rest of her clothes and walked back to the camp with Gregor. Although the lack of love words troubled her, she found that his easy manner made it easier for her to feel comfortable with him despite what they had just done. On the bank of the river. In the full light of day. Alana shook her head in amazement at her own daring.

As she readied the fire, Gregor cleaned the fish. She sat and watched them cook as he went on a hunt for more wood. It all seemed so normal, so ordinary, that she felt a little dazed. It was hard to believe that just a short time ago she had lost her maidenhead on the riverbank. Only a faint soreness between her legs told her it had not all been just some strange dream. Alana wondered if this was how all lovers acted, their lives as normal as everyone else's except for brief, heady moments of passion.

Nay, she thought, there should be more. She doubted Gregor bedded down with virgins every day of the week. There should have been a compliment or two if nothing else. It was almost as if he was purposely saying as little as possible, although she could not think why he would do so. She supposed she could just ask him how he felt, but she shied away from such a direct approach, fearing his answer.

She had said nothing, either, she reminded herself. There had certainly been a lot of words dancing on her tongue, but they would have come straight from her heart and she did not believe Gregor was ready to hear them. Alana had made love with Gregor because she loved him, but she knew men did not have to feel so deeply when they bedded a woman. Gregor lusted after her, of that she had no more doubt, but she needed so much more from the man. From tales the other women in her family had told her, getting that more from a man could take some time. Alana hoped she had the patience.

Gregor struggled to keep the conversation between him and Alana light as they ate the fish she had cooked, almost too light to be interesting. He knew he was acting as if nothing momentous had happened down by the river, but he was still too confused to trust himself to speak of all that had passed between them. He could tell by the look in her eyes that she was troubled by how he behaved, but he needed time to find a safe middle path to walk with her. Although he did not want to offer her promises or vows of love, neither did he wish to appear so unmoved by what they had shared that she was hurt or, worse, withdrew her favors.

When they climbed beneath the blankets, Gregor could feel the chill in her begin and knew he had to do something. He pulled her into his arms and kissed her, relieved when her brief resistance quickly melted and she returned his kiss. As he reached down to stroke her slim thigh, he kissed her ear and felt her shiver.

"Ah, lass, my bonnie wee Alana, ye do shake a mon to his roots," he murmured as he kissed the hollow at the base of her throat.

"Ye didnae appear verra shaken," she felt compelled to say.

"And that didnae seem odd to ye? Wheesht, do ye think I ravish virgins upon riverbanks every day?"

She smiled faintly as she stroked his arm, realizing that she had been so caught up in her increasingly morose thoughts that she had not even noticed he had stripped off all his clothes before joining her in their rough bed. "Weel, nay. From what little I have heard, most men avoid our ilk."

And they both knew why, he thought, for taking the maidenhead of a wellborn virgin was often a quick route to the altar, but that was a subject he desperately wished to avoid. "'Twas a wondrous gift ye gave me," he said softly, "and I am nay speaking of that wee shield of your innocence. Ye gave me fire, lass, a passion more fierce and satisfying than any I have e'er tasted. Sweeter, too. I did fear that I had hurt ye badly, especially when I grew so rough near the end."

"Nay, ye didnae really hurt me, nay more than was necessary. And I didnae find ye rough at all."

"'Tis good of ye to say so, but I ken weel that I failed to be as gentle with ye as I should have near the end."

Alana lightly trailed her fingers over his chest. He sounded disgusted with himself. She suspected a man like Gregor did not like to lose control, and she was sure he had. Although she found it unsettling to speak of the act itself, she could not leave him thinking he had hurt her or been too rough. She had savored those final moments when his desire had possessed him so completely, just as hers had done to her. It had been exactly what she had needed and would undoubtedly need again. She did not want some well-practiced minstrel in her arms concentrating on each move he made instead of on her and on the pleasure they could share. She wanted Gregor, just Gregor, even if that meant rough and greedy.

"I rather liked it when ye were a wee bit rough," she said softly, daring a quick glance at his face before fixing her gaze upon his chest. "'Struth, I wanted faster and harder."

She was a precious jewel, Gregor thought, as

he tilted her face up to his and kissed her. "Or slow and gentle?"

"Any way ye wish it 'tis what gives ye pleasure, for yours is mine."

"Tell me, my sweet treasure, are ye sore?"

"Nay. I told ye, 'twas just a wee sting and it has long since faded."

"Good, for I feel suddenly compelled to make love to ye again." He started to remove her shift.

There was an odd note of tension in his voice, but Alana decided it was due to his desire. She could feel his erection brushing against her leg as he undressed her. He still had not spoken of love, but she no longer felt so uneasy. From all that he had said, he had suffered from the same sense of awkwardness that she had. His words had not carried the taint of empty, well-used flattery, either. Such open expressions of his desire and how much pleasure she gave him would be enough for now, she told herself firmly and then turned all of her attention to the delight she could find in Gregor's arms.

Gregor held the back of a sleeping Alana close against his chest and pressed a kiss to the top of her head. He idly stroked her flat belly and smiled when she murmured his name in her sleep and briefly rubbed her taut little backside against his groin. He should be exhausted, such was the ferocity of the passion they had just shared, but he could feel the willingness to start all over again tingle in his groin. She was making him insatiable, he mused, and grinned. Insatiable was good.

He had taken her words to heart as the full truth

and allowed himself to just give and take pleasure, his only concern being that Alana gained as much enjoyment from their lovemaking as he did. For once he had not thought carefully about every touch, every kiss, and every thrust of his body. It had been the most sensual interlude he had ever enjoyed. The fact that Alana was a very responsive woman, willing and eager to share in the passion that flared between them, only made it easier for him.

As he watched Charlemagne curl up against Alana's chest, Gregor yawned and closed his eyes. If the weather held fine, they would stay here for a day or two and revel in their passion. All too quickly life and all its trials would intrude again, from the need to find Alana's sister to extracting himself from the courtship of Mavis. And he would extract himself from that tangle the moment he reached Scarglas, he vowed. Mavis was a good woman, but there was no passion there. He tightened his hold on Alana a little as he made himself another vow. No matter what the future did or did not hold for him and Alana, never again would he consider marrying for anything less than a true, fierce passion.

CHAPTER 11

Gregor was inside her. Alana woke slowly, a soft murmur of delight escaping her when she realized it was not a dream. One of Gregor's hands was on her breast and the other was moving down her body. A flicker of surprise cut through her desire when she realized he had joined their bodies while still behind her. Then his clever fingers found that spot between her legs that could drive her utterly mad and she lost all ability to think. Alana let passion grasp hold of her as tightly as Gregor did as he took them both to paradise.

Light shivers of pleasure still rippled through her body as she stroked the arm Gregor had wrapped around her waist. She had not realized there were so many ways to make love. For the past two days, Gregor had taught her a great deal. Alana did not want to think about where he had learned such things, however. She was not fool enough to think Gregor had come to her as innocent as she had come to him, but she truly did not want to know exactly how much experience he had. It would be too easy to start comparing herself to all the beautiful women he had known before her. Beautiful women with big, lush handfuls for breasts and plump, rounded bottoms.

Such thoughts quickly cooled the lingering warmth in her blood and she slipped free of Gregor's hold. Hastily donning the shift he had removed from her last night, she grabbed her pack and sought out a private spot in the woods. Alana knew she had to stop allowing thoughts of other women to spoil the time she and Gregor had together. He was hers now. He might not be hers for as long as she wanted him, but for right now, she had to do her best to suppress the attacks of jealousy she kept suffering from. Since she had taken such a big risk, it was foolish to waste one single moment of whatever time she might have with Gregor worrying over women he had known before her.

Once she had seen to her personal needs, Alana hurried to the river to bathe. Glancing around to make sure she was alone, she stripped off her shift and plunged into the water. She gritted her teeth against the sharp cold and bathed as quickly as she could. Since she was growing as tired of fish as she was of rabbit, she ignored the ones swimming by her as she soaped her hair and then sank beneath the water to rinse the soap away. Once that was done, Alana fled the water and rubbed herself dry as briskly as she could to try and return the warmth to her body.

The very first chance she got, she was going to have a long—very long—hot bath, Alana promised herself. As she dressed and braided her hair, Alana savored the thought of that bath, idly wondering how long she could soak in the hot water before she looked as wrinkled as an ancient crone. And this time, it would be her bath and only hers, so that there would be no need to hurry. Gregor could find his own.

When they did finally reach a place where she could pamper herself so, it would probably be time for Gregor to decide if he wanted to stay with her or continue on his own, she thought with a heavy sigh. She was so torn. She needed to find Keira, to know her sister was safe, but finding Keira meant the end of her journey with Gregor. Despite the dearth of any words of love from him, she felt certain that he cared for her. It was there to see in the way he held her close as they slept, in his smile, and even in the way he spoke to her. Yet for all she knew, Gregor treated all his lovers so tenderly, right up until he left them behind.

So she would just have to work harder to make Gregor want to keep her by his side. If they were at his home, she could show him what a good helpmate she could be. She had certainly done her share in keeping them fed and warm in their travels, but she doubted that was quite the same thing in Gregor's eyes. She knew he liked to talk with her about anything and everything, and he liked the fact that she could give him a challenging game of chess, but all that had been true from the start and had brought her no whispers of loving words yet.

That left one thing—lovemaking. Gregor was a very sensual man and she knew he enjoyed every part of making love, for she could feel his desire as if it were her own. As Alana started back to the camp, she decided that she was going to be the best lover Gregor had ever known. Perhaps that was the key to his heart. She was willing to try anything now, for all her instincts told her that the time she had left to find that key was rapidly running out.

* * *

The moment Alana returned to the camp, Gregor gave her a kiss and wandered off to see to his own personal needs. Life was good, he thought as he relieved himself under the curious gaze of Charlemagne and then headed to the river to wash. The place they were camped in had plenty of food and water, although it was a little humiliating to discover that Alana was a better hunter of small game than he was. The weather was exceptionally good, as if nature itself had decided they deserved a respite from the cold and the damp.

Ah, and then there was sweet Alana, who was proving to be a lover beyond compare, he thought with what he suspected was a besotted grin. The cold water of the river quickly doused the desire that thought had stirred. As he hastily washed, he tried to decide what it was that made her so much better than all of the others he had known. He had always believed that, as concerned the actual act of lovemaking, one woman was much the same as another. Alana had proven him wrong about that from the start.

There was no question that knowing he was the only man who had ever been with her stirred feelings inside of him he was hard pressed to describe. Arrogant and hypocritical though it was, he liked the fact that no man had ever touched that soft skin, kissed those beautiful breasts, or felt her tight heat clench around him as she cried out his name. He had never before cared who or how many other men a woman had known before or after him, but the mere thought of another man even kissing Alana made him feel decidedly murderous. Yet he did not think the gift of her innocence was what made her feel so right.

Stepping up onto the bank, Gregor nudged Charlemagne off the coarse linen cloth he had taken from the inn and briskly rubbed himself dry, his mind still set on trying to work out the puzzle that was Alana. She gave him the freedom to be himself above and beneath the blankets, he thought and smiled. He had not realized how coldly precise he had become, how carefully he judged every touch and movement. It had been the best way to arouse the woman enough so that he could get what he was after. He had been called a good lover, but he now knew he had also been a selfish one, his skills learned not for the woman's sake, but for his own. And with Alana, he did not seem to have to plan or calculate. Not only did her passion match his perfectly, but it was almost as if he could feel her desire, sense the pleasure she felt when he touched her. He was no romantic fool, but he could swear that when that sweet release swept over them, they truly were one, their sense of pleasure as united as their bodies. It was something he suspected he would never understand, but he was starting to crave it.

As he began to walk back to camp, he decided it was time to continue their journey, and he sighed. He hated to leave this idyll, but he had promised Alana he would help her find Keira, and that would not be accomplished by living in the forest like a pair of carefree wood sprites. There was also the chance that his family had gotten word of how he had disappeared somewhere between Mavis's home and Scarglas. They would worry and start to search for him. Alana's family had to be worried, too. Although a selfish part of him wanted to shrug aside those concerns and spend a few more days frolicking in the woods with Alana, he knew he could not give in to it.

There was such a serious look upon Gregor's face as he sat down beside her and helped himself to some of the porridge she had made that Alana felt compelled to ask, "Is something wrong?"

"Nay, I had just decided that we had best start walking again and wasnae feeling too happy about it," he replied and smiled at her.

Alana did not feel too happy about it, either, but she smiled back at him. "Aye, it is time. I have been feeling as though Keira is close at hand for a while now."

"Close at hand, but nay in trouble?" He decided he liked the way Alana had flavored the porridge with a finely chopped apple. A good cook, he thought, and then felt a little ashamed of himself for making a tally of her good points before coming to any decision about her.

"Nay, not in trouble, but troubled. That evil mon I dreamed about is gone now. I am hoping that is because he is dead." She grimaced. "Bloodthirsty of me, I ken it, but I think he was a mon with a lot of blood on his hands and he would ne'er leave Keira alone unless he or she was dead."

"A hard truth, but one that cannae be ignored when ye must face it. I suspicion your sister has. Now, if ye can feel her as ye say ye can, then she cannae be too far away."

"I shouldnae think so, but I dinnae ken where *we* are."

"If we set a brisk pace, we should reach the monastery of Saint Bearnard before nightfall."

Alana stared at him in surprise and disbelief. "The monastery near Muirlan?"

"Aye. Do ye ken where that is?" Gregor savored the last few mouthfuls of the wine Mistress Dunn had given them.

"I do. My cousin Matthew is there. Weel, he is Brother Matthew now."

Gregor shook his head. "Is there anywhere in this land where there isnae a Murray lurking about?"

She laughed and shrugged. "There *are* a lot of us, but in truth, Matthew is a Kirkcaldy. That is my grandmother's family." Alana suddenly gasped as a realization swept over her. "Of course! *That* is why I have been feeling Keira."

"Do ye think she went to your cousin for help, then?"

"She went to him to hide." Alana thought about that for a moment and only became even more convinced of it. "Aye, she went to Cousin Matthew when she was hurt, which means that Ardgleann cannae be all that far away from Muirlan and the monastery."

"I cannae say where Ardgleann is, but I do ken that Muirlan isnae verra far from Scarglas." He shrugged when Alana looked at him with faint curiosity, for he knew most men had a much better knowledge of the land around them for many days' ride than he did. "Because my father had such a keen skill for making enemies, we were surrounded by them. One clan, the Grays, felt it was their right to kill any MacFingal they found. We didnae travel far because of that and we tended to stay on the most sheltered trails when we did. I can tell ye a great deal about every clan encircling Scarglas, a wee bit about how to get to Dubheidland, where my cousin Sigimor is laird, and some of us have been to Deilcladach, where Fiona's brother Connor rules, but little else. E'en though it is no longer as dangerous as it was, old habits die hard and we still dinnae travel verra far."

Suddenly realizing that Alana might ask him why he was so far from home when the Gowans captured him, Gregor quickly asked her what she knew about the monastery. He breathed an inner sigh of relief when she began to tell him all she could recall from the things Matthew had told her family over the years. Keeping secrets from Alana was proving to be very hard work and making him feel guilty. He shook aside that thought and forced himself to listen closely to all she told him about Muirlan.

Within an hour they were ready to begin the walk to Muirlan. Alana looked around the campsite, both sorry to leave and eager to start the journey that might well take her to her sister. She knew she could not linger here with Gregor and hide away from the world any longer, but it was impossible to completely rid herself of the sadness that knowledge brought her. Smiling faintly at Gregor, who took her by the hand as he started to walk, she fell into step at his side. She would not think on how near the end of their journey was, an end that could hold both joy and great sorrow for her. The only consolation she could see ahead of her was that the joy of finding Keira would help her survive the pain of losing Gregor if she failed to win his heart.

Gregor decided they could take a rest at midday, for they had covered a lot of ground already. He sat on a rock warmed by the sun and watched Alana trail Charlemagne, who had insisted upon getting out of his sling and doing a little exploring. That, he decided with a brief grin, was a very odd cat, and then he laughed softly before taking a drink of water.

"Do ye want some of these oatcakes, lass?" he called out to Alana. "They are the last of the bounty Mistress Dunn sent with us."

"Aye," Alana replied from the small cairn she was intently studying. "I will be there in a moment."

Gregor frowned when, as Alana crouched down by the bottom of the cairn, she suddenly became very tense and still. "Did ye find something?"

"Oh, aye," she replied in a slightly high voice, but still she did not move as much as a finger. "An adder."

A chill rushed through Gregor as he leapt to his feet and drew his dagger. Walking as softly yet as swiftly as he could, he approached Alana. It took him a moment to see the snake, for the shadows cast by the rocks hid it very well. It was within striking distance of the wrist of Alana's outstretched hand. She must have reached right over it, he thought in horror. The way the snake was poised upon the ground eyeing Alana's wrist told Gregor that the adder could well strike soon even if Alana did not make a move.

Just as Gregor readied his dagger and took aim, praying that he could kill the snake before it bit Alana, Charlemagne leapt through the air from someplace to his right. Alana cried out in alarm, but Gregor grabbed her and yanked her away before she could move to try and stop the cat. Holding her in his arms, he stepped several feet away from the snake and began to feel truly sorry that the cat would soon die. Even as that touch of grief began to creep over him, Charlemagne started to walk toward them, a very limp snake hanging from his mouth. Still holding Alana, Gregor began to step back from the approaching cat.

"Jesu! Drop that!" Gregor ordered, a little surprised when the cat obeyed him.

"Is it dead?" Alana asked, fighting the urge to rush to Charlemagne and pick him up.

"It looks verra dead to me," Gregor replied after looking closely at the snake. He picked a stick up off the ground and poked at the adder, but it showed no sign of life. "Aye, 'tis dead."

"Oh, Charlemagne!" Alana broke free of Gregor's now-light hold upon her arm and rushed to gather her cat up in her arms, although she took care to give the dead snake a wide berth. "Do ye think he was bitten, Gregor?" she asked even as she began to carefully look the cat over for some sign of a wound.

"Being that he is such a small creature, love, I suspicion ye would see him sickening already if he had been bitten."

Gregor rolled his eyes and scowled at the cat as Alana fawned over it, telling it what a *brave wee mon* it was and other such nonsense. As he followed her back to where they had set down their packs, Gregor did not know whether to laugh or cry. He had been outmaneuvered by a cat. One thing he was learning from this journey with Alana was humility, he mused and inwardly grinned. Sitting back down on the rock, he watched Alana feed the cat some of the rabbit they had carefully tucked away in their supplies for later.

"I was planning to sup on that," he murmured.

"There is still plenty left," Alana said as she sat back on her heels and watched Charlemagne eat. "He seems to be weel, aye? I think ye are right. He would be sickening already if the snake had bitten him."

The cat finished the meat and began to wash itself.

Gregor shook his head. "I didnae ken that cats would hunt and kill adders."

"Nay, neither did I. I am nay sure they do. Howbeit, Charlemagne did it verra weel. Quick and deadly."

"So, ye arenae useless, then, are ye?" Gregor said to the cat, biting back a smile at Alana's look of outrage.

"He is a verra fine cat," Alana mumbled, feeling a little foolish yet not certain why.

Gregor smiled. "Aye, he is, e'en if he did ruin my chance to play the gallant rescuer."

"Oh." Alana bit her lip but was unable to fully suppress a giggle. "Weel, mayhap next time."

Still tasting the fear he had felt for Alana, Gregor just grunted. The poison of an adder's bite did not kill everyone unlucky enough to be bitten, but it could kill some. Alana was so small and slender, Gregor felt certain she would have died if she had been bitten. He had felt chilled to the bone until the threat to her life had ended. In truth, he still felt shaken. As she sat on the ground next to the rock he sat on to eat her oatcakes, he stroked her hair, feeling an urge to reassure himself that she was unharmed.

She had become important to him, he realized. Very important. Gregor knew that should tell him something very precise about his feelings for her, but he was not sure he wanted to know what it was. From all he had seen in the past, when a man let his heart gain the reins, he became an idiot. He was determined to make his decisions concerning Alana with cold, calm reason. It was what he had thought he had been doing with Mavis, but he now knew that greed for her dowry had interfered, as well as a compulsion to have what Sigimor and Ewan had. He still felt that urge, but this time, the woman he sought to share the rest of his life with would *fit*.

"It looks as if the cat will survive," he said as he stood up, needing to start moving and shake free of his thoughts.

"Aye." Alana smiled, stood up, and brushed off her skirts. "I still cannae believe he did that."

"Neither can I. I believe Charlemagne thinks he is a dog. He follows one about like a faithful hound, travels about with us like one, and protects ye like one. Aye, that cat thinks it is a dog." He looked down at the cat that waited patiently by Alana's feet as she donned the sling she carried him in. "He is sadly confused."

"Nay, he is just afraid to be left alone," Alana said, a hint of laughter over his nonsense tinting her voice as she settled the cat in the sling and picked up her pack.

Gregor could understand that. It was one reason he had decided to search for a wife. Fleeting moments of pleasure with too many women he did not really care about were no longer enough. Far too often the pleasure gained rapidly faded into dissatisfaction and emptiness. He had also thought to step away from his large family, to make his own life. That was no longer so important to him, not if it meant he had to bind himself to the wrong woman for life in order to do it.

Taking Alana by the hand, Gregor started walking. He tried to imagine Mavis spending so many days walking, sleeping beneath the stars, and catching dinner as well as cooking it, but it was impossible to see her doing any of it. It would not have mattered so much if Alana had lacked such skills, but he found he was very pleased that she had them. There was something almost comforting about it. It had certainly made this journey a lot easier.

"Do ye think your sister will still be at the monastery?" he asked and then frowned as she tugged free of his grasp and went back to the small cairn. "'Ware, lass, there may be more adders nesting there."

Alana picked up the stick Gregor had used to poke at the snake. She stood back from the piled rocks forming the marker and used the stick to carefully knock toward her what she had been reaching for when she had confronted the adder. Picking it up, she hurried back to Gregor's side and took his hand in hers.

"Weel? What treasure did ye think was worth facing another adder?" he asked as they started walking again. He frowned when she blushed and slowly opened her other hand to show him her prize. "Alana, that is a rock."

"Aye, and a verra pretty rock, too."

"I see. Ye have decided that the cat and a full pack arenae enough weight for ye to carry and so ye have decided to add a few rocks to it all. For this ye risked getting poisoned by an adder's bite?" He knew he was revealing a little of the anger he had felt when she had put herself at risk again.

She sighed. She recognized the look that had settled upon his handsome face. It was the one men wore when they thought they were dealing with some strange womanly whim. Or, she thought with a faint smile, someone who was not quite right in the head. To many men, the two things were often very similar. Alana doubted she could make Gregor understand, but she hoped an explanation would help, if only in easing the anger he had clearly felt over the way she had returned to a place where danger might still lurk. After all, it was already proving very difficult to reach his heart without him thinking she was slightly mad.

"'Tis pretty," she said, "and I like pretty things. 'Tis all swirling colors and it feels cool and pleasant in my hand." She carefully placed the rock in his free hand. "I like rocks. They are a creation of God and nature, and that one has probably been lying about for more years than we could e'er count."

That was true, Gregor thought, not that he had ever considered the matter before. Rocks were everywhere, and if he thought of them at all, it was that they could trip one and they hurt if one fell on them. This rock did feel cool, and it fit nicely in the hollow of his palm. He even supposed one could say it was pretty. All that did not really explain why she had felt so compelled to collect it that she had returned to what could have been a nesting ground for adders.

"'Tis also a memory," she continued. "Years from now, I can pick that rock up in my hand and it will stir all the memories of this adventure." She accepted the rock when Gregor handed it back to her and then placed it in the small pouch hidden in the folds of her skirt. "I often select a rock from places where something important happens or to mark a special moment."

"And staring death in the eye wasnae enough to help ye hold fast to the memory of this moment and this place?"

"Ah, weel, the adder was certainly frightening. I couldnae move or e'en think, just stare at it and wait all asweat for it to bite me. But ye and Charlemagne came most gallantly to my rescue. Now, each time I pick up this rock, I shall see it all again most clearly."

She shrugged. "Many people have things to, weel, celebrate certain events."

True enough, Gregor thought. He was not sure he wanted her to remember that a cat had saved her life whilst he stood by like a dumb bullock, however. Still, he could understand keeping something to stir one's memory, which too often grew cloudy as time passed. He knew one woman who kept a lock of hair from every lover she had had, but he decided that was not a tale to tell Alana. She might ask how he knew about it, and he did not want her to know that a lock of his hair was a part of that woman's ever-growing collection.

"That one rock is all ye need to recall this whole journey?" he asked, wondering why he felt an increasingly sharp pinch of guilt and embarrassment whenever he thought of his somewhat licentious past.

Alana blushed. "Weel, I do have one I found down by the river." He did not need to know about the one from the oubliette, or the cottage, or the inn where she had first seen him naked, or from the camp where they had made love by the fire, she decided. Her pouch was starting to get a little heavy.

Gregor nodded and started walking, but inside he was grinning like a fool. The time by the riverbank when he had finally claimed her was *definitely* a memory he wanted her to keep sharp. He found he was a little sorry he had not collected one himself.

The sun was just beginning to disappear beneath the horizon when they reached the monastery. The heavy doors that would allow them within the surrounding walls were already shut tight. Alana felt tense with anticipation and fear as Gregor loudly rang the bell hanging beside the doors to call someone to the gates. A few moments passed, which felt like hours to Alana, before a round-faced monk opened one big door just enough to peer out at them.

"What do ye want?" he asked in what Alana thought was a rather unfriendly greeting from a monk.

"I need to see Brother Matthew," she replied. "I am his cousin Alana Murray of Donncoill."

"Murray?"

Alana widened her eyes in shock at the note of alarm in the man's voce. "Aye, Alana Murray of Donncoill. I am hoping that Brother Matthew will have some news concerning my sister, Keira Murray MacKail."

"Are your brothers with ye?" The man stuck his head out farther, stared at Gregor for a moment, and then looked around. "Ye dinnae have those two savages with ye, do ye? They have already been here twice. Twice, mind ye!"

"Savages?" Alana was starting to get annoyed by the way this man spoke of her family. "Let me speak to Brother Matthew."

"Nay!" the man snapped. "No more Murray lasses!" he bellowed and slammed the door shut.

Chapter 12

Blinking at the door that had been vigorously shut in her face, Alana heard the monk drop the bar in place on the other side. He was muttering angrily but, although she could easily discern the tone of his voice, she could not make out the words. A moment later she heard other voices. Some other monks had arrived, and there was obviously a fierce argument going on just inside the doors. She looked at Gregor, who had leaned against the rough stone wall and crossed his arms over his chest. He looked far too amused for her liking.

"I believe Keira did indeed seek out our cousin Matthew," she said.

"Och, aye, I would have to agree with ye, lass." Gregor could not help himself, he started to laugh, and the disgusted and slightly offended look Alana gave him only made him laugh harder. "And it appears your brothers came avisiting as weel," he added and laughed some more.

"'Tisnae *that* funny," she muttered, wondering

what her family could have possibly done to so upset the monks of Saint Bearnard's.

"Pardons, lass, but, aye, 'tis just that funny," Gregor said as he started to calm down. "Do ye think he means the brothers ye were following?"

She sighed and nodded. "Aye, and I fear Artan and Lucas can be, weel, a wee bit intimidating if they choose to be, although I cannae believe they behave so with monks. And why would they come here twice? They do like Matthew, but they say that monks make them nervous. Something about how they may truly have God's ear and the vow of celibacy." This time she had to smile when Gregor laughed, but the opening of the door quickly drew her full attention. "Matthew!" she cried when she saw who was standing there, but the door was not open enough for her to embrace him as she wished to, and he appeared to be fighting to keep it open even that much. "Am I truly unwelcome here?"

"Nay, of course not!" protested Matthew, speaking loudly in the vain hope of hiding the fact that several other voices said aye. "There has been a bit of trouble lately, is all, and the brethren are a wee bit nervous." He looked at Gregor. "Who do ye have with ye, lass?"

"Gregor MacFingal Cameron," she replied and heard someone cry out, *Och, nay, we cannae have another one of them here, too!*

Alana looked at Gregor and cocked one brow. "It appears that 'tis nay only my kinsmen causing trouble."

"Nay, nay, no trouble, cousin," protested Matthew as he continued to fight to keep the door open as someone just out of her sight was trying very hard to close it. "Wait there, lass, and ye, sir. I will join ye in but a few moments. Do ye have need of some food and drink?"

"Aye, if ye would be so kind. And I am seeking some word of Keira's fate."

"Weel, I have plenty to tell ye about that. Be patient for just a few moments and I will join ye. Wait there."

The door was forcefully shut again and Alana heard more raised voices. She looked at Gregor again. "This is all verra strange, aye? But I think there is a verra interesting tale to be told and I am most anxious to hear it."

"I wonder if one of my kinsmen was here," Gregor murmured as he frowned at the door, "or just some mon named Cameron."

"It could have been one of your kinsmen. The question is why? And why were my brothers here twice? Keira coming here is the only thing I can understand or guess at the reasons for the visit. I certainly cannae guess what trouble she may have stirred up, for Keira ne'er causes trouble."

Alana was just about to bang on the door when Matthew appeared, struggling with two large baskets full of food. He barely missed getting slapped on the backside by the heavy doors, they were shut so quickly behind him. Gregor relieved Matthew of the burden of one of the baskets, and her cousin started to lead her and Gregor along a winding path.

"Where are we going, cousin?" Alana asked Matthew.

"To the cottage we keep for guests of the monastery," replied Brother Matthew. "Is that a cat ye are carrying about like a bairn?"

"Aye. I call it Charlemagne."

As they walked Alana explained about the cat and answered all of her cousin's many questions about how she had come to be knocking on the gates of the monastery. Although she wanted to shake Matthew until he told her everything he knew about Keira, she struggled to remain calm and let him tell her all the news when he was ready. By the time they reached the little cottage he led them to, however, Alana was gritting her teeth in rising impatience. The fact that Gregor appeared to find it all highly amusing only added to her rapidly rising temper.

"Come in and sit here," Matthew said as he set his basket on the table. "We can talk as ye eat."

"She was here. Right here in this cottage," Alana whispered, feeling Keira's presence so strongly she was surprised she could not see her standing there. "She stayed here and she was afraid of something. Or someone."

"Someone," said Brother Matthew. "Please, Alana, come and sit down and allow me to tell ye what I can about Keira."

Ignoring the sudden sharp look Brother Matthew gave him, Gregor put his arm around Alana's shoulders and held her close for a moment. "We have found her trail, love. Now let us hear her story." He kissed the top of her head when she nodded and then led her over to the table, where her cousin waited.

"I cannae believe that both ye and Keira have had such adventures," said Brother Matthew as he poured some wine into the sturdy wooden goblets he had set out on the table. "By God's grace, ye have both survived."

"I wasnae really hurt, cousin," Alana said. "I ken weel that Keira was hurt, and badly, so I think."

"Aye, her injuries were grave ones."

"Mayhap ye should begin at the beginning," Gregor said between bites of bread. "All Alana kens is that her sister's husband is dead, that Keira was hurt when Ardgleann was taken, and that she has disappeared."

"Eat, eat," Brother Matthew gently urged Alana, "and allow me to tell the tale. When I am done ye can question me as ye will. Now, an outlaw named Rauf Mowbray murdered Keira's husband, the laird of Ardgleann. Rauf and his men took Ardgleann at great cost to its people. Aye, Keira was badly hurt, for Rauf wished to claim the laird's wife along with his lands. Your sister sustained her injuries when she fought him."

"Did he—" Alana began to ask, terrified of the answer even though she felt almost certain her sister had escaped that fate.

"Nay!" Brother Matthew hastily patted her hand where Alana had clenched it on the table edge. "She escaped him ere he could commit that sin against her."

Alana nodded and forced herself to relax. She had been horrified and frightened by the mere mention of such a crime against her sister. Now that she thought about it more carefully, she knew what her cousin said was true. If Keira had been raped, she would have known it. Such brutality could never have been committed against her twin without her having felt something, having been aware of the pain Keira felt in some way. It did, however, explain the fear she knew had clung to Keira while she had stayed in this cottage.

"Keira stayed here to heal," Brother Matthew continued. "At first she stayed in the guest quarters within the monastery, but I moved her here as soon as she had healed enough to care for herself."

A quick exchange of a look with Gregor told Alana that he was thinking the same thing she was. One of the monks had some trouble with that vow of celibacy and had made life difficult for Keira. Alana said nothing, however, just began to eat and wait for her cousin to continue.

"Keira had a dream about a mon who needed help," said Brother Matthew. "It was Liam Cameron."

Gregor sat up straighter in his seat. "Liam? Was my cousin badly hurt?"

"Och, aye." Brother Matthew shook his head. "Beaten sorely and either fell or was pushed off a hillside onto some rocks. Broke his leg. A woman had him beaten. She was jealous for she thought he had, er, wooed her sister when he refused to woo her. They are both married ladies, ye see."

"Nay, it didnae happen. Liam ne'er beds down with wedded lasses." Gregor smiled faintly when Brother Matthew blushed at the word *beds*.

"I ken it. He healed weel. Keira saw to that. She has the touch, ye ken. Then that woman came here seeking Liam, and her jealous husband was close behind her, demanding Liam's blood. Liam and Keira fled here and traveled on to Scarglas." He looked at Alana. "Ere he was so cruelly murdered, Keira had promised her husband that she would help the people of Ardgleann get free of Rauf Mowbray, and she decided it was past time to fulfill that promise. Liam swore himself to help her in that quest and he felt his kinsmen would be eager to help as weel." He pulled a letter from inside of his robes and handed it to Alana. "I have but just received a full accounting of all that happened after they left here. I think Keira's own words say it all much better than I can."

Alana read the letter twice before handing it to Gregor so that he could have a look. She knew Keira had been precise but no more and would not care if her letter was shared around. Very few of Keira's feelings about her new husband Liam Cameron or the evils done to the people of Ardgleann could be read there. Some matters were still unsettled, and Alana could sense her sister's worries and doubts behind the unemotional words she had written. The threat of Rauf Mowbray was gone and Ardgleann would heal, but Keira was still sadly troubled and uncertain.

Gregor inwardly frowned as he read the letter. Alana's sister wrote cleanly, in script as well as in word, but there was very little emotion revealed in the letter. It read like some cold report from a bailiff, a simple recitation of facts and not the letter of a young woman who had seen her worst enemy defeated and who had married a man like Liam. He suspected Keira Murray MacKail, now Cameron, was hiding something.

A quick glance at Alana revealed that she was frowning in concern. Liam was undoubtedly the beautiful man she had seen in her dreams. Most women would sell their own grandmothers to be married to a man like Liam, but there was no real sense of that triumph or joy in Keira's letter, and Gregor suspected *feelings* were involved. What concerned him the most was what Alana thought of it all. Liam was his kinsman and had benefited greatly from the marriage to Keira, yet if he sensed something wrong, he was certain that Alana could sense a great deal more.

The very last thing he wanted was trouble between him and Alana because one of his kinsmen was not making her sister happy.

"Liam Cameron is a good mon, lass," Brother Matthew said quietly. "He trained right here, thinking to become a monk, but he didnae have the true calling." He accepted the letter back from Gregor with a faint, absent smile, most of his attention remaining fixed upon Alana. "He will be a good husband to Keira, kind and faithful, and a good laird to the people of Ardgleann. Aye, and Liam has the wit to ken what must be done to keep them all safe and prosperous. Ye shouldnae worry so." He glanced at the letter before tucking it back inside his robe. "I ken she doesnae say so, and that there may be a few things still worrying her, but Liam will soon end whatever doubts she clings to."

Alana sighed and hastily finished a bite of apple. "Mayhap. But I am close now and can go to her side if need be."

"True, and I am certain she will be most pleased to see ye as weel, for word of your disappearance has spread."

"Oh. That is why Artan and Lucas came here twice, isnae it. Once because of Keira and once because of me. Were they so verra much trouble, then?"

Brother Matthew chuckled. "The brethren here arenae the bravest group of men, and your brothers were in an ill mood. As Artan said, they had just finished hunting down one sister, and ere they could rest, they had to go out and hunt down another." He smiled when Alana groaned. "Word had reached them that ye had followed them, but since ye hadnae appeared, they were concerned. They were following their own trail back to the start in hopes of finding ye. That is why they stopped here. 'Tis a wonder ye didnae meet with them somewhere along your route."

"Let us pray that my brothers dinnae meet with the Gowans."

"They were looking verra rough, lass. I dinnae think the Gowans would see them as a good choice for ransoming."

"Actually, cousin, I was worrying about the Gowans," drawled Alana and shared a laugh with Matthew. "At least now I ken why we were so unwelcome."

"That was wrong and so I told them. It wasnae Keira and Liam who caused us trouble, but others such as that woman and her enraged husband and Brother Peter, who still claims Keira bewitched him. And nay, he didnae hurt her. Liam threw him into a wall. Just punishment, I say, but men of the church do tend to cling to the idea that such sinful thoughts and deeds are all the fault of the woman. As for your brothers, 'tis the brethren's own cowardice that makes them reluctant to see those two again." Brother Matthew shook his head in disgust over the behavior of his fellow monks. "Your brothers didnae hurt anyone or break anything."

"Ah, so they were on their best behavior."

He laughed again and nodded. "Weel, except for threatening Brother Peter when they returned here for the second time. A lad who had been sent here by his family decided to follow Keira and stay at Ardgleann. I fear he told your brothers what Brother Peter had tried to do to Keira. They didnae hurt the mon, although I feel they had every right to. The mon's robes shouldnae protect him from such as that.

But as Artan said, there isnae much satisfaction in hurting a mon who soils himself at the mere sight of a clenched fist."

"Artan is quite the font of wisdom," muttered Alana.

For a while they ate and talked quietly, sharing what news they had each gathered over time. Even old news was welcome, for it could always warn of some future trouble or explain why something had happened. It was not until Brother Matthew stood up, ready to return to the monastery, that Alana realized the full awkwardness of her situation. She breathed a hearty sigh of relief when Gregor grasped her cousin by the arm and led him out of the cottage, talking all the while about Matthew's kind hospitality, the good food, and the rigors of travel. Cowardly though it was, Alana was more than happy to allow Gregor to deal with whatever lectures, demands, or protests Matthew intended to offer.

Gregor stopped several feet away from the cottage and looked at Brother Matthew. The man scowled at him. "Naught ye can say will change my mind. Or hers. We stay together."

"She is a weelborn lass," began Matthew.

"I ken it. I also ken she is the sort one marries. That is for us to decide, however. She is two-and-twenty, nay some young, sweet bairn of a lass just cut loose of her nurse's apron strings."

"She is an innocent nonetheless."

Gregor decided it would not be wise to correct the man about that. He suspected Brother Matthew was not really referring to the innocence of Alana's body anyway. The man was right, too. Alana was not the sort of woman a man used for his pleasure and then walked away from. As her kinsman, the good monk also had every right to be angry and concerned. It was, perhaps, only fair to speak the truth. For the last few miles, calm, cold reason had been telling Gregor that he would be a complete fool if he did not hold fast to Alana and he told Brother Matthew as much. He also told the man all about the complication called Mavis.

"Oh, I see." Brother Matthew frowned. "Are ye verra certain ye arenae legally betrothed to the woman?"

"Verra certain. No vows have been exchanged, no papers have been signed, and I havenae e'en asked her. Aye, it was made plain that I was there with an eye to making her my wife, and for that I feel I owe her an explanation for why that isnae going to happen."

"Aye, ye do." He sighed and shook his head. "I just pray that Alana doesnae find out what ye are hiding ere ye can speak all I think ye are keeping hidden in your heart, for your sake as weel as for hers."

Brother Matthew's words kept tumbling through his mind as Gregor watched the man leave. He then went to the well and pulled up a bucket full of water. Standing there by the well, he washed up before returning to Alana. There was certainly a risk in not speaking plainly to Alana about what he wanted and what he had to do, and he knew it, but he would take it. He knew Alana would step away from him if he told her about Mavis, if only because she would feel he was not truly free. He could not allow that.

"Is my cousin verra angry?" Alana asked the moment Gregor returned to the cottage.

"Nay. I think your sister and my cousin caused him the same concerns. Dinnae trouble yourself o'er him.

'Tis but that, as your kinsman, he feels he must say something. There is a well just outside if ye wish some water to wash with."

Alana hurried away and Gregor turned his attention to building up the fire. Tonight he and Alana would make love in a proper bed, and he was looking forward to it. A good fire would make certain that the night's chill air did not invade the cottage and it would give him light to see her by.

Brother Matthew's words continued to make Gregor uneasy. However small, there certainly was a chance that Alana could discover the truth he was keeping from her on her own. Gregor did not need to know the depth of her feelings for him to know that would hurt her. It could also cost him dearly, for she would surely see it as a huge betrayal, a lie great enough to put into question everything he had said and done while they had been together. He had to bind her to him in every way he could without breaking his vow to himself that he would offer her no promises until he had ended all ties to Mavis, no matter how tenuous those ties were. And, he thought as he watched Alana come into the cottage, he knew one way to do that.

When Alana looked at Gregor, she felt herself blush at the look in his eyes. She also felt her blood warm. It was obvious what he had been thinking of while she had been outside washing off the dust of their journey. For a brief moment, she felt the pinch of shame and embarrassment, but she shook free of it. She knew it was because of her cousin knowing what was going on between her and Gregor, but she would not pretend that there was nothing just to please him and ease his worries about her. Alana also suspected that Brother Matthew was not so pious as to condemn her, and he understood Murray women too well to press her too hard about this.

Gregor slowly rose from where he crouched by the fire and started to walk toward her. He moved like some great cat stalking its prey. Alana trembled faintly beneath the power of the sensual promise glittering in his eyes. He pulled her into his arms and smiled at her in a way that made her feel a little breathless. Alana wondered if his ability to stir her in such a way would ever fade.

"We have a bed, my sweet treasure," Gregor said as he began to unlace her gown. "A proper bed, nay one of blankets spread o'er the hard ground."

"Aye, so we do."

She stood still as he removed her clothing piece by piece, brushing fleeting kisses over her skin as he uncovered it. Her modesty tried to make her flinch away from such exposure, but she wrestled it into submission. Now was the perfect time to begin her plan to reach his heart through the one thing she felt sure of—his desire for her. He liked looking at her, so she would let him. She quickly discovered that, with her modesty silenced, the way Gregor looked at her naked body was very exciting. It was as if the heat of his gaze seeped right into her veins.

"My bonnie wee Alana," he murmured as he began to kiss her throat, pleased by this sudden boldness she was revealing, "ye are as soft as eiderdown and as sweet as clover honey." He gently nipped the hardened tip of each breast before picking her up and carrying her to the bed. "Aye, and the sight of ye nearly made me forget we have a real bed to lie upon this night."

He set her on the bed, rapidly shed his clothes, and joined her there. Alana murmured her delight as she ran her hands over his lean body, savoring the feel of every ridge and hollow. She returned his kiss with a hunger she made no attempt to hide or soften. The boldness that had allowed her to stand naked before him without blushing freed her in many ways. Alana had not thought lovemaking could get any better than it was with Gregor, but she had been wrong. What few tethers she had unknowingly kept upon her passion were now cut, and she took brazen delight in his every kiss and caress. Her own caresses of his long, strong body grew more daring as well.

A soft protest escaped her when he moved his kisses downward from the breast he had been feasting upon. Alana tried to touch him in all the places she knew he liked, but he proved surprisingly elusive all of a sudden. When he slid his hand between her legs, she opened herself to the intimate caress. It was not until his kisses reached the juncture of her thighs, his mouth replacing his fingers there, that he suffered a check in her bold new demeanor.

"Gregor," she whispered in shock, yet her body was already greedily welcoming this new intimacy.

"Hush, love," he whispered back and lightly nipped the tender inside of her thighs. "I think ye will like this. Wheesht, I think *I* am going to like it verra much indeed. Let me, loving. Let me please you."

She did. With but a few strokes of his tongue, he banished all of her hesitation. Alana not only let him, she soon encouraged him. Then the tight burning she recognized as the start of her release gripped her and she tried to tug him up into her arms. He ignored her, sending her tumbling fast and hard into desire's abyss. Alana was still caught firmly in the grip of her release when he thrust inside her, and she wrapped her body tightly around his as he fiercely pushed her right over the edge a second time before he joined her there.

It took Gregor a long time to recover enough strength to flop onto his back and tug a limp Alana into his arms. He grinned as she muttered and curled her sleek body around his. His grand plans to make love to her all night were probably ruined, but he was not too disappointed since it was his lovemaking that had put her into such an exhausted stupor.

In his mind he patted himself on the back, pleased that he had heeded Liam's advice years ago. There certainly was satisfaction in knowing he had given Alana something he had never given another woman. It was small payment in return for the gift of her innocence, but it still pleased him. He had thought his cousin a bit of a fool for not taking his fill of every sensual experience he could, but something had caused him to heed the man's advice. Not quite understanding why, he had found himself holding back a little and he was now very glad of that. There were things he could do with Alana that he had never done with another woman, and he was eager to try every one.

He was not sure he could ever share that knowledge with her, however, for it could remind her a little too clearly that he had vast experience, but it was still satisfying. The fact that she had gone wild with desire as he had kissed her so intimately had certainly pleased him. He had every intention of doing it again.

And, he thought as he felt Charlemagne curl up by his side, he had every intention of keeping Alana.

Now that the decision had been made, he wondered why he had hesitated to face the truth for so long. She was his mate. There was no doubt in his mind that Alana felt *right*; she *fit*.

Gregor inwardly shook his head. There was no comparison between the cold, somewhat mercenary plans he had been making concerning Mavis and the ones he now made concerning Alana. Letting his heart lead him in deciding what to do in this matter was not what made him a fool. Trying to use calm, cold reason and nothing else when it concerned something so sweet and hot as what they shared together did, however. It did not even matter if he felt he could use the word *love* when describing what flared between them and what made him feel bound to her in so many ways. He could sort out those feelings later. As soon as he released Mavis, he intended to tie Alana to his side in every possible way known to man. She did not know it yet, but she was caught and he would never let her go. He had been her first lover, and he intended to be her last.

Chapter 13

"We have a horse," Gregor announced as he stepped into the cottage, his hair still damp from his morning wash. "Your cousin has been verra kind to us and given us a horse to ride to Scarglas." He handed Alana a short letter that had been tied to the horse's saddle along with a pack full to bursting with food.

Alana smiled as she read her cousin's farewell, one surrounded by apologies for not being able to say it in person. A part of her relaxed, the small part that had feared his disapproval and scorn. Matthew also asked that she be sure to send him word of everything that happened once she got to Scarglas and was eventually reunited with Keira. Alana was not sure what Matthew expected to happen to her, for Scarglas surely marked the end of her journey, but she silently vowed to write him a very long letter as soon as possible. As she tucked the small letter into her pouch, she had to smile over the way he had said he felt sure they could borrow Brother Peter's horse. There was still a lot of mischief in her cousin.

When she followed Gregor outside, she nearly gasped

aloud. Brother Peter had a very fine horse, so fine that Alana was a little wary about taking it. It seemed strange, however, that a monk would keep such an elegant animal. Big, mottled gray, and strong, this was a knight's horse, the mount of a warrior, not a monk.

"Cease your frowning, love," Gregor advised as he mounted the big stallion and pulled Alana up behind him. "I truly do mean to return this horse." He patted the animal's strong neck. "Or pay weel for him if he proves a weel-behaved lad. The poor beast must be weary of standing about and doing nay more than pulling a cart or taking a monk on a slow amble down the road."

"I was thinking much the same." Alana looked up at the sky and grimaced. "I believe our spell of verra fine weather is soon to come to an unpleasant end."

After a quick glance up at the sky, Gregor nudged the horse into a slow trot. "It certainly doesnae look promising, but at least we can ride through it now instead of walking."

Alana was not sure that would make travel in the rain all that much better. Twisting the sling that held Charlemagne off to her side, Alana put her arms around Gregor's waist and rested her cheek against his back. She yawned widely and then grinned even as she felt herself blush. Gregor had wakened her once during the night to make love to her, and she had greeted the morning with him making love to her again. She had become utterly shameless and, despite the shyness and embarrassment she had not yet fully conquered, she fully intended to be shameless again.

She had discovered more than a blinding passion in Gregor's arms last night. Alana knew she had discovered something about herself. When she set that wanton part of her free, she felt beautiful and more womanly than she had ever felt before. The way her boldness so clearly enflamed Gregor gave her a sense of power. Although she knew she would never abuse it, she had liked the taste of it. She also recognized the threat to herself in such feelings, for they could make her feel too confident, even make her think she had already won the battle for Gregor's heart. That could be very dangerous indeed, she thought as she closed her eyes. If she lost her battle to win Gregor as her own, that confidence would ensure that the fall she suffered when he walked away would be very hard indeed.

The feel of chilly water falling on her face woke Alana from a very pleasant dream of Gregor holding their child and smiling at her with love in his fine eyes. She scowled up at the sky, knowing by the ominous roiling of the dark clouds that the gentle rain falling now would soon become a deluge. A sharp *meow* drew her attention and she quickly adjusted the sling so that a very cross-looking Charlemagne was sheltered from the rain. It would serve only for a little while, however, as the blanket was no real protection against a cold, hard rain. Neither was her cloak.

"Awake now, are ye?" asked Gregor.

"Aye. Sorry I was such poor company," she replied. "We are soon to be thoroughly soaked, I am thinking."

"Mayhap, but there is a wee shepherd's hut but a short ride from here. Your cousin left me a verra detailed map. I think he suspected that the weather could easily turn against us."

"Matthew has always had a keen skill at judging such things."

"He also seems to ken the importance of marking each and every possible place to shelter from the rain when he draws a map."

"Ah, weel, Matthew has also always hated to get wet."

"That explains the map, then. I thought it odd that he would leave me a map to show me the way to my own home. 'Struth, I was a wee bit insulted. But now I see that he was but showing me where shelters were along the way that I might nay ken about. Mostly for your sake, I am sure."

"Mayhap it was for Charlemagne's sake," she drawled and smiled when he chuckled.

The rain was falling harder and the wind had gained strength by the time they reached the tiny shepherd's hut. Alana stood huddled in her cloak, Charlemagne tucked beneath it, as Gregor carefully checked the inside to be sure that it was empty, of men and of wild animals. And adders, she thought, touched by how her experience with the adder seemed to have truly frightened him. The moment that he signaled that it was all right for her to enter, she hurried inside, grateful to be out of the cold rain no matter how mean their shelter.

She set her pack down on the floor of hard-packed earth and then released Charlemagne. The cross look the cat wore as it glanced around the hut nearly made her laugh. Charlemagne was becoming one very spoiled cat.

"Aye, 'tis a sad, wee place," she said as she took off her cloak, shook it out, and hung it on a nail near the door. "But at least it has a door," she murmured, quickly stepping out of the way when it started to open.

Gregor stepped inside and closed the door. He dropped the two packs he had carried in down next to Alana's things, hung his cloak on a nail next to hers, and looked around. It was a poor little place, with a firepit in the center of the room and a hole in the roof for a chimney. It was also very dark, the only light in the room coming through two very narrow slits in the front and back walls. The pile of wood and peat against one wall suggested that the place had become a regular stopping place for cattle drovers or travelers. He had seen no sheep as they had ridden here, so he doubted it was still a shepherd's hut. At least it had a solid slate roof and thick stone walls. And, he thought as he glanced up at the smoke-darkened roof beams, was high enough within that he did not have to crouch. Seeing a bucket tipped on its side in a far corner of the room, he picked it up and set it outside the door to catch some rain.

"At least this time ye willnae have to catch our food," he said to Alana as he started to build a fire. "Your cousin packed us a feast."

"Matthew felt embarrassed by the way the monks treated us, I think," she said as she sat down near the fire he was building, eager for the warmth it would provide.

"Och, weel, as he said, his brethren arenae the bravest of men, and such men oftimes are as afraid of the lasses as they are of big, armed men."

"It probably helps them to hold to their vows to think all women are sin on two legs."

He chuckled and sat down next to her. "It was non-sense such as that which made Liam decide that he didnae want to be a monk. The mon has a verra strong faith, but he had no tolerance for some of the foolish ideas the cloistered men cling to." He winked at Alana as he warmed his hands by the fire. "He also missed the lasses."

"Ah, I see." She lightly bit her bottom lip and then asked tenuously, "He *will* be good to Keira, will he not?"

"Aye, lass." He wrapped his arm around her shoulders and held her close, smiling faintly when Charlemagne squeezed himself between them and faced the fire. "Liam truly is a good mon. He just didnae have a true calling, as your cousin calls it. Yet when Liam left the monastery, he didnae walk away from all he had learned or all that had taken him there to begin with. He gave your sister vows and he will hold fast to them. E'en before he wed her, he held fast to vows he had made only to himself. Aye, he liked the lasses and they adored him, but he bedded no virgins, no wives, and no women who were betrothed, even ones who claimed they didnae want the mon they would have to marry. And e'en though Liam and Keira were forced to marry, trust me in this, Liam could ne'er have said his vows unless he wanted to and meant to hold fast to them."

She nodded, wanting to believe all these assurances she was getting concerning her sister's new husband. Yet she still felt that Keira was troubled, even sad. If it was not Liam Cameron causing Keira to feel so, then what was it? She knew she would have to see Liam and Keira together before she could make any true judgments. Alana knew that men did not always see what a woman did, that sometimes the men they thought to be so good and honorable made very poor husbands. All the goodness the man revealed to his male companions was not extended to his wife.

Although she desperately wanted to believe that Keira would not allow herself to be married to a man she could not trust or love, Alana was no longer so naïve. She also knew that her sister had not really loved her first husband but had hoped the fact that she had liked and respected him would lead to love. It had not, of that Alana had no doubt at all. Yet she now knew the power desire could have over a woman. It was possible that Keira had fallen into a powerful lusting for Liam Cameron and was now discovering that such a thing did not always lead to love, either. Or, worse, Keira loved, but it was not and might never be returned. That would certainly explain the sadness she felt her sister was suffering from.

"Cease fretting o'er it, lass," Gregor said as he unpacked some of the food her cousin had given them. "Ye can do naught about it. I dinnae think there is aught ye need to fret about, but I understand that ye will need to see that for yourself or hear the assurance that all is weel from your sister's own lips."

"Aye, ye are right." She took her eating knife out of the sheath hanging at her waist and cut herself a bit of cheese. "'Tis just that I ken her first marriage wasnae a good one and now, so soon after she was widowed, she is married again. Och, and to such a beautiful mon who has married women mad with jealousy and chasing him all about the land."

Gregor was getting very tired of hearing Alana refer to Liam as a beautiful man. When she went to see her sister, he would go with her. Only a fool would let his woman get too near a man like Liam, one who seemed able to turn a woman's mind to warm gruel with just a smile, unless he was standing right at her side. With a sword. He no longer found the jealousy Ewan, Sigimor, and others suffered over the man all that funny.

"The lasses have always chased Liam," he said as he cut up a few bits of chicken and set it before Charlemagne. "It didnae stop him from turning his back on them and entering the monastery for several years."

"Ah, true. Weel, Keira will tell me what troubles her when I see her, so I shall cease to fret o'er it. Mayhap by the time we reach Scarglas the sadness I feel she is suffering now will have passed." She frowned as the wind blew so strongly it rattled the door. "'Tis going to be a verra fierce storm. Do ye think we ought to bring the horse in here with us?"

He bit back a smile. Only Alana would fret about such a big, strong horse being caught out in a storm and actually suggest they share their small shelter with the beast. She had a very soft heart as concerned animals. He was glad she did not allow it to make her hesitate to catch a fish or a rabbit, although he suspected she would swiftly and gladly give up her hunting when their journey ended.

"There is a wee shelter for him at the back of this hut, and this place also shelters it from the worst of the wind. I think the monks, and others, may use this place when they travel, for 'tis weel supplied with wood and peat for the fire and hay for the horse. Those who use it must replace what they use whilst here. We are following a weel-traveled drover's trail and they, too, like to have some shelter along the way as they take the cattle to market."

Gregor had been planning to stop at an inn between

the monastery and Scarglas, but he was now glad they would not be spending the night there. He had suddenly recalled that there was a buxom maid or two there who knew him very well. Alana knew he was no innocent, but he did not want her actually meeting any women from his past. Even worse, there was absolutely no chance his frolics there had been forgotten, for they had been frequent and he had spent a lively night there just before traveling to begin his courtship of Mavis. He really had been a greedy piglet, he thought ruefully.

Alana looked at Gregor as she drank from the wine-skin Matthew had sent along with them, enjoying the way the sight of him and the heady drink warmed her insides. Suddenly she felt guilty for not telling him about her father's plans for her. Trust was an important part of the marriage she was longing for. By not telling him, she was, in a way, lying to him, and there was always the chance that he would find out. It would be even worse if her father had broken with Murray tradition and actually arranged a betrothal, binding her to someone without asking her approval of the man first. She did not think he would do so, but it was not impossible, and there was a good chance he could come very close to doing so. That would set a complication in her path that would prove very awkward to step around. And, she thought, Gregor's reaction to the possibility that she might be given to another man could tell her something important about how he felt about her.

"Still troubled about your sister?" Gregor asked when he caught her staring at him.

"Nay, not so much anymore." She grimaced. "I was but thinking of my family. I left them a note and all, but they will still worry about me. My disappearance could also prove a wee bit awkward for my father."

"Awkward? How so?"

"Weel, I didnae lie to ye when I said I was neither married nor betrothed, because I wasnae when I left Donncoill. Howbeit, my father was searching for a husband for me," she admitted quietly. "It isnae the way we Murrays usually do it, but—" She shrugged.

Gregor violently disliked the idea that some man might, even now, be given the right to lay claim to Alana. "But what?"

"I am two-and-twenty, ye ken. Many years past the age when a lass is usually married. Many women my age have a few bairns clinging to their skirts by now. I hadnae e'en been properly kissed, as I think ye ken weel by now. So, my father suggested that he find a husband for me and I decided he may as weel do so as I was a sad failure at it. He was setting about the chore when I decided I had to find Keira."

It was an awkward conversation for him to get tangled up in, Gregor mused. He did not believe that Alana was telling him this in some sly attempt to get him to offer her marriage. This was a confession, nothing more. They were lovers and she obviously felt he was owed the full truth about her circumstances.

He was going to have to tread warily. He wanted to assure her that she need not worry, that she was his and he would be more than willing to face down any man who tried to say elsewise, but he had to bite back the words. It would be just his poor luck to speak so fulsomely to Alana and then have her discover his courtship of Mavis. Alana would think him some faithless idiot who made a habit of offering marriage to a woman.

"If 'tis the custom amongst the Murrays to allow their women to choose their mates, I suspicion your father will hold to it," he murmured. "I doubt he continued at the task once ye disappeared anyway. He would be putting all his time and wits to the matter of finding ye."

For a moment, when she had told him of the possibility that a marriage could have been arranged for her, Gregor had looked gratifyingly fierce. But only for a moment. Alana sighed. She had seen the hint of jealousy or possessiveness in his eyes, but not enough to make her certain he felt it very deeply. It was enough that she had been fully honest with him, she told herself, but she did not really believe it. She was growing weary of telling herself that something was enough when it was not enough at all. She simply nodded in response to his words and went to fetch the bucket he had set outside and then placed it near the fire in the hope that it would take a little of the chill off the rainwater.

Gregor inwardly cursed and moved away to collect their blankets and make a bed for them near the fire. He told himself that his complication was not the same as Alana's. It was not unusual for a father to search out a husband for his daughter, whereas he was his own man and had purposely set out to find a wife who could give him land and coin. She had confessed to something she had no real power over, something that may or may not have been settled while she was running around trying to find her sister. His confession, if he roused the courage to give it, was about something he had chosen to do, something that had already happened and that he now knew had been a mistake.

When Alana stepped out for a moment of privacy, he cursed himself for a complete coward. He could list all the good reasons he could think of for not grabbing this chance to confess about Mavis, but his silence was born of fear. There was so little time left to be alone with Alana that he did not wish to give her any reason to pull away from him now. A woman he was but a few words and a signature away from being betrothed to would be a very good reason to Alana.

The moment Alana dashed back inside, he hurried out. It was cold and the wind was so strong it made the rain sting as it struck him. Gregor took care of his needs, checked on the welfare of the horse, and hurried back inside. He barred the door even though it looked as if a strong man could easily knock it down, barred or not, and then turned toward Alana. She was already curled up beneath the blankets, her clothing folded neatly on top of her pack. Gregor did not hesitate to strip off his clothes, have a quick wash, and crawl beneath the blanket with her.

He pulled her into his arms, pleased that she was already as naked as he was. "Thank God that your cousin doesnae like to get wet," he said as he stroked her slim back. "'Tis a braw storm and I am that glad we are out of it."

"And the horse isnae suffering?" she asked, idly caressing his hip.

"The horse is fine," he said, laughter tinting his voice, and he kissed her on the cheek when she blushed. "Trust me, if I thought any harm would come to the animal, I would bring him in here whether ye liked it or nay. A mon who doesnae care for his horse as if it is his own blood kin is a fool."

She nodded and huddled a little closer to him as the wind howled around the hut. Alana shook aside the disappointment she still felt over his lack of any easily read response to her confession. It had been foolish to think it would be enough to reveal any great secret about his feelings for her. She was fortunate that he had not thought she was trying to prod some declaration or vow out of him. From what she had learned about men and women from the men in her family, trickery such as that was something that could make them very angry. She wanted to build upon Gregor's trust in her, not rip it all down. And she had added to that trust he felt; she was certain of it. That would have to be enough for now.

Gregor tilted her face up to his and kissed her, the desire he stirred so effortlessly quickly banishing her troubled thoughts. Alana clung to him as he gently urged her onto her back. She hoped her troubles never grew so great that Gregor could not kiss them away. A little voice in her head added the words *if he stays with ye*, but she ignored it. Their time to be alone together, to act freely upon their desires, was rapidly fading and she would not waste any more of that precious time fretting about the future.

Hungry for the way his lovemaking could make her feel, for the way it cleared her mind and heart of all worries, she gave herself over to the passion soaring within her body. She only tensed a little when his kisses moved down her body and she felt the heat of his mouth upon that part she had no name for. The way his intimate kiss made her feel, however, was too good to resist, even though the wildness that seized her was a little frightening. She could feel Gregor's pleasure flowing into her and knew he was almost as stirred by the act as she was. The fleeting thought that he might like her to do something similar to him skipped through her passion-dazed mind but was swiftly gone as blind desire left her with no ability to do any more thinking.

As she felt herself teetering on that sharp edge he could so easily lead her to, Alana heard herself call out for him to join her. She could barely recognize herself in that hoarse, demanding voice. Gregor laughed as he kissed his way back up her body, feasting upon her breasts as he thrust inside her. His possession of her was fierce, his movements hard and fast, and she reveled in it all. The way he joined her in her release only added to the glory of it all. The way his cry of completion blended with hers was sweet music to her ears.

Struggling to catch her breath, Alana trailed her fingers up and down his spine. He was careful not to rest his full weight on top of her and she was able to enjoy the feel of his body pressed so close to hers. His breath was hot against the curve of her neck and it warmed her. She smiled faintly as she realized she even liked the way he slowly grew soft and slipped free of her body.

Her thoughts clearer, she was able to carefully consider the small differences she had felt in Gregor as they had made love. There had been a strong hint of possessiveness within him, a fierce, manly urge to claim her and hold fast to that claim. She had been so completely caught up in the force of her own desire and need, she had barely acknowledged the intrusion of such a feeling, but she could not ignore it now. It was possible that he had not been as unmoved by the thought of her being given to another man as he had appeared or wanted her to believe.

Hope stirred within her heart and she was unable to fully banish it. Gregor had just tried to mark her in

some strange, manly way. She was sure of it. Alana
knew a man could feel possessive about something
or someone without wanting to keep it forever. Men
could even feel possessive about their dagger, and yet
they would never attach any of the softer emotions to
that feeling. Nonetheless, she decided, there was no
harm in thinking it was a good sign. She would
remain cautious, but she would allow herself to see
some small hope for success in the way he had repeated one word over and over again.

   With each thrust of his body, he had spoken the
word *mine*.

Chapter 14

Gregor woke from a very sensuous dream about Alana. It was a moment before he woke up enough to realize it was not really a dream. Alana's warm lips and soft little hands were making a thorough exploration of his body. He groaned and trembled slightly when she wrapped her hand around his erection and gently stroked him. Glancing down his body, he caught her peering up at him through a tangled mass of her thick hair, a blush and a faint smile upon her face.

"Good morning," she murmured, casting him a decidedly sultry look from beneath her long lashes as she slowly ran her tongue up his ribs.

"Och, aye, 'tis that," he replied, clenching his fists at his sides as she slipped a little lower down his body to kiss his belly as she continued to stroke him with her long, slender fingers.

It took all his willpower not to grab her and take control over their lovemaking. He was hard and aching to be inside her, but he fought to rein in that mindless need. Alana was being very bold and he did not wish to stop her. He was tense with hope and anticipation over just how bold she might choose to be. She was certainly headed in the right direction, he thought, groaning again as he felt the hard tip of her breast move against his thigh.

When her kisses moved to his thighs instead of the place that so ached for the touch of her lips, her soft hair brushing over his groin, he felt his desire grow despite his disappointment. He was just thinking that it was foolish to expect her to do something she had probably never heard of when he felt her run her tongue slowly up the length of him. Gregor could not stop himself from arching slightly, silently asking her for what he now desperately wanted her to do.

"Jesu, lass," he groaned when the heat of her mouth surrounded him, only to curse when she swiftly pulled away.

"Wrong?" she asked in a very small voice.

"Nay! Right! Verra right," he said, threading his fingers in her hair and gently urging her to do it again. "There's a good lass."

What a stupid thing to say, he thought a little wildly. He was not surprised to feel the faint gust of her breath against his skin as she giggled. His idiocy did not stop her, however, and he sent up a silent prayer of thanks as the damp warmth of her mouth again encircled him.

Closing his eyes, he fought to keep a tight rein upon his passion so that he could enjoy this delight for as long as possible. It was something he had indulged in only twice. Once when he was a mere lad learning the art of love from a much older widow and any caress could finish him and once again as a young man with a few years of experience under his belt. That last time he had enjoyed in some ways, but

the woman had performed the act with such a strong
air of self-sacrifice that he had never requested it
again. The feel of Alana's mouth, however, was driving him mad with pure, hot pleasure, one heightened
by the feeling that she was only trying to give him
pleasure, a pleasure he began to think she was gaining as well as giving.

Too soon he knew he could not hold back any
longer and he grabbed her beneath the arms to drag
her up his body. "Now, lass, take me inside ye and
ride me hard," he said as he settled her on top of him.

Intrigued, Alana straddled his hips and slowly
joined their bodies. She closed her eyes as pleasure
swept over her with such force it made her feel a bit
light-headed. Then Gregor grabbed her by the hips
and urged her to move. She quickly took the lead
from him, inspired by his husky words of passion
and encouragement. This time she could almost feel
his release build and she was right there to share it
with him. Still trembling from the strength of what
she had experienced in his arms, she collapsed on top
of him. Beneath the ear she pressed against his broad
chest, she could hear his heart pounding as hard as
hers was.

It was not until Gregor's hand ceased stroking her
back and slipped to the side that she realized he had
gone back to sleep. As carefully as she could, Alana
got off him, stood up, and quickly dressed. She
smiled as she studied the way he was sprawled on
his back sleeping soundly. It was strangely invigorating to think that she had exhausted such a big,
strong man.

She opened the door, looked outside, and smiled.
It was a beautiful day. Recalling a small burn they

had crossed just before reaching their small shelter, she collected the things she would need to have a thorough wash. The water would undoubtedly be cold, as the burn was running downhill and probably came from somewhere in the high hills she could see in the distance, but she felt she could endure it long enough to get completely clean. If she hurried she might even be able to return before Gregor woke up, which would save her from a lecture about wandering around alone and unprotected, she mused as she hurried out of the cottage, quickly shutting the door before Charlemagne could follow.

The water proved far colder than she had anticipated, and Alana did not think she had ever bathed with greater speed. Even when she had dried herself off and put her clean clothes on, she continued to shiver faintly. She headed toward a sunnier spot where the water tumbled over the side of a shallow gorge. Sitting on the ground, she rubbed her hair dry and began to braid it. Although it was pleasant to sit in the sun and let its warmth flow through her, she knew she could not enjoy the pleasure for too long. Gregor would worry when he woke up to find her gone, and that worry would increase with each moment that passed with no sight of her return. She might not know how he felt about her in so many other ways, but she had no doubt that he felt very protective.

She was unable to stop her thoughts from drifting to what she had done this morning. It astonished her that she could ever have dared to be so bold. If Gregor had not been so obvious in his enjoyment of her attentions, she would worry that she had shocked him, perhaps even pushed him away with her boldness.

She had no fear of that, however. She also knew that she would do it all again the first chance she got. It had been exciting beyond words to make love to him like that, to lead the dance for a change.

Alana shook aside the arousing thought of all the ways she could make love to Gregor and stood up. She was just moving to collect her things when six men stepped out of the shelter of the surrounding trees. Just over their shoulders she glimpsed another man standing with their horses and wondered how she had missed hearing their approach. They looked ragged and filthy and she felt her stomach knot with fear. They stood between her and the hut where Gregor waited for her. Worse, she had not even brought her dagger with her.

"Weel, 'tis a bonnie wee prize we have found ourselves, eh, laddies?" said a short, barrel-chested man whose face was so covered in hair she could see little more than his eyes.

"I am nay alone," Alana warned. "'Twould be best if ye get back on your ponies and ride away. Fast."

As a bluff it was a very weak one. The area all around where they stood was open and there was no sign of anyone but her. Alana was not surprised when the man facing her looked around and then glared at her.

"Do ye think me a fool?" he snapped. "Now, come here."

"Och, nay, I dinnae think so." Did the man truly think she was so witless that she would just walk to his side and surrender?

"Now, lass, ye really dinnae want to be making me angry. We willnae hurt ye," he added in a faintly soft tone of voice.

The man's attempt to smile reassuringly made Alana shiver with distaste. What little she could see of his teeth through his thick, snarled beard revealed that they were rotting in his mouth. Alana knew she had to decide what to do next and she had to do it quickly. This was not a man who would patiently trade words with her in an attempt to coax her into doing what he wanted. As subtly as she could, she glanced all around her and tried to determine the best route of escape. She prayed her ability to run and hide would not fail her again, for these men made the Gowans look like saints.

"I am afraid I dinnae believe ye, sir," she said calmly even as her heart raced almost painfully with growing fear.

"Are ye calling me a liar?"

"Aye, I believe I am."

"Ye had best cease this foolish game, woman, or it willnae go weel for ye when I catch ye. Believe that."

"I think ye should say *if* ye catch me."

A growl rumbled in the man's chest and Alana understood that warning. She bolted and headed for the trees behind her. A cry rose up from the men as they started to chase her, a sound that reminded her far too much of the ones hunters made as they ran down their prey. One voice kept bellowing out threats that made her blood run cold.

It quickly became evident that these men were not all as stupid as they looked. While three of them ran after her, the other three ran back to their horses. A glance behind her showed Alana that she could certainly outrun the men who came after her on foot, but the men on the horses were rapidly closing in on her. Even she could not outrun a horse, but she just might be able to evade it if she could just reach the trees, she thought. If luck was with her, she might even be able to escape pursuit long enough to climb up into one of those trees and hide. She suspected these men would not linger in the area long if they lost sight of her. They were undoubtedly outlaws, broken men who were long overdue for a hanging.

Good fortune completely deserted her at the very edge of the trees she struggled to reach. Two men on horseback rode between her and the trees. They reined in so close to her that she could feel the breath of the horses on her face as she stumbled to a halt. Alana tried to dart around them, but they were quick to block her each time. Just as she realized why they were not attacking her, were merely holding her in place, she felt someone slam into her from behind. Even putting her arms out to try and break her fall, she hit the ground hard enough to knock the breath out of her.

She was still struggling to breathe when the man who had knocked her down turned her onto her back, slapped her hard across the face, and then sat on her. Straddling her, he glared at her. It was the one who had first spoken to her, and he looked more than eager to carry out all the threats he had bellowed after her when she had bolted for the trees. Alana did not think she had ever seen a man as filthy as this one or one who smelled so foul. She would not have thought that *who* the man was who violated her would matter, the abuse being horror enough to bear, but the fact that it was this foul creature who intended to rape her did indeed make it all the more horrifying. She doubted she would ever feel clean again—if she even survived.

Then she thought of Gregor, of all they had shared

together, and wanted to scream. Only the thought that this man was the sort who would like to see her fear kept her silent. It was not easy, for hand in hand with the fear was a growing rage. He was going to ruin all the sweet memories she had made with Gregor, taint all that beauty with filth and violence. Before she could consider the wisdom of it, she curled up one hand into a tight fist and punched him in the nose as hard as she could. She was so angry that the blood and the sound of bones cracking did not even trouble her.

The man howled, clutched his nose, and rolled off her as he cursed and threatened her. Alana took quick advantage of her freedom, leapt to her feet, and ran. Another man tried to grab her, but as he yanked her toward him, she kicked him in the groin. She knew she was running blindly now but could not completely still the panic that gripped her so tightly. The fact that the men had not yet come at her all at once this time was all that was saving her, and she knew that, too. Yet each way she turned there was another man forcing her in yet another direction, and never in the one direction she truly wanted to go. Her body ached from being thrown to the ground and having a man fall on her and she was not sure how much longer she could continue to run and fight.

Alana felt the bitter taste of defeat sting the back of her throat when she suddenly realized she had been herded to the very edge of a shallow gorge. Each way she looked now, a man stood in her way. Behind them were arranged the four horsemen. The man who had slapped her walked toward her, and she braced herself for a fight. She knew she would lose in the end, but she fully intended to make him suffer before he took what he wanted.

"Ye will pay for this, ye stupid bitch," the man snapped, lightly touching his bleeding nose. "I was intending to be gentle with ye and all, but nay more. Nay, now I intend to make ye bleed."

He lunged at her and Alana tried to avoid his attack, but when she tried to move to the side another man darted toward her. A snarl of warning escaped the first man, halting him, but the move had cost Alana her chance to get out of the way. The man she had punched grabbed her and tried to wrestle her to the ground. She heard one of the other men yell out, "'Ware the edge, Rob!" and knew both she and her attacker were in danger of plunging to the bottom of the gorge.

Rob grunted and tried to pull her back, away from the crumbling ground at the edge of the gorge. As Alana struggled in his arms, he bit her on the neck and she screamed as much from surprise and horror as from pain. Realizing suddenly that Rob was so busy trying to tear off her gown he had not protected his body well, Alana butted her head against his, trying to inflict enough pain that he loosened his grip on her. It seemed that all she had accomplished was to hurt her head and make him curse. Then she saw that her leg was situated in the perfect place for a hard strike to the groin. She was already bringing her knee up when the man realized his mistake and his vulnerability, but it was too late for him to save himself. Alana rammed her knee up between his legs. He screamed and shoved her away before dropping to his knees, clutching himself and retching.

Her sense of triumph lasted for only a heartbeat.

Pushed back to the very edge of the gorge, she felt the ground slowly disappear from beneath her feet. She grabbed out at empty air even as she began to fall. Her frantic attempts to catch onto something to halt her fall only succeeded in causing her to slide and bounce her way down the rocky wall of the gorge. She hit the ground at the bottom hard on her back. The last thing she was aware of before darkness swallowed her was a sound very much like that of an enraged beast.

Gregor woke, stretched lazily, and looked around for Alana, frowning when he did not see her. Deciding that she must have slipped outside for a few moments of privacy, he dressed and did the same. It was not until he had seen to the horse, washed up, and tended to the fire that he began to be concerned. Alana should not be taking so long. When Charlemagne came to sit beside him, his worry for Alana increased. If Alana had only stepped out to relieve herself, she would have let Charlemagne out as well.

He sighed and told himself he was acting like an old woman. Alana had wandered all through the woods around the camps they had stayed at and never come to harm. She knew how to care for herself in the forest, and on her own. Had he not felt useless from time to time because she was so capable at caring for herself?

Then again, she had been caught by the Gowans, he mused as he chewed on a honey-sweetened oat-cake. But so had he, he admitted reluctantly, so he could not count that against her. There was also the incident with the adder to consider. That could have happened to anyone, but it did reveal that there were dangers out there one could not always protect oneself against. Hidden dangers, both of nature and of man.

Scowling at the door, he carefully debated going out to look for her. There was probably nothing wrong. She might even have decided to catch a fish in the burn they had crossed, or a rabbit. Although he suspected the water in the burn was icy cold, she might have even gone to take a quick bath in it. There were a dozen good reasons for her not to be in the cottage to smile at him when he woke up. He could look very foolish if he went out looking for her.

"Curse it," he muttered as he stood up and reached for his sword. "I cannae shake the feeling that something is wrong," he said and cursed again when he realized he was talking to the cat. "That lass is driving me mad. I am talking to a cat and fretting o'er her like an old woman. 'Tisnae to be born and I shall tell her so. She cannae keep skipping off on her own as if the world is a peaceful haven where naught will e'er happen to a lass."

When Charlemagne meowed, Gregor scowled at him and then strode out of the cottage. He had to shut the door quickly to halt the cat's attempt to follow him. The animal was a strange one and, he thought, he was even stranger to be thinking about what a cat did and did not understand when his woman was missing.

His woman, he repeated in his mind and decided it sounded right and gave him a great sense of satisfaction. He had felt a bit of satisfaction over the possibility of marrying Mavis, but it had been over the prospect of gaining his own land and a heavy purse. With Alana, he simply did not care what she had. He would take her if all she brought to him was herself and that annoying cat. Today they would reach Scarglas if they encountered no trouble, and he would immediately begin to untangle himself from the Kerrs. The only thing that would take time was the need to be kind to Mavis when he did so, but he would not allow it to take too much time. He needed to openly claim Alana as his own, to convince her to stay at his side as his wife before she rejoined her family, and he could not do so until he dealt with the Kerrs.

The way she had made love to him this morning gave him confidence that she would be willing to be his wife, even if he did not have all that much to offer her besides himself. No woman could do that to a man with the tenderness and passion she had if she did not care for him. Her every kiss and caress had held the promise of a depth of feeling that he now craved.

Gregor suddenly realized that he wanted her to do more than care for him and desire him; he wanted her to love him. It was probably unfair of him to expect her to love him when he was not ready to put that name to what he felt, but he still wanted it. He would care for her, give her pleasure and give her bairns, and he would never betray her with another. That, he decided, should satisfy any woman.

A little voice in his head scoffed at him as he made his way through the trees to the burn. He was being a hypocrite but he did not care. Despite how content Sigimor and Ewan appeared in their marriages and how clearly they revealed their love for their wives even if they did not speak of it, Gregor mistrusted the emotion. He had also seen far too many suffer for it. It stirred the sort of fierce emotion he wanted nothing to do with.

At the fording place they had crossed yesterday, Gregor could not see Alana and he felt his concern grow stronger. Crouching down near the bank of the burn, he found signs that she had been there but had left. Since she had not returned to his side, he had to wonder where she had gone.

The sound of shouting drew his attention, and he looked through the thinning trees toward a clearing. At first he thought he was watching hunters trying to catch a bit of meat for the table, although he saw no sign of a buck or doe. Then he saw Alana and realized these men were hunting her. There was no doubt in his mind as to what they intended to do when they caught her, and the thought of any man touching his Alana with violence made the bloodlust rise swiftly in his heart.

He leapt to his feet when he saw a man tackle her to the ground, but struggled to restrain the keen urge to race into the crowd of men with his sword swinging. That would just get him killed, and then Alana would be at their mercy. It was hard to move cautiously as he watched the man turn her over and slap her face, but he knew the only way he could possibly win against such greater odds was with stealth.

A sigh of relief escaped him when he saw Alana break free of the man, but his relief was short-lived. As he moved closer it was easy to see that they were herding her, slowly surrounding her. Even as far away as he still was, Gregor could see the exact moment Alana realized what was happening, but it was too late for her to save herself. He had to bite his tongue to stop himself from calling out some words of encouragement, so strong was his need to ease the fear she had to be feeling.

Despite how desperately he wanted to cut to pieces the man who threatened her and then grabbed her, Gregor forced himself to take advantage of the way all the men watched Alana struggle with the man. He felt pride in the way she did not cower, and almost smiled when she nearly gelded the man with her knee. Those good feelings faded fast, however, rapidly replaced by a cold, hard knot of fear when he saw the way she stumbled at the very edge of the gorge. He stood watching helplessly as she disappeared over the edge. The silence that followed was chilling.

Gregor heard a bellow of pain and rage and realized it came from him. He charged the men gathered near the edge of the gorge, too blind with fury and grief to weigh the odds against him. All he wanted was to kill the men who had taken Alana away from him. In a small part of his mind he noticed that the men on horseback did not wait to see that he was alone but fled, leaving him with only three men to face. Instead of being pleased by the evening of the odds against him, he only became angrier that he would not be able to rid the world of all these vermin.

The first man fell quickly to his sword, and now Gregor faced only two. For all the trouble his feckless father had caused over the years, one thing the man had taught his many sons was how to fight and fight well. Gregor had no fear that he would fail to kill these two men. He only had to decide whether to do it quickly or make them suffer for stealing the joy out of his life.

When a small, sane voice in his mind whispered that he could not be certain Alana was dead, he decided on killing the men quickly. The chances of her surviving such a fall were small, but he could not risk leaving her there too long just to satisfy the need to make these men suffer as much pain as he could possibly inflict. Alana might be in need of his help, and he could not hesitate just to satisfy his strong need for vengeance.

He killed the one who had caused her fall first, slicing the man through the middle as he held the second man back with his dagger. For just a moment he let the man think he would be left to die the slow, agonizing death such a wound brought, and then he stabbed him through the heart. When Gregor turned to face the second man, he could see the sweat of fear running down the man's face, but he offered him no chance of mercy. Impatient to get to Alana now, he quickly put an end to the man's fear, feinting with his sword to draw the man's attention and then sinking his dagger into the man's heart.

After looking to make sure that the cowards who had left their companions to die were not creeping back, Gregor moved cautiously to the edge of the gorge. The sight of Alana sprawled on her back on the bottom nearly made him cry out again. She was not moving, but he told himself that could just be because she was unconscious.

He cleaned his sword on the jupon of the closest dead man, sheathed it, and started to climb down into the gorge. When he reached the bottom, he stood and stared at her for a moment, afraid to touch her and find only the coldness of death. Shaking free of his unease, he knelt by her side. When he saw her chest rise and fall, he felt weak with relief. Placing his hands over his face as he struggled to calm himself, he was not all that surprised to find tears upon his cheeks. That brief moment in which he had thought she was dead had stripped him of all his defenses and made him accept the truth he had been denying to himself for too long. She was more than important to him; she was his heart. He loved her.

As gently as he could he tried to ascertain the extent of her wounds. Her braies were intact, which implied that she had been saved from the horror of rape, or so he prayed. From what little knowledge he possessed he did not believe she had broken any limbs, but he needed her awake to tell him how she felt and to move before he could be sure of that. What frightened him the most was that she had fallen onto her back. An injury there could leave her unable to walk. She would have cracked the back of her head against the ground as well, and he had seen the sad results of such head wounds. There could also be injuries he could not see, ones deep inside of her that would not stop bleeding.

She was alive, he told himself in the hope of stilling the worries building inside of him. He had to decide how to safely get her back to the hut and then to Scarglas. Fiona had skill in the healing arts and he would get Alana to her as quickly as he could. Sitting by her side, he lightly stroked her head and prayed for the first time in far too long. *Just let her wake up and smile at me*, he asked.

A soft moan escaped Alana, and he tensed. There was a little movement of her body and he took hope in that, seeing it as a sign that she might have escaped the pain of broken bones. Crouching over her, he waited for her to open her eyes, needing her to look at him, recognize him, before he could begin to relax and have hope that she had survived this ordeal with no more than bruises and scrapes.

Chapter 15

Alana slowly opened her eyes and found Gregor crouched over her. "Ye are looking verra pale," she said and wondered why her voice sounded so soft and weak.

"Pale? Aye, I suspect I am. Watching ye plummet off a cliff did worry me a wee bit."

"A cliff?" she asked and then the memory of the reivers returned a heartbeat before the pain struck.

"Nay! Dinnae move yet," he ordered her when she tried to curl up into a ball, whispering curses all the while. "I need ye to help me see if ye have suffered any broken bones." He gently stroked her forehead until she grew still and quiet. "I dinnae think ye have, and ye just moved about as if naught is broken, but I need ye to slowly, carefully move each limb. Easy, lass. Do it easy."

"Those men?" she asked as she cautiously tested the soundness of her right arm and then her left, relieved to feel none of the excruciating pain a broken bone would give her.

"Three are dead and the rest ran away."

"Three? Three are dead?" She moved each leg and, although there was some pain, she knew she had not broken them, either.

"I was angry." He sighed and dragged his hand through his hair. "Ye fell off a cliff!" He took a few deep breaths to calm himself down. "When I saw ye fall, driven to the edge by those animals, I went half mad. So I gave them no mercy. The ones who lived were the ones who ran away, and I am certain they willnae be back."

"Ah, weel, thank ye for coming to my rescue."

He grunted. "A good rescue would have been if I had saved ye from falling off a cliff. Now, can ye tell me if ye have hurt your back at all, love? I was afeared of moving ye at all in case ye have broken something there."

"Naught has been broken in my back, Gregor. I once saw a mon who had broken his back and he couldnae move his arms or his legs. I can move both, as ye just saw. They arenae broken, either. 'Tis certain that I have bruised my back verra badly, as weel as the rest of me, but I havenae broken it."

"And your head?"

"Aches, but it isnae broken, either," she said with a smile.

Gregor felt such a wave of relief wash over him that he was afraid he would unman himself again. A few tears were acceptable when shed in private, but he did not wish Alana to see him shed any. He sat down and tried to calm himself. When he had first seen her sprawled upon the ground, he had feared the worst, and he had obviously not fully recovered from that fright. It was hard to believe that she had survived the fall at all, let alone with only bruises and scrapes. He did not completely trust such good fortune and it would take him a while to fully accept it.

"We need to get ye back up those rocks and then take ye to Scarglas so that Fiona can tend to your injuries," he said.

That hard truth made Alana wince in anticipation of the pain she would soon suffer. She had not broken anything, but every bone in her body felt as if it had taken a vicious beating. There were bruises and painful scrapes all over her body. She did not need to search for them to know they were there. Her head throbbed so badly it made her feel nauseous. Alana really wanted to just lie there on the ground for a little while until the pain eased.

She sighed and glanced at the rocky slope she had fallen down. It was going to hurt almost as much going up as it had coming down, even with Gregor's help. Although she did not consider it as the cliff Gregor kept calling it, it would not be an easy climb. Alana knew she had no choice, however. Delaying the ordeal would not save her from it, either.

Carefully, with Gregor's strong arm around her shoulders to help her, Alana sat up. She slumped against him as a wave of pain and dizziness swept over her. Slow, deep breaths cleared her head and pushed the pain back a little, but she clung to Gregor for a few more minutes.

Fear still writhed inside of her, Alana realized. She had been absolutely terrified from the moment she had realized there was no escape from those men. That did not really shame her, for she had put up a good fight, but it was clearly going to take a while to completely shake free of that fear. The fear of dying had not been the sharpest, either. It had been the knowledge that those men intended to rape her, all of them, that had caused the greatest part of her terror. If, by some miracle, she had survived such a brutal assault, she had known even in her panic that it could mean an end to all the beauty she had shared with Gregor. Alana did not think Gregor would turn away from her because of it, but she would have turned away from him. All chance of a future for them would have been irrevocably ended.

"Easy now, love," Gregor murmured, unsettled by the faint trembling of her body. If just sitting up caused her to be so weak and unsteady, he did not know how he was going to get her back to the cottage. "Ye can rest here for a wee bit if ye want."

"That would be nice, but nay, we must get up that slope, to the hut, and then continue our journey."

"But ye are shaking, ye are so weak. Or it is the pain that causes ye to tremble so?"

"Ah, that. 'Tis fear, Gregor. Blind, unreasoning fear." She sat back a little and gave him a faint smile.

"They didnae—" Gregor began, nearly choking on the words, for he was coldly horrified that those men had succeeded, at least once, in abusing her even though he had seen no sign of it. He did not care about the act itself, for it would have been rape which, in his mind, was no more than another kind of beating. What concerned him was how such an intimate assault might affect Alana's ability to return to his arms with all the passionate fire she had gifted him with before the attack.

"Nay, they didnae rape me," she said, "although they planned to." Just saying the words made her shiver with fear and she looked up toward the top of the slope she had fallen down. "The moment I realized I was cornered, I was very, very afraid."

"Of course ye were," Gregor said, sharing her remembered fear if for different reasons, some of which he knew were selfish ones. "Ye could have died."

"Och, aye. Either from the abuse they inflicted or because they didnae wish to leave me alive to tell anyone about it. Yet it wasnae dying I was so afraid of. I just kenned that even if I survived, e'en if I recovered in mind and body, they would have destroyed something precious to me." She spoke softly now, knowing she would be revealing something about her feelings for Gregor if he cared to look closely. "They would have tainted all we have shared, stolen away all the beauty of it." She could tell he was moved by her words by the way he ever so slightly tightened his hold on her.

"I wouldnae have turned away from ye," he said, his certainty of that weighting his every word. "I am nay one of those fools who think that, somehow, a woman invites such violence."

Alana smiled. "I ken it. I dinnae understand why I do, but I do. That was one fear I ne'er felt."

"Thank ye for that, love." He kissed her cheek, deeply touched that she would have such faith in him, especially when he gave her no words of love or promises that they would stay together past the time their journey ended.

She started to shrug, quickly lessening the motion when it caused her pain. "It will just take a wee while for me to shake free of that fear. I just didnae want them to ruin everything, e'en the memories." She frowned up the slope. "They *are* gone, aye?"

"Aye. Three have gone to hell where they belong and, as I told ye, the others have run for their lives. I was quite awe-inspiring," he drawled and was pleased to hear her laugh. "Are ye ready to give it a try?" he asked, nodding at the slope.

"Ready," she said as he helped her stand up, "but nay too happy about it."

Gregor quickly put his arm around her again as she swayed slightly. She was recovering well despite this sign of weakness. That such a small, delicate woman could even stand up after such a fall said a lot about her strength. Yet he did not think she had regained enough of that strength to climb up that rocky slope. Unsteady as she was, she could easily slip and fall, and this time she might well break something. She could also all too easily take him down with her.

"Do ye think ye could hold on fast to me if I carry ye up?" he asked. "On my back," he added when she frowned. "Ye must be certain ye can hang on, for if ye fall from my back, I willnae be able to catch ye."

"'Twould test my strength far less than trying to climb up there myself, but 'twill make it verra awkward for you."

"Nay, ye arenae verra heavy and I trust ye to keep as still as a weel-stuffed pack."

"Then aye, I will get on your back. It galls me a wee bit to need such help, but far better that pinch to my pride than falling back down and breaking something. I would probably take ye down with me as weel."

"'Tis what I was thinking. Although I suspicion ye would break my fall, as ye would go down first."

"That would surely finish me off. Weel, let us get this over with."

Gregor had to smile when he got her settled upon his back, her legs wrapped around his waist and her arms around his neck. It had obviously pained her and even though she had muttered curses in a near whisper, he now knew that she had learned an intriguing array of colorful oaths. Her brothers or male cousins had clearly not taken much care in watching what they said around her.

"Do ye feel secure, lass?" he asked, for even though he could feel the strength in her arms and legs as she gripped him, there was still a faint tremor rippling through her body.

"Secure enough to hang on until we reach the top," she replied, willing herself to speak in a firm, steady voice.

He nodded and started to climb up the rocks. Alana fought to ignore the pain coursing through her body and concentrate only on holding on and not moving. There had been a note of humor in Gregor's voice when he had spoken of her staying as still as a well-stuffed pack, but she had understood the seriousness of that gentle command. Any movement she made could cause Gregor to slip, and that would send them both tumbling back down onto the hard ground.

The moment they reached the top, she started to loosen her grip on him, the strength in her battered body fleeing her in a rush. Gregor quickly steadied her and helped her stagger to a spot several feet away from the edge. She sat down and struggled to ease the pain and conquer the weakness that had her trembling so badly. Taking slow, deep breaths, she reached out for enough strength to get back to the little cottage as she watched Gregor search each of the dead men sprawled upon the ground for anything of value. It was a morbid chore, but Alana knew the men in her family would do the same. If it was one of their own, they did it to make certain his things would be sent back to his family, and if it was the enemy, it was considered the spoils of war.

"Ye are looking a wee bit steadier, love," Gregor said as he crouched by her side and kissed her cheek. "Shall I carry ye back to the cottage?"

"Let me try to walk first," she said. "My cloak and other things are just o'er there and they look as if they are unharmed. Ye could use my cloak to make a sack to carry those things."

"Aye, good idea. They were verra poor thieves, I think, for they had but a verra few things which I am fair sure arenae theirs." He made a sack of her cloak and shoved the swords in the sheaths and the daggers he had collected into it, as well as one small sack of coins and a few rings and pendants that he suspected had been stolen. "The ones who fled here paused long enough to grab the rest of the horses, which would have been the truly valuable boon."

"And left their three companions to fend for themselves," she said and shook her head.

"They may have had some arrangement and are waiting for their friends at some hiding place, but aye, I think they just deserted them without even one look back."

"No loyalty at all, then."

"None." He helped her to her feet and placed a steadying arm around her waist. "Are ye sure ye want to walk, lass?"

"For a bit, aye. We must continue our journey, and riding on the horse will undoubtedly make me all stiff and sore. Mayhap if I walk a wee bit now, I can lessen that suffering later."

"I wish we could wait a wee bit, until ye feel better and stronger, but I have no knowledge of the healing arts. Aye, right now ye could advise me, but what if ye fall ill or swoon? Nay, I would really like Fiona to have a look at you. Aye, and get ye into a soft, warm bed with maids and all to help care for ye."

"The latter certainly sounds welcome," she murmured, concentrating on putting one foot in front of the other.

By the time they reached the cottage, Alana felt as if her legs were made of porridge and her head throbbed. She had to smile, however, at how noisily Charlemagne greeted them. When Gregor urged her down onto their bed of blankets, the cat quickly curled up at her side, purring loudly. She idly scratched his ears as she watched Gregor pack up their things.

"I think he was afeared that we had left him behind," she said.

Gregor shook his head. "He hasnae realized that cats are supposed to be aloof, sly, and solitary in their habits. I told ye, he is confused. And so am I, for I am calling it a he."

"That is naught but rumor and lies. A cat can be as friendly and as in need of affection as any dog. Most people dinnae show them any, however, but leave them in the stables or the kitchens expecting them to work for their scraps by keeping the vermin out of the meal. Most of the cats my family has are verra friendly."

"Weel, I am nay sure ye ought to be carrying this friendly fool cat this time," he said.

"Aye, I can do it. 'Tisnae a big cat."

"We can try it. Now, do ye need anything to eat? I doubt ye broke your fast."

"Are there any oatcakes left?"

Gregor handed her the last of the honey-sweetened oatcakes and went out to ready the horse for their journey. He would have to keep a close watch on her. Alana seemed determined to push herself to the very limits of her strength and, until he was certain she had not hurt anything inside of her, he could not allow her to do that. He was worried enough about taking her on a ride so soon after her fall, but she needed the kind of care he could not give her.

He caught her yawning when he returned to the cottage and smiled. That suited him just fine. If she was sleeping then she could not try to do too much too soon. It would also make the journey a lot easier on her battered body.

They had barely gone two miles before Alana fell fast asleep. Gregor tightened his grip on her just a little and settled her more comfortably in front of him. It would be a little difficult to travel this way, but he felt it was best. She would not be able to find such respite from her pain for the whole trip, but at least this rest might give her the strength to endure it.

He found himself constantly looking down at her as they rode along, checking to make sure her color was good and that the fear she had spoken of had not invaded her dreams. Gregor could remember very clearly what she had said concerning that fear, and it still moved him. She saw what they shared as beautiful and claimed it was precious to her. That had to mean that she more than just desired him. Now that he knew how he felt about her, he needed to know that she returned his love. Having her love him was no longer just a good thing; it was a necessity.

And if she did love him, that love would be sorely tested in the next few days. He would probably have to leave her in Fiona's care while he went to speak to Mavis and her father and he would not be able to tell her why he was leaving her alone so quickly after reaching Scarglas. There were also his two bastard sons waiting for him at home. That was something he should have mentioned, and could have, but he had been so concerned about keeping Alana yet not committing himself to her until he was free that he had never given a thought to mentioning his children. It was too late to do so now, for he had no time to softly, subtly prepare her for such news or say the words that could ease her concerns over his lecherous past.

Well, he would deal with it all when he got there, he decided. Since she would need to rest, Alana would not be able to run off. That would give him time to deal with the Kerrs and then woo Alana with all the words he had been keeping inside him for so long. It was a tangle he could easily drive himself mad thinking about, so he would deal with it all as it happened and hope that Alana loved and needed him at her side enough to be forgiving.

Alana winced as the horse moved a little faster and jarred her more in the saddle. The way Gregor held her eased some of the discomfort, but after hours of riding, there was not much that could help except a nice soft bed. Sleeping for several hours had been a blessing and renewed her strength a little, but now she ached so badly she knew she could not seek that respite again. They had stopped a few times so that she could stretch her aching legs, but that had only made getting back on the horse harder each time. Now she just wanted to get to Scarglas and go lie down.

"Scarglas is just on the other side of those trees," Gregor said.

"Oh, how wonderful," she murmured.

"I would be verra pleased and flattered if I actually thought ye were speaking just of seeing my home, but I ken ye are thinking of a soft bed."

She laughed. "Aye, and a long hot bath."

"And ye shall have both as quickly as I can get them for ye."

"That will be pure bliss."

"Ye havenae noticed any new pains, have ye?"

"Nay, just the ones I started out with. I think I am safe from any complications. I am exactly as we thought I was—bruised and scraped and nay more."

Gregor nodded as he reined in the horse. "There is Scarglas."

Alana stared at the dark, forbidding fortress ahead of them. Even if she had not heard Gregor's tales of the troubled years now thankfully in the past, she would have known that the men of Scarglas were men of war, willingly or not. It was buit for defense. Even the approach to the place was littered with ways to hold back an enemy.

"'Tisnae a verra pretty place," he murmured as he nudged the horse into a gentle trot.

"Nay, but it was safe, wasnae it," she said.

"Aye, it was. And although my brother Ewan has defeated or wooed most of our enemies, we will keep it like this. The future could hold troubles that cannae be fought successfully or ended with a treaty."

"After all ye have told me about how it used to be, I suspicion none of ye will e'er grow lax in making sure your home can be defended against all comers."

"Nay, 'tis a lesson one ne'er forgets."

"That isnae such a bad thing, Gregor," she said quietly.

"Nay, mayhap it isnae." He certainly liked knowing that she would be safe behind those dark walls.

Before Alana could think of any questions to ask about the people she was about to meet, they were riding into a very crowded inner bailey. Gregor was quickly surrounded by a horde of dark, handsome men all asking questions at the same time. It was clear to see that most of them were his brothers and she had to marvel at his father's virility. It was also a little unsettling to be surrounded by so many men who bore such a striking resemblance to Gregor.

When he helped her down from the horse and introduced her, the sudden silence was even more unsettling. The crowd of MacFingals began to slowly thin out, one after another of the men slipping away. A quick glance at Gregor revealed him frowning, looking as puzzled and suspicious as she felt. Since none of these men knew her, Alana could not believe she was the cause of the silent retreat.

Gregor watched all of his brothers slip away muttering a few welcomes to Alana and saying they would see him in the great hall later. Something was amiss, but it was obvious none of them wanted to tell him what. Everything had been as chaotic as normal until he had introduced Alana. For a moment they had all stared at him as if they recognized something in the way he said her name and held her close to his side, and then the retreat had begun. It made no sense and he knew he would get no answers from them, even if he chased after them.

"Do ye need me to carry ye inside, lass?" he asked, turning his attention to Alana.

"Nay," she replied. "I can make it on my own. Weel, on my own with your help."

"Then let us go and see if we can find out what has made my brothers all flee us as if we carry the plague."

She laughed and leaned against him as he helped her into the keep. Once inside, some of the dark, forbidding air of Scarglas faded. Alana suspected Fiona had been busy softening the hard edges of what had been nearly an all-male household. There was light, tapestries, and cushions upon the chairs flanking the alms table.

As if her thoughts of the woman were a command, Fiona strode out of the great hall and gaped at Gregor. She then turned her gaze on Alana. Although she smiled in greeting, there was a wariness in her expression that made Alana nervous. Something was indeed going on at Scarglas, and even though she could think of no reason why, she seemed to be part of the trouble. Alana wondered if her brothers had come here looking for her and offended everyone.

"Ye remember Alana Murray, dinnae ye, Fiona?" Gregor asked.

"Aye, although it has been years since we have seen each other."

Before anything else could be said, a plump, pretty young woman hurried out of the great hall. Realizing the way she was tucked under Gregor's arm and held close by his side, Alana carefully stepped away from him. She frowned up at him when she noticed that he was standing very still, his body had tensed, and he was gaping at the woman who had just come out of the great hall.

Before she could ask Gregor anything, a burly man with gray hair and a scowl on his face came out and stood next to the young woman. "'Tis past time ye wandered home, lad," he snapped. "We heard ye had disappeared near a fortnight ago and have been waiting here to find out what happened to ye for a sennight now. Naturally, as your betrothed wife, Mavis felt it was her duty to be here, waiting with your family to find out if ye were alive or dead."

Out of all the man said, only one word truly concerned Alana. It struck her like a dagger to the heart. She was so shocked, so hurt, she barely flinched when the young woman flung herself into Gregor's arms. Alana fleetingly thought that this was a very poor way to find out that she had been an utter fool. She looked at Gregor and fixed her mind on that one word, needing him to immediately accept or deny the title.

Chapter 16

"Betrothed?"

It was not only astonishment over how much fury could be contained in that one word that caused Gregor to look over Mavis's head and meet Alana's gaze. He wanted to ease what must appear to be a gross betrayal with a look or a few words. With Mavis clinging to him it was impossible to say anything, however. The way Alana was looking at him, as if he was lower than a worm, told him she was in no mood to listen to him anyway.

And why was Mavis even here? he thought. He had issued no invitation. Gregor was certain he had made it clear that he would return to her once he had spoken to his family. He had been most careful not to make any unbreakable promises. There had been no papers signed, no betrothal ceremony, and no proposal made. Expectations had been raised, he could not deny that, but although there might be some hard feelings stirred over his not meeting those expectations, he had thought he could back away from them with quiet dignity.

Now he stood with a woman in his arms he did not want, while the one he wanted looked as if she would welcome a chance to gut him. Worse, he could not humiliate Mavis by loudly disputing her claim to him. Expectations might not be promises, but since he had been the one to raise them with his courtship and talks with her father, he owed Mavis a gentle, private explanation for why matters between them had changed.

"When we didnae hear from ye for so verra long, we were most concerned," said Mavis as she stepped back a little.

Gregor opened his mouth to speak only to realize that he did not know what to say. His family and Mavis's father were beginning to look at him with suspicion. He looked helplessly at Fiona. She glared at him but, to his great relief, quickly moved to Alana's side.

"Come with me, Mistress Murray," said Fiona as she hooked her arm through Alana's. "Ye must be sorely tired. I suspicion ye would like a bath as weel, aye?"

"Aye," replied Alana, allowing Fiona to lead her away.

Alana felt dazed and a little numb. The fury that had swept over Alana when that woman had greeted Gregor so lovingly and laid claim to him had slowly left her. When it did, it seemed to have taken every other emotion with it, leaving only a stunned realization that she had been the greatest of fools. Gregor belonged to someone else and could never be hers. She hoped she stayed numb, for she feared there was a searing pain lurking beneath that chill.

Fiona shaking her slightly brought Alana to her

senses, and she realized they were inside a bed-chamber. "Oh. 'Tis a verra fine room."

"Satan's teeth, Alana, ye act as though ye have been knocked on the head."

"Oh, ye just called me Alana, nay Mistress Murray. So, ye remember me now?"

"I remembered ye before." Fiona shrugged. "I just thought it suited the moment to be more formal."

"Ah, I suppose it did." Increasingly aware of how her body ached, Alana moved to the bed and sat down, letting Charlemagne out of the sack so that he could explore their new home.

"Why are ye limping?" asked Fiona as she moved to scratch the cat's ears.

"Weel, there was a wee confrontation with some thieves and I had a fall. 'Tis but a wide collection of bruises and scrapes."

"Let me be the judge of that."

Before Alana could protest, Fiona was unlacing her clothes and demanding the full story about the thieves. Eager to keep her mind off Gregor's betrayal, Alana complied. It was not until she was bathed, dressed in a clean shift, and all her little wounds salved that she began to suspect Fiona had skillfully aided her in keeping her mind occupied. By the look upon Fiona's face, however, that reprieve was over. With a heavy sigh, Alana sat on a stool before the fireplace.

"I think that tale about the thieves is but one of many ye have to tell," Fiona said as she began to gently brush the snarls from Alana's wet hair. "How long have ye and Gregor been together?"

"Too long, and yet he ne'er mentioned he was be-trothed." Alana inwardly cursed, for even she could hear the hurt and anger behind her words. She did not need the knowing look upon Fiona's face to tell her she had given herself away. "It matters not. I will join Keira as soon as possible and—"

"Ye are going nowhere until those bruises fade a wee bit. Just because ye were fortunate enough to nay break any bones doesnae mean ye are hale enough to ride off again."

"I rode here—" Alana began.

"As ye had to, although a litter would have been much wiser. Your body took a beating. Ye need to let it rest."

"If I go to Keira, she can help and I can rest once I reach her keep."

"And I will be verra fortunate if she doesnae come right here to give me the sharp edge of her tongue for letting ye leave your bed and bounce about on the back of a horse. Ye had to do so to get here, but ye dinnae have to do so to then travel to her side."

"I could ride in a cart."

Fiona crossed her arms over her chest and scowled at Alana. "Nay. I assume ye have learned all that has happened concerning Keira, so ye must ken that she has work aplenty to do without ye adding to it. Now, as I finish brushing dry your hair, ye can tell me what ye and Gregor have been doing these last few weeks and why ye both looked so wretchedly unhappy to see Mavis."

"He was embracing her," Alana muttered. "He couldnae be that unhappy."

"Tell me what has happened to you and I shall tell ye anything ye may wish to hear about Keira."

Alana thought about refusing again and then decided it would be useless. Fiona was determined and,

from what she could recall of the woman, a determined Fiona was a mighty force to be reckoned with.
As Alana told her tale, she did her best to try to avoid
all hint that she and Gregor had become lovers, as
well as any indication of the feelings she had for him.
A few covert glances at Fiona told Alana that she was
probably tying her tongue into knots for nothing.
Fiona appeared to be rapidly filling in all the holes
Alana had left in her story.

"Weel, ye have certainly had an adventure," Fiona
said when Alana was finished. "Ye have also answered a question or two I have had concerning this
betrothal between Gregor and Mavis."

"How did I do that? I didnae e'en mention the
lying swine's betrothal." And Alana heartily wished
no one else would, either, for she could feel all the
hurt inside of her writhing to be set free.

Fiona pulled up a stool and sat down facing Alana.
"But that is just it, ye see."

"Nay, nary a glimmer."

"Gregor isnae a lying swine. Oh, he is as big a rutting fool as the rest of these MacFingals, but he is an
honest mon. True, there must be some reason Mavis's
father claims a betrothal, and Gregor was on the hunt
for a wife, but I feel verra sure he would ne'er break
a vow if he made one. When Mavis and her father arrived and talked of a betrothal, we were all puzzled,
for Gregor hadnae sent word to us and we were all
certain that he would."

"He was riding home to Scarglas. Mayhap it was
to tell ye that he had finally chosen his bride." Alana
heard her voice waver as she spoke that last word and
reached out for that anger or that numbness that had
thus far shielded her from pain.

"Mayhap, but he looked completely stunned, and then, weel, upset. Verra upset."

"Wheesht, of course he looked upset. He was just caught out, wasnae he."

"I dinnae think so. Oh, I suspect a betrothal was talked about between the men, but I truly dinnae think it was settled. Mavis's father would like it to be and that may be why he speaks so boldly, as if all were settled and done, but I dinnae think so. Nay, kenning Gregor as I do, I think he was coming here to think on it all, mayhap e'en talk it all o'er with Ewan. This wasnae a match born of passion or love, so I feel certain Gregor would step carefully nay matter what he would gain from the marriage."

That did sound like Gregor, Alana thought and then hastily pushed that thought aside. Fiona was offering hope and Alana did not dare grasp at it. She still had not dealt with the hurt of seeing another woman claim Gregor. If she let hope seep into her heart and it proved fruitless, the pain that would bring her did not bear thinking on. There was also the fact that Gregor had never once hinted that he was not a free man. It was a lie of silence, but it was still a lie. That made her wonder just how many other lies he had told her.

"Weel, it doesnae matter. Gregor and I were but prisoners and then travelers together," Alana said.

"Ye are a verra poor liar, Alana Murray. I dinnae ask that ye confess all that passed between ye and Gregor, but I dinnae believe ye were naught but fellow prisoners who escaped together and then made your way here. If naught else, the look upon Gregor's face when Mavis appeared tells me that the two of ye shared far more than a cell and a horse."

"Whate'er we shared is now over. He is to be wed to Mavis."

Fiona rose and braided Alana's hair. "We shall see. Now, do ye want to hide here in this room or shall ye come down to the great hall to sup with us?"

"I thought ye said I needed to take good care of my poor, battered self."

"I said ye shouldnae be traveling about and adding to your many bruises. Donning a gown, coming down to the great hall, and eating something will-nae add to your injuries."

The very last thing Alana wished to do was sit at a table and watch Gregor with his betrothed. It might not add to all the bruises and scrapes she had, but it would certainly add to her pain. Yet her pride quailed at the thought of hiding in her bedchamber as if she had done something wrong. Such a cowardly act would also tell Gregor that he had hurt her, and she did not want him to know that she felt anything more than a righteous fury over his lies. It would mean she could not succumb to all the feelings churning inside of her, but if she clung to her anger she might be able to hide her pain from everyone for a few more hours.

"I doubt I shall be able to eat much," she said and could tell by Fiona's smile that the woman recognized those grumbled words for the acceptance she had been waiting for.

Gregor ached to go after Alana and try to explain things, but he knew he could not do so. It was also going to be difficult to deal with Mavis and her father for a while. Not only were there too many people around, he needed to think carefully about exactly what he should say to Mavis. After assuring her that he was well, Gregor escaped to his bedchamber to bathe and don some clean clothes. He was not really surprised when, within minutes after he had finished his bath, his brother Ewan arrived.

"Ye arenae acting much like a mon who has finally found the lass he wishes to marry," said Ewan as he sprawled on Gregor's bed.

"Ah, but I have," said Gregor as he began to dress. "Unfortunately, it isnae Mavis Kerr."

"Nay? She and her father feel verra certain that it is. If ye werenae certain yourself, ye shouldnae have gotten yourself betrothed to the lass."

"Actually, I didnae. I did court her, and her father and I talked round it a few times, that I cannae deny. I didnae ask for her hand, however, nor did I put my mark on any papers. In truth, I was coming here to talk it o'er with ye and think on it verra carefully ere I made any vows. The Gowans interfered with that plan."

"Yet ye made no denials when she ran into your arms."

"Aside from the fact that I was stunned stupid to find Mavis waiting for me, and everyone claiming she is my betrothed, I couldnae humiliate her so by denying it before all of you. Mavis is a good woman and, weel, I did raise expectations. My plan was to return to her and gently end those expectations. I think this is her father's doing and he has made it all far more difficult than it needed to be. Here, amongst all my kinsmen, it will be difficult to avoid offering her an insult or causing her some humiliation."

"Weel, I would like to help ye untangle this, but I must leave in the morning."

"For where?"

"Ardgleann. Do ye ken anything about it? I mean, aside from the fact that Alana's sister Keira is alive and married again."

Gregor told his brother all that Brother Matthew had told him and Alana. "He was pleased to hear that Liam had married Keira and would be laird of Ardgleann."

"Liam has done verra weel for himself and will be a good laird. He has also found his soul mate." Ewan smiled faintly. "He is having a wee bit of trouble convincing the lass of that, as his past hangs o'er him like a dark cloud, but I have faith that they will soon be settled."

"Mayhap that can be used to keep Alana from rushing to her sister's side," Gregor mused aloud.

"Fiona has already put a stop to Alana rushing off to Ardgleann. She told the lass she cannae go anywhere until her injuries heal more. When that cannae hold her any longer, I suspicion Fiona will convince her that it would be best to leave Liam and Keira alone a wee bit longer so that they can sort out their troubles. That is, if ye wish Alana to stay here."

"Aye, I do. *She* is my mate."

Ewan nodded. "I had wondered. The way ye looked at Alana when Mavis flung herself into your arms made me think that ye had changed your mind about your choice of bride."

"I had begun to change my mind shortly after being tossed into the Gowans' oubliette. Sitting alone in the dark with nowhere to go can greatly clarify a mon's thought. Mavis really is a fine woman, nay too hard to look at, with a fine purse as a dowry, and a bit of land, but she doesnae move me. I suspicion I could grow to care for her, feel some true affection for her, but I suddenly didnae want to bind myself for the rest of my days to a woman I could, at best, feel a mild affection for."

"Nay, that path can lead to misery and the breaking of vows made. Which, as we ken all too weel, leads to e'en more misery. Yet 'tis true that ye cannae just cast her aside."

"I ken it." Gregor sighed. "It all requires a tact and skill with words I am nay sure I am capable of."

"Then come with me to Ardgleann. That bastard Mowbray stripped the place of food and I am taking them some supplies. Ye can explain the need for such a journey, for there are many good reasons for it. And Mavis and her father did come here uninvited, so they cannae complain too loudly. They have also lied to all of us. We will be gone for several days, so that should give ye time to think o'er what ye will say."

"A sound plan, e'en if it tastes a wee bit too much like a cowardly retreat from a mess of my own making."

Ewan laughed softly as he stood up. "Think of it more as a strategic withdrawal to allow yourself to prepare for a battle."

"That does sound much better." Gregor hastily brushed his hair. "I wonder if Alana will brave the great hall tonight or also employ a strategic withdrawal."

"Is she a proud lass?"

"Aye, for all that she doesnae think much good of herself."

"Then she will be there. She willnae want to give ye the idea that she is hurt by what she may see as a gross betrayal."

"Och, I dinnae think there is any *may* about it."

"Seduced her, did ye?"

"We were lovers, aye." Gregor heard the tone of defensiveness in his voice and inwardly cursed.

"We willnae argue o'er whether or not ye should have told her about Mavis but, weel, it doesnae surprise me that ye and Alana became lovers. Nay if ye are certain that she is your true mate."

"Aye, she is. Although after this, it will be cursed difficult to convince her of that."

"A prize is all the sweeter when 'tis hard won. And dinnae forget that she took ye as her lover. From all Fiona tells me of the Murray lasses, they are verra particular about whom they give their favors to."

"I pray she is right. But first, I must get through a meal sitting near one lass who thinks she is betrothed to me and another who is the one I wish to marry, but who would probably like to see my head on a pike right now."

Alana tried very hard not to stare at Gregor, who sat between Mavis and her father. Every bite of food she put into her mouth tasted like sand on her tongue and sat in her belly like a rock. Each smile Gregor gave Mavis stabbed Alana to the heart. He certainly did not act as if the betrothal was false. In truth, Alana was beginning to think Fiona was the only one who had any doubts about it.

In the few hours between arriving at Scarglas and this interminable meal, everything Alana had found out about Gregor only added to her sense of being the greatest fool in the Christian world. Not only had he neglected to tell her he was betrothed, he had also neglected to mention that he had two children, each born of a different mother, and neither woman one whom Gregor had been married to. He was obviously a lecherous dog and she had just been one more conquest amongst far too many. All his pretty words had been no more than empty flatteries meant to lift her skirts. The thought made her so angry she wished she could see his pretty head on a pike, or, more fitting, another far too well used part of him.

Gregor was pressed to tell everyone about his adventures. Alana noticed how carefully he told the tale, cleverly dancing around any hint that she might be more than a fellow prisoner, a woman caught up in the adventure whom he had been kind enough to bring home. He was far better at that than she had been when talking to Fiona. She knew he could not boldly announce to the crowd gathered in the great hall that she had been his lover, nor did she wish him to. Yet he did not act as if he had any intention of pushing Mavis aside, either, even in the most subtle of ways. Alana did not believe the look of warmth in his eyes when he occasionally turned his gaze on her. For all she knew, he looked at Mavis in the same way.

The question was—where did that leave her? He had used her, taken her innocence, yet she was not at all inclined to demand that he marry her. Alana did not want anyone to know how easily she had fallen for his smiles and sweet words. The truly sad thing was that she still wanted him, even as he sat there talking softly to his betrothed.

The only thing she could do was to ignore him, she decided. There would be no more kisses, no more lovemaking, and if possible, no more talking. Talking with Gregor was dangerous. Not only could he easily woo her back into his bed, he could probably persuade her to stay there even after he married Mavis. Alana knew that she could never shame her family in such a way. Or herself.

When Mavis laughingly fed Gregor a piece of apple, Alana decided she had had enough, more than enough. Pride had demanded that she attend this meal, that she show Gregor that she had not been crushed by his betrayal and his lies. As far as she was concerned, her pride had been placated now. Watching Gregor and his soon-to-be bride woo each other was putting Alana into such a passionate fury, she would undoubtedly spew out all the hurt and anger she was trying to hide if she did not leave very soon. Murmuring the excuse of enduring a very long journey and a multitude of aches and pains, Alana excused herself and headed for her bedchamber. She had already gotten halfway up the stairs when she heard someone hurriedly approach her and she had the sinking feeling it was the one person she would rather not see right now, perhaps not ever again.

"Alana, wait," Gregor called as he climbed the stairs after her.

"For what?" she asked, slowly turning to look at him. "An invitation to the wedding?" The bite behind her words told Alana that she was rapidly losing control over her hurt and anger. She was pleased, however, to see that her furious response had caused Gregor to halt his advance on her.

"I can explain—" he began.

"Can ye? Forgot her, did ye? From what I heard, that required only a matter of days, for ye had only just left her side when the Gowans captured you. That doesnae say much about your constancy, does it?"

"Alana, this is all a misunderstanding."

"Aye, mine. I believed all of your pretty words, fool that I am. I dinnae believe I want to hear any more of them," she said, turning to continue up the stairs.

She heard Gregor start after her again, but then Mavis called to him. Alana looked over her shoulder to see the woman standing at the foot of the stairs, frowning up at them, looking more curious than worried. Gregor looked down at Mavis and then looked back at Alana, his expression an odd mixture of annoyance and pleading. Alana directed a faint curtsey toward Mavis and then hurried away before Gregor could try to stop her again.

Once inside her bedchamber, Alana shut the door, barred it, and slumped against it. She was both relieved and sharply disappointed when, after several minutes of silence, it became obvious that Gregor had chosen to rejoin Mavis in the great hall. It hurt. It hurt more than anything else had ever done. Alana was torn between the wish to hurt Gregor as he had hurt her and an urge to leave Scarglas as swiftly as possible.

Stripping off her clothes, she donned the night shift Fiona had left out for her and crawled into bed. There was nothing she could do to hurt Gregor, although thoughts of taking a stick to him provided her with a few minutes of vengeful pleasure. She could not leave Scarglas yet, either. Fiona was right. Alana could feel her battered body protesting the journey down to the great hall to sup. Traveling anywhere now would be an agony. Even with Gregor's aid, the last part of their journey to Scarglas had certainly given her more pain than she wished to experience again.

It appeared she had a choice between two sources of pain. She could endure physical pain by going to her sister at Ardgleann, perhaps even making her injuries worse before they got better. Or she could stay at Scarglas to heal from her injuries and endure the emotional pain of seeing her lover with his betrothed. This was most definitely one of those choices between a rock and a hard place, she mused.

"Then I shall stay here and be damned to the lying swine," she muttered and burst into tears.

For a moment she tried to fight the urge to keep crying until sleep shut her eyes, but then decided to give her shattered emotions free rein. She had been thinking of winning Gregor's heart, while it was now clear that he had none to give. Such a crushing disappointment was worth a few tears. Alana decided she would cry, then she would sleep, and then she would spend her remaining time at Scarglas pretending that Gregor MacFingal Cameron meant absolutely nothing to her, that she had completely cut him out of her heart and mind. Perhaps, if she lived that pretense for long enough and well enough, she would begin to believe it herself.

Chapter 17

"Gone? When? Where?"

Alana knew she was not hiding her shock well as she looked at Fiona for the answers to her snapped-out questions. She had come to the great hall to break her fast determined to be cool and aloof, to treat Gregor as if he were no more than a passing acquaintance. Instead, she had arrived too late to eat with anyone aside from Fiona and Charlemagne, and that woman had blithely announced that Gregor was gone. While it was true that maintaining her calm and hiding her pain would be a great deal easier if Gregor was not around, Alana still felt annoyed.

And a little bereft, she realized, and inwardly cursed. Alana was dismayed that she could be so pathetic as to be disappointed that she could not at least see the man who had so deeply betrayed her. Love, she decided, had no respect for a woman's pride or dignity. Such feelings also told her that she had a dangerous weakness Gregor could make use of if he chose to. A mere day ago she would never have thought that he would sink so low as to take advantage of her feelings for him, but now she was not so sure. He had, after all, seduced her even though he was betrothed to another.

Suddenly realizing that Mavis was not around, either, she asked, "Did he go away with his bride?"

"Nay, and I still think she isnae his betrothed," replied Fiona as she slathered honey on a chunk of bread.

"He didnae deny it," Alana reminded her, dismissing Gregor's claim that there had been some misunderstanding.

"I suspicion he wishes to sort this matter out in privacy, and there was none of that once ye arrived. How do ye feel this morning?"

It took Alana a moment to realize that Fiona was asking about her bodily injuries and not the state of her heart. "Still battered but nay as sore as I was yestereve."

"Good. Ye probably havenae hurt anything inside of ye, then, or done more than raise a wee bump on your head. I didnae think so, but it was a worry. The pain will ease more each day."

The pain of her body's injuries would, but Alana doubted the pain in her heart would ever heal. Crying half the night had not lessened it, nor did anger. The outrage she felt over how she had been used and betrayed only helped her hide her pain. It did nothing to end it.

"So where did Gregor go?" she asked and inwardly cursed herself for a weak fool for even asking.

"To Ardgleann with Ewan," replied Fiona as she peeled an apple.

"Without me? Without e'en telling me so that I might send word to Keira?"

"Ewan and Gregor will tell your sister all about

your adventures and how ye fare. I think 'tis enough that she will hear how hard ye tried to reach her in her time of need and that as soon as ye are healed and strong again, ye will come and see her. The journey was planned ere ye and Gregor arrived and, considering all that occurred last eve, there wasnae much opportunity to tell ye. 'Struth, I was quite surprised when Gregor left with Ewan at dawn." Fiona scowled. "My husband didnae see fit to tell me."

And the man would pay for that, Alana thought and almost smiled. "It would have been nice to send e'en just a few words to Keira, a wee letter mayhap."

"There is naught to stop ye from writing her one now. I believe there will be a lot of travel between the two keeps for quite a while. That swine Mowbray left little food for the people and made them late in starting the planting of their fields."

"Can ye tell me much about this mon Liam Cameron? Brother Matthew swears that he is a good mon and will make my sister a good husband, but Brother Matthew sees good in everyone. Gregor said the same, but Liam is his cousin, and men cannae always see those faults in a mon that would make a poor husband. I feel certain Keira's first marriage wasnae happy and I would like to think this one will be. He is a handsome mon, aye?"

"Liam is beautiful, although saying so tends to make other men gnash their teeth."

Alana laughed, but quickly grew serious again. "And will he be a good and faithful husband?"

"Aye, I have no doubt of it. He and Keira are true mates." Fiona filled a bowl with porridge and poured thick cream on it. "Your sister loves him and I truly believe Liam loves her. I am pleased ye have asked

about them, for I think ye should wait to visit Keira
until she and Liam can sort themselves out."

"They are having some problems?"

"Just those problems two people can have when
they love each other but havenae the courage to tell
each other so."

"I hope ye are right. I have dreams about her, ye
ken," Alana admitted quietly, a little uneasy about
telling Fiona even though the woman had spent a lot of
time with the Murrays before her marriage to Ewan.

"Havenae they told ye that she is happy?"

"Aye and nay. The dreams that made me come in
search of her were verra precise. I e'en had a few ere
I reached Brother Matthew and learned so much
about what had happened to Keira. Since that time,
I have had one that told me she was sad, verra sad."

"Probably when she was grieving for all the harm
done to Ardgleann and its people."

"'Tis what I thought. But then, I have had a few
others that are more feelings than dreams and she is
happy, yet there is also a sadness in her heart." Alana
frowned, struggling to recall all she had felt. "And
doubts. Definitely doubts. And, I think, a few fears,
but of what I dinnae ken."

Fiona nodded. "Now, doesnae that sound verra
much like a woman who loves a mon but isnae certain how he feels about her? Such a thing can make
a woman doubt herself, doubt him, and fear for her
future."

Alana thought about that for a moment, comparing
it to how she had felt about Gregor before she had
discovered his lie. "Aye, that does make sense. I think
Keira may be with child."

"That wouldnae surprise me. Liam is a verra virile

mon." Fiona looked at Alana and cocked one brow. "All the Camerons are."

As the meaning of Fiona's words settled into Alana's mind, she almost choked on the honey-sweetened oatcake she was eating. Virile men made bairns. Gregor had already made two. She prayed he had not made a third. She would love the child and so would her family, but others would see only the shame, and her child would be only one of the many who could suffer for her recklessness. There was also the fact that she would spend a lot of time trying to convince the men in her family that nothing would be gained by killing Gregor. She had been right to think that passion had consequences for women and very wrong to think she could blithely ignore them.

"Weel, dinnae worry, I willnae let them hurt the fool," she assured Fiona.

"I thank ye for that e'en though I ne'er thought ye would." Fiona winked at her. "'Tis one thing for a woman to think of all the gruesome tortures and deaths she wishes to inflict upon the mon she loves because he hurt or angered her, but she would ne'er let such things really happen to him."

"And I have ne'er said that I love that liar."

Fiona rolled her eyes and reached for an oatcake. "Of course not. My mistake."

"Och, weel, have the truth then, if ye must."

"I do prefer it."

Alana ignored that, scowling at the apple she had just picked up. "I *do* love him. At the moment, I would also like to see him ripped apart by wolves and a certain part he is so proud of nailed to a wall."

Fiona giggled and nodded. "Sounds like love to me."

Surprised she could do so, Alana smiled but then

recalled all of Gregor's crimes against her. "If he is truly betrothed to Mavis, then why didnae he tell me about her? Aye, I wouldnae have liked hearing that he had seriously courted another woman, was e'en thinking of marrying her, but at least I would have been armed with the truth when I met her. Instead, the Kerrs claim there is a betrothal, Gregor tells me there is a misunderstanding, and no one about Scarglas can assure me that they ken the truth of it all one way or the other."

"Aye, that must be a torment. I suspicion there is a part of you that doesnae want to believe he could treat ye so poorly."

Alana nodded. "That foolish part of me that loves him, but I intend to kill it, ruthlessly, mercilessly, and quickly. E'en if the Kerrs are lying or have misunderstood something, that doesnae change the fact that Gregor lied to me. That lie has made all that passed between us seem like no more than a, a heartless frolic on his part. It was all naught but rutting."

"Och, now, Alana, ye dinnae really believe that, do ye?"

"I have to. It appears that Gregor is betrothed, and only he and the Kerrs ken the truth of it. Weel, if he is, then I *have* been a great fool, and if I dinnae believe that, he could easily woo me into becoming an even greater one."

"Ah, I see. Mayhap there simply wasnae a good time to tell ye about Mavis."

"A good time would have been before he bedded me. Another good time would have been when I told him all about my father's plans to find me a husband."

Fiona gasped. "Ye arenae betrothed, are ye?"

"Nay. 'Tis just that I am two-and-twenty and have

ne'er e'en been wooed. I want a home of my own. I want bairns. So my father said he would find me a husband. He was looking, but he hadnae asked me to approve any choices yet, so nay, I am still free. My father would ne'er betroth me to a mon without my approval."

"Of course not. The Murrays give their lasses the freedom of choice. I mean to do the same for whatever daughters I might have. And aye, that would have been the best time for Gregor to tell ye about Mavis. I think he just turned cowardly or thought he could untangle the mess without ye ever learning about her. Men often get such foolish ideas. This should teach Gregor that it isnae wise to keep secrets from ye in the future."

Alana was about to tell Fiona there would be no future for her and Gregor when Mavis arrived with a handsome young man Fiona hailed as Brian. It was obvious that he was one of Gregor's vast horde of brothers. It was also obvious that he and Mavis were very friendly. The blush that colored Mavis's plump cheeks as she let go of Brian's arm and sat down at the table bespoke guilt. Alana exchanged a brief look of mingled surprise and suspicion with Fiona before turning her attention back on Mavis and Brian.

Mavis was an attractive woman with thick, dark auburn hair and bright hazel eyes. She was also somewhat voluptuous, and Alana hastily beat down the sting of envy that swept over her. Pushing all thought of how this woman had a claim on Gregor from her mind, Alana made a careful study of Brian and Mavis as they ate and talked with her and Fiona. By the time the couple left, Alana was not sure if she was happy for herself or outraged for Gregor's sake.

She looked at Fiona, who stared after the couple with an intense frown upon her face.

"Do ye think Mavis is playing Gregor false with his own brother?" she asked Fiona.

"Nay, Mavis isnae the type of woman to break a vow," replied Fiona.

"Then I have let my own foolish hope make me see what isnae there. 'Tis clear that I am still a besotted fool."

"Oh, ye saw clearly enough. If those two arenae lovers already, they soon will be."

"But ye said—"

"That Mavis wouldnae break a vow, aye. Since she is besotted with Brian and he with her, and they appear to be acting upon those feelings, then we must conclude that Mavis kens verra weel that she isnae betrothed to Gregor."

Alana slumped in her seat and gently rubbed her temples, not surprised to feel the beginnings of a very bad headache. "Why would she, and her father, lie about it?"

"'Tis most likely her father who lies, and Mavis is the sort of sweet, biddable lass who would ne'er dream of arguing with him or defying him. As to why her father would lie? Weel, Mavis is his only surviving child and he has no male heir, or at least none whom he likes. He wants a strong mon who can hold his lands for Mavis once he is gone. He wants grandsons and 'tis clear to all that this clan produces sons in abundance. Since Mavis is a wee bit older than ye are, one can only guess at why she is still unwed, but her father grows anxious. So, he has clutched at our Gregor."

It made sense, but Alana was reluctant to allow

herself to hope. Even if the betrothal was false and Gregor ended it, there were still his lie and his lecherous past to consider. There was also the fact that he had never spoken to her of love or marriage. Gregor might not marry Mavis, but that did not mean he would turn around and marry her, either.

"If Mavis is such a sweet, biddable lass who would never defy her father, then the betrothal between her and Gregor still stands."

"I dinnae think so. Mavis probably kens that her father isnae so much set on Gregor as he is set upon a strong mon who will give him grandsons. For that, our Brian will do as weel as Gregor. I am just nay sure how this will end. Mavis's father is a stubborn mon who doesnae like to change his mind. He has set his mind on Gregor. This could be quite interesting." Fiona drummed her fingers on the table and frowned. "And I get the feeling my husband kenned all about Brian and Mavis. I suspicion that is why he convinced Gregor to go with him to Ardgleann."

"To clear the path for Brian?"

"Aye. Ewan had a long talk with Gregor ere we supped last night and told me that I was right, that no official betrothal existed. He said Gregor felt he owed Mavis as gentle a fareweel as possible and one that wouldnae humiliate her, for even though he wasnae betrothed to her, he had raised expectations with his courtship. Ewan also told me that he might take Gregor with him so that the mon could most carefully plan how he would do that. He said it wouldnae be possible if Gregor was trapped here with Mavis and her father dogging his heels. The fool could find himself married to the wrong woman." Fiona cast Alana a telling glance that she ignored. "It all sounded verra wise. Now? Weel, I am fair certain Ewan took Gregor away so that Brian could woo and claim Mavis."

"So much intrigue. Weel, no one should be forced into a marriage they dinnae want, even lecherous, lying dogs like Gregor. So if Mavis wants Brian and he wants her, I wish them both luck. I dinnae think it will change my situation, however."

Fiona scowled at her. "Why not? Gregor will be free."

"Free, aye, but he still lied to me and he ne'er told me about his sons, proof of a verra lecherous past."

"Och, most men try verra hard to have a lecherous past."

Alana ignored that even as she acknowledged it as the hard truth. "He has also ne'er told me that he feels anything beyond lust for me or spoken of a future for us."

"He couldnae until he set Mavis aside." Fiona grimaced. "That sounds harsh. He really hadnae promised her anything. Still, she was a knot he needed to untie." Fiona reached out and grasped Alana's hand. "Aye, he lied and he was a lecherous pig in his past. He isnae perfect. What mon is? Or what woman, either? But, Alana, ye love him and I have kenned enough Murray women for long enough to ken that ye would ne'er have become his lover unless ye were certain he was your true mate. I think Mavis will soon take herself away, ending this complication and, sadly, with less care for Gregor's feelings or pride than he had for hers. So wait. Just wait. See what happens and what he does when he finds himself free. Is he nay worth that little effort?"

He was, but Alana wished she did not think so.

Everything Fiona said concerning why Gregor had never told her about Mavis made perfect sense. Alana could even understand why he had hesitated to tell her about his sons. He had tried to speak to her last night, but she had been too angry and hurt to listen. And then, Mavis had come to take him away.

And that, Alana realized, was the source of yet another wound. Gregor was full of consideration for Mavis, for her feelings and her pride. Where was his consideration for hers? He could not be so blind that he did not know how hurt she was, how betrayed and humiliated she felt, yet it was Mavis he was concerned about. It made her doubt that he had any deep feelings for her at all, that, perhaps, she truly had been no more than a convenient lover.

"I dinnae like that look upon your face," murmured Fiona.

"I am thinking just as ye told me to do."

"Aye, but I dinnae think they are the kindly, loving, forgiving types of thoughts I was hoping for."

"Fiona, I will wait as ye have asked me to, and despite the fact that Gregor has ne'er spoken of love or marriage. I will wait, and think, but I willnae let myself hope. When he is free, I will see what he does next and then decide what I should do. Ye cannae ask any more of me."

"Nay, that is more than enough. Just try not to think too harshly about him and too poorly about yourself."

Alana tried. She rested so that her scrapes and bruises could heal, and she spent a lot of time lost in her own thoughts. For three days she carefully examined every word Gregor had ever said and how he had treated her when they had been together. She could find forgiveness within her, but she did not allow hope to enter her heart.

She also kept a very close watch on Brian and Mavis. The romance between Mavis and Gregor's brother was obvious to all except, it seemed, Mavis's father Ian. The man grumbled about being deserted by his soon-to-be son-in-law, talked far too much about how quickly the marriage could take place after Gregor returned, and remained oblivious to the fact that his daughter was falling in love with Brian. Mavis was sweet and biddable, but she was also skilled at keeping secrets. Alana grew more certain every day that Brian and Mavis did not plan to ask Laird Ian for his blessing.

It was late on the fourth day when Alana stood at the window in her bedchamber staring out at the moonlit bailey and saw that she was right about the lovers. She had been thinking of Gregor as she too often did when a movement near the stables caught her eye. A man led two horses out of the stables and, from such a distance, all Alana could be sure of was that it was one of Gregor's brothers. It was the sudden appearance of Mavis at his side that told her it was Brian. The couple briefly embraced and then Brian helped Mavis into her saddle. He mounted his horse, grasped Mavis by the hand and spoke to her. Mavis smiled and nodded and they rode out through the suspiciously wide-open gates and away from Scarglas.

For a brief moment, Alana actually considered raising the alarm. She realized she was seeing it all as a great insult to Gregor and felt outraged for him. He had been so considerate of Mavis, so concerned that she not be hurt or humiliated, and this was a wretched way for her to repay that kindness.

"And ye are a wretched great idiot," she told herself as she went over to her bed, where Charlemagne waited for her.

As she settled herself beneath the covers, she realized that a little of the pain in her heart had eased and she cursed. She had obviously not been completely successful in killing all hope. That worried her enough that she seriously considered following Brian and Mavis's example and fleeing Scarglas. Only her promise to Fiona to wait and see what Gregor did once he was free held her in place. She feared suffering more pain but struggled to grasp firm at a little courage. Gregor was worth at least one more chance. The love she could not kill demanded it of her. Alana did think, however, that there was no need to make it easy for him.

Alana started down the steps toward the great hall looking to break her fast when she saw a red-faced Ian Kerr come striding out of the great hall. He threw open the door leading out into the inner bailey and bellowed for someone to get him a fast horse. The moment he was gone, Alana hurried to the door to the great hall and looked inside. Fiona sat in her husband's big chair at the head table calmly eating. Charlemagne slipped past Alana and hurried toward Fiona. He was immediately gifted with a piece of chicken.

"I had thought I was early enough today to break my fast in the company of everyone else," Alana said as she walked to the head table and sat down next to Fiona.

"They were all here ere the sun had fully risen and then did their verra best to disappear," said Fiona.

"So that they wouldnae have to face Mavis's verra angry father?"

"Saw him, did ye?" Fiona shrugged when Alana nodded. "I dinnae envy Brian that mon for a father-in-law."

"I saw Mavis and Brian leave last night, riding quickly through some surprisingly wide-open gates."

"Weel, dinnae look at me. I didnae have anything to do with it. Ewan probably had a word with the lads before he left. 'Tis the only reason I can think of for why none of Gregor's other brothers stopped Brian from wooing Mavis. Someone had told them that Mavis wasnae really betrothed to Gregor. They can all be lecherous swine, but they never touch a woman who belongs to one of their brethren."

Alana helped herself to some porridge, sweetening it with honey and thick cream. "They might have learned that Mavis wasnae really betrothed to Gregor, but that doesnae mean they knew for certain whether or not Gregor wanted her."

"True, so somehow they learned that he didnae."

"Do ye ken, for a moment I almost raised the alarm and stopped them."

Fiona laughed and nodded. "Aye, so did I. I could only think how dare they humiliate Gregor like this."

"Exactly. Howbeit, good sense prevailed and not just because this frees Gregor. Mavis has ne'er done me any harm and seems a good woman. She deserves her happiness as much as anyone else does."

"Aye, she does. And now, we wait for Gregor to return."

"Aye, and now we wait."

"Ye *will* at least listen to the fool, will ye not?"

"I will listen if he wishes to talk, but I cannae just allow him to woo me back to where we were before Mavis intruded. I thought he was a free mon and that I was taking a risk in order to win his heart, his free and open heart. Weel, now he can work to win *my* heart, and to win my trust back. I trusted him once and, all good reasons for the lie aside, he betrayed that trust." She was relieved when Fiona nodded in agreement. "Last night I decided that I am willing to give him a chance, but I have no intention of making it easy for him."

"Good. It shouldnae be."

"And, Fiona, if he doesnae act as ye think he will, if he really doesnae care for me beyond the lusting, I *will* leave here."

"Fair enough."

"Ye think I will be staying, dinnae ye."

"I do, but I understand why ye shy from letting yourself hope. I offer only one wee bit of advice."

"And what is that?"

"Be verra sure ye recognize when ye have ceased to be reasonably difficult to win and have become pigheaded and impossible."

Alana laughed. "As ye like to say—fair enough."

CHAPTER 18

"Gone? When? Where?"

Gregor stared at Fiona in shock and wondered why Ewan looked as if he wanted to smile. He had spent six days away from Scarglas readying himself to face Mavis and her father, carefully planning each and every word he would say to them. For most of the last ten miles of the ride home, he had repeated his speech over and over in his mind so that he would not stumble over the words once he confronted Mavis and her father. He had even made the effort to shake free of the anger he felt over the fact that they had come to his home uninvited, claimed a betrothal they knew did not exist, and caused Alana pain.

He looked around the great hall and realized that there were only Fiona, Ewan, and himself in the room. Gregor was a little surprised that none of his large family had gathered to find out if they had brought back any interesting news, and then he began to get suspicious. Even the men they had ridden in with had disappeared, without even quenching their thirst. By the time Fiona finished the apple she had been eating, Gregor was close to demanding that she hurry and answer his questions. All that held his tongue was the knowledge that not only would Fiona be completely unmoved by his demands, but Ewan would probably knock him flat for yelling at her.

"Mavis ran off with Brian," Fiona finally said.

After staring at her in disbelief for a moment, Gregor sat down and poured himself an ale. It took several deep drinks of the heady brew before his shock began to fade enough for him to think clearly. Ewan and Fiona both looked a little amused and decidedly smug as they watched him. That, added to the strange absence of any of his vast family, told Gregor that this was no great surprise to anyone but him.

"And Laird Kerr?" he asked.

"Set out after them the verra next morning, but he had verra little chance of catching them ere they were married, for they had many hours' start on him."

"Ye suspected this would happen, didnae ye, Ewan," Gregor said, fixing a hard stare on his elder brother. "'Tis why ye talked me into going to Ardgleann with ye. Ye wished to give Mavis and Brian time to decide that they were right for each other."

Ewan picked Fiona up in his arms, sat down in his chair, and settled her on his lap. "Oh, I think they had already decided upon that ere ye came home. Mavis had already been here for a sennight."

"Did ye want her, then?" asked Fiona.

"Nay, but that doesnae mean that I like being made a fool of. I ken weel that I am the verra last to hear about this. If someone had e'en hinted at what was going on, I could have saved myself six long days of struggling to decide what to do and say to untangle this mess."

"Ah, but then ye would have stayed here, and I do think it was for the best that ye left," said Ewan. "Mavis was a wee bit cowed by her father. The moment ye returned, she began to stay close by your side. I feared Laird Kerr could convince her that she had to marry you and she was too much the dutiful daughter to tell him that she wished to have another mon for her husband. With ye gone, Brian had the freedom to woo her and convince her to do as she wished to anyway."

Gregor slowly drank a little more ale. He did wonder why he felt so annoyed. He should be pleased, should be skipping about the room in unbridled joy. The tangle he had fretted over for so long had been neatly untied with no effort needed on his part. Brian now had himself a good wife, land, and a full purse. He also had Ian Kerr for a father-in-law, but Gregor suspected Brian would know how to deal with the man. It was his pride that was hurting, he realized. Gregor suspected no man would like to discover that a woman preferred another man over him, even if it was a woman he was about to set aside for another. The fact that he was the last to know what had been going on stung, for it made him look like a complete fool.

He quickly pushed those feelings aside. This was what he had wanted, even before he had met Alana. He should be pleased no matter how it had come about or how much it had cost his pride. Now he could turn all of his attention on Alana and soothe the hurt he had inflicted. Gregor felt a flicker of fear enter his heart as he began to wonder exactly why he had not seen her yet.

"Where is Alana?" he asked, eager to settle matters between them.

"In her bedchamber," replied Fiona. "She fled there when she heard ye had returned."

That stung, but Gregor could understand. He had hurt her and, even though it was not widely known that they had been lovers, he had shamed her, at least in her own mind. There was every chance she thought he had simply used her to pass the time and feed his manly needs while they journeyed to Scarglas, where he would be reunited with his betrothed.

Gregor did not dare to even guess how that had made Alana feel, and she had not allowed him to explain everything. Worse, he had spent a lot of time during his journey to and from Ardgleann planning what to say to Mavis, but had not thought of anything he could say to Alana. The idea that he could just apologize most humbly and kiss her into forgiving him was a foolish one, but he had clung to it with a desperation he winced to acknowledge.

Meeting Alana's twin sister had proven very uncomfortable, although the sisters looked nothing alike except in size and the shapes of their faces. Keira was a lovely woman and obviously had the same bond with Alana that Alana had with her. Gregor was not able to shake the feeling that Keira knew what he and Alana had shared and that he had hurt her sister. It had been tempting to ask the woman if she knew what Alana was feeling now, even if she knew if Alana loved him, but he had shied away from indulging in any confidences with the woman. Unfortunately, Keira had shared no confidences with him, either, so he had little to tell Alana to soothe her concerns about Keira's happiness.

Liam had been much more forthcoming, and he could try to reassure Alana with those confidences.

Gregor suspected it would not be enough, however. Not only was he going to be giving her a man's view of it all, but she could probably still sense her sister's lingering unhappiness. He had not needed to reveal any of that to Liam, for the man had already known about the bond between the sisters. Worse, it was Liam's past that was making it difficult for him to win his wife's trust. Gregor was concerned that his past was going to prove a problem as well. At least Liam had no bastard children under his roof who would constantly remind his wife of that past.

"Ye willnae sort anything out by sitting there and scowling into your ale," said Fiona.

Gregor scowled at her instead. "I doubt Alana wishes to see me. 'Struth, she has made that verra clear by fleeing to her room when I arrived."

"Ye should have told her about Mavis," said Fiona, ignoring her husband's murmured protest about her interfering. "Nay, I will say my piece. After all, he left me here to deal with his betrothed and his lover beneath the same roof. It could have proven verra awkward for me."

"I ken that I made a mistake when I didnae tell Alana about Mavis, but 'tis verra hard to correct that mistake when she willnae listen to what I have to say."

"Aye, ye made a big mistake by nay telling her the truth ere she arrived here to face the woman, but ye made an even bigger one by fretting more about Mavis's pride and feelings than ye did about Alana's."

"That isnae true," Gregor protested a little weakly because he had the sudden realization that it might well have appeared so to Alana.

As he thought over how he had behaved in the few short hours he had been at Scarglas, he decided that *might* was the wrong word. It had undoubtedly appeared so to Alana. He had been still reeling with the shock of finding Mavis here claiming him as her betrothed and facing Alana's hurt and anger, and he had not been thinking too clearly. All he had been able to think of was the need to keep Mavis and her father happy until he could quietly end the misunderstanding and get them out of Scarglas. Guilt over having wooed the woman for her dowry as much as anything else had kept him concerned for her feelings, for not humiliating her by disclaiming her before one and all. Instead, he had disclaimed Alana.

He cursed. The number of missteps he had made with Alana continued to pile up. He should have done something, even forced her to listen to him, but he had played the kind groom to Mavis's smiling bride. If it had been Alana who had done that to him, had acted so before his eyes, he would not have been so quiet about it all. No, there would have been one dead man before the meal had ended.

But, he thought a little crossly, he would have at least allowed Alana to explain. If she had just listened to him for a minute, all he had done at the meal that night would have been understandable. Gregor knew Alana would never have wanted her pride to take precedence over anyone else's. She would not have wanted Mavis hurt or humiliated, either.

"Ye shall have to make her sit down and listen to ye," said Fiona.

"That easy, is it?" he asked, his voice sharp with an anger that was mostly directed at himself.

"Easy would have been if ye had told her about Mavis. Now ye must not only explain that, but why ye didnae tell her." Fiona sighed. "Can ye nay see? Ye have made Alana think that all she was to ye was a convenient woman, someone to warm the blankets ere ye arrived home to marry another."

"Ye speak verra freely."

"I must, or this tangle could become a knot that will ne'er be untied, and that would cost both ye and Alana far too dearly. I think ye held back a lot of words as the two of ye traveled here, perhaps afraid to give her any promises or the like until ye were completely free, but it has cost ye now. Alana has naught from ye, nay, not e'en a few whispered words, to cling to and believe that this is all just a mistake. Ye gave her naught to set her trust in. Ewan says ye consider Alana your mate, but I fear ye have given her naught to make *her* think the same."

There was no denying that. His reasons had seemed all that was honorable. It was wrong to make any vows or promises to one woman when one had just come from wooing another for his wife and had not let it be known that that was not going to happen. But it had put him in the tight corner Fiona now described. The woman he wanted now had nothing to tell her why she should trust him or believe that anything aside from passion had passed between them.

"And of course, she now kens about your sons."

Gregor stared down at the top of the table and wondered if it would help if he banged his head on it a few times. "I wasnae really hiding them." He grimaced. "I had just forgotten about them. The trouble with Mavis was all I could think of, aside from what was happening between Alana and me." He frowned. "If I can sort this all out in my favor, she will accept the lads, willnae she?" he asked, and he knew she would even as he presented the question to Fiona. He accepted the disgusted look she gave him as his due.

"Of course she will and ye ken it. Now, I believe she is actually in the solar. All I will say is that she promised me she would listen to you. The rest is up to you. If ye cannae convince her, soothe her hurt and all of that, she will leave for Ardgleann and I willnae stop her this time."

"Ye are a verra managing woman, Fiona," he said and grinned when she just smiled. "I shall do what I can. Since I ken she wanted news of her sister and now I ken about her promise to ye, at least I can get a foot in the door to plead my case."

He made his way to the solar feeling both hopeful and terrified. This was why he had shied away from love. It was undignified for a man to go to a woman feeling as if he was facing the hardest battle of his life and was actually considering the possibility of a craven retreat.

Gregor sighed as he stared at the door to the solar and tried to brace himself for the coming confrontation. He was facing the most important battle of his life, if not the hardest, for he knew the future would be cold and empty without Alana at his side. That emptiness he had felt before deciding he would cease tumbling any woman when the mood struck and get himself a wife seemed like nothing of any real importance compared to what he would feel if he could not win Alana's heart. In the time he had been away from Scarglas, he had become all too aware of how he liked having her at his side all night, waking to her in the morning, and knowing she was close at hand during the day. Nay, not liked, he told himself, determined to cease deceiving himself—needed.

His tap upon the door did not immediately bring an invitation to enter. He waited only for a moment before he considered just marching in there. Common sense told him that was hardly the way to soften Alana's anger, but the longer he stood outside the door like some sad penitent, the more annoyed he got. Gregor was just reaching out to open the door when he heard Alana's voice issue a clearly reluctant invitation to enter. As he opened the door, he prayed that he could find all the appropriate words to bring her back into his arms.

Alana watched Gregor enter the room, softly close the door behind him, and turn to look at her. The sight of him made her heart skip and she cursed herself for a witless fool. While it was true that he was now completely free, it did not change matters between them very much. He still had a lot of lies to explain and she still had no idea of how he felt about her beyond desire.

She thought of how happy she had been that those thieves had not been able to abuse her and kill all the beauty of what she and Gregor had shared. What violence had not killed, Gregor's lies had. At the moment, with the pain of betrayal still a hard knot inside her and no words of love to cling to, she could not recall those moments in his arms without wincing in pain and embarrassment over her foolish innocence. It would probably pass with time and the memories would grow beautiful again, undoubtedly tinged with a bit of melancholy for things lost, but right now she tried her best not to remember one single moment of their passion.

"Did ye have a pleasant journey?" she asked as he sat down in the chair facing her before the fireplace.

The way his eyes narrowed at the cool, polite tone she used made her feel better. Alana knew it was probably petty of her to gain some satisfaction from being able to annoy him, but she did not care. He had left her here to wallow in her own pain and fury for six days, side by side with a woman he had courted and who claimed she was his betrothed. If he had been anxious to explain things to her or sort out what he had claimed was a misunderstanding, it would seem he could have stayed at Scarglas and put some effort into it.

"My journey was pleasant enough," he replied, "although I sorely missed my usual companion."

"Ah, such a shame, but I felt Charlemagne needed a respite from travel."

Alana could get nasty when she was angry, Gregor thought, torn between an urge to grin and one to give her a little shake. Now that he thought on it, their time with the Gowans should have warned him of that. She had slapped those men with the sharp side of her tongue many times. He would accept it as his penance for his mistakes, but only for a little while. He knew he had hurt her even if he did not know how deeply or badly, and he could understand that she would feel a need to try and hurt him back. It could also be her way to keep him at a distance, but she would find that did not work for long.

"Where is the cat?" he asked, looking around for the animal that had never strayed far from her side.

"Your sons have taken a liking to him and Charlemagne is gracing them with his presence."

Gregor felt himself blush and inwardly cursed. He had not anticipated that she would slap him in the face with one of his lies quite so quickly. Although, he mused, it was not really a lie, but he suspected trying to explain how he had forgotten them because he had been thinking about the problem with Mavis would not endear him to her. In truth, he was a little embarrassed about that himself.

"Ah, that is good." And now he was apparently reduced to stuttering out polite idiocies, he thought. "Do ye wish to ken how your sister is?" Even more idiotic, he mused, not surprised when she looked at him as if he had been beaten on the head once too often.

"Aye, how is Keira?"

She sat up very straight with her hands folded in her lap, just as she had been taught to do since childhood. It was the way one sat when meeting guests, and Alana suspected Gregor knew it, if his scowl was any indication. If he thought she would be all smiles and soft welcome just because Mavis had run off with Brian, he had another thing coming. He would be treated as no more than an acquaintance until he gave her very good reason to treat him otherwise.

"She is fine," he said. "That sorrow ye feel could be from the hurt done to Ardgleann and its people. He treated the lasses there as his own private stable, he and his men. Took them away from their homes and families and held them in the keep for their own amusement. They dinnae fault her, but I think she still blames herself for nay coming to their aid sooner than she did. Ah, and there was damage done to some of the beautiful things Ardgleann seems to abound with. All the food stores and livestock were tossed down the gullets of the men and the fields werenae planted on time. Aye, there are a lot of things there that could bring her sorrow, although things are improving."

It took a moment for Alana to shake aside the

horror she had felt over what the women of Ardgleann had been forced to endure. She could
understand how Keira would feel it was her fault because she had not returned to oust the invader almost
immediately. Alana suspected she would feel the
same no matter how foolish it was to do so. For a
moment she concentrated on all she had felt concerning her sister and then slowly shook her head.

"Aye, that is the way of it. There is the weight of
an unearned guilt upon her heart, but there is more.
I truly believe there is something wrong with her
marriage."

"Nay, Alana, there isnae anything wrong. There is
just a wee bit of, weel, unease. Some matters must be
settled between her and Liam, but nay more than
that. Liam truly cares for her, but she remains uncon-
vinced, or so he believes. As ye have said yourself, he
is a mon most women find beautiful and your sister
is troubled by that. They but need time to learn about
each other and for her to believe that he willnae play
her false with another woman, nay matter how foolishly that woman may pursue him."

"Ah, like the one who came to the monastery, the
one who had him beaten because she was jealous."

"Exactly. The people of Ardgleann already trust
him and look to him as their laird. Can ye nay take
some comfort in their opinion of the mon?"

"Some, aye, but I still feel the need to see Keira."

"Soon. Let her and Liam have time to settle things
between them. She didnae appear truly unhappy with
him and showed no resentment o'er everyone looking to him as the new laird e'en though Ardgleann
was bequeathed to her. He openly marks her as his

equal in all things, sending people to her for some of the decisions."

Alana was heartily pleased by that and saw it as very promising. Although she understood that marriages were often made with an eye to a gain in land or purse or an alliance, Keira had not needed to make such a match. She had wondered if Liam had been mercenary in his pursuit of her sister. That he shared the power of the laird's place made it seem far more probable that he had married her sister for more reasons than her inheritance.

She suddenly noticed that Gregor had leaned forward in his chair and was looking at her intently. He was obviously finished telling her the news from Ardgleann. She had relaxed with him as they had discussed Liam and Keira and she fleetingly wondered if that had been his intention. The expression in his eyes told her he was about to try and discuss them, and she was not sure she was quite ready for that.

"Alana, I ken ye think I but played some game with ye, using ye when I had no right to," he said, taking one of her hands in his and ignoring her brief effort to tug it free.

"Ye should have told me about Mavis, told me that ye were a betrothed mon."

"But I wasnae betrothed. Aye, I courted her. I decided it was time I ceased playing about with women I couldnae remember from one day to the next and get me a wife. Most men reach an age when they start to think like that. I heard about Mavis Kerr and went to see if she would suit me. She had land and a nice fat purse, and I am sorry if that sounds callous, but 'tis what most men think on when they go looking about for a wife. I did court her, but I never became betrothed to her. Aye, it was all done with a marriage in the offing, but naught had been promised or signed."

"So why did she need to be kept some great dark secret?"

"In the beginning I didnae think it was of any importance. I had already decided I couldnae marry her, that tempting though her dowry was, I couldnae feel any more than a mild affection for her. While I sat alone in the dark at the Gowans', I realized I didnae want to tie myself for life to a woman I could only, weel, like."

"All that is verra understandable, so I ask again, why couldnae ye tell me about it? Why say naught e'en after we had become lovers? At that point it did become my business, didnae it?"

He dragged his hand through his hair. This was going to be difficult. He did not want to tell her how he had been more or less judging her suitability as his wife, testing his own feelings to be certain they were strong enough to take her as his wife. If it sounded callous to him, and it did, it was certain to offend her. He would not like to hear that she had been judging him in a like manner.

"Aye, it did," he said. "By the time we were lovers, however, I kenned ye weel enough that I was sure ye wouldnae come to my bed again until I had ended the tenuous relationship with the Kerrs. Selfish bastard that I am, I didnae want ye to step back, right out of my bed. I thought I could get here and then quietly settle matters with the Kerrs. When ye told me what your father was about, I ken weel that it was the perfect time to tell ye about Mavis, but there was that fear that ye would leave my bed, and it choked the words right off."

That was flattering in a way, but Alana tried not to be swayed by it. She might like the reasons he did not tell her, but that did not change the fact that he had lied to her. There were some other, murky reasons for his silence about Mavis, she was sure of it, but she did not press him. They did not really matter and she suspected his reasons for being silent had changed over the days they had been together.

"Come, love, can ye nay understand? I didnae want to lose your warmth." He sighed when she just frowned. "And when we got here and there stood Mavis, her father loudly claiming us betrothed, it stunned me. Aye, stunned me as if someone had just slapped me in the head with a rock. I couldnae think of what to say and I didnae want to humiliate Mavis by decrying her in front of my family. She wasnae at fault in any of this and I had raised her expectations, so I felt honor bound to be as gentle and quiet about it all as I could be. It and the fact that I had hurt ye, made ye believe everything we had shared was a lie, left me as unsteady as I have e'er felt. I fixed my mind on gently removing Mavis and all talk of betrothal. Now I see that, by doing so, I made ye think I truly was just a bastard who used ye and walked away."

"That did pass through my mind," she murmured.

"All I could think of was removing Mavis and then I felt ye and I could settle matters, but that we couldnae settle anything until Mavis understood that there would be no marriage. 'Tis as if I blinded myself to anything and everything else but ending this connection to the Kerrs first. If ye would have let me explain—" he began.

"I might have, but Mavis didnae seem inclined to leave ye alone long enough for ye to convince me that there was a reason for what ye had done and that ye werenae just some lecherous cur." She ignored his expression, which was an odd mixture of amused and irritated, and stood up. "So, ye have explained and I have listened. Now I need to think. It will take me a while to decide if I can e'er trust a mon who would forget to mention he had two bastard children, especially when they are such bright, handsome wee lads, and decide that his lover didnae need to ken that some other woman felt she had a claim to him. And a mon who ne'er once hinted at exactly what he wants from me."

Gregor stood up and pulled her into his arms, ignoring the way she tensed. He kissed her with all the passion that had gone unfed for nearly a week as well as all the desperation he still felt. She quickly softened in his arms, and he took some hope from that sign that she had not turned completely cold toward him. Knowing how easily he could be stirred to the point of pushing her too far and too fast, he released her and walked to the door. He opened it and stepped out of the solar, looking at her over his shoulder.

"As for what I want from ye? 'Tis quite simple, lass—everything. I want everything ye have to give." He softly shut the door behind him as he left.

CHAPTER 19

"What happened to him?" Alana asked Fiona as she entered the solar to find the woman putting salve on the bruised face of Gregor's half brother James.

"Gregor doesnae take kindly to being teased about his wooing skills," drawled Fiona as she wiped her hands and frowned at young James. "Leave the poor mon be, Jamie."

James grinned as he started to leave, but he paused by Alana and whispered, "Have mercy on the poor lad, mistress."

Alana sighed as he left, and then looked at Fiona. The expression on the woman's face told Alana she was facing a lecture. It had been a fortnight since Gregor had explained himself and told her he wanted everything. It had taken Alana but a few days to realize he really meant everything—including marriage. She did not know why she was being so hesitant to accept him. Alana began to think she was afraid, the memory of the pain she had felt when she had thought him betrothed to another woman making her too cautious. There was also the chance that she had not really forgiven him, at least not enough to trust in him again.

"How are ye feeling this morning?" Fiona asked.

"Quite weel," Alana replied as she moved to sit in the chair near the fire. "I didnae feel a single twinge or ache when I rose from my bed this morning."

That was the truth, but not the complete truth, Alana thought as she tried not to feel guilty. She had not felt any remaining pain from her wounds. She had, however, found it a little painful to have to scramble for a pot to empty her belly in. The way Fiona watched her as she sat down in the seat across from her nearly made Alana wriggle in her chair. Her mind told her that there was no way Fiona could know what ailed her now, yet that steady gaze made Alana think the truth was written on her forehead.

"Good, then mayhap ye can cease playing such a game with Gregor and make up your mind about him," Fiona said. "Dinnae ye think ye have dangled him from your fingers long enough?"

"That isnae what I am doing," Alana protested.

"Isnae it? Ye listened to what he had to say, and ye have stayed at Scarglas when we both ken ye were weel enough to travel to your sister a week past, if nay sooner. When ye stayed I believed ye had forgiven him."

Alana grimaced. "I thought I had, if not then, verra soon after. Now I am nay so sure."

"I think he means to marry you."

"I think so, too, although he hasnae said those precise words yet. This was what I wanted, so I dinnae understand why I am nay grabbing it with both hands. Oh, aye, there are things he hasnae said and all of that, but I wasnae so worried about that before."

"'Tis a matter of trust, isnae it," Fiona said quietly. "He lost your trust."

"Aye, I think that may be it. I can feel myself drawing close to him and then I halt, e'en pull back. Ach, it hurt, Fiona. It hurt like fire when I heard Mavis's father say Gregor was her betrothed and I realized I had been lied to, mayhap used, and most certainly made a fool. I think I am afraid that he will hurt me again and I am too much the coward to risk it."

Fiona nodded. "I can understand that and I suspicion Gregor can, too, but, Alana, just how can he prove himself? It isnae something one can just do. He can tell ye why he did what he did, and he has. It may seem to be all monly idiocy to us, but dinnae think that means it is all a lie. He can swear he will ne'er lie again, but ye must believe him or that isnae any good. No matter how one looks at the problem, it comes down to the fact that ye have to forgive him and trust him again. Aye, 'tis a risk and I weel ken how one can doubt one's own judgment, but I think there is always a risk when it comes to love, and ye do still love him, aye?"

Alana smiled faintly. "Oh, aye, I do and that frightens me, too. See? A coward."

"Nay. Ye are still here, aye? A true coward would have run verra far away. There is a part of ye that wishes to give him a chance and I think ye should give in to it. Just dinnae ask him to make any impossible promises."

"Such as what?"

"Such as never keeping a secret from ye. That one would soon be broken and then ye will be thinking he cannae be trusted again. Or he will be so intent upon keeping that promise that he will tell ye all sorts of things ye dinnae really want to hear about just to be sure ye can ne'er catch him in a secret."

For a moment Alana just stared at Fiona as she thought that over, and then she laughed. "Och, aye, that would be terrible." She quickly sobered and sighed. "Weel, I best decide soon, if only to put a stop to all these fights. An untamed lot, these MacFingals."

"Verra much so. Wait until ye meet the father." Fiona rolled her eyes.

"I suppose I will have to." She stood up, suddenly felt a little dizzy, and quickly sat down again.

"Ah, I thought that may be the way of it," said Fiona as she rose from her seat and fetched Alana a tankard of cool cider. "Sip it slow. Ye just stood up too quickly, is all. That is something ye will have to take care with." She crossed her arms over her chest and watched as Alana took several cautious sips of the cider. "And that is why ye are suddenly fretting o'er how to make yourself come to some decision about Gregor."

"My moment of light-headedness?"

"Wheesht, ye dinnae think me a fool, do ye?"

"Nay, I was but hoping that ye might just decide to be politely ignorant of it all."

Fiona snorted as she sat down. "I wouldnae ken how to do that. So, ye carry his child."

Alana nodded and then frowned. "I might just be sick," she said almost hopefully.

"Weel, I could always physic ye and see if ye get better."

All too aware of what kind of foul brews Fiona would try to pour down her throat, Alana slowly shook her head. "Nay, I am with child. I was just thinking that a wee ague would be better right now than this."

Fiona laughed and leaned forward to pat Alana on the knee. "I think there will be quite a flurry of bairns in this family come seven or eight months from now." She nodded when Alana looked at her in surprise. "Aye. I hope ye didnae think I always eat enough to feed the king's army. And I think ye may like to ken that Keira is probably with child as weel."

"Gregor didnae tell me that."

"He didnae ken it. Liam asked Ewan about how a woman with child might behave, what are the signs that she is carrying and all of that. Since all the signs Ewan told him about were being shown by Keira, Ewan said he felt sure she was carrying. She hadnae told Liam yet, however. Since no word has come from Ardgleann about the chance of a child, then I must assume she still hasnae told him."

"That would certainly explain some of the odd things I have felt." Alana's joy for her sister faded quickly as she recalled her own condition. "Weel, at least she is already married and doesnae have to decide it all because a child is on the way."

"Tsk, arenae we feeling sorry for ourself. Did ye think that Ewan and I were all sweet and loving from the moment we met? Or any of your cousins? I am sure ye have heard many a tale about their trials and tribulations ere they found happiness. Nay, 'tis rare when it is all clear to see and there are no doubts and no fears and no mistakes. Do ye love the fool?"

"Aye."

"Then naught else matters. He wants ye, ye love him, and there is a bairn on its way."

"That does rather settle the whole matter, doesnae

it. Yet I dinnae really wish to walk up to him and tell him he is about to be a father. He will, of course, immediately say we must be wed, and he hasnae been all that clear about his feelings for me yet."

"Ye mean he hasnae said he loves ye."

"Aye, he hasnae."

"Weel, give it a wee bit more time if ye wish, but let him ken that ye have softened to his wooing. The words might come if he thinks he is finally winning your heart. Believe me in this—a mon can choke on those words nay matter how strongly he feels the emotion."

"I suspicion women can, too." She smiled. "After all, I havenae told him I love him, either." She shared a brief laugh with Fiona. "I will soften; I promise you. And I will silence that voice of cowardice and mistrust. Ye are right. I said I would give him a chance, that he was worth it, and yet I havenae done so." Alana lightly stroked her still-flat belly. "This wee life is reason enough to set aside my foolish doubts and fears and take that chance. After all, if he proves a sad choice for a husband, I can always blame you."

"Fair enough," drawled Fiona and they both laughed.

Gregor saw Alana walking toward the large rowan tree at the far end of the garden and hurried to meet her there. He was becoming highly frustrated. It was almost a relief when one of his brothers teased him about his courtship and he was forced to pound him into the mud, for it helped ease the knot of tension that had become a permanent part of him. Wooing a woman was hard work, he thought, and almost smiled at his own nonsense.

Yet he did wonder why she had not softened to him

after all his efforts to woo her properly. There were times when he thought she had, that all was forgiven, and then she seemed to pull away from him. He knew he had failed her, had betrayed her trust in him, and yet he had thought she had accepted his explanation and that all he had to do was convince her that she meant something to him, that he wanted her, and that his plans for their future were all that was honorable.

When she turned and smiled at him as he drew near, he felt a spurt of hope. It was a smile much like the ones she had given him before she had found out about Mavis. "I believe the last of your bruises have finally faded," he said as he reached out to tuck a stray lock of her hair behind her ear.

"Aye, my fall from the cliff is now but a distant memory in all ways," she said.

Alana studied him as he stood there smiling at her. He looked at her as he always had, with warmth and interest. She was being foolish in holding fast to her mistrust. He had explained everything, and there was reason of a sort behind all he had done. She certainly would not have wanted him to treat Mavis harshly. The fact that he had tried to be kind to her was actually something in his favor, and she had to try harder to think of it that way. She had not been eager to tell him about her father's plans for finding her a husband, so it was a little unfair to think he should have been more honest about his entanglements.

"There has been word from Brian and Mavis at last," he said.

She heard the reluctance in his voice and cursed herself for a hard-hearted fool. The man should not feel hesitant about giving her such news. "And all is weel?"

"Aye. They were married and her father didnae find them until two days later. Brian tells me that the mon took it weel, although he suspects it will be many a month before the mon ceases to complain about ungrateful children and all of that." He breathed an inner sigh of relief when she laughed, for he had been afraid of what mention of Mavis might do to what little progress he had made.

"I am glad," she said. "It was obvious that they cared for each other."

"Obvious to everyone but me."

"Ah, but ye left within hours after coming home and so couldnae watch them together as the rest of us did. Fiona hadnae seen it before then, either, yet she kens that Ewan did."

And Ewan had not told Fiona, she realized, yet Fiona did not seem terribly upset about that. She had obviously been sunk so deeply in her own sense of injury that she had failed to think clearly, Alana decided. Yes, Gregor had lied to her and he had hurt her, but he was honestly contrite and aware of what he had done wrong. It was time to cauterize that wound and start living again, she told herself firmly.

"Aye, the wretch."

Gregor cautiously put his arm around her shoulders and walked her toward a stone bench set amidst a tangle of ivy and roses. He felt his hopes rise a little more when she did not tense beneath his touch or try to pull away. There was a change in her; he was certain of it. He doubted the change had much to do with his wooing of her, but he did not care. Whether the change was born of some thought she had finally grasped hold of, a talk with someone, or simply a change of heart, it was there and he intended to take full advantage of it.

After seating her on the bench, he sat beside her and put his arm back around her shoulders. His whole body ached with need for her and the strain of acting as if they had never been lovers. In the beginning of his courtship, he had thought to use the passion they shared to win her back, but had decided that would be wrong. He was paying for that restraint now with long sleepless nights spent thinking of her in her bed and how much he would like to join her there.

After three weeks surely he could steal a kiss, he thought as he looked at her and caught her looking at him from beneath her lashes. Tentatively, he lowered his mouth to hers, watchful for any sign that she might not wish him to kiss her. Instead, she ever so slightly lifted her mouth toward his in silent invitation. Gregor groaned softly and accepted that invitation before it could be withdrawn.

The sweet warmth of her mouth, a taste he had not savored for far too long, had him hard and aching in a heartbeat. He wrapped his arms around her and deepened the kiss, not even trying to hide the hunger and need twisting his insides. For three long weeks he had slept alone and been forced to keep a very tight rein on his desire when he was with her. Gregor was not sure how well those restraints he had put on himself would hold now that he had her in his arms again, warm and increasingly eager.

The moment Gregor kissed her Alana wondered what strange whim had made her think she could turn away from this man. Her desire roared to life at the first touch of his lips. She wrapped her arms around his neck and pressed close to his body. Memories of his every touch, of the pleasure he could give her, flooded her mind and heart.

This was the man she loved, she thought as he pushed her down onto her back. He had made a mistake in judgment and hurt her feelings. It was hardly a sin worthy of ripping out her own heart just to protect it from any further pain, and that was just what she had been doing by holding Gregor at a distance. Now that she held him close again for the first time in weeks, she had to wonder at what madness had seized her to make her turn away from all they could share.

She did trust him, she realized. She trusted him to protect her and the children she would give him, to be kind to her, and to provide for her. So he was not perfect. As Fiona said—what man or woman was? And she had forgotten her second promise to Fiona until right now. Fiona had asked that she be careful not to cross that line from being reasonably difficult to win to being pigheaded and impossible. Holding Gregor at a distance for something he had explained and apologized for was definitely being pigheaded. There was also something she was surprised she had taken so long to understand. Gregor was not a man to repeat his mistakes.

"Oh, lass, my sweet treasure, I have missed ye," he whispered against her neck as he unlaced her bodice with shaking fingers.

"I have missed ye, too, Gregor," she said in an equally quiet voice.

"Have ye forgiven me, then?"

"Oh, aye," she said and meant it, the last of her resistance fading. "I was just afraid."

"That I would treat ye unkindly?"

"That I couldnae trust my own judgment."

"Ah, I can understand that fear verra weel indeed."

He slipped his hand inside her bodice and stroked her breast, trembling from the strength of the hunger raging inside of him. She trembled, too, and arched into his caress, sending his passion soaring. She had come back to him, he thought dazedly, and felt an emptiness that had haunted him for weeks start to fade away.

Feeling his hands on her body again was pure bliss, Alana thought, but she grasped enough sanity to recall where they were. The gardens in the middle of the day were not the place for this type of reunion. Groaning softly as frustration gripped her, she put her hands on his chest and gave him a slight push. The look he gave her was one of crushing disappointment and Alana suddenly realized that, although it might not be the love she wanted, Gregor did feel something for her. She could feel his desire within her, smell the heat of his on his skin, and she should have known that such a thing would not be possible unless the man felt more than a simple lusting for her.

"We are in the garden, Gregor," she said, not surprised to hear the husky note of passion in her voice, for her blood still ran hot with it.

"Aye, we are." He frowned and looked around as he slowly came to his senses.

"And 'tis the middle of the day."

"Aye, so it is."

"And I can hear your brothers on the training ground nay so verra far away."

"The bastards."

She laughed and was pleased to see him grin. He shook his head and relaced her bodice with such a heavy sigh of regret that she had to laugh again. It felt good to laugh, to feel that joy he had always stirred within her. She had allowed herself to become mired in self-pity, fear, and doubt for too long.

As he helped her sit up and then hugged her close to his side, she considered telling him that she carried his child. After a moment's thought she discarded the idea. There were a few things still left unsaid and undone between them, and she did not want the fact that she was with child to make him do or say anything he did not feel wholeheartedly. She was going to keep a secret from him, she realized, and almost grinned.

Gregor gently stroked her cheek, pleased to see the glow in her eyes again. Whatever had troubled her so had truly faded. In a way, he had simply been standing in place as she had struggled with her thoughts and feelings. Now the true wooing could begin.

Suddenly he felt almost shy. It was not so hard to speak pretty flatteries and give her little gifts in an effort to soothe the hurt he had dealt. Those would not be enough now, however. Now he was going to have to speak of his feelings, speak of the future and the thousands of other things that he had never spoken of with a woman before. He felt all the words he had thought of telling her dry up in his mouth.

When had he become such a coward, he wondered? He loved this woman. He wanted her to sleep at his side every night. He wanted children with her. He wanted to know that she would be within reach whenever he needed to see her smile or touch her. Such things should not be hard to say aloud, and yet his throat had closed up, refusing to allow the words out of his mouth. Perhaps, he thought, he needed to practice saying them a few times before he actually spoke them to her. It seemed a foolish idea, but sitting there like a dumb ox was embarrassing.

"We need to talk, lass," he said.

"Aye, we do." She frowned, for he looked a little agitated and had gone somewhat pale. "Ye dinnae have another secret ye havenae told me, do ye, Gregor?" she asked nervously.

"Nay," he said firmly. "Jesu, lass, ye ken more about me than any woman e'er has. I cannae seem to shut up around ye."

She had to bite back a smile, for he sounded very disgruntled about that. "I like to ken what ye think and hear about what ye are doing."

"I feel the same about ye, lass."

He relaxed a bit, thinking that it might be possible to edge up to a confession of what was in his heart. Perhaps if he let the words out slowly, speaking of one hope and need at a time, it would not choke him so. Gregor had not considered how difficult it would be to bare his heart and soul, even to a woman he knew would never abuse the heart he wanted to set in her small hands. He could recall advising his brother Ewan on what to say and do concerning Fiona and cursed himself for a hypocrite. Advice was a lot easier to give than to take.

The feel of Alana's soft fingers stroking his cheek drew him from his thoughts and he smiled at her. She looked confused, and well she might. He had been pursuing her for a fortnight, and now that she had finally softened toward him, he stuttered and fumbled about like a beardless boy with his first lass. If this were happening to any of his brothers, he would have teased them without mercy. He thanked God none of them could see or hear him now.

Deciding that Gregor was not going to be offering her any sweet words for the moment, Alana looked up at the sky. "'Tis time to go to the great hall for a meal."

"The nooning," he murmured, unable to resist another taste of her.

Alana shivered with pleasure as he kissed the curve of her neck. "The what?"

"My father calls it the nooning."

"But the church calls it—"

"Aye, but as my father says, he doesnae care what the church calls it. He isnae praying, he is eating." He grinned against her skin when she laughed. "Ye are right. 'Tis time to eat, and if we dinnae hurry into the great hall, Fiona will probably eat everything herself." He laughed when she lightly punched him on the arm, for she was grinning as she did so.

He sat up straighter and grasped her by the shoulders. "I truly have missed ye sorely, love," he said softly.

"I have been right here at Scarglas, Gregor."

"Ye ken what I mean. And, aye, ye have been here, close at hand, but this is the first time that I have felt that ye are really back at my side."

She felt the pinch of guilt for the way she had been treating him but quickly shook it aside. He was not without fault in what had gone wrong between them. While it was true that she had clung to her hurt and anger longer than was necessary, he had put it there to begin with. Nevertheless, she felt some sympathy for him. Leaning forward, she kissed him, and after a moment of a gentle brushing of their lips, he pulled her hard against him and deepened the kiss. The strong passion they shared had obviously been left unsatisfied for too long for them to be able to indulge in sweet, gentle kisses.

Then, so abruptly she almost fell off the bench, Gregor was yanked out of her arms. Alana blinked when she saw him dangling several inches off the ground. Then she looked up from the strange sight of Gregor's feet in the air and saw who held him in a tight grip by the back of his jupon. Artan and Lucas had finally tracked her down.

CHAPTER 20

Gregor was so amazed to find himself dangling in the air that it took him a moment to realize that he could be in danger. He quickly looked at Alana to assure himself that she was safe only to find her glaring at the man who held him by the back of his jupon. Something in her manner told him that he was not in any real danger, nor was she. He glanced over his shoulder at the two men behind him and stared into two angry faces. They were big; they were handsome; they were absolutely identical in looks.

"Ah, Alana, I believe your brothers have arrived," he drawled.

"Put him down this minute," Alana ordered her brothers and then cursed when Lucas shrugged and tossed Gregor at her feet. "That was unnecessary," she snapped as she moved to help Gregor to his feet.

Gregor smiled at her as she helped him brush the dirt off his clothes. "Mayhap ye should introduce me, love."

"These are my brothers. Artan is to the right and

Lucas is to the left. These are the ones I was following when the Gowans grabbed me."

"I am more concerned about who was grabbing ye here in the garden," said Artan.

"This is Gregor MacFingal Cameron," she said.

"Cannae decide on a name?"

"Ye have met my cousins and some of my brothers, so dinnae pretend ye dinnae understand," said Gregor.

Artan shrugged and then glared at him. "Mayhap ye would like to tell us what ye were doing with our sister?"

"I believe I was kissing her."

"And I believe I am about to break your head."

Alana quickly stepped between Gregor and her brothers. She was used to their somewhat belligerent natures, but she was a little surprised at how Gregor was behaving. That last remark had been intended to goad her brothers, if she was any judge of such things. Under the circumstances it seemed to be a foolish thing to do.

"There will be none of that," she said.

"That was what I was about to tell you," drawled Lucas. "'Tis nay like ye to be sitting in a garden letting some fool put his tongue down your throat."

Although she blushed over such blunt language, Alana refused to back down. "I am a grown woman, and 'tis none of your business whose tongue I let go down my throat." She nearly groaned. "I cannae believe I just said that," she muttered and then glared at all three men, who looked far too amused. "How did ye find me? Did the mon we sent out to find ye bring ye here?"

"Nay. He didnae find us. We found him."

"What do ye mean, ye found him?"

"Perhaps we ought to go inside and talk about this as we eat," said Gregor.

"Now that sounds a fine idea," said Artan, and he grabbed Alana by the hand and pulled her away from Gregor.

Alana kicked her brother in the shin and quickly returned to Gregor's side. She hooked her arm through Gregor's and walked beside him as they started toward the keep. For a moment her brothers scowled after her, but then the thought of food softened their mood and set them moving. Within a few steps she found herself and Gregor following her brothers. Then she caught sight of two horses being led to the stables.

"Gregor, arenae those our horses?" she asked, unable to believe her eyes.

"Aye, they are. I wonder how they got here?" Gregor had the feeling her brothers had brought them, and the thought galled him beyond words.

Looking for her brothers, she realized they had already entered the keep. "Those wretches have a few things to explain," she muttered as she hurried into the keep, dragging a grinning Gregor along with her.

Gregor could not help but be amused by the way Alana acted with her brothers. They were big men with a rough manner and, he suspected, very hard when they needed to be, yet she had absolutely no fear of them. Even though he found something about them that set his hackles up, he knew they would never hurt her and it was clear that she knew it, too. He suspected that one of the things he found so threatening about Alana's brothers was that they might try to take her away from him and, worse, they had the right to do so.

As they entered the great hall, Gregor saw his brother scowling at the way the Murray twins were charming Fiona, and he chuckled. He escorted Alana to her seat and sat down beside her while the two men were distracted. The identical glares they sent him as they sat down opposite him and Alana made him smile.

"Gregor," Alana said as she tugged on his sleeve, "isnae that the mon we sent to find my brothers and tell them that I was here? It certainly looks like young Simon."

Looking in the direction she was pointing, he saw his young half brother Simon, the one they had sent to find the Murray twins, sitting with a group of his brothers and laughing, and then Gregor looked at the Murrays. "Ye met up with Simon, I see."

"Aye, we found him at the Gowans," said Artan as he filled his plate with venison and some of the vegetables Fiona was so fond of.

"They had taken Simon for ransom?"

"Aye, that was their game."

"Ye must let us repay ye for the cost of freeing the mon," said Ewan.

"Och, it didnae cost us anything," Artan said almost sweetly as he spread a thick layer of honey on his bread.

"Artan, I wouldnae wish ye to give yourself a brain fever, but do ye think ye could just tell your tale from beginning to end instead of forcing us to pull it out of ye word by word?" asked Alana, her sharp words spoken in a too-sweet voice as she fought to keep her temper.

"Ye werenae beaten enough as a child."

"I was ne'er beaten. Now, please, the story about how ye found Simon and our horses."

"She is getting to be a verra ordering sort of female, dinnae ye think, Lucas?"

"Artan!"

"Aye," replied Lucas, "but best ye do as she says ere she sets after ye with that wee dagger she is clutching so tightly."

"Weel, we followed ye to the Gowans' keep and heard all that had happened. The tale of your escape is a favorite one of the men in the alehouse. 'Tis there we heard about this new fellow they had captured, and so we went to have a wee word with them. We convinced them that it would be in their best interest to give us the horses they had stolen from ye and Gregor MacFingal and that, if they didnae mind, we would be taking the mon they had tossed in the oubliette with us as weel, for we believed that they had played that game long enough. Then we headed here, for young Simon was certain this would be where this mon would take ye."

Alana stared at her brother as she fought the urge to hit him over the head with her heavy tankard—repeatedly. She knew he could speak well when he chose to and could weave a tale that left one spellbound. He was being so terse in the telling of this tale that she knew he was doing it on purpose.

"That was not a proper tale, Artan; it was lacking a great deal of information, for one thing."

Lucas grinned. "Aye, it was short. Near as short as the wren here." He winked at her.

"I am nay short. The two of ye are just far too tall," she replied nearly word for word as she had for years.

"Aye, we did keep on growing long after we should have stopped."

"How did ye get the Gowans to give ye the horses and Simon without having to pay their ransom or join Simon in that dreadful hole in the ground?"

"Artan met the laird's wife."

"Oh dear," Alana murmured, having a dreadful suspicion as to where this part of the tale was headed. Women did seem to be drawn to her brothers, and she suspected some of the fascination was that there were two of them and they were nearly exactly alike.

"Aye, that fine woman took a liking to our Artan and told him all about the Gowans, the ransoming, and the keep. She isnae a happy wife."

"I cannae accept the laurels for the information about the keep, Lucas," said Artan. "She told ye about that."

"Only because she thought I was you, brother."

Alana exchanged a wide-eyed look with Fiona and then took a long drink of cider to calm herself. She was torn between an urge to laugh and one that would have her sliding beneath the table and hiding in embarrassment. It was a common problem when dealing with her brothers. Ewan and Gregor were doing a very poor job of hiding their amusement. Alana suddenly wondered if Lady Gowan truly had been confused about which twin she was with or had simply let her brothers think she was so that she could enjoy both of them. She then scolded herself for having such an unkind thought about the woman, only to realize that she had betrayed her husband with two men.

"To continue," said Lucas, much to her relief, "we got inside the keep late one night and quickly convinced the laird that it would be a fine gesture on his part if he returned your horses and let us take Simon home. I told him that would probably be enough to soothe my ire and sense of grave insult o'er the way he had treated my sister."

Artan nodded. "The laird decided he didnae want to be nailed to the floor and," he glanced at Fiona, "other such playful diversions and let us take the horses and Simon."

Lucas suddenly grinned. "The laird's wife wanted us to take her with us, too, but Artan told her he didnae think the two wives he already had would ken what to do with a third." He chuckled when Alana groaned softly.

"Several Gowans tried to come after us, but we made them understand that we didnae want the company."

"Ye didnae leave dead Gowans scattered about, did ye?" asked Alana, feeling a little sorry for the inept Gowans, for she knew with what deadly swiftness her brothers would react to any perceived threat.

"Wheesht, we would ne'er be so untidy."

"Lucas," she said warningly, although she knew they would ignore her threats as easily as she ignored theirs.

"Nay," replied Lucas. "We remembered what Maman taught us." He winked at Alana.

"Which lesson was that?"

"The one in which she said that although the world might be the better for it, ye cannae kill a mon just because he is an idiot." He smiled sweetly at Fiona when she laughed and smiled even more widely when Ewan scowled at him.

"Ah, that one." Alana began to think that there might be a lot more of her mother in the twins than she had realized. "I thank ye for getting our horses back and bringing Simon home. It was kind of ye." She hid a smile at the way they both winced at being called kind. "Actually, ye might be able to do us a favor when ye leave. We had to borrow Brother Peter's horse when we left the monastery and—"

"'Tis your horse now," said Lucas as he peeled and cored an apple with an awe-inspiring speed and skill.

"Nay, 'tis Brother Peter's. Cousin Matthew said so."

"Aye, so he told us when we stopped at the monastery on our way back here. 'Tis yours now."

"Oh, dear. Ye didnae threaten the mon again, did ye?"

"Nay, we just convinced him that it would be a fine gesture if he gave us the horse so that none of us would be troubled with bringing the beast back. Told him we would see it as a gracious mea culpa for what he tried to do to our sister. He agreed."

"Then 'tis Keira's horse. She was the one he wronged."

"Aye, but one thing Ardgleann has a lot of now is horses, and she doesnae need another. So, 'tis yours."

Alana decided not to argue the matter. One thing was certain. It was not Brother Peter's horse any longer. Alana idly wondered if she would give it to Gregor, perhaps as a wedding gift if he ever got around to speaking of marriage. She then realized that there would be few chances for some private conversation or kisses with her brothers here and turned her mind to thinking of a way to get them to leave without insisting she go with them.

"And we willnae be leaving until after the wedding," said Artan, and Lucas grunted in agreement.

"Wedding? What wedding?" she asked, startled out

of making plans to hurry them on their way home
to Donncoill.

"Yours and this laddie's."

She heard Ewan choke on a laugh and suspected it
was because very few people called Gregor a laddie.
The way her brothers were eyeing her told her they
were prepared for an argument and she decided there
was no need to disappoint them. It was true that she
wanted nothing more than to be Gregor's wife, but she
wanted him to go to the altar willingly, not dragged
there by her brothers. There were enough missteps between them without adding a forced marriage and all
the anger and resentment that could stir up.

"Nay, there is no reason for ye to be demanding
marriage between Gregor and me."

"That isnae what Cousin Matthew said."

As soon as she was able, Alana intended to write
her cousin a scolding letter about having a big
mouth. "Weel, Cousin Matthew doesnae ken what he
is talking about."

"He had his tongue down your throat," Artan said
and watched her closely over the rim of his tankard
as he had a deep drink of ale.

Alana felt herself blush fiercely. "That doesnae
mean he must marry me. I am certain ye have had
your tongues down the throats of many women and
ye havenae married them." She could not believe the
things she was saying and decided it was all her
brothers' fault.

"Of course we havenae. Most of them arenae the
sort of women a mon marries. Ye are."

"A mon shouldnae be forced to marry a lass just
because he kissed her in the garden!" Arguing with
her brothers was akin to banging her head against a

wall and Alana decided she had had enough. "I believe this discussion is over and nay more of any use or sense will be said," she said, quite proud of how dignified she sounded as she started to stand up.

"Ye run along then, lass," said Lucas. "We dinnae mind having this talk with Gregor. The mon cannae seem to decide what his name is, but I suspicion we can talk some sense into him."

Alana quickly sat down again. Her brothers' discussions with other men could swiftly become brawls, and she had the feeling the MacFingals were ones to join in such a thing wholeheartedly.

"They are the kind of brothers that make ye always find yourself looking for something to hit them o'er the head with, arenae they," murmured Fiona.

"Most certainly. Something verra heavy, but nay so heavy that ye cannae hit them o'er the head again and again without getting tired." She ignored the way her brothers just grinned.

"There is no need for ye to insist upon a marriage. I dinnae care what Brother Matthew has told ye. He wasnae with us in that cottage, was he? And just because two people share a cottage, it doesnae mean that they share anything else. Wheesht, for the first week Gregor and I were together, he thought I was a child. And he rescued me from the Gowans and got me all the way here safely, most of it on foot. In fact, there were several times he saved my life. Ye ought to be ashamed of yourselves for impugning his honor in this way."

"Weel said, lass," murmured Gregor, his voice shaking with laughter.

As soon as she was done beating her brothers, she would beat Gregor, Alana decided. "This isnae the way Maman taught us to behave when guests in a mon's home." For a brief moment her brothers looked uneasy, but then Lucas's eyes narrowed, and she knew that ploy to get them to be quiet had failed.

"A mon's honor demands that he wed the wellborn lass he has been frolicking with," said Lucas.

"Oh! And now ye impugn *my* honor!"

Gregor could not help it, he grinned as he listened to the ensuing argument. Alana never lied to her brothers, never denied what had happened between them, but never admitted it, either. When she had first refused to be married to him, he had felt a sharp pain, seeing it as the rejection of him he realized he had been half expecting all along. Then he started to understand what she was doing. She did not wish to have them both forced to the altar, and he could only agree with that. Until they had talked and he had found the courage to tell her all he felt, it would not be good for them to be forced into marriage. There was also the fact that he simply did not like these men telling him what he must do.

For a brief moment he considered the possibility of letting them have their way. It would get him what he wanted without his having to spit out words that seemed to be stuck in his throat. Alana would be his, which was exactly what he needed, and he would be free of the burden of having to expose all that was in his heart.

He inwardly shook his head, forcing that idea out of his mind. His first thought had been the wiser one. He and Alana needed to talk openly about all they felt for each other and all they wanted and expected from each other. Despite how he had hurt her, she had given him a second chance. Gregor knew he owed it to her to give her the full truth about how he felt. If they were forced to marry, Gregor suspected he would let his cowardice rule him, for, after all, he would have what he wanted already.

There was another reason he wished to have a serious talk with Alana—an exchange of all the truths they had kept hidden from each other or from themselves. He had no real idea of what she felt for him. He could guess, and Gregor admitted that he did a lot of that, but she had said no more about what lay in her heart than he had. Although he could still hear her call what they shared beautiful and precious to her, those were not really words of love, but of passion. What he needed from her was the deeper, the more binding emotions such as love.

Never had he been so concerned about what a woman felt and he supposed he ought to be ashamed of that. It was his past, however, and now he looked to his future. Alana was his future, and he wanted her to come to him willingly. He hoped she could convince her brothers that there was no need for them to be dragged before a priest.

"And have ye thought about our father and what he may be doing right now?" Alana asked, hoping her father had not selected a man for her but more than willing to use the possibility to stop her brothers from forcing Gregor to marry her.

She thought it a little odd that Gregor just sat there, apparently lost in his own thoughts. He occasionally grinned at some exchange between her and her pig-headed brothers but made no attempt to defend himself or protest the plans her brothers had for him. Alana did not want him to loudly declare that he had no intention of marrying her no matter what he was threatened with, or something of that ilk, but she did think he might say something. Most men would be raging at her brothers simply because they did not like to be ordered to do anything.

Her brothers had their heads together and were whispering, and Alana scowled. That was always a bad sign. Either they knew something about what her father was doing, which they were soon to use to counter her argument, or they were planning some attack, verbal or physical. It was not that unusual for her brothers to decide that there had been enough talking and start to use their fists to settle a dispute. Since they would never hurt her, they would go after Gregor. An attack on him could bring forth the whole family. Good as they were in all the arts of battle, she doubted her brothers could hold off Gregor and his army of brothers. Nor did she wish a fight between members of her blood family and those of the family she wished to join.

She took a sip of cider and tried to act as if she had just struck them a telling blow and won the dispute. There was a faint humming in her ears and she feared she had allowed herself to become too warm. The way Lucas raised his head and looked at her told her there would be some further argument, however, and she sighed before bracing herself to face it.

"The last we kenned, our father hadnae found any mon fool enough to have ye," Lucas growled. "And I doubt ye have heard from our father since leaving Donncoill."

"There is no need to become insulting just because ye cannae win the argument," she said. "Ye havenae heard from our father since leaving Donncoill, either, so ye cannae be any more sure than I am about what he may have done."

"Ah, then we shall just take the both of ye back to Donncoill and speak to Father about this," said Artan and then he smiled. "'Tis his right to decide such things anyway."

"'Tis *my* right and weel ye ken it," she snapped and jumped to her feet. Even as she wondered why Fiona muttered a curse, Alana felt all the blood slowly drain from her head. "Oh dear. This isnae good," she whispered and started to sink to the floor.

Gregor watched all the color flee Alana's cheeks. One moment she had been prettily flushed with the rigors of her dispute with her brothers, the next she had gone as white as snow. He lunged for her as she started to crumple to the floor with a surprising grace. Catching her in his arms, he barely kept her head from hitting the floor.

Perhaps there had been some damage done inside her when she had fallen off that cliff, he thought in horror. There was always the chance that it had taken some time for it to reveal itself in any way. Gregor looked to Fiona for some answers and found himself staring into the angry, cold silver eyes of Alana's impressively big, strong brothers.

CHAPTER 21

"I think ye have been sticking more than your tongue in—"

Artan's angry and slightly crude words ended on a grunt as Lucas slapped him on the back of his head. Gregor knew he would be eager to answer the belligerence he sensed in the twins if he were not so concerned about Alana. Holding her close as he stood up with her cradled in his arms, he started to walk out of the great hall. He could hear the twins, Ewan, and Fiona hurrying after him. The only one he was glad to have following him was Fiona, for he had great confidence in her healing skills.

The moment he put Alana down on her bed, Fiona rushed to her side, muttering, "I told her nay to stand up too quickly or move too fast."

Gregor thought nothing of her words until she blushed and cast him a brief look weighted with guilt and secret knowledge before turning her full attention back on Alana. Then he began to consider what would make a healthy woman who was enjoying a rousing argument with her pigheaded brothers faint simply because she stood up too quickly. At first he had feared that Alana had finally succumbed to some hidden injury gained in her fall, but not now. Although not by choice, he had been around enough women who were carrying a child to know exactly what Alana's sudden faint meant. Alana was carrying his child.

Why had she not told him? he wondered, feeling a deep hurt as he rapidly considered all the bad reasons for such silence. Then he grimaced over his own idiocy. She had not told him about the child because of what had happened with Mavis. It had taken a fortnight of assiduously courting her to ease the hurt he had inflicted and regain her trust. There was even the chance that Alana had only just realized that she was carrying his child. He hoped that was not why she had suddenly softened toward him, but he did not care all that much if it was. Once she was irrevocably his, once he had her back in his bed, he could continue to mend things between them.

The soft but sharp clearing of a throat brought Gregor out of his rambling thoughts. He turned toward the sound and found Alana's two brothers standing at the foot of her bed glaring at him. They had obviously guessed what her condition was as well.

"Ye Camerons are becoming a sharp pain in my arse," snapped Lucas.

"Actually, I am a MacFingal," Gregor drawled.

It did not surprise Gregor when both Fiona and Ewan looked at him as if he had lost his mind. Every time one of Alana's brothers spoke to him, he felt a compelling urge to respond in a manner that was certain to anger them. They had every right to their anger and he knew it. Their sister had been a virgin, was a woman of good family, and he had made her his leman. He did not think of her that way but knew most everyone else would if they discovered she had been his lover. He had given the Murray twins no more reason to think his intentions toward their sister were honorable than he had given Alana herself. If their situations were reversed, Gregor knew he would be eager to do them some injury.

"Ye will be married to Alana as soon as we can find a priest."

"That should be something decided between Alana and myself, dinnae ye think?"

"It should have been decided ere ye put your bairn in her belly."

"Now, we cannae be sure that is why she had fainted, can we?"

Lucas snorted and looked at Gregor with disgust. "We can be." He nodded toward Fiona. "She is. And, I am thinking, so are ye, for all ye are acting like a cocksure bastard who needs his neck wrung."

"Mayhap we should take him outside and have us a wee talk with him," said Artan.

The way Artan was clenching and unclenching his fists at his side made it very clear to Gregor just how Artan wished to make his point. Gregor suddenly realized that he could tell which twin was which and he almost grinned. Maybe he ought to let them take him outside and toss him around the bailey for a while. He had clearly lost his wits, and they might be able to knock some sense back into him.

"Gregor," said Ewan as he moved to stand next to his brother, "the decision is yours to make. I willnae tell ye what to do. But heed me, if ye dinnae want the lass, I will stand by ye and help ye deal with her kinsmen."

Leave it to Ewan to put it all so succinctly that all posturing became useless, thought Gregor. With that one quiet statement of support, Ewan had nicely recalled Gregor to the cold fact that this was not just a private matter between him and Alana. His family would not meekly accept any harm or insult done to him, and her family would not quietly accept any harm or insult done to her. It was time to cease trading glares and insults with Alana's irritating brothers, no matter how enjoyable he found it, and face a few facts.

Of course he wanted Alana. She carried his child. She was his mate and he had known that for a fact for quite a while. He loved her and wanted her by his side for the rest of his life. As much fun as it was to refuse the demands of her brothers, in the end the ones who would suffer the most for that game were Alana, him, and the child they had created.

"Nay, Ewan, there will be none of that," Gregor said. "Ye ken weel that I want her."

"Then why are ye arguing with us about this?" demanded Artan.

"Because ye irritate me," replied Gregor, and he shrugged.

Artan blinked slowly and then grinned. "Och, weel, fair enough, then." He looked at Ewan. "Where can we find us a priest?" he asked.

The moment Ewan told them, the two men left, and Gregor looked at his brother. "Those are two verra odd men."

"But good men, I think," said Fiona as she tucked the bedclothes around Alana. "Far more clever than they seem to want people to think, too. And just consider for a moment all they have been through in these last weeks. They go out looking for one sister, fearing the worst due to all sorts of chilling rumors, they find her with our Liam, fight a battle, and then have to go hunting for another sister who has disappeared. I suspicion they ken all that happened to ye and Alana on your journey. And what do they find when they return to Scarglas—Alana with you in the garden, kissing her quite thoroughly from all they said. 'Struth, one must wonder why they havenae just gutted ye and taken her home."

Gregor thought over all she had said and grinned when she nodded. "Aye, ye are right." He quickly grew serious and a little concerned as he moved to the side of the bed and lightly stroked Alana's hair. "Why has she nay awakened yet?"

"She sleeps," replied Fiona. "This last fortnight has been a trial for her, I think. Aye, 'tis more like the last three weeks. I suspicion the bairn she carries hasnae helped. Whilst ye and her brothers glared and snarled at each other, she did stir a wee bit, but then she went from a faint to a much-needed sleep."

"Her brothers will return soon with that priest."

"And then we will wake her, but we should let her rest for a wee while." Fiona smiled her thanks to Ewan when he set a chair near the bed and then she sat down to begin her vigil. "Go away," she said, "and see to the preparations. We can at least try to make it all a wee bit festive."

"But I should tell her what has happened and what has been decided," protested Gregor.

"I can do that. It may be for the best that I do. She willnae just say nay and refuse to listen to another word about the matter if I am the one talking to her. Ye may need to talk some more with her brothers, too."

Gregor nodded and left the room with Ewan. It

seemed that he and Alana would have to have that serious discussion *after* they were married. That troubled him, but then he realized what else this sudden marriage meant. Alana would be back in his bed tonight. Significantly cheered, he made his way down to the great hall, where he and Ewan busied themselves preparing the room for a wedding.

"A wedding? Right now?"

Alana stared at Fiona in horror as she slowly sat up. When she had first opened her eyes, she had been greatly relieved that her brothers were not there. She had been a little disappointed to find Fiona at her bedside instead of Gregor, but then had decided that that was probably for the best. She had known she would need to prepare herself for any awkward questions asked concerning her faint. Then Fiona had told her that it was good she had had herself some rest, as she would be in need of all her strength for the wedding.

"The wedding between ye and Gregor, of course."

"Ooh, nay, those brothers of mine havenae threatened Gregor into marrying me, have they?"

"Weel, a few threats were tossed out, but that shouldnae surprise ye. Ye were most convincing in all of your arguments and may have e'en won the day if ye hadnae fainted. Weel, once your brothers realized ye were with child, there wasnae a single argument any of us could muster that would have changed their minds about fetching a priest and getting the two of ye married."

"They ken about the bairn?" Alana groaned when Fiona nodded. "Gregor does, too?" Fiona nodded again and Alana cursed. "Why did ye tell them?" she asked, but there was no accusation or anger behind her question.

"I didnae tell any of them," Fiona replied. "Didnae have to. Your brothers kenned it before Gregor did, but he wasnae slow to guess it, either."

Alana supposed that should not surprise her. For all they sometimes acted as if they did not have a brain between them, her brothers were not the idiots they sometimes pretended to be and they were very observant men. Their family was a large one and there always seemed to be some woman with child around them. One could not help but learn all the signs that told one when a woman was carrying. Considering how many brothers and nephews Gregor had, he would undoubtedly know all the signs as well. Alana was rather embarrassed that she had missed them up until she had been so ill in the morning.

"I didnae want Gregor to be forced to marry me," she said in a small voice, wondering how things could have gone so wrong when everything had just seemed to being going right.

"The *when* of the marriage is all that is being forced upon the two of you. Gregor was intending to marry ye anyway."

"He has ne'er said so, Fiona."

"Wheesht, what do ye think this last fortnight was all about?"

"Getting me back into his bed?" Alana had to smile over the thoroughly disgusted look Fiona gave her.

"That goes without saying. E'en the best of men tends to think with the wrong head first when it

comes to a woman he desires. Howbeit, a mon doesnae woo a lass as doggedly as Gregor has been
wooing ye if he doesnae plan to marry ye. Nay, especially not when he has a horde of brothers teasing
him about it at every turn. Aye, Gregor put up a wee
bit of a fight e'en when he kenned that ye are carrying his child, but it was just because any mon would
bristle when ordered to do so. Gregor also seemed inclined to argue with your brothers for no good reason
at all except that, as he told your brother Artan, they
irritated him."

Alana surprised herself by laughing. "Aye, my
brothers irritate a lot of people. They are verra skilled
at it. Sometimes I think 'tis but a game they play."

Fiona smiled. "Possibly. Nay, I would say definitely. Ewan's cousin Sigimor is much the same." She
stood up, stretched a little, and idly rubbed at the
small of her back. "Do ye think ye are rested enough
to prepare for your wedding?"

"Aye, but I dinnae like this," Alana muttered as she
cautiously stood up, waited a moment to see how she
felt, and then sighed with relief when there was no
hint of dizziness. "There are still so many things left
unsettled between Gregor and me. We have only this
day begun to return to what we were before I found
out about Mavis."

"'Tis a beginning." Fiona helped Alana undress
and brush the wrinkles from the clean clothing she
had set out while Alana had slept. "Ye can continue
to sort out your troubles after ye are married."

Alana thought about that as Fiona helped her wash
up and get dressed in a very fine dark blue gown that
had obviously come from Fiona's own supply. She
and Gregor had cleared one hurdle in the garden—

the one she had set around her badly bruised heart. Their passion had flared hot again, although she suspected it had never really cooled. Hers had simply been buried by her hurt and anger for a while. Soon they could feed that hunger again. She could not see how that could hurt her cause which was, once again, to win Gregor's heart.

And there was the child to consider, she thought, smoothing her hand over her stomach even as Fiona pushed her down onto a stool and began to tidy her sleep-tangled hair. Gregor's sons were good boys, handsome and strong, but they would always carry the stain of being bastards, unfair though that was. She did not want that for her child. It was not the best reason to marry, but it was as good as or better than many of the others that set a man and a woman before a priest.

"Come, now, Alana, dinnae look so fretful," urged Fiona. "Ye must see that Gregor wants ye as his wife. Aye, mayhap ye cannae be sure of much else, but there has to be something between the two of ye or ye wouldnae be carrying that child now, would ye?"

"Lust, Fiona. It need be only lust on Gregor's part, and we both ken how easily a mon can feel that for nearly any woman who isnae too ugly, too old, or too foul of smell."

Fiona chuckled as she helped Alana stand up again and idly brushed down the skirts of her gown. "True enough, but if lust were all that ailed Gregor, he would have had ye and still married Mavis for her fine dowry. He also wouldnae have played the monk all the while he did his best to woo ye back into his arms."

Alana stared at Fiona in surprise. "How verra odd and contrary of me. I thought I had lost all trust in

him, yet I ne'er once thought that he might seek all I
was denying him in the arms of another woman. Despite Mavis, despite those two bonnie lads of his
born of his licentious past, I have ne'er thought
Gregor would bed down with another whilst he was
courting me."

"And that should tell ye that, despite all the hurt
and anger that has clouded your thoughts of late,
deep in your heart, ye do trust Gregor."

"I suppose I must."

"And so ye should. When he takes those vows, he
will mean them. Aye, his father was a rutting pig, unfaithful to every wife and lover he had—until Mab.
The old fool truly cares for her, as ye will see when
they return from their travels and ye can finally meet
him. It was a long time coming, but when he said
those vows to Mab, he meant every one. His sons
took heed of the turmoil their father's faithlessness
caused in this place and none of them mean to follow
his lead. 'Tis probably why none of them are rushing
to the altar, either. They need to be certain of the lass
when they wed, for they ken that will be the end of
all their roaming. My Ewan also made certain that
they understood that such vows before God should
be taken verra seriously. 'Struth, I dinnae think
Gregor really needed to be taught that, for he had
already accepted that. And now, he has made his
choice."

"Och, weel, there really isnae much choice being
offered here, is there?"

"Of course there is. They arenae verra good ones,
but they are there."

"The choices being get married or watch a fight
develop between our clans. It may stop at violence,

but it will still cause a great deal of trouble for all of you." Alana sighed. "It doesnae matter. I may fret and bemoan my poor, miserable fate," she briefly exchanged a grin with Fiona, " but I want the fool."

"'Twill all turn out weel."

"I hope Gregor thinks so as weel."

Gregor grimaced as he tugged on the bottom of the ornately embroidered doublet he wore. It was surprising how quickly he had gotten used to wearing the more comfortable plaid and a shirt. He felt it was important to look his best for the wedding, however. After all, he had worn all his finery for Mavis. He owed Alana no less.

"Are ye still certain this is what ye wish to do?" Ewan asked as he moved to stand near Gregor.

"Aye, as I have told ye before this complication. 'Struth, I kenned it long ago, but I was verra good at lying to myself," Gregor murmured.

Ewan nodded. "'Tis an easy thing for a mon to do. It isnae really a weakness, ye ken, but a strength," he added softly.

Gregor was surprised to see the faintest hint of a blush upon Ewan's cheeks, and the man would not meet his gaze squarely. He knew Ewan was speaking of love, and Gregor felt a little uncomfortable himself. It was difficult for a man to accept that his happiness rested firmly in the soft, delicate hands of a woman. Gregor was still a little reluctant to face that truth. A man was, after all, supposed to be the strong one, the leader, the warrior, and the protector.

He tried to look at his love for Alana as a strength, but it was not an easy thing to see. "I am nay so verra sure of that. It certainly doesnae feel that way." He realized that he had just confessed to the fact that he loved Alana even if he had not used the word itself.

"Ye will be as soon as ye feel certain that ye arenae alone in it all. 'Tis the uncertainty that makes it all so verra hard. I ken ye willnae heed what I think on it, not deep in your heart, but I dinnae think ye have aught to worry about."

"There are times when hope nudges close to certainty, but it doesnae matter. It will all sort itself out in the end. There really isnae any choice for me." Gregor smiled faintly. "And who can say, mayhap that is one of the things that troubles me the most."

There was no answer from Ewan, for Fiona and Alana arrived. Gregor fixed his full attention on his bride as she walked toward him. It had both relieved him and worried him to leave telling Alana about the marriage to Fiona, yet he saw no sign of anger upon Alana's face. She looked nervous, uncertain, and a little afraid. That he could understand. He was feeling much the same.

She looked lovely in the dark blue gown she wore. He had to wonder yet again how she could have been left unwooed and untouched for two-and-twenty years. Glancing toward where the Murray twins stood with their legs braced and their arms crossed over their broad chests, it was easy for Gregor to think that they had had something to do with that. It would really gall him beyond words if he discovered that he owed them anything.

Alana felt torn between the urge to crow triumphantly over the husband she was about to gain and one to flee into the wilderness. Gregor looked so handsome in his black and red finery that he made her feel a little breathless. She had to be mad to think she could make a man like him love her or that she could keep him content for years. All too readily she thought of all her faults, from being too thin to being afraid of the dark.

"Steady, Alana," whispered Fiona, who walked at her side. "'Tis usually the mon who flees when faced with marriage, and Gregor doesnae look like he has any intention of doing so before that knot is tied and tied tightly."

"Trapping him," Alana whispered back.

"Idiot. If ye must think such foolish things, ye might try to recall that ye didnae breed that bairn all by yourself and that it has ensnared ye as weel."

That was true, Alana thought as she stopped in front of Gregor. Fiona slipped around her and went to stand next to Ewan. Alana watched them exchange an intimate smile and nearly sighed with envy. That was what she wanted but was suddenly afraid she would never have. There was little she could do about it, however, she mused as Gregor bowed elegantly over her hand. The warmth left behind by the brush of his lips flowed through her body and she suddenly did not care what woes and doubts plagued her.

This man was her mate, and fate had pushed her into his path. She had to have faith that she was not wrong in all she felt for him. He felt something more than desire for her, and she was sure of that in her more confident moments. It was there in the way he spoke to her and always seemed to have to touch her in some way. There had to be some depth of feeling in his heart for her or he would not have spent so much time courting her and enduring the teasing of his family even though she had remained cool to his efforts for so long. He had also planned to turn aside Mavis despite the land and coin she would have given him and that, too, had to be considered.

Now was not the time to do all that, however. The priest was waiting and, from the disgruntled look he wore, she suspected her brothers had dragged him away from something. They were not known for their patience. In fact, Alana suspected they would soon begin growling over the way she was dawdling and, with the great hall filled with Gregor's brothers and half brothers, nephews, and sons, she did not think it would be wise to test the limits of her brothers's patience.

"'Twill be fine, lass," Gregor whispered as he kissed her cheek.

"They shouldnae have threatened ye," she murmured, eyeing her brothers with displeasure.

"Aye, they should have. Many a mon would have done far worse than threaten me. One question ere we stand before that highly irritated priest—why didnae ye tell me about the bairn?"

Alana blushed and shrugged. "I really wasnae aware of it until today. Aye, I had the occasional suspicion for the last week, but I didnae really consider it all until I had my head in a bucket this morning."

"Och, poor wee lass. Mayhap Fiona has a potion that can ease that."

"I suspicion she does and I will be sure to ask her."

"Are ye ready then, love?"

She looked from the darkening scowls upon her brothers's faces to the equally frowning priest. "Aye, let us go and be done with it." She blushed. "Oh, I didnae mean—"

"I ken exactly what ye mean and take no offense. 'Tis galling to have those two lord it o'er you."

"Verra galling."

With Gregor holding her hand in his, they moved to kneel before the priest. As he began to read the words that would bind her and Gregor together for as long as they lived, Alana had one cheering thought. In a few moments her brothers would no longer have the rule of her and she could tell them to go away.

CHAPTER 22

"'Tis my wedding night," Alana said as she paced her room, Charlemagne at her side. "Do ye happen to notice that something is a wee bit strange, Charlemagne? Weel, I will tell ye exactly what is wrong. 'Tis my wedding night and I am all alone, pacing the floor and talking to a cat." She stopped pacing, put her hands on her hips, and glared at the door. "Where is my new and much-anticipated husband?"

Charlemagne sprawled on his back at her feet, silently begging to have his belly scratched.

"The many trials and tribulations of us poor mortals simply dinnae interest ye at all, do they?" she asked as she crouched down and began to scratch his belly.

Alana felt both angry and terrified. Everything had seemed well enough at the wedding. Gregor had acted not only accepting of his fate, but even a little pleased. He had spoken his vows clearly, without any hesitation. The kiss he had given her to seal their vows had shocked the priest and left her reeling. She had not even had the wit left to blush beneath the hoots and bawdy suggestions flung at them by his kinsmen. Then he had walked off with her brothers while she had come to the bedchamber they would now share. And disappeared.

She stood up and glared at the door again. If her brothers had done anything to hurt Gregor she would see that they paid dearly for it. Yet she could not think why they would do anything to him now that they had gotten all they had demanded. Neither did she think all three men were sitting in Gregor's bedchamber, drinking and becoming close friends. Alana hoped that they would become friends, but it was far too early for that to happen. Nevertheless, now her anxiety and her curiosity were roused.

Biting her lip, she reached for the door latch and then quickly snatched her hand back. *He* was supposed to come to *her*. She was freshly bathed, softly perfumed, and dressed in a night rail so thin it was useless as a shield for her modesty. She was all that a new bride should be, but the groom seemed to have forgotten about her.

Anger quickly overcame her fears and doubts. She grabbed a blanket from the bed, wrapped it around herself, and went to find Gregor. All during the wedding celebration he had been making her promises of a night filled with passion with every kiss and every subtle caress of his hand. As her newly wedded husband it was past time he set about fulfilling those promises that had made her so eager she had been counting the minutes left before she could go to their bedchamber and get ready for their wedding night. It was time he stopped whatever else he was doing and joined her there.

* * *

Gregor stared into the tankard of ale he held and wondered what he should do. He had been feeling quite smug, even a little self-righteous, for marrying Alana without a thought or care to what her dowry might be. Finding out that she had a dowry that made Mavis's look paltry in comparison was like a hard blow to the stomach. Since Keira had gained all her husband owned, she had given her dowry to Alana, adding enough to Alana's already generous dowry to make her a very rich bride indeed. A bride far too rich for a man like him.

Why had she never mentioned that she had a dowry so large it was absolutely astounding that there was not a man behind every tree and shrub ready to leap out and grab her and force her to marry him? Men snatched brides with far less for a dowry. No one would believe that he had married Alana for anything else but the lure of her fortune. Seeking a bride with a dowry the size of Mavis's would have been seen by most people as the act of a smart man. Taking a bride with a dowry the size of Alana's made him look greedy.

The hard truth was that she was far too good for him in all ways. She deserved so much better. For a woman like Alana to marry a man like him was much akin to a princess marrying a blacksmith. Now, just when he finally held her firmly in his grasp, he knew he had to let her go. That was the truly honorable thing to do.

Even though Gregor knew he had already had far too much ale to drink, he lifted his tankard to his lips and had another long draught. He had begun to drink from the moment Artan and Lucas had left him reeling from the news of all Alana was bringing to the marriage, and it was not helping him to overcome that shock. In truth, it was making him feel morose, and he hated morose drunks.

When he lowered his tankard, Gregor found himself staring at Alana's breasts. They were covered with a very fine linen, so fine he could see her nipples. He really liked Alana's breasts, he thought and sighed. He blinked and suddenly a thick blanket was pulled over that intoxicating view. Slowly Gregor looked up from Alana's chest and found himself staring into her golden brown eyes. She was glaring at him. Now, he thought, he would face all the anger she had kept hidden, anger over the fact that her brothers had forced her to marry a peasant.

"Mayhap ye can explain to me why ye are sitting here, all alone and swilling ale on our wedding night."

The cold, precise tone in her voice made him wince. "There cannae be a wedding night."

Alana wondered just how much he had drunk. Considering how long it had been since he had left the great hall with her brothers, Gregor could have swallowed a prodigious amount of ale by now. "Oh, I see," she said, unable to hide her keen disappointment. "I have heard that too much drink can soften—"

"Soften?" Gregor grabbed her hand and placed it upon the erection he had not been able to fully shake free of since the kiss they had shared in the garden. "Nay, I am not soft. I could never drink enough ale to suffer like that."

She ignored that boast. "Then why do ye say there can be no wedding night?"

"Because ye are too fine a bride for a mon like me. Your brothers had a wee talk with me about your dowry, as is right and proper. What they told me near knocked me down. Why didnae ye tell me ye are as rich as a prince?"

Her eyes widened at the note of accusation in his voice. "I didnae tell ye because there was ne'er any indication that ye might be interested. In me as a wife, I mean. When the mon is courting a lass and hinting at a marriage is usually the time the talk of a dowry takes place."

That was true, but he liked the idea of feeling the injured party more than he did just sitting there feeling sorry for himself. "Ye should have told me. 'Twas a bit of a shock, ye ken. If I had learned about it earlier, we ne'er would have been married. Now, weel, we shall just have to leave it unconsummated until I can think of a way to cut ye loose. Ye deserve a better mon than me, a mon with naught but a few fine clothes and a good horse and a family that isnae the most respected in the land. Wheesht, most people think my father is a madmon. E'en we did until but a while ago." He shook his head and felt a little dizzy. "Nay, I cannae think what rattles in your brothers' heads that they would think me a fit husband for ye."

Setting down his tankard, he stood up very carefully and went over to the washbowl to douse his head with the cold water there. He had suddenly realized that he was far too drunk to have this conversation. Since this was his wedding night, he could not tell her to go away and that they would talk about it all on the morrow when his head was clear. Alana was owed an explanation for why she was alone in the bedchamber that had been chosen for them.

His body did not even soften when he let the cold water run down inside his shirt. The very last thing he wanted to do was leave her alone tonight, or any night ever again. She obviously wore a night rail designed to seduce a man, and smelled sweetly of roses and clean skin. He ached to taste that soft skin again. Instead of easing, his desire for her grew even fiercer and he cursed as he grabbed a soft drying cloth and scrubbed his face dry. He did not feel dazed by drink any longer, but by need.

Wrong though it was, he would have to tell her to leave and that they would talk in the morning. If she did not move out of his reach soon, he would weaken and take her into his arms. There would be no turning back then, no doing the honorable thing and setting her free so that she could find herself a husband to make her proud. He tossed aside the cloth, looked at her, and frowned. She had her arms crossed over her chest and he could see one bare little foot tapping on the floor. Even worse, she was wearing an expression that was part amusement and part that look that women gave men when they thought they were behaving like complete idiots.

"Gregor, I do not believe, in this situation, leaving the marriage unconsummated will make any difference at all."

Her tone was that patient, sweet one some women used when trying to explain something to a small child, and it set his teeth on edge. "A marriage can be set aside if it isnae consummated, although I shall have to find out exactly how one does that."

"Did ye forget that I am nay longer a virgin? That I am, in fact, carrying your child?"

For a moment he just stared at her as the last of the ale fumes cleared from his head. He *was* an idiot. He had forgotten those very important things for a little while. Shock had pushed everything from his mind except for the fact that she was too rich a bride for a man like him. Too much ale had assured that his wits had stayed scattered. Gregor wondered if he could bluff his way out of this embarrassment. He prayed she was not one of those women who insisted a man openly admit that he was being a complete fool.

"Lass," he began, struggling to find the right words, "ye dinnae need a mon like me e'en if I was your lover and ye carry my child. With a dowry like yours, ye could still have any mon ye wanted, and I think ye ken it. Why, if your father e'en hinted at what would come with ye as a dowry, the men would be lining up at the gates e'en if ye had a dozen fatherless children clinging to your skirts." The mere thought of never seeing the child they had created, of having some other man raise that child, cut him to the bone, but he still felt he was doing what was best for her.

Alana studied him for a moment. There was a look of misery in his face, and so she discarded the painful thought that he was just trying to be rid of her. He really thought that she was now too good for him because of the size of her dowry. It was time, she thought, to stop guarding her heart, to stop holding fast to all the words she had wanted to say to him for weeks. He would not accept logic in this, so she would have to sway him with feelings.

"But my child willnae be fatherless, will he? He has a father, a verra fine mon who makes his mother's blood heat with a smile."

He felt his manhood twitch. The thing was leaning out toward her like some hound on a scent. A simple, if very flattering compliment, and he was acting like a heedless boy facing his first lover. A flicker of laughter passed over her face and he scowled at her, almost daring her to say something. And it was not just a smile he wanted to use to make her blood heat, he thought, and inwardly groaned.

"Did ye not woo Mavis for her dowry?" she asked. "Ye said ye sought her out because ye had heard of it. Why would ye think it acceptable to go after hers and yet shy away from taking mine?"

"Because next to yours, hers is a pittance, but a pittance that was good enough to live on and was suitable for a mon like me."

"Gregor, do ye think my sister brought naught to her marriage to Liam? Aye, she handed o'er to me a goodly part of her dowry because Ardgleann would be hers and 'tis a rich place. Do ye fault Liam for accepting it?"

A logical woman could be a curse, he mused. He had not only let shock and then ale scatter his wits; he had lost them completely. There really was no way he could make all he had been thinking sound sensible, probably not even sane. Gregor suspected he was going to have to admit that he had been, for a little while and under the influence of strong drink, a complete idiot, and he hoped he could find the right words to soften the blow to his pride, at least in her eyes.

"I was in shock," he admitted. "Deeply in shock. All I could see was that ye were a verra rich woman, one who would never had been within my reach except that fate put ye in the same oubliette as I was. I thought the whole world would think that all I married ye for was that massive dowry, and I couldnae stomach that."

"Ah, pride." She stepped closer to him and slowly put her arms around his neck.

"Aye, I was worried about my own wee monly pride,

but I also didnae want the world and its mother to think that that was the only reason I had married ye, that that was the only way ye could get a husband."

His ability to think clearly began to slip away fast as she brushed soft, quick kisses over his face and neck. His whole body shook with need for her. And, he thought, since the marriage really could not be annulled, why was he hesitating?

"'Tis most kind of ye to be so concerned with my pride that ye would set me aside e'en though ye want me." She began to unlace his shirt. "And ye do want me, dinnae ye, Gregor?"

Grasping her by the hips, he pressed her close to his throbbing erection. "How can ye e'en need to ask, love? Aye, I need ye like a fish needs the water to live. I need ye to face each morning with hope and an eagerness to keep on living." He slid his hand over her still-flat belly. "I need ye to give me bonnie wee lasses with thick hair and golden brown eyes. Aye, I need ye, and 'tis sorry I am that I e'er left ye in doubt of that."

Alana was so moved by his words that she could only stare at him, the sting of tears in her eyes. This was the most he had said about his feelings since they had met, and she was shaken by the fierce tone of truth behind each word. He had not said he loved her, but now that lack did not sting as much. When a man could speak so to a woman, surely he was in love or very near to it.

"I think we shall forget my plan to annul the marriage," he growled and picked her up in his arms.

"What about our verra fine marriage bed?" she asked as she curled her arms around his neck to steady herself as he carried her to the bed.

"We can move to it later."

* * *

Alana opened her eyes and blinked, uncertain of where she was. Then she felt Gregor move and heard Charlemagne jump off the bed and smiled. Now she remembered. After making love in his bedchamber, they had hurried down the hall to the bridal chamber to make love again. Wild, greedy, frenzied love, she thought with a smile as she felt Gregor kiss the back of her neck.

"I have been waiting for ye to wake up," he murmured as he gently nudged her onto her back.

Gregor brushed a kiss over her lips and slid his hand down to her belly. He was eager to feel the child they had made move inside her. He loved his two sons and would never think of them as somehow less than this child, but the fact that he had created this one with the woman he loved and not just because he had been careless did make it all different in some strange, unfathomable way. Instinct told him that he did not need to worry that Alana would ignore his bastard sons for her own child, either. He lightly kissed her belly.

"Are ye feeling weel?" he asked. "I ken that we behaved a wee bit, er, wildly and I shouldnae want to hurt ye or our bairn."

"Nay, ye cannae hurt the bairn that way," she murmured as she ran her hands over his back. "I dinnae ken much about this save for some very simple goods and bads and how to birth it, but all we lasses are told that lovemaking cannae hurt the bairn."

"That is a relief, for I intend to do a lot of it."

She sighed her pleasure as he kissed his way to her breasts. Threading her fingers in his thick hair, she held him close as he kissed and suckled her. She

badly wished to speak more about their future and
their feelings for each other, but she was a coward.
However, she had the strongest feeling that, if she did
not push just a little now, the chance would be gone,
that Gregor would settle in and think all was well. If
that happened, she could face months, even years
without knowing what he truly felt for her.

"I have missed ye in my bed, my sweet treasure,"
he said against her stomach as he slipped his fingers
between her thighs to tease her passion to a greater
height. "I had feared that, in my idiocy, I had lost
ye, had killed all we had shared just when I had realized how much it meant to me."

Wondering a little wildly if he had read her
thoughts in some way and had decided to take the
first step, Alana tensed. Even though she desperately
wanted to hear all he had to say, the desire he was
stirring within her was starting to make it hard to
concentrate. She would not be surprised if that was
his intention, but she refused to let him hide from her
as he told her all the things she had needed to hear
for so long.

"Ye cannae lose me, Gregor," she said softly and
felt him tremble faintly beneath her hand. "Ye can
ne'er lose me, didnae ye ken that?"

"I had hoped. And why is it that I can ne'er lose ye?"
he asked as he brushed kisses over the soft inside of her
slim thighs.

Alana knew she was being played with, pushed in
the direction he wanted her to go, but she did not
care. The feel of his soft hair brushing against her
womanhood was driving her mad. She blushed to
admit it even to herself, but she ached to feel his kiss

there and she suspected he knew it. He was silently telling her that if she bared her soul to him, he would reward her with pleasure. Tightly gripping his broad shoulders, she decided that one of them had to go first to cure the cowardice of the other, and it might as well be her.

"Ye cannae lose me, Gregor, because I am yours in body, in mind, in heart, and in soul. I love ye with all that I am and all I will become," she whispered.

Gregor groaned and kissed her just where she so desperately wanted him to, ravishing her with his mouth until she was nearly screaming at him to come inside her. He joined their bodies with one hard, fast thrust and then held himself still as he looked down at her. Her pretty face was flushed with passion and her eyes were black with it. He did not think he had ever seen a finer sight.

"Say it again, my love," he said softly.

"I love ye," she said and gasped when he pulled out almost completely and then thrust back inside her.

They played that game for several minutes until Alana thought she would go mad or beat him. Then as she told him that she loved him yet again, his control broke and she almost cheered. Before she could ask him if he felt the same, however, passion stole her wits as he drove them both to the very heights of desire and sent them tumbling back down together.

It was several minutes after Gregor had collapsed in her arms that Alana began to recover her wits again. Although she was pleased that Gregor found her declaration of love so exciting and was driven to hear her say it again and again, she felt a little irritated as well. He must love her if he was so hungry to hear her say the words to him, yet he had not given her that same comfort. That seemed grossly unfair to her. She prayed Gregor was not one of those men who demanded his wife love him, but did not see that it was equally important to the happiness of their union that he love her, too.

"Ye have gone verra tense, love," he said as he lifted his head and brushed a kiss over her mouth.

"I was but wondering about why it was so important that ye hear how I feel about ye," she asked, trying not to sound as upset as she was beginning to feel.

Closing his eyes, Gregor nuzzled his nose into the soft place where her neck met her shoulder and somewhat absently said, "Why, I should think that was clear to see. Of course I wish to ken that I am nay the only one who loves. I just wished to be assured that my love was returned." When she grew even tenser, he warily ceased what he was doing and looked at her again. "What is wrong? Are ye crying?" he asked with a touch of panic even as he saw the tears trickle down her cheeks.

"Nay," she snapped as she wiped the tears from her cheeks with a corner of the sheet. "Ye love me?"

"Aye, of course I do."

"How could I ken that when ye have ne'er said so!"

"I am sure I did and just a few hours ago, when I was ravishing ye to make sure our marriage was undisputedly consummated. Twice." He smiled in remembered satisfaction.

Alana frowned as she tried to recall those frenzied times of lovemaking when they were both so starved for each other they had gone a little mad. She could faintly recall Gregor pressing his face into the side of her neck as he thrust inside of her and feeling his mouth move against her skin. That was when he had told her he loved her? And she had missed it. Just as he had thought she would, the coward, she decided and hit him on the arm.

Gregor eyed her warily as he rubbed his abused arm. "I see ye remember."

"I recall ye muttering into the side of my neck. I also recall verra clearly that ye demanded I say it loud and clear several times."

"Ah, I see. Ye want me to say it loud and clear."

She frowned when she saw the hint of a blush on his cheeks and then had to bite back a smile. "It doesnae hurt," she said quietly.

"I wouldnae ken, as ye are the only woman I have e'er said it to," he grumbled, eyeing that soft curve of her neck covetously only to see her put her hand over the place.

"Dinnae ye wish to love me?"

"Aye, love, as I cannae think of any woman I could trust more, but it isnae easy for a mon." He sighed and gently pressed his forehead against hers. "I love ye." His eyes widened when he saw the glitter of tears in her eyes again. "Dinnae ye start crying again."

Alana laughed softly and hugged him. "Tears of happiness, Gregor. Naught to worry about. When did ye ken ye loved me?"

"When ye fell off that cliff." He smiled when she laughed again and he decided it was not so very painful to speak of such things while holding each other close. "When did ye ken it?"

"Oh, probably when I decided I would take ye as my lover," she drawled and giggled when he lightly pinched her side. "I just needed to ken that ye loved me, Gregor. I willnae ask ye to say it thrice a day or the like, although I certainly wouldnae mind. Nay, I ken it now and it has made some lingering fears within me just fade away like the morning mists. It gives me strength. Aye, and a welcome confidence that we can have a verra good marriage."

"We will, love. A verra good marriage indeed."

Looking into her eyes, he could see that the last of the shadows that had lurked there for too long were gone. He had known he had made a mistake by not telling her about Mavis, but he now saw he could have saved them all that heartache if he had just said a few loving words, given her something to cling to when trouble came their way. He swore he would not be so cautious again. Unused to revealing all he felt, he knew it would take time to overcome that reluctance, but he swore that he would try. That glow of happiness, of serenity on her face was worth the effort.

"I dinnae ken how ye could have been in doubt of my feelings for ye, lass," he said. "I thought they were clear for all to see."

"I dinnae ken why ye should think that. Ye are verra good at hiding what ye are feeling or thinking."

"Ah, but there was a clue if ye had just kenned what to look for."

"And what was that clue?"

"Why, the way I kept acting like a complete idiot." He grinned when she laughed and hugged him again. "'Tis the surest sign there is that a mon has lost his heart to a lass. 'Tis also the reason I was determined to stay out of that trap. I have ne'er liked to be an idiot."

"I see. Weel, it appears I have developed a great fondness for idiots."

"A great fondness, is it?"

"A verra great fondness indeed. 'Struth, I am quite madly in love with my idiot."

"And will love him forever?" he asked softly, his lips against hers.

"And for the day after that as weel."

Epilogue

Six months later . . .

Groaning softly, Alana sat down on the stone bench next to Keira. This would be the last visit with her sister for months, she thought as she smoothed her hand over her well-rounded stomach. Since Keira was as round as she was, her ankles as swollen, and her movements as awkward, Alana knew neither of them would be able to travel again for quite a while, especially not with winter on the horizon.

"Ardgleann is looking more prosperous, nearly returned to its former glory," Alana said, admiring the flowers surrounding them, "and your garden looks verra bright for so late in the season."

"The weather has been mild for far longer than is customary, which is a blessing. We will actually have a crop to harvest this year, e'en though we were so late in the planting of it. 'Twill be a small one, for there was no time to plant all the fields, but it will serve to keep the wolves from the door. As will all the help of our families. How fares Craigdene?"

"Verra weel, thank ye." Alana exchanged a broad grin with Keira over the extremely polite tone of her voice, and then softened it. "It isnae such a grand place as this is, but 'tis more than enough to please us. Gregor was certainly pleased that it didnae visibly declare the fact that he had married a rich woman. The size of my dowry can still make him wince. And Craigdene is nicely placed right in the midst of so many we care about, making visits such as these easy enough."

"I am going to have a son, ye ken," Keira said abruptly.

"Aye, so am I," Alana said, laughter tinting her voice. "And a lass. Mab says so."

"Aye, so am I."

Alana shared a laugh with Keira and then they waved at their husbands, who looked their way from where they stood talking together at the far end of the garden. "We found ourselves some verra bonnie men, didnae we."

Keira nodded. "Verra bonnie, indeed, and so verra good to us, although it took a wee bit of work to find the happiness we are now so blessed with. I still feel a wee bit guilty at times for finding mine in the midst of such tragedy."

"Nay, ye must ne'er feel so." Alana shrugged. "Sometimes that is just the way 'tis meant to be. Who would e'er have believed that I would find my happiness at the bottom of the Gowans' oubliette?"

Both of them looked at their husbands and sighed, which made Alana laugh. "I suspicion I shall always do that when I look upon Gregor. He is such a fine-looking mon. I sometimes watch him sleep and wonder why such a mon would choose me, would love me of all women."

"I do the same. As ye said, sometimes that is just the way 'tis meant to be. We found our mates."

"That we did. And 'twill be interesting to see just how our big, strong husbands act when we present them with a son and a daughter in a few months. Have ye told Liam?"

"Nay, I thought I would let it be a surprise."

"As did I."

"Do ye think that might be just a wee bit cruel?"

"Nay, not at all. Besides, if I tell Gregor about it, he will become even more protective of me than he is now."

"And that would be unbearable," Keira agreed. "Liam would be the same."

"And, of course, it would spoil the surprise." Alana laughed along with Keira.

Gregor smiled faintly as he watched Alana and Keira laughing together. "I am nay sure I want to ken what they find so verra funny."

Liam chuckled. "'Twould be best for the sake of our wee monly pride if we dinnae ask any questions, I think."

"Having a wife and learning that I will be a father soon is taking a wee bit of time to get used to. I ken I have two children already, but I wasnae about as they were carried and born by their mothers. They just appeared at the gates. This, weel, this is both wonderful and terrifying."

"Exactly so. I could say the same about being

married to a twin, one who is so verra closely tied to her sister."

"That is indeed hard to understand at times. I suspicion I will ken exactly when your wife takes to her childbed."

"And I yours. Och, weel, there are worse things. I nearly became a monk."

"And I nearly married the wrong woman."

"I think ye would have paid far more dearly for your choice than I would have with mine."

"Without question. There is one thing about all of this that does truly gall me, however."

Liam looked at Gregor a little warily. "And what would that be?"

"The realization that Sigimor was right all along."

"That certainly is galling, but exactly what was he right about?"

"About how we would ken the woman we were meant to marry because she felt *right*."

"And she *fits*," added Liam and laughed with Gregor. "I now recall thinking the same thing. So, ye love the lass, do ye?"

"Aye, although it took watching her fall off a cliff for me to admit it." Gregor shook his head. "I didnae want it, ye ken. I thought love made a mon act like an idiot. Instead, I denied it and acted like an idiot anyway."

"But now ye are a verra happy idiot, arenae ye."

"I am. A verra happy idiot indeed."

Liam looked at Keira and started to walk toward her. "Ah, weel, there are some verra fine rewards for being an idiot."

Quickly falling into step, his gaze fixed upon his smiling wife, Gregor had to agree.

Please turn the page for an exciting sneak peek of

Hannah Howell's

HIGHLAND BARBARIAN

coming in December 2006!

Scotland, Summer 1480

"Ye dinnae look dead, though I think ye might be trying to smell like ye are."

Angus MacReith scowled at the young man towering over his bed. Artan Murray was big, strongly built, and handsome. His cousin had done well, he thought. Far better than all his nearer kin who had born no children at all or left him with ones like young Malcolm. Angus scowled even more fiercely as he thought about that man. Untrustworthy, greedy, and cowardly, he thought. Artan had the blood of the MacReiths in him and it showed, just as it did in his twin Lucas. it was only then that Angus realized Artan stood there alone.

"Where is the other one?" he asked.

"Lucas had his leg broken," Artan replied.

"Bad?"

"Could be. I was looking for the ones who did it when ye sent word."

"Ye dinnae ken who did it?"

"I have a good idea who did it. A verra good idea." Artan shrugged. "I will find them."

Angus nodded. "Aye, ye will, lad. Suspicion they will be hiding now, eh?"

"Aye. As time passes and I dinnae come to take my reckoning they will begin to feel themselves safe.

'Twill be most enjoyable to show them how mistaken they are."

"Ye have a devious mind, Artan," Angus said in obvious admiration.

"Thank ye." Artan moved to lean against the bedpost at the head of the bed. "I dinnae think ye are dying, Angus."

"I am nay weel!"

"Och, nay, ye arenae, but ye arenae dying."

"What do ye ken about it?" grumbled Angus, pushing himself upright enough to collapse against the pillows Artan quickly set behind him.

"Dinnae ye recall that I am a Murray? I have spent near all my life surrounded by healers. Aye, ye are ailing, but I dinnae think ye will die if ye are careful. Ye dinnae have the odor of a mon with one foot in the grave. And, for all ye do stink some, 'tisnae really the smell of death."

"Death has a smell ere it e'en takes hold of a mon's soul?"

"Aye, I think it does. And since ye are nay dying, I will return to hunting the men who hurt Lucas."

Angus grabbed Artan by the arm, halting the younger man as he started to move away. "Nay! I could die and ye ken it weel. I hold three score years. E'en the smallest chill could set me firm in the grave."

That was true enough, Artan thought as he studied the man who had fostered him and Lucas for nearly ten years. Angus was still a big strong man, but age sometimes weakened a body in ways one could not see. The fact that Angus was in bed in the middle of the day was proof enough that whatever ailed him was serious. Artan wondered if he was just refusing to accept the fact that Angus was old and would die soon.

"So ye have brought me here to stand watch o'er your deathbed?" he asked, frowning for he doubted Angus would ask such a thing of him.

"Nay, I need ye to do something for me. This ague, or whate'er it is that ails me, has made me face the hard fact that, e'en if I recover from this, I dinnae have many years left to me. 'Tis past time I start thinking on what must be done to ensure the well-being of Glascreag and the clan when I am nay longer here."

"Then ye should be speaking with Malcolm."

"Bah, that craven whelp is naught but a stain upon the name MacReith. Sly, whining little wretch. I wouldnae trust him to care for my dogs let alone these lands and the people living here. He couldnae hold fast to this place for a fortnight. Nay, I willnae have him as my heir."

"Ye dinnae have another one that I ken of."

"Aye, I do, although I have kept it quiet. Glad of that now. My youngest sister bore a child two and twenty years ago. Poor Moira died a few years later bearing another child," he murmured, the shadow of old memories briefly darkening his eyes.

"Then where is he? Why wasnae he sent here to train to be the laird? Why isnae he kicking that wee timid mousie named Malcolm out of Glascreag?"

"'Tis a lass."

Artan opened his mouth to loudly decry naming a lass the heir to Glascreag and then quickly shut it. He resisted the temptation to look behind him to see if his kinswomen were bearing down on him, well armed and ready to beat some sense into him. They would all be sorely aggrieved if they knew what thoughts were whirling about in his head. Words like too weak, too sentimental, too trusting, and made to have bairns not lead armies were the sort of thoughts that would have his kinswomen grinding their teeth in fury.

But Glascreag was no Donncoill, he thought. Deep in the Highlands, it was surrounded by rough lands and even rougher men. In the years he and Lucas had trained with Angus they had fought reivers, other clans, and some who wanted Angus's lands. Glascreag required constant vigilance and a strong sword arm. Murray women were strong and clever, but they were healers, not warriors, not deep in their hearts. Artan also considered his kinswomen unique and doubted Angus's niece was of their ilk.

"If ye name a lass as your heir, Angus, every mon who has e'er coveted your lands will come kicking down yer gates." Artan crossed his arms over his chest and scowled at the man. "Malcolm is a spineless weasel, but a mon, more or less. Naming him yer heir would at least make men pause as they girded themselves for battle. Aye, and yer men would heed his orders far more quickly than they would those of a lass and ye ken it weel."

Angus nodded and ran one scarred hand through his black hair, which was still thick and long but was now well threaded with white. "I ken it, but I have a plan."

A tickle of unease passed through Artan. Angus's plans could often mean trouble. At the very least, they meant hard work for him. The way the man's eyes, a silvery blue like his own, were shielded by his half-lowered lids warned Artan that even Angus knew he was not going to like this particular plan.

"I want ye to go and fetch my niece for me and bring her here to Glascreag where she belongs. I wish to see her once more before I die." Angus sighed, slumped heavily against the pillows, and closed his eyes.

Artan grunted, making his disgust with such a pitiful play for sympathy very clear. "Then send word and have her people bring her here."

Sitting up straight, Angus glared at him. "I did. I have been writing to the lass for years, e'en sent for her when her father and brother died ten, nay, twelve years ago. Her father's kinsmen refused to give her into my care e'en though nary a one of them is as close in blood to her as I am."

"Why didnae ye just go and get her? Ye are a laird. Ye could have claimed her as yer legal heir and taken her. 'Tis easy to refuse letters and emissaries, but nay so easy to refuse a mon to his face. Ye could have saved yerself the misery of dealing with Malcolm."

"I wanted the lass to want to come to Glascreag, didnae I."

"'Tis past time ye ceased trying to coax her or her father's kinsmen."

"Exactly! That is why I want *ye* to go and fetch her here. Ach, laddie, I am sure ye can do it, Ye can charm and threaten with equal skill. Aye, and ye can do it without making them all hot for yer blood. I would surely start a feud I dinnae need. Ye have a way with folk that I dinnae, that ye do."

Artan listened to Angus's flattery and grew even more uneasy. Angus was not only a little desperate to have his niece brought home to Glascreag, but he also knew Artan would probably refuse to do him this favor. The question was why would Angus think Artan would refuse to go and get the woman. It could not be because it was dangerous, for the man knew well that only something foolishly suicidal would cause Artan to, perhaps, hesitate. Although his mind was quickly crowded with possibilities ranging from illegal to just plain disgusting, Artan decided he had played this game long enough.

"Shut it, Angus," he said, standing up straighter and putting his hands on his hips. "*Why* havenae ye gone after the woman yourself and *why* do ye think I will refuse to go?"

"Ye would refuse to help a mon on his deathbed?"

"Just spit it out, Angus, or I will leave right now and ye will ne'er ken which I might have said, aye or nay."

"Och, ye will say nay," Angus mumbled. "Cecily lives near Kirkfalls."

"In Kirkfalls? Kirkfalls?" Artan muttered and then he swore. "That is in the Lowlands." Artan's voice was soft yet sharp with loathing.

"Weel, just a few miles into the Lowlands."

"Now I ken why ye ne'er went after the lass yerself. Ye couldnae stomach the thought of going there. Yet ye would send *me* into that hellhole?"

"'Tisnae as bad as all that."

"'Tis as bad as if ye wanted me to ride to London. I willnae do it," Artan said and started to leave.

"I need an heir of my own blood!"

"Then ye should ne'er have let your sister marry a Lowlander. 'Tis near as bad as if ye had let her run off with a Sassanach. Best ye leave the lass where she is. She is weel ruined by now."

"Wait! Ye havenae heard the whole of my plan!"

Artan opened the door and stared at Malcolm who was crouched on the floor, obviously having had his large ear pressed against the door. The thin, pale young man grew even paler and stood up. He staggered back a few steps and then bolted down the hall. Artan sighed. He did not need such a stark reminder of the pathetic choice Angus had for an heir now.

Curiosity also halted him at the door. Every instinct he had told him to keep on moving, that he would be a fool to listen to anything else Angus had to say. A voice in his head whispered that his next step could change his life forever. Artan wished that voice would tell him if that change would be for the better. Praying he was not about to make a very bad choice, he slowly turned to look at Angus, but he did not move away from the door.

Angus looked a little smug and Artan inwardly cursed. The old man had judged his victim well. Curiosity had always been Artan's weakness. It had caused him trouble and several injuries more times than he cared to recall. He wished Lucas were with him for his brother was the cautious one. Then Artan quickly shook that thought aside. He was a grown man now, not a reckless child, and he had wit enough to make his own decisions with care and wisdom.

"What is the rest of your plan?" he asked Angus.

"Weel, 'tis verra simple. I need a strong mon to take my place as laird once I die or decide 'tis time I rested. Malcolm isnae it and neither is Cecily. Howbeit, there has to be someone of MacReith blood to step into my place, the closer to me the better."

"Aye, 'tis the way it should be."

"So e'en though ye have MacReith blood, 'tis but from a distant cousin. Howbeit, if ye marry Cecily—"

"Marry!"

"Wheesht, what are ye looking so horrified about,

eh? Ye arenae getting any younger, laddie. Past time ye were wed."

"I have naught against marriage. I fully intend to *choose* a bride some day."

Angus grunted. "*Some day* can sneak up on a body, laddie. I ken it weel. Now, cease your fretting for a moment and let me finish. If ye were to marry my niece, ye could be laird here. I would name ye my heir and nary a one of my men would protest it. E'en better, Malcolm couldnae get anyone to heed him if he cried foul. Cecily is my closest blood kin and ye are nearly as close to me as Malcolm is. So, ye marry the lass and, one day, Glascreag is yers."

Artan stepped back into the room and slowly closed the door. Angus was offering him something he had never thought to have—the chance to be a laird, to hold lands of his own. As the second born of the twins, his future had always been as Lucas's second, or as the next in line to be the laird of Donncoill if anything happened to Lucas, something he never cared to think about. There had always been only one possibility of changing that future. Marriage to a woman with lands as part of her dowry.

Which was exactly what Angus was offering him, he mused, and felt temptation tease at his mind and heart. Marry Cecily and become heir to Glascreag, a place he truly loved as much as he did his own homelands. Any man with wit enough to recall his own name would grab at this chance with both hands, yet, despite the strong temptation of it all, he hesitated. Since Artan considered his wits sound and sharp, he had to wonder why.

Because he wanted a marriage like his parents had, like his grandparents had, and like so many of his clan had, he realized. He wanted a marriage of choice, of passion, of a bonding that held firm for life. When it was land, coin, or alliances that tied a couple together the chances of such a good marriage were sadly dimmed. He had been offered the favors of too many unhappy wives to doubt that conclusion. If the thought of taking part in committing adultery did not trouble him so much, he would now be a very experienced lover, he mused and hastily shook aside a pinch of regret. He certainly did not want his wife to become one of those women and he did not want to be one of those men who felt so little bond with his wife that he repeatedly broke his vows. Or worse, find himself trapped in a cold marriage and, bound tightly by his own beliefs, unable to find passion elsewhere.

He looked at Angus who was waiting for an answer with an ill-concealed impatience. Although he could not agree to marry a woman he had never met, no matter how tempting her dowry, there was no harm in agreeing to consider it. He could go and get the woman and decide on marrying her once he saw her. As they traveled back to Glascreag together he would have ample time to decide if she was a woman he could share the rest of his life with.

Then he recalled where she lived and how long she had lived there. "She is a Lowlander."

"She is a MacReith," Angus snapped.

Angus was looking smug again. Artan ignored it for the man was right in thinking he might get what he wanted. In many ways, it was what Artan wanted as well. It all depended upon what this woman Cecily was like.

"Cecily," he murmured, "sounds like a Sassanach

name." He almost smiled when Angus glared at him, the old man's pale cheeks now flushed with anger.

"'Tis nae an English name! 'Tis the name of a martyr, ye great heathen, and weel ye ken it. My sister was a pious lass. She didnae change the child's christening name as some folk do. Kept the saint's name. I call the lass Sile. Use the Gaelic, ye ken."

"Because ye think Cecily sounds English." Artan ignored Angus's stuttering denial. "When did ye last see this lass?"

"Her father brought her and her wee brother here just before he and the lad died."

"How did they die?"

"Killed whilst traveling back home from visiting me. Thieves. Poor wee lass saw it all. Old Meg, her maid, got her to safety, though. Some of their escort survived, chased away the thieves, and then got Cecily, Old Meg, and the dead back to their home. The moment I heard I sent for the lass, but the cousins had already taken hold of her and wouldnae let go."

"Was her father a mon of wealth or property?"

"Aye, he was. He had both and the cousins now control it all. For the lass's sake they say. And, aye, I wonder on the killing. His kinsmen could have had a hand in it."

"Yet they havenae rid themselves of the lass."

"She made it home and has ne'er left there again. They also have control of all that she has since she is a woman, aye?"

"Aye, and it probably helps muzzle any suspicions about the other deaths."

Angus nodded. "'Tis what I think. So will ye go to Kirkfalls and fetch my niece?"

"Aye, I will fetch her, but I make no promises about marrying her."

"Not e'en to become my heir?"

"Nay, not e'en for that, tempting as it is. I willnae tie myself to a woman for that alone. There has to be more."

"She is a bonnie wee lass with dark red hair and big green eyes."

That sounded promising, but Artan fixed a stern gaze upon the old man. "Ye havenae set eyes on her since she was a child and ye dinnae ken what sort of woman she has become. A lass can be so bonnie on the outside she makes a mon's innards clench. But then the blind lust clears away, and he finds himself with a bonnie lass who is as cold as ice, or mean of spirit, or any of a dozen things that would make living with her a pure misery. Nay, I willnae promise to wed your niece now. I will only promise to consider it. There will be time to come to know the lass as we travel here from Kirkfalls."

"Fair enough, but ye will see. Ye will be wanting to marry her. She is a sweet, gentle, biddable lass. A true lady raised to be a mon's comfort."

Artan wondered just how much of that effusive praise was true, then shrugged and began to plan his journey.

About the Author

Hannah Howell is an award-winning author who lives with her family in Massachusetts. She is the author of twenty Zebra historical romances and is currently working on a new Highland historical romance, HIGHLAND BARBARIAN (the first of a two book series focusing on twin brothers), which will be published in December 2006. Hannah loves hearing from readers and you may visit her website: *www.hannahhowell.com.*

BOOK YOUR PLACE ON OUR WEBSITE AND MAKE THE READING CONNECTION!

We've created a customized website just for our very special readers, where you can get the inside scoop on everything that's going on with Zebra, Pinnacle and Kensington books.

When you come online, you'll have the exciting opportunity to:

- View covers of upcoming books
- Read sample chapters
- Learn about our future publishing schedule (listed by publication month *and author*)
- Find out when your favorite authors will be visiting a city near you
- Search for and order backlist books from our online catalog
- Check out author bios and background information
- Send e-mail to your favorite authors
- Meet the Kensington staff online
- Join us in weekly chats with authors, readers and other guests
- Get writing guidelines
- AND MUCH MORE!

**Visit our website at
http://www.kensingtonbooks.com**